THE PENGUIN CLASSICS

FOUNDER EDITOR (1944–64): E. V. RIEU

HONORÉ DE BALZAC was born in Tours in 1799, the son of a civil servant. He spent nearly six years as a boarder in a Vendôme school, then went to live in Paris, working as a lawyer's clerk then as a hack-writer. Between 1820 and 1824 he wrote a number of novels under various pseudonyms, many of them in collaboration, after which he unsuccessfully tried his luck at publishing, printing and type-founding. At the age of thirty, heavily in debt, he returned to literature with a dedicated fury and wrote the first novel to appear under his own name, *The Chouans*. During the next twenty years he wrote about ninety novels and shorter stories, among them many masterpieces, to which he gave the comprehensive title *The Human Comedy*. He died in 1850, a few months after his marriage to Eveline Hanska, the Polish countess with whom he had maintained amorous relations for eighteen years.

HERBERT J. HUNT was educated at Lichfield Cathedral Choir School, the Lichfield Grammar School and Magdalen College, Oxford. He was a Tutor and Fellow at St Edmund Hall from 1927 to 1944, then until 1966 he was Professor of French Literature and Language at London University and from 1966 to 1970 was Senior Fellow of Warwick University. He published books on literature and thought in nineteenth-century France; he was also the author of a biography of Balzac, and a comprehensive study of Balzac's writings: *Balzac's 'Comédie Humaine'* (1959, paperback 1964). His translation of Balzac's *Cousin Pons* appeared in the Penguin Classics in 1968, followed by *Lost Illusions* (1971), *A Murky Business* (1972) and *History of the Thirteen* (1974). He died in 1973.

Honoré de Balzac

THE WILD ASS'S SKIN

(*La Peau de Chagrin*)

TRANSLATED AND
WITH AN INTRODUCTION BY
HERBERT J. HUNT

PENGUIN BOOKS

Penguin Books Ltd, Harmondsworth, Middlesex, England
Penguin Books, 40 West 23rd Street, New York, New York 10010, U.S.A.
Penguin Books Australia Ltd, Ringwood, Victoria, Australia
Penguin Books Canada Ltd, 2801 John Street, Markham, Ontario, Canada L3R 1B4
Penguin Books (N.Z.) Ltd, 182–190 Wairau Road, Auckland 10, New Zealand

—

This translation published 1977
Reprinted 1979, 1981, 1984

—

Copyright © the Estate of Herbert J. Hunt, 1977
All rights reserved

—

Made and printed in Great Britain by
Hazell Watson & Viney Limited,
Member of the BPCC Group,
Aylesbury, Bucks
Set in Linotype Granjon

Contents

Introduction 7

Select Bibliography 17

THE WILD ASS'S SKIN

1. The Talisman 21

2. The Woman without a Heart 91

3. The Death-Agony 195

Epilogue 284

Introduction

AFTER several years of relatively abortive literary effort (from 1819), Honoré de Balzac began signing his works with his own name in 1829, the first being his historical novel now known as *Les Chouans* whose subject is the failure of the royalist rising against the Directoire in Britanny in 1799. Between 1829 and 1834 he laid the foundation of his vast work, which by 1834 he was already organizing into 'studies': Studies of Manners, Philosophical Studies and Analytical Studies. These he was to expand throughout the years; between 1842 and 1848, and while still adding to them, he re-published them under the Dantesque title of *The Human Comedy*.[1]

It was as a historian of his own times (1799 to 1848 approximately) as the 'secretary of society', that Balzac achieved his reputation as one of the world's greatest novelists. But he was never content to be a mere story-teller or 'realist'. He regarded himself as a philosopher and sage whose business it was to explain man to himself, also to study man's position in society and the impact of society on the individual. Yet it is perhaps true that his primary impulse was to study manners. From 1829 he was producing a large number of short stories which as he elaborated them tended to develop into 'nouvelles' – an intermediate form of fiction whose interest lies in the study of psychological cases rather than the mere narration of events – or even into full sized novels. Hence the earliest *Scenes of Private Life* (1830 and 1832), swiftly followed (or accompanied) by studies of life in Paris and the provinces which gave him the clue for the six types of 'scenes' (Balzac had a strong sense of drama) into which before long he was to subdivide his 'Studies of Manners' – those of private, provincial, Parisian, political, military and country life. But at the

1. For general accounts of Balzac's life and work see below, Select Bibliography, p. 17.

same time he was producing a series of philosophical tales,[2] of which *The Wild Ass's Skin* (*La Peau de chagrin*)[3] is the most important. Nor was he content with that. A trio of fictions: *The Exiles*, the semi-autobiographical *Louis Lambert* and the Sweden-borgist novel *Séraphîta* were collected in 1835 into one volume bearing the title *The Mystical Book* (*Le Livre mystique*). It is also important to note that, although his Studies of Manners became more numerous in the later 1830s and 1840s, he continued to produce 'philosophical studies' throughout his career; moreover, the philosophical system he had thought out finds its way into and informs many of his most 'realist' studies of manners, e.g. *Ursule Mirouët* of 1841. Indeed, the Philosophical Studies were intended to stand in relation to the Studies of Manners as the study of *causes* in relation to that of *effects*. 'In the *Studies of Manners* I shall have depicted human feelings and their action, life and its tendencies. In the *Philosophical Studies* I shall explain the cause of those feelings and the foundation on which life rests.' (Letter to Madame Hanska of 26 October 1834.)[4] The *Analytical Studies* were to examine *principles*; but this was a category he never succeeded in developing.

It is the novel *Louis Lambert* which represents his most deter-mined effort to present the philosophy on which his Studies of Manners were to repose. It is not too easy to follow, thanks per-haps to the fact that it is a sort of compromise between material-ism and illuminism,[5] between occultism and the belief that human science, especially physiology and its derivatives, was destined to provide the key to all knowledge, once it had ex-

2. The three-volume collection of *Philosophical Novels and Tales* in 1831, and the one-volume collection of *New Philosophical Tales*, 1832.

3. See below, pp. 226–8, for information about the onager or wild ass. The French *chagrin* has two meanings, significant in the context of the story: *shagreen* and *grief* or *vexation*.

4. *Lettres à Madame Hanska*, Éditions du Delta, Vol. I, pp. 269–70.

5. A tradition of semi-mystical thoughts from Jakob Boehme in the seven-teenth century to Willermoz, Martinès de Pasqually, Saint-Martin and Swedenborg in the eighteenth and early nineteenth centuries. The illuminists professed to inherit a 'revelation' from primitive times, and also to possess a special intuition of religious truth. The occultists were believers in alchemy, magic, necromancy, etc.

panded in the direction in which Balzac expected it to expand. This compromise is due to Balzac's effort to get away from the dualist conception of reality – which holds that there are two irreducible substances, spirit and matter – by postulating one essential and fundamental reality which he defines as a 'fluid', a 'substance éthérée' (analogous to electric current, heat or light waves) of which all phenomena and all forms of activity, both what we call spiritual and what we call physical, are manifestations. It is difficult not to suspect an element of superstitious credulity in his adherence to such questionable sciences as the physiology of Broussais and Lavater, the phrenology of Gall and Mesmer's theory of animal magnetism. But he was convinced that they were real sciences whose postulates future research and discovery would confirm.

There would be little point in carrying the matter further, for *The Wild Ass's Skin* was conceived and written before Balzac had completely thought out his system. What, however, must be said here is that there is an autobiographical substratum also in this earlier novel, and that the fiction itself – the story of the magic skin – is an attempt to present in allegorical form what Balzac was even then ready to postulate about that mysterious force we call the Will. Just as Louis Lambert, Balzac's *alter ego* in the novel of that name, was occupied when still at school with a *Treatise of the Will*, so does Raphael de Valentin, during his spell as an austere and virtuous student, apply himself devotedly to the composition of a *Theory of the Will*. In an attempt to capture Fœdora's interest Raphael sketches out for her the Balzacian theory of the 'substance éthérée'.

'She seemed quite intrigued to learn that the human will was a material force similar to steam-power; that nothing in the moral world could resist it when a man trained himself to concentrate it, to control the sum of it, and constantly to direct upon other men's minds the projection of that fluid mass; and that such a man could modify as he pleased everything relating to mankind, even the absolute laws of nature' (p. 124).

This idea of the concentration of the will is only expressed here *en passant*, but it lies behind many of Balzac's major psychological conceptions and accounts for his creation of numerous 'monomaniacs' like Gobseck the moneylender (*Gobseck*, 1830–35), Grandet the amasser of gold (*Eugénie Grandet*, 1833), Balthazar Claës the alchemist (*Quest of the Absolute*, 1834), Goriot the man with the daughter fixation (*Old Goriot*, 1834–5) and many others. But *The Wild Ass's Skin* is more remarkable still for its expounding of a wider aspect of the interplay of the human faculties. This exposition is entrusted to the mysterious and sardonic antiquary:

'I am going to reveal to you, in a few words, one of the great mysteries of human life. Man exhausts himself by two acts, instinctively accomplished, which dry up the sources of his existence. Two words[6] express all the forms that these two causes of death can assume: will and power. Between these two terms of human action there is another formula which wise men cling to, and to it I owe happiness and my long life. The exercise of the *will* consumes us; the exercise of *power* destroys us; but the pursuit of *knowledge* leaves our feeble organization in a state of perpetual calm. So desire or volition is dead in me, killed by thought. Movement, or power, has been dissolved by the natural play of my organs. In short, I have invested my life, not in the heart, so easily broken, not in the senses, which are so readily blunted, but in the brain which does not wear out and outlasts everything. No kind of excess has galled either my soul or my body.' (p. 52).

This principle, expressed elsewhere in a broader context,[7] is summed up in the phrase *l'usure par la pensée*: the abrasive action of thought, a term which is widened to include all forms of psychological activity – the passions and the imagination – but with volition having the priority since all thinking involves willing. The antiquary's basic idea is that each human being is endowed with a certain quantity of the *masse fluide*, which he may husband carefully or expend rashly, and his span of life depends

6. The French has here an advantage over the English in that *vouloir*, *pouvoir* and *savoir* are all three verbs as well as nouns. Hence in the original we have 'deux *verbes*'.

7. Notably by Balzac's friend and spokesman Félix Davin, who late in 1834 wrote an Introduction for the Werdet edition of the *Philosophical Studies*. It is collected in Spoelberch de Lovenjoul's *Histoire des œuvres de H. de B*, 1886 (now photographically reproduced, pp. 171–7).

on the choice he makes. The magic skin, with the dramatic rapidity of its contraction, symbolizes this choice. In a review that Philarète Chasles, a friend of Balzac's, wrote of the novel in 1831, he borrowed a Byronic phrase to express this truth: 'the blade wears out the scabbard'. The antiquarian has eked out his life for over a century, whereas Raphael clutches the skin, cries out: 'I want to live to excess!' and immediately finds himself doomed to pay the price. The same choice is taken by the prostitutes Aquilina and Euphrasie. Fœdora refuses to expend herself. Then in this strange minuet there is a swift change-over. Raphael makes frenzied attempts to slow down his pace of life, and the antiquary, thanks to a malicious wish expressed by Raphael, begins to make up for lost time: 'I had taken life the wrong way round. A man's life is contained in one hour of love!'

The view has sometimes been expressed that Balzac did not intend the magic power of the skin to be taken literally, that it is a mere hallucination, a figment of Raphael's frenzied imagination. I do not think this view is tenable. I believe that, because of rather than despite a visible symmetry in the quasi-allegorical role played by the different characters, the supernatural fiction is tangibly and effectively used. There is effective symmetry also in the apposition and interweaving of the three parts of the story. In *The Talisman* Raphael has already determined on suicide; the same determination and the process by which it is accomplished are lengthily described in *The Woman without a Heart*. Then *The Death-Agony* converts this suicide ('only postponed', the Antiquary has said on page 55) into a lurid and excruciating tragedy which is slightly more lengthily narrated but still with a pressing and terrifying rapidity that only the inexorable power of the talisman can convey.

The Wild Ass's Skin is, strictly speaking, only the second novel written by the mature Balzac, but it is probably to be counted among his most powerful ones. It is well known how indefatigable in revision Balzac was. *The Wild Ass's Skin* is one of the novels to which he most unremittingly returned in the effort to polish and perfect. It contains a great deal of fine and vigorous descriptive writing – the gambling den, the old curiosity shop, the orgy given by Taillefer, Raphael's visits to the scientists and doctors where his satiric intentions are most manifest, the land-scapes of the Lac du Bourget and Mont Dore, the hostility of the guests and the duel, and the devastating closing scenes.

While not forgetting the profundity of Balzac's philosophical intentions, we must also recognize the fact that his role as a social historian is well to the fore in this novel. The Revolution of July 1830, which replaced the legitimate Bourbon line with that astute opportunist Louis-Philippe, Duke of Orleans, did not meet with Balzac's approval. He regarded the new régime as a speed-ing-up of the process whereby, since the fall of Napoleon, France had launched into a career of rapacious individualism and acquis-itiveness. Although he had inherited from his father some sym-pathy with liberalism, he quickly receded from the liberal posi-tion, regarded the accession of Louis-Philippe as a masterpiece of political skulduggery and refused to believe either in democracy or representative government. Hence the unprincipled cynicism attributed at Taillefer's dining-table to politicians, journalists and financiers alike. And, finally, we must note the deep strain of pessimism running through the novel and the emphasis he lays on human selfishness, relieved only by the selfless devotion of Pauline and her mother and the stupid devotion of Jonathas. It becomes even more incisive towards the end when Balzac re-flects on the treatment meted out to Raphael at Aix. Few denun-ciations of human egoism could be more trenchant:

'*Death to the weak!* That is the watchword of what we might call the equestrian order established in every nation of the earth, for there is a wealthy class in every country, and that death-sentence is deeply engraved on the heart of every nobleman or millionaire. Take any collection of children in a school: this microcosm of society, reflect-ing it all the more accurately because it does so frankly and ingen-uously, always contains specimens of the poor helots, creatures made for sorrow and suffering, subject always either to pity or to contempt: the Kingdom of Heaven is theirs, say the Scriptures. Take a few steps farther down the ladder of creation: if a barnyard fowl falls sick, the other hens hunt it around, attack it, scratch out its feathers and peck it to death.' (p. 255).

Readers of *The Human Comedy* will be familiar with the ingenious device which Balzac began to adopt from 1834 onwards – that of the 'reappearing characters'. His idea was, as his sister Laure Surville puts it, 'to bind all his characters together in order to form them into a complete social world'; to provide as it were a pool of characters, families and milieux, so that he might move from one to another in different works, throwing the limelight on each one in turn while leaving the others in the shade. He would thus give the impression of a society portrayed in depth. He first began to apply this system methodically in *Old Goriot* (1834), and as he progressively created new characters in his novels of the succeeding years, he adopted the habit of working them back into novels first published before 1834. *The Wild Ass's Skin* gives much evidence of this process in the seven editions published from 1831 to 1845. For instance, in 1831, many of the guests at the Taillefer banquet were either anonymous[8] or actual living figures (Victor Hugo, Delacroix, Henri Monnier, etc.); as edition followed edition they were replaced by Balzac's invented characters. 'Emile' for example settles down as Emile Blondet, one of the most ubiquitous journalists of *The Human Comedy*, while Raphael's anonymous general practitioner becomes identified (1838 edition) with Horace Bianchon, first conceived in *Old Goriot*, who makes innumerable appearances in Balzac's works as a medical genius and of whom it is related that, as Balzac lay dying in August 1850, he exclaimed: 'I need Bianchon. Bianchon would save me!'

Sometimes such identifications created psychological difficulties. In *The Wild Ass's Skin*, for instance, Eugène de Rastignac is presented to us (from 1824 to 1830) as a cynical rake and opportunist. When Balzac was (in 1834) writing *Old Goriot*, he first of all called his young Gascon law-student, who befriends the daughter-besotted Goriot and becomes the lover of the latter's daughter Delphine, by the name of Eugène de Massiac, an impecunious young aristocrat struggling to make his way in the Paris of 1819, and about to become the well-rewarded catspaw of Delphine's husband, the banker and speculator Baron de

8. Like Taillefer himself, he had first appeared in *The Red Inn*, one of the Philosophic Tales of 1831. But there his name was Mauricey. He figures also in the background of *Old Goriot*, but it was not until 1836 that he was identified in all three works as Taillefer.

Nucingen. Balzac was suddenly inspired to re-baptize this young man as Eugène de Rastignac, but the not uncongenial careerist of 1819 whom we meet in *Old Goriot* does not easily identify with the blasé friend and corrupter of Raphael de Valentin: mainly because, by 1830, the Rastignac who had started life as Massiac had made good and was on the threshold of a brilliant political career. There is no suggestion of such already achieved success in the career of the Rastignac of *The Wild Ass's Skin*.

Incompatibilities of this nature need not disconcert readers of *The Wild Ass's Skin*. The other main characters never reappear in *The Human Comedy*: Raphael for the obvious reason that he dies at the end of the story, Fœdora because she has a mainly symbolic role as the incarnation of hard-hearted and hard-faced Society,[9] and Pauline because, as the Epilogue shows, she represents Balzac's ideal woman, a vision glimpsed in the flames of the fireside or in the misty skies of reverie. And yet: may we not maintain that these symbolic values do not prevent either Fœdora or Pauline from carrying conviction as the incarnations of two opposite types of real and living women? It is interesting to pass from Fœdora to Antoinette de Langeais in *History of the Thirteen* (1834). A lady of whom Balzac became enamoured in 1832 – the Marquise de Castries – was no doubt his main inspiration when he created the Duchesse de Langeais.[10] But it might not perhaps be too fanciful to surmise that both Fœdora and Pauline entered into her composition.

The translator has used, for the sake of convenience, the Classiques Garnier edition of the novel. It is divided into three fairly long parts. Balzac's practice as concerns chapter divisions varied, and in the 1842–8 edition of the *Human Comedy* he virtually abolished them. Nor is he beyond criticism as regards division into paragraphs: often he makes a very palpable transition in the middle of one. The translator has therefore taken some liberties with the text in this respect. He has also to some extent arbitrarily, but perhaps helpfully, broken up the narrative into significant episodes by the use of double spaces and asterisks.

9. The final sentence of the Epilogue clinches this: 'She is, if you like, Society' (p. 285). But it was not added until 1845.
10. See the Penguin translation of *History of the Thirteen*, Introduction.

A note is called for about the strange device adopted by the novelist on page 19: a borrowing from Laurence Sterne in *Tristram Shandy*, this curious squiggle merely represents the flourish made by Corporal Trim with his stick as an illustration of the freedom enjoyed by bachelors. 'A thousand of my father's most subtle syllogisms,' says Tristram, 'could not have said more for celibacy.' It is not easy to see why Balzac, enthusiastic admirer of Sterne though he was, adopted it – perhaps in order to symbolize by contrast the constraint under which Raphael de Valentin lives once he has accepted the magic skin. In the earlier editions it remained a mere squiggle, but from 1855 onwards it was given the form of a snake.

Select Bibliography

BIOGRAPHY

André Maurois, *Prometheus: the Life of Balzac*, Bodley Head, 1965.

H. J. Hunt, *Honoré de Balzac. A Biography*, Athlone Press, 1957. Reprinted 1969, Greenwood Press, New York, with indispensable corrigendum sheet bringing it up to date.

V. S. Pritchett, *Balzac*, Chatto and Windus, 1973.

GENERAL STUDIES

Philippe Bertault, *Balzac and the Human Comedy*, New York University Press, 1963.

H. J. Hunt, *Balzac's Comédie Humaine*, Athlone Press, 1959 (paperback edition, ibid., 1964): an analysis of Balzac's work in the course of its evolution.

F. W. J. Hemmings, *Balzac. An Interpretation of La Comédie Humaine*, Random House, New York, 1967.

Félicien Marceau, *Balzac and his World*, W. H. Allen, 1967: a study of the characters in *The Human Comedy* which unfortunately takes no account of the stages by which these characters came into being in Balzac's imagination.

A MONSIEUR SAVARY[1]

MEMBRE DE L'ACADÉMIE DES SCIENCES

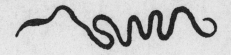

STERNE. *Tristram Shandy*, ch. cccxii

---

1. M. Savary (1797–1841), was a professor of applied mathematics at the
École Polytechnique.

1. *The Talisman*

Towards the end of October 1830 a young man entered the Palais-Royal[1] just as the gambling-houses were opening in conformity with the law which protects an essentially taxable passion. Without too much hesitation he walked up the staircase of the gambling-den designated as No. 36.

'Your hat, sir, if you please!' This cry, ejaculated in a sharp and scolding voice, came from a small, pallid old man squatting in the shadow behind a barrier, who suddenly rose to his feet and displayed a very ignoble type of countenance.

When you enter a gambling-house, the first thing the law does is to deprive you of your hat. Is this as it were a parable from the Gospel or a providential warning? Or is it not rather a way of concluding an infernal pact with you by exacting a sort of pledge? Might it not be devised in order to force you to show due respect to those who are about to win your money from you? Or do the police, lurking near every social sewer, insist on knowing the name of your hatter or your own if you have written it on the lining? Or indeed is it their purpose to take the measure of your skull and to draw up illuminating statistics on the cerebral capacity of gamblers? Administrative authorities remain completely silent on this point. But make no mistake about this: scarcely have you taken one step towards the green table before your hat no longer belongs to you any more than you belong to yourself: you are yourself at stake – you, your fortune, your headgear, your cane and your cloak. When you go out, the Spirit of Gaming will show you, by putting an atrocious epigram into action, that it is still leaving you something by restoring your personal belongings. But if your hat happens to be a new one, you will learn to your cost that if you go gambling, you need to dress the part.

1. The thoroughfares and shopping centres surrounding the palace which for a long time belonged to the Dukes of Orleans. Notorious in this period as a centre for prostitution and gambling.

The young man's astonishment as he received a numbered ticket in exchange for his hat, of which the brim was luckily slightly shabby, was proof that he was still innocent of soul; reason enough for the little old man, who no doubt had wallowed since youth in the scalding pleasures of a gamester's life, to give him a lack-lustre, lukewarm glance into which a thinking man might well have read the sufferings of doss-house inmates, the vagrancy of down-and-outs, the inquests held on innumerable charcoal-fume fatalities, sentences to penal servitude and transportation to overseas colonies. This man, who to judge by his haggard white face lived on nothing more nourishing than the gelatinous soups provided by popular caterers, offered the pale image of passion reduced to its simplest terms. Old torments had left their mark in the wrinkles on his brow: obviously he was in the habit of staking his meagre wages the very day he drew them. Like jaded horses no longer responsive to the whip, he was impervious to any thrill: the muffled groans of ruined gamesters, their mute imprecations, their vacant stares made no impression on him at all. He was the very incarnation of the gaming table. If the young man had paused to contemplate this dreary-looking Cerberus, he might perhaps have told himself: 'Nothing but a pack of cards is left in that man's heart!'

But the young stranger paid no heed to this warning in human guise, placed there no doubt by the same Providence which has set the seal of disgust over the threshold of all disorderly houses. He stepped boldly into the gaming-room in which the chink of gold coins was exercising its dazzling fascination over the senses driven by the desire for gain. The young man had probably come here in obedience to the most logical and most eloquently expressed of Jean-Jacques Rousseau's thoughts – a sad one. 'Yes, I can understand a man taking to gambling, but only when he can no longer see anything but one last florin between him and death.'

In the evenings, gaming-houses have but a commonplace poetry about them, even though the effect of it is as assured as that of a gory melodrama. The various salons are teeming with spectators and players; indigent old men who shuffle along there to find warmth; tormented faces belonging to those whose orgies began in wine and will end up in the Seine. Though there is passion in abundance, the multitude of actors prevents you from staring the demon of gambling full in the face. The evening session is a genuine concert-piece to which the entire company contributes, in which every orchestral instrument has its phrase to execute. You may well see many respectable people who come there for distraction and pay for it just as they would pay for the pleasure of an evening at the theatre or that of a lavish meal, or just as they might climb up to a garret to buy on the cheap three months of sharp regret. But can you realize what delirium, what frenzy possesses the mind of a man impatiently waiting for a gambling-den to open? Between the evening and the morning gambler the same difference exists as between the nonchalant husband and the ecstatic lover waiting under his mistress's window. It is only in the morning that quivering passion and stark need manifest themselves in all their horror. At that time of day you may stare in wonderment at the true gambler who has not eaten or slept, lived or thought, so cruelly has he been scourged by the scorpion of his vice, so sorely has he been itching to make his throw at *trente-et-quarante*. At that baleful hour you will meet with eyes whose steady calm is frightening, with faces that hold you spellbound; you will intercept gazes which lift the cards and greedily peer beneath them.

Gaming-houses then reach sublimity only at opening time. Spain has its bull-fights. Rome had its gladiators. But Paris takes pride in its Palais-Royal, whose teasing roulette wheels afford spectators in the pit the pleasure of seeing blood flow freely without running the risk of their feet slithering in it. Cast a furtive glance into this arena! Venture down into it! . . . How bare it all is! The walls, covered with greasy wallpaper up to head height, show nothing that might refresh the spirit. There is not even a nail there to make it easier to hang oneself. The floor is worn and dirty. An oblong table occupies the middle of the room. The plainness of the straw-bottomed chairs crowded round the baize cloth, worn threadbare by the raking-in of gold coins, bespeaks a strange indifference to luxury in people who come there to perish in their quest of the fortune that can buy luxury.

23

This very human contradiction may be discovered wherever the soul reacts powerfully on itself. A man in love wants to clothe his mistress in silk, drape her in a soft, oriental gauze. Yet, most of the time, he makes love to her on a truckle-bed. The ambitious man dreams that he is at the pinnacle of power while he is still grovelling in the mire of servility. The tradesman vegetates in the depths of a damp, unhealthy shop while he builds a huge mansion from which his son, having taken premature possession, will be ousted by fraternal litigation.[2] But, when all is said and done, does anything less pleasureable exist than a 'house of pleasure'? A singular problem! Man, always at war with himself, finding his hopes cheated by his present ills and cheating his present ills with hopes for a future over which he has no control, imprints all his actions with the stamp of inconsistency and feebleness. Here below only calamity is ever complete.

At the moment when the young man entered the *salon de jeu* a few gamblers were already there. Three bald-headed old men were nonchalantly sitting round the green cloth; their plaster-white faces, as impassive as those of diplomats, betokened jaded souls and hearts which long since had forgotten how to beat even after they had staked not only their own, but also their wives', personal property. A young black-haired olive-skinned Italian was placidly leaning his elbows on the end of the table and appeared to be listening to that inner voice which gives prophetic warning to gamblers: 'Yes! – No!' His southerner's head was breathing fire and dreaming gold. Seven or eight onlookers were standing round in anticipation of the dramatic scenes which were being prepared by the vagaries of chance, the expressiveness of the gamblers' faces and the to-and-fro movement of coins under the croupier's rake. They stood idly by, silent and motionless, as watchful as a crowd gathered on the Place de Grève to see an execution.

A tall, spare man in a threadbare coat was holding a register in one hand and in the other a pin for pricking off the sequences of Red and Black. He was like a modern Tantalus, one of those men who live just out of reach of the enjoyments of their times,

2. An auction sale enforced by the heir's brothers.

a miser with no store of coins, one who can only lay imaginary stakes: a kind of reasoning madman who consoled himself for his poverty by nursing a chimæra, who in fact dallied with vice and hazard as young priests do with the sacred elements when they are rehearsing for their first Mass. Sitting opposite the bank were one or two of those shrewd punters, expert in gambling odds and very like hardened convicts no longer afraid of the hulks, who had come there to risk three throws and carry off on the spot their likely winnings which were what they lived on. Two elderly attendants were walking unconcernedly up and down with arms crossed, and every now and then they stood at the windows overlooking the gardens as if to exhibit their featureless faces to passers-by as a sort of shop-sign.

The banker and the croupier had just cast on the punters their characteristically ashen and chilling glance and were uttering their high-pitched call: 'Lay your stakes!' when the young man opened the door. The silence grew somewhat more profound and heads were turned towards the newcomer. Wonder of wonders, the old men with dulled senses, the stony-faced attendants, the onlookers, and even the single-minded Italian, the whole assembly in fact, when they saw the stranger appear, experienced an appalling kind of emotion. Must not a man be inordinately unhappy to awaken pity, extremely enfeebled to excite sympathy, or else very sinister-looking to cause a shudder to pass through those who frequent such a den as this where grief has to be muted, where indigence must pretend to be gay, where even despair must behave in a seemly fashion? Such factors did indeed enter into the unprecedented sensation which stirred these icy hearts when the young man stepped in. But have not even executioners been moved to tears over maidens whose fair heads were about to be severed at the bidding of the Revolution?

At their first glance the gamblers were able to read some horrible mystery in the newcomer's face. His youthful features were stamped with a clouded grace and the look in his eyes bore witness to efforts betrayed and to a thousand hopes deceived. The gloomy passivity of intended suicide imparted to his brow a dull, unhealthy pallor, a bitter smile drew creases round the corners of his mouth, and his whole physiognomy expressed a resignation which was distressing to behold.

Some spark of undiscovered genius flashed deep down in those eyes, upon which pleasure perhaps had cast a veil of fatigue. Was it debauchery that had put its noisome seal upon that noble face, once bright and innocent, but now degraded? Doctors would no doubt have attributed to lesions of heart or lungs the yellow ring around the eyelids and the hectic flush on the cheeks, whereas poets would have discerned in these signs the ravages of knowledge, the traces of nights spent under the gleam of the student's lamp. But a passion more fatal than disease, a disease more pitiless than study and genius were robbing this young head of its beauty, contracting those still vigorous muscles, wringing the heart as yet only lightly touched by orgy, illness and the pursuit of knowledge. Just as, when a famous criminal arrives at the galleys he is respectfully welcomed by the convicts, so all these human demons, well-versed in torture, acclaimed an exorbitant sorrow and a wound whose depths their gaze could probe; they acknowledged him as a prince of their tribe thanks to the majesty of his mute irony and the elegant shabbiness of his attire.

Admittedly the young man had a stylish evening coat, but the junction of his waistcoat and cravat was too carefully preserved for one to suppose that he was wearing linen underneath. His hands, as dainty as a woman's, were none too clean; in fact, for the last two days he had worn no gloves. If the banker and his assistants shuddered, it was because some vestiges of the charm of innocence still bloomed in his slender, delicate proportions, his sparse, fair and naturally curly hair. He still had the face of a young man of twenty-five, and vice looked only to have touched it lightly. The vitality of youth was still warring with the enervating effects of dissipation; the struggle between light and darkness, between the forces of death and those of life gave an impression of grace as well as horror. The young man was standing there like an angel stripped of his halo, one who had strayed from his path. And so each of those emeritus professors of vice and infamy, like toothless old women seized with pity at the sight of a beautiful girl offering herself up to corruption, was ready to call out to the novice: 'Leave this place!' But the young man walked straight up to the table, remained standing, and blindly threw on to the cloth a gold coin he had been holding. It rolled on to black. Then, with the fortitude of such souls as abhor pettifogging uncertainties, he looked at the banker with a glance which was at once turbulent and calm.

This throw aroused such great interest that the old men laid no stake. But the Italian, in passionate single-mindedness, seized on an idea which took his fancy: he laid his pile of gold on the red in opposition to the stranger's play. The banker forgot to utter the conventional phrases which by dint of repetition have degenerated into a raucous and unintelligible cry:

'Place your bets!'

'The bets are placed!'

'Betting is closed!'

The dealer spread out the cards and seemed to be wishing good luck to the latest arrival, indifferent as he was to the loss or gain sustained by those addicted to those sombre pleasures. All the watchers guessed that the melodramatic closing scene of a noble life hung on the fate of that one gold coin; their eyes glittered as they studied the fateful scraps of pasteboard. And yet, in spite of the intentness with which they scrutinized turn by turn the young man and the cards, they could perceive no sign of emotion on his cold, resigned face.

'Red wins,' the dealer proclaimed. 'And even numbers over eighteen.'

A strange, muffled rattle issued from the Italian's throat as he saw the crumpled bank-notes falling one by one as the banker threw them down to him. As for the young man, he did not realize he had lost until the croupier stretched out his rake to pull in his last napoleon. The ivory hit the gold with a sharp click and the coin, fast as an arrow, shot across the table to join the pile of gold spread out in front of the bank. The stranger gently closed his eyes and the colour faded from his lips. But he soon lifted his eyelids again, his mouth regained its coral redness, he put on the air of an Englishman who sees no further mystery in life, and disappeared without even one of those pleading looks which despairing gamblers often cast around the ring of bystanders, hoping for some consolation. How many events can be crowded into the space of a second! How much depends on the throw of a dice!

'I bet that was the last shot in his locker!' the croupier said with a grin, after a moment's silence while he held the gold coin between his forefinger and thumb to show it to the assembled company.

'A young idiot who's going to jump into the river!' said an old *habitué*, looking round him at the gamblers, who all knew one another.

'Likely enough!' exclaimed an attendant as he took a pinch of snuff.

'If only we had followed that gentleman's example!' one of the old men said to his cronies as he pointed to the Italian.

All eyes were turned to the lucky gambler, whose hands shook as he counted his bank-notes.

'I heard,' he said, 'a voice crying in my ear: "The Game will get the better of that young man's despair."'

'He's no gambler,' the banker responded. 'Otherwise he would have divided his money into three lots to stand a better chance.'

The young man was leaving without claiming his hat, but the old watchdog, having noticed its battered condition, returned it to him without a word. The young gamester automatically gave up the check and went downstairs whistling *Di tanto palpiti*[3] so softly that he himself could scarcely hear its charming notes.

*

He soon found himself under the arcades of the Palais-Royal, went through to the Rue Saint-Honoré, made for the Tuileries Gardens and crossed them with hesitant step. He was plodding along as in the middle of a desert, elbowed by men he did not see, attentive, through the hubbub of the crowd, to one voice only – that of death. He was in fact lost in a daze of meditation similar to that which used to fasten on criminals as the tumbril conveyed them from the Palais de Justice to the Place de Grève,

3. From Rossini's *Tancred*. Balzac was a great admirer of Rossini.

towards the scaffold reddened with all the blood shed there since 1793.

There is something grandiose and awe-inspiring about suicide. A multitude of people may fall like children, who tumble from too low down to hurt themselves. But when one of the great is dashed to pieces he must have dropped from a great height after soaring to the skies and catching sight of some inaccessible paradise. How fierce must be the hurricanes which force him to seek peace of soul from the muzzle of a pistol! How many young men of talent, shut up in a garret, wither and perish for lack of a friend, for lack of a woman to console them, alone in the midst of a million fellow beings, while a bored crowd, glutted with gold, looks on.

Seen from this angle, suicide assumes gigantic proportions. Between self-slaughter and the burgeoning hope that summoned a man to Paris in his youth, God alone knows what a chaos there lies of abandoned projects and poems, of stifled cries of despair, of fruitless efforts and birth-strangled masterpieces! Every suicide is a poem sublime in its melancholy. Where will you find, emerging from the ocean of literature, a book that can vie in genius with a news-item such as:

Yesterday, at four o'clock, a woman threw herself into the Seine from the Pont des Arts.

Compared with this laconic sentence from a Paris evening paper, everything pales – melodramas, novels, and even the ancient title-page, *The Lamentations of the glorious King of Kaernavan, thrown into prison by his own Children*: the last fragment of a lost book, the mere reading of which reduced Sterne to tears, at a time when he was himself leaving his wife and children in want.

The stranger was a prey to countless thoughts of this kind which flitted through his brain like tattered flags fluttering amid the stress of battle. If for a moment he laid down the burden of intelligence and memory in order to pause in front of a clump of flowers whose heads swayed languidly in the breeze amid mounds of verdure, instantly seized by a spasm of life still rebelling against the oppressive idea of suicide, he lifted his eyes to heaven, and there grey clouds, gusts of wind laden with melancholy and a leaden atmosphere still counselled death. He made his way towards the Pont Royal, thinking of the last fantasies of his predecessors. He smiled as he remembered that Lord Castlereagh had satisfied the humblest of our needs before cutting his throat, and that Auger, of the French Academy, had searched for his snuff-box in order to take a pinch as he walked out to meet his death. He was analysing these eccentricities of conduct and examining his own reactions when, as he pressed against the parapet of the bridge in order to let a burly costermonger go by, this man having lightly brushed against his coat-sleeve, he was surprised to find himself carefully shaking the dust off it. Having reached the middle of the bridge, he gave a black look at the water.

'Bad weather to drown yourself!' a ragged old woman said to him with a laugh. 'It's filthy and it's cold, the Seine is!'

He answered with an unaffected smile that bore witness to the pitch of delirium his courage had reached; but he gave a sudden shudder when he saw in the distance, on the Tuileries landing stage, the hut with a notice-board over it on which the following words are traced in letters a foot high: FIRST-AID FOR THE DROWNING. M. Dacheux[4] appeared before him armed with charitable intentions, leaping into activity and setting in motion the virtuous oars that break drowning people's skulls when they are unfortunate enough to come to the surface. He could see him shouting at the inquisitive onlookers, sending for a doctor, getting his fumigating apparatus ready.[5] He could read the articles, deploring the accident, written by journalists in the interval between enjoying themselves at dinner and watching a ballet-dancer's smile; he could hear the chink of silver paid to boatmen by the prefect of police for the recovery of his body. Once dead, he was worth fifty francs; alive, he was merely a man of talent, without friends or patrons, with nowhere to sleep and no one to sing his praises: a social cipher, of no use to the State which had no concern for him. But death in full daylight seemed sordid to him, and so he decided to die by

4. Inspector of river-side first-aid posts.
5. Rectal injections of tobacco smoke then formed part of the first-aid treatment given to the drowned.

night, in order to deliver an unrecognizable corpse to the society which had not appreciated his greatness while alive. So he strolled along, making for the Quai Voltaire while affecting the idolent gait of an idler bent on killing time.

When he descended the steps at the end of the footpath over the bridge, at the corner of the quay, his attention was drawn to the array of second-hand books on the parapet. He only just stopped himself bargaining for a few of them. He broke into a smile, philosophically thrust his hands back into his waistcoat pockets, and was about to walk on again with an air of unconcern tinged with cold disdain, when he was surprised to hear some coins jingling in a truly fantastic manner in the depth of his pocket. A smile of hope stole from his lips to every feature, lit up his brow, and brought a gleam of joy to his eyes and haggard cheeks. This spark of gladness was like the glow that runs through the remains of a piece of paper already consumed in the flame. But his face darkened as such ashes do: it grew as gloomy as before when, pulling his hand hastily from his pocket, the stranger saw there were three copper coins.

'Ah! Kind gentleman! *La carita*! *La carita*! *Caterina*! Just a penny to buy bread!'

A young chimney-sweep, with a black, puffy face, a sooty brown skin and ragged clothes, held his hand out to grasp the young man's last coppers.

Two paces away from the little Savoyard, a poor old man, shamefaced, infirm, decrepit, wearing a wretched coat cut out of some curtain material, murmured to him in a low, raucous voice:

'Good sir, give me what you will. I will pray to God for you ...'

But, when the young man had looked at him, the old man said no more and did not repeat his request, perhaps because he recognized on his sad countenance the signs of a harsher poverty than his own.

'*La carita*! *La carita*!'

The stranger threw his small change to the boy and the old pauper as he stepped off the pavement to go towards the houses: he could no longer stand the heart-rending sight of the Seine.

'We will pray to God to keep you in long life,' the two beg-gars told him.

As he arrived at the window of a print-seller's shop, this man so near to death, met a young woman alighting from a smart carriage-and-pair. Ravished, he eyed this delightful apparition, whose pale features were harmoniously framed in the satin of an elegant hat. He was enchanted by her slender waist and graceful movements. Her dress, which lifted slightly as she stepped down, gave him a glimpse of a leg whose dainty curves were outlined by a white, close-fitting stocking. She entered the shop, discussed the price of certain albums and collections of lithographs, and paid for them with several gold coins which glittered and jingled on the counter.

The young man lingered on the threshold, ostensibly in order to study the engravings in the show-case, and quickly ex-changed with the beautiful stranger the most penetrating glance a man can cast in return for one of those careless looks casually thrown at passers-by. He for his part was bidding farewell to woman and love; but this ultimate, insistently questioning gaze went uncomprehended, failed to stir the heart of this frivolous woman, did not raise a blush or cause her to drop her eyes. What did it mean to her? One more tribute of admiration, one more desire aroused which, that evening, would bring her the pleasing thought: 'I was looking my best today.'

The young man quickly turned to another show-case and did not look round when the unknown woman stepped back into her carriage. The horses trotted off and this last picture of luxury and elegance faded away, just as his own life was about to fade away. He walked with melancholy step alongside the shops, listlessly examining the merchandise displayed. When the shops came to an end he studied the Louvre, the Institute, the towers of Notre-Dame, the turrets of the Palace and the Pont des Arts. These monuments appeared to be taking on a dreary look as they reflected the grey tints of the sky, whose rare gleams of sunlight imparted a menacing air to Paris which, like a pretty woman, is subject to inexplicable whims, to alternations of ugliness and beauty. Thus, nature itself was conspiring to plunge the dying man into a painful kind of ecstasy. A prey to that maleficent force whose solvent action finds a vehicle in the fluid that circulates in our nerves, he felt his frame imperceptibly invaded by the phenomena of fluidity. The tempestuous blasts of this death-agony seemed to toss him hither and thither as waves toss a boat, so that he saw buildings and men through a haze in which everything was swaying. Wishing to shake free of the titillation produced by the action of his physical nature upon his mind, he walked towards an old curiosity shop with the intention of finding something to occupy his senses, or else to pass the time before nightfall bargaining over the price of *objets d'art*. He was as it were soliciting courage and begging for a stimulant, like criminals afraid of breaking down on their way to the scaffold; but the consciousness of impending death momentarily gave the young man the self-assurance of a duchess who has two lovers, and he entered the old curiosity shop with a free-and-easy air, showing on his lips a forced smile like that of a drunkard. Was he not indeed drunk with life, or perhaps with death? Soon his dizziness came back, and he continued to perceive things in strange colours or starting into slight movement, an effect no doubt of the irregular circulation of his blood, which now was foaming like a cascade, now still and dull like tepid water.

In simple terms, he asked to be taken round the show-rooms in order too find out if they contained any interesting objects which might take his fancy. A young assistant with a fresh and chubby face and red hair, wearing an otter-skin cap, handed over the care of the shop to an old peasant woman, a sort of female Caliban employed in cleaning a stove whose marvellous handiwork was due to the genius of Bernard Palissy; then he said to the stranger with an air of unconcern:

'Look round, sir, look round! On the ground floor we have only fairly ordinary things, but if you will take the trouble to go up to the first floor I can show you some very fine mummies from Cairo, several pieces of inlaid pottery, a few carvings in ebony, *genuine renaissance*, which have recently come in and are incredibly beautiful.'

In the deplorable situation in which the stranger found himself, this guide's patter, this idiotic salesman's talk affected his nerves like the irritating commonplaces by which narrow minds torture a man of genius. Carrying his cross to the end, he appeared to be listening to his guide and answered him with gestures or monosyllables; but little by little he was able to assert the right to be silent and to give himself over without constraint to his last terrible meditations. He had the soul of a poet and here, chance had given it an immense pasture on which to graze: he was to see in advance the debris of a score of civilizations.

*

At first sight the show-rooms offered him a chaotic medley of human and divine works. Crocodiles, apes and stuffed boas grinned at stained-glass windows, seemed to be about to snap at carved busts, to be running after lacquer-ware or to be clambering up chandeliers. A Sèvres vase on which Madame Jaquetot had painted Napoleon was standing next to a sphinx dedicated to Sesostris. The beginnings of creation and the events of yesterday were paired off with grotesque good humour. A roasting-jack was posed on a monstrance, a Republican sabre on a medieval arquebus. Madame du Barry, painted in pastel by Latour, with a star on her head, nude and enveloped in cloud, seemed to be concupiscently contemplating an Indian chibouk and trying to divine some purpose in the spirals of smoke which were drifting towards her.

Instruments of death, poniards, quaint pistols, weapons with secret springs were hobnobbing with instruments of life: porcelain soup-tureens, Dresden china plates, translucent porcelain cups from China, antique salt-cellars, comfit-dishes from feudal times. An ivory ship was sailing under full canvas on the back of an immovable tortoise. A pneumatic machine was poking out the eye of the Emperor Augustus, who remained majestic and unmoved. Several portraits of French aldermen and Dutch burgomasters, insensible now as during their life-time, rose above this chaos of antiques and cast a cold and disapproving glance at them.

All the countries on earth seemed to have brought here some

remnants of their sciences and a sample of their arts. It was a sort of philosophical midden in which nothing was lacking, neither the Red Indian's calumet nor the green and gold slipper of the seraglio, nor the yatogan of the Moor, nor the brazen image of the Tartar. There was even the soldier's tobacco-pouch, the ciborium of the priest and the plumes from a throne. Furthermore, these monstrous tableaux were subjected to a thousand accidents of lighting by the whimsical effects of a multitude of reflected gleams due to the confusion of tints and the abrupt contrasts of light and shade. The ear fancied it heard stifled cries, the mind imagined that it caught the thread of unfinished dramas, and the eye that it perceived half-smothered glimmers. Lastly, persistent dust had cast its thin coating over all these objects, whose multiple angles and numerous sinuosities produced the most picturesque of impressions.

To begin with, the stranger compared these three showrooms, crammed with the relics of civilizations and religions, deities, royalties, masterpieces of art, the products of debauchery, reason and unreason, to a mirror of many facets, each one representing a whole world. After registering this hazy impression, he tried to make a choice of specimens to be enjoyed; but, in the process of gazing, pondering, dreaming, he was overcome by a fever which was perhaps due to the hunger which was gnawing at his vitals. His senses ended by being numbed at the sight of so many national and individual existences, their authenticity guaranteed by the human pledges which had survived them. The longing that had caused him to visit the shop was satisfied: he left real life behind him, ascended by degrees to an ideal world, and reached the enchanted palaces of ecstasy where the universe appeared to him in transitory gleams and tongues of fire; just as, long ago, the future of mankind had filed past in flaming visions before the gaze of Saint John of Patmos.

A multitude of sorrowing faces, gracious or terrifying, dimly or clearly descried, remote or near at hand, rose up before him in masses, in myriads, in generations. Egypt in its mysterious rigidity, emerged from its sands, represented by a mummy swathed in black bandages; then came the Pharaohs burying entire peoples in order to build a tomb for themselves; then Moses and the Hebrews and the wilderness: the whole of the ancient world, in all its solemnity, drifted before his eyes. But here, cool and graceful, a marble statue posed on a wreathed column, radiantly white, spoke to him of the voluptuous myths of Greece and Ionia. Oh, who would not have smiled, as he did, to see upon a red background, in the fine clay of an Etruscan vase, the brown girl dancing before the god Priapus and joyously saluting him? Facing her was a Latin queen lovingly fondling her chimaera! The capricious pleasures of imperial Rome were there in every aspect: the bath, the couch, the dressing-table ritual of some indolent, pensive Julia awaiting her Tibullus. Armed with the power of Arabian talismans, the head of Cicero evoked the memories of republican Rome and unwound for him the scroll of Livy's histories. The young man gazed on the *Senatus populusque romanus*: the consul, the lictors, the purple-edged togas, the fights in the Forum, the plebs aroused to wrath. All this filed past him like the insubstantial figures of a dream.

Then Christian Rome became the dominant theme in these presentations. One painting showed the heavens opened and in it he saw the Virgin Mary bathed in a cloud of gold in the midst of angels, eclipsing the sun in glory, lending an ear to the lamentations of the sufferer on whom this regenerate Eve smiled gently. As he fingered a mosaic made of different lavas from Vesuvius and Etna, in imagination he emerged into sundrenched and tawny Italy: he was an onlooker at the Borgias' feasts, he rode through the Abruzzi, sighed after Italian mistresses, worshipping their pale cheeks and dark, elongated eyes.

Espying a medieval dagger with a hilt as cunningly wrought as a piece of lace, with rust patches on it like bloodstains, he thought with a shudder of mighty trysts interrupted by the cold blade of a husband's sword. India and its religions lived again in an idol dressed in gold and silk with conical cap and lozenge-shaped ear-flaps folded upwards and adorned with bells. Near this grotesque figure a rush mat, as pretty as the Indian dancer who had once rolled herself in it, still exhaled the perfume of sandalwood. The mind was startled into perceptiveness by a monster from China with twisted gaze, contorted mouth and writhing limbs: the creation of an inventive people weary of unvarying beauty and drawing ineffable pleasure from the luxuriant diversity of ugliness.

A salt-cellar from Benvenuto Cellini's workshop brought him back to the bosom of the Renaissance at a period when art and licence flourished together, when sovereign princes found diversion in torture and prelates at Church Councils rested from their labours in the arms of courtesans after decreeing chastity for mere priests. He saw the conquests of Alexander carved on a cameo, the massacres of Pizarro etched on a match-lock arquebus, the wars of religion – frenzied, seething, pitiless – engraved on the base of a helmet. Then the charming pageantry of chivalry sprang up from a Milanese suit of armour, brightly furbished, superbly damascened, beneath whose visor the eyes of a paladin still gleamed.

For him this ocean of furnishings, inventions, fashions, works of art and relics made up an endless poem. Forms, colours, concepts of thought came to life again; but nothing complete presented itself to his mind. The poet in him had to finish these sketches by the great painter who had composed the vast palette on to which the innumerable accidents of human life had been thrown in such disdainful profusion. Having encompassed the whole world, having contemplated whole countries, reigns and eras, the young man returned to individual existences. He embodied himself once more in individuals, thrusting the life of nations into the background as being too overwhelming for one man to take stock of them.

Here a child modelled in wax lay sleeping, saved from the cabinet of Ruysch,[6] and this ravishing creation reminded him of the joys of his early years. At the fascinating sight of the virginal loin-cloth of a girl from Tahiti, his fervid imagination conjured up a picture of the simple life of nature, the chaste nudity of genuine purity, the delights of indolence, so natural to man, a whole lifetime of tranquillity spent on the banks of a cool and

6. Actually Fredrik Ruysch (1638–1731) had made a collection of embalmed corpses which gained some renown as a museum of anatomy.

gentle stream or beneath a banana plant which, untended by man, bestows its delectable manna on him. But suddenly he became a corsair and wrapped himself in the terrible poetry which marks the role of Lara, having taken rapid inspiration from the pearly tints of numberless sea-shells, his imagination stirred by the sight of corals still smelling of the kelp and sea-wrack torn from its bed by Atlantic storms.

Admiring farther on the delicate miniatures, the arabesques of azure and gold which enriched a priceless illuminated missal, he forgot the tumults of the sea. Rocked in the cradle of peaceful thought, he turned once more to study and science, longed for the easeful life of a monk, free from pain and free from pleasure, sleeping snug in a cell and gazing out through its Gothic window on to the meadows, woods and vineyards of his monastery. Confronted with a Teniers canvas, he donned a soldier's uniform or a workman's rags; he had the fancy to wear the dirty, smoky cap of the Flemings, to get fuddled with their beer, play cards with them and to throw a smile at a big, attractively plump peasant-girl. He shivered as he looked at a snow scene by Mieris, fought doughtily at the sight of a battle-scene by Salvator Rosa. He ran a finger across an Illinois tomahawk and felt himself scalped by a Cherokee's hunting-knife. Enchanted to discover a rebec, he entrusted it to the hand of a chatelaine, thrilled to the tuneful ballads she sang and declared his love for her in an evening setting beside a Gothic fireplace, in a half-light which scarcely allowed her consenting glance to be seen. He clutched at every joy, grasped at every grief, made all the formulas of existence his own and so generously dispersed his life and feelings over the images of that empty, plastic nature that the tread of his own footsteps echoed within himself like far-off sounds from another world, like the roar of Paris heard from the topmost towers of Notre-Dame.

As he climbed the inner staircase leading to the rooms of the first floor, he saw votive bucklers, panoplies, carved tabernacles, wooden figures fixed to the walls and standing on every stair. Pursued by the strangest of forms, by fabulous creations poised on the confines between life and death, he walked along as in the enchantment of a dream. Indeed, in some doubt as to his own existence, he felt himself at one with these curious objects: neither altogether living nor altogether dead. When he entered the new series of show-rooms, daylight was fading; but one scarcely needed light to distinguish the treasures of gold and silver piled up here.

The most extravagant whims of spendthrifts who had died in garrets after owning millions were to be found in this vast museum of human folly. A little writing-desk that had cost a hundred thousand francs and had been bought back for a five-franc piece stood next to a secret lock whose price would formerly have sufficed for a king's ransom. The human race appeared there in all its petty pomp, in all the splendour of its pretentious triviality. An ebony table, a gem of artistic creation, carved from designs by Jean Goujon, which had cost years of toil, had perhaps been picked up for the price of a load of firewood. Precious caskets and furniture wrought by the hands of magicians were jumbled together with a fine indifference.

'You have millions here!' the young man exclaimed as he arrived at the last of an immense suite of rooms, gilded and sculptured by artists of the previous century.

'Say rather thousands of millions,' rejoined the stout, plump-cheeked attendant. 'But that's nothing to what you'll see if you go up to the third floor.'

The visitor followed his guide and came to a fourth gallery, where his tired eyes were greeted by, in turn, a number of paintings by Poussin, a sublime statue by Michelangelo, several enchanting landscapes by Claude Lorrain, a Gerard Dow which resembled a page of Sterne, Rembrandts and Murillos, some Velasquez canvases as sombre and vivid as a poem by Lord Byron; then ancient bas-reliefs, goblets in agate, wonderful pieces of onyx! In short, works that would discourage anyone from working, so many masterpieces brought together as to wear down enthusiasm and turn one against the arts. He came to a Virgin by Raphael, but he was tired of Raphael. A face by Correggio demanded his attention but failed to obtain it. A priceless vase of ancient porphyry, chased round with carvings figuring the most grotesquely licentious of all Roman priapic orgies – how it would have delighted some Corinna of five centuries before Christ![7] – drew scarcely a smile from him. He felt smothered under the debris of fifty vanished centuries, nauseated with this surfeit of human thought, crushed under the weight of luxury and art, oppressed by these constantly recurring shapes which, like monsters springing up under his feet, engendered by some wicked genie, engaged him in endless combat.

Alike in its caprices to our modern chemistry, which would reduce creation to one single gas, does not the soul distil fearful poisons in the rapid concentration of its pleasures, its powers, or its ideas? Do not many men perish through the lightning action of some moral acid or other suddenly injected into their innermost being?[8]

'What does this box contain?' he asked as they came to a large cabinet, the last of these treasure-houses of glorious achievement, human effort and ingenuity, and artistic wealth. He was pointing to a big, square mahogany chest which was hanging from a nail by a silver chain.

'Oh, the master has the key to that,' the stout assistant said with an air of mystery. 'If you wish to see the portrait inside, I will gladly venture to inform him.'

'Venture?' the young man said, 'Is your master a prince?'.

'I really don't know,' the attendant replied.

They looked at each other for a moment, each of them as astonished as the other. Having interpreted the stranger's silence as the expression of a wish, the assistant left him alone in the cabinet.

Have you ever plunged into the immensity of space and time by reading the geological treatises of Cuvier? Borne away on the wings of his genius, have you hovered over the illimitable abyss of the past as if a magician's hand were holding you aloft? As one penetrates from seam to seam, from stratum to stratum and discovers, under the quarries of Montmartre or in the schists of the Urals, those animals whose fossilized remains belong to

7. The reference is either to a lyric poetess of ancient Greece, a contemporary of Pindar, or to the heroine of Mme de Staël's novel *Corinne* (1807).

8. These two rather obscure sentences have a general reference to Balzac's eccentric psychological doctrine. Their immediate import is that Raphael de Valentin is about to reach the point of no return.

antediluvian civilizations, the mind is startled to catch a vista of the milliards of years and the millions of peoples which the feeble memory of man and an indestructible divine tradition[9] have forgotten and whose ashes heaped on the surface of our globe, form the two feet of earth which furnish us with bread and flowers. Is not Cuvier the greatest poet of our century? Certainly Lord Byron has expressed in words some aspects of spiritual turmoil; but our immortal natural historian has reconstructed worlds from bleached bones, has, like Cadmus, rebuilt cities by means of teeth, peopled anew a thousand forests with all the wonders of zoology thanks to a few chips of coal and rediscovered races of giants in a mammoth's foot. These figures rise from the soil, tower up and people whole regions whose dimensions are in harmony with their colossal stature. He writes poems in numbers, he is sublime in the way he places cyphers after a seven.[10] He calls æons back into being without pronouncing the abracadabra of magic; he digs out a fragment of gypsum, descries a footprint in it, and cries out: 'Behold!' And suddenly marble turns into animals, dead things live anew and lost worlds are unfolded before us! After countless dynasties of gigantic creatures, after endless generations of fishes, innumerable clans of molluscs, comes at last the human race, the degenerate product of a grandiose type whose mould was perhaps broken by the Creator Himself.[11] Their imagination enflamed by his retrospective glance, these puny men, born only yesterday, are able to stride across chaos, intone an endless hymn and imagine the shape of the past history of the universe in a sort of retrogressive apocalypse. In the presence of this awesome resurrection due

9. As stated in the Introduction, Balzac blended science with mysticism (above, p. 8). The 'divine tradition' here referred to is the special communication vouchsafed to man by God from primitive times: obscured but recoverable by specially gifted, in fact 'illuminated' souls.

10. After the supposed 6,000 or so years of Creation according to the Bible, archaeology was now computing in hundreds of thousands, and then millions of years. Hence Balzac's amazement.

11. Balzac's admiration of Cuvier may seem naïve to us today. But his palæological discoveries, like those of Geoffrey de Saint-Hilaire, whom Balzac admired even more, prepared the way for Darwin and the Origin of Species.

to the voice of a single man, that tiny grain granted to our use in this nameless infinity, which is common to all spheres and which we have baptized as TIME, that minute of life seems pitiable. We wonder, crushed as we are under so many worlds in ruin, what can our glories avail, our hatreds and our loves, and if it is worth living at all if we are to become, for future generations, an imperceptible speck in the past. Having lost our footing in the present, we are become as though dead – until our footman comes in to tell us: 'Sir, my lady answers that she is expecting your visit this evening.'

The wonderful objects the sight of which had just revealed the whole of known creation to the young man plunged his soul in the dejection which the scientific vision of unknown creations produces in a philosophic mind. More than ever he wished to die. Collapsing into a curule chair, he allowed his gaze to wander over this phantasmagoric panorama of the past. The pictures lighted up, the faces of the Virgin smiled at him, the statues took on the deceptive colouring of life. These works of art, under the favour of the half-light, set dancing by the feverish turmoil fermenting in his stricken brain, stirred and whirled before his eyes. Each of the idols grinned at him, each face in every picture blinked its eyes as if to rest them. Every one of these strange shapes shuddered, quivered, moved gravely, lightly, gracefully or clumsily aside in accordance with its habits, character or composition. It was a weird witches' sabbath worthy of the fantasies glimpsed by Dr Faust on the Brocken. But these optical illusions born of weariness, the strain resulting from ocular tension or from the play of twilight shadows, had no power to frighten the stranger. The terrors of life had no hold on a soul which had already become familiar with the terrors of death. He even favoured with a sort of mocking complicity the bizarre elements in this moral galvanism whose prodigious manifestations were coupled with the last thoughts which gave him the feeling that he still existed. The silence around him was so profound that presently he allowed himself to drift into a gentle reverie whose impressions, growing more and more opaque, followed from nuance to nuance, as if by magic, the slow degradations of the daylight.

A glimmer falling from the sky threw out a last red gleam in its struggle with oncoming night. He looked up and saw the dim form of a skeleton sceptically wagging his skull from left to right as if to tell him: 'The dead are not yet ready to receive you!' Passing his hand over his brow to drive away sleep, the young man distinctly felt a cool breeze produced by some hairy thing which brushed his cheeks, and he shuddered. As the window-panes rattled under a dull blow, he supposed that this cold caress worthy of the mysteries of the tomb had been given him by a bat. For yet one more moment the vague glimmers of the setting sun enabled him to catch an indistinct view of the phantoms surrounding him; then the whole of this still life was effaced in a uniform tint of black.

Night, and his appointment with death, had suddenly come upon him. From then on there occurred a certain lapse of time during which he had no clear perception of terrestrial things, whether because he was buried in deep reverie or because he had yielded to the sleepiness provoked by fatigue and the crowding thoughts which were rending his heart. Suddenly he thought he heard himself called by a terrifying voice, and he shuddered just as when, in the middle of a lurid nightmare, we feel ourselves being hurled headlong to the bottom of an abyss. He closed his eyes, dazzled by the rays of a bright light. Then he saw, shining in the darkness, an orb of glowing red, and in the centre of it was a little old man, erect, turning the beam of a lamp upon him. He had neither heard him approach, speak nor move.

In this apparition there was something magical. The bravest of men, being thus startled awake, would surely have quailed at the sight of this individual who looked as if he had stepped out of a nearby sarcophagus. The amazing youthfulness that sparkled in the steady gaze of this spectral creature made it impossible for the stranger to believe in any supernatural effects; and yet, during the short space of time which separated his somnambulistic dream from his return to real life, he remained in the state of philosophic doubt recommended by Descartes, and in consequence, in spite of himself, was a prey to these inexplicable hallucinations whose mysteries our pride urges us to deny or which our impotent science strives in vain to analyse.

Picture to yourself a thin, wizened little old man, dressed in a black velvet gown pulled tight round the waist by a thick silk cord. On his head, a skull-cap, also of black velvet, allowed the long wisps of his white hair to fall down either temple; but it was pressed down on his skull in such a way as to provide a close frame for his forehead. His dressing-gown was swathed round his body like a voluminous shroud, so that the only human outline visible was his pale, narrow face. Had it not been for his skinny arm resembling a stick with a piece of material hanging from it and which the old man held aloft in order to bring the whole light of the lamp to bear on the young man, the face in question would have seemed to be suspended in mid-air. A grey, pointed beard concealed this odd person's chin and gave him the appearance of those Hebraic heads which serve as types to artists when they wish to portray the prophet Moses.

The man's lips were so colourless and so thin that one had to look with particular care to distinguish the line traced by his mouth in his white face. His wide, wrinkled brow, his pale and hollow cheeks, the implacable severity of his small green eyes, devoid of eyelashes and eyebrows, might well have made the stranger believe that Gerald Dow's *Money-Changer* had stepped down from his frame. The cunning of an inquisitor, indicated by the sinuosity of his wrinkles and the circular puckers on his temples, betokened a profound knowledge of earthly matters.

It was impossible to deceive this man, for he seemed to possess the gift of reading thoughts lurking deep in the most secretive of souls. The morality of every nation on the globe, their wisdom too, were summed up on his chilly countenance, just as the products of the entire world were piled up in his dusty showrooms. You could read in it the lucid serenity of an all-seeing God or else the arrogant self-sufficiency of a man who indeed has seen everything. A painter, using two different expressions and two touches of the brush, could have turned this figure either into a fine image of the eternal Father or the jeering mask of Mephistopheles, for at one and the same time there was supreme power in the forehead and sinister raillery playing about his mouth. By grinding all human grief to powder beneath a

44

pestle of enormous power, this man had doubtless suppressed all terrestrial joy. The doomed man shuddered at the thought that this aged genie inhabited a sphere remote from normal society, a sphere in which he lived in solitude, having no pleasures because he had no illusions left and suffering no pains because he no longer knew what pleasure meant. He stood erect, motionless, as fixed as a star in the midst of a luminous nebula. His green eyes, flashing with an indescribably imperturbable malice, seemed to light up the world of the mind in the same way as his lamp was lighting up the mysterious cabinet.

Such was the strange spectacle which met the young man's gaze as he opened his eyes after being lulled with thoughts of death and fanciful images. If he remained in a half daze, if for a moment he yielded to superstitions fit only for children listening to the tales told them by their nurses, this lapse must be attributed to the veil spread over his life and understanding by his meditations, to the jarring of his exasperated nerves, to the violent drama whose successive scenes had just now lavished on him such atrocious delights as can be contained in a pinch of opium. This vision was taking place in Paris, on the Quai Voltaire, in the nineteenth century, at a time and place which should surely rule out the possibility of magic. Close to the house in which the apostle of French scepticism [12] had breathed his last, the stranger, a disciple of Gay-Lussac and Arago, [13] one who scorned the sleight-of-hand tricks performed by the men in power, was no doubt giving in to the poetic hallucinations to which we often succumb in our desperate flight from heartbreaking truths, as if we wished to test the power of God. He therefore trembled before the light and the old man, perturbed by the inexplicable intuition of being confronted by some strange power, an emotion similar to that we have all felt in the presence of Napoleon or of some illustrious man of genius covered in glory.

'The gentleman wishes to see the portrait of Jesus Christ painted by Raphael?' the old man politely asked him in a voice whose clear and sharp sonority had a metallic quality. He placed

12. Voltaire.
13. Two outstanding physicists of the first half of the nineteenth century.

45

the lamp on the shaft of a broken column so as to flood the mahogany cabinet with its light.

At the hallowed names of Jesus Christ and Raphael, the young man gave the gesture of curiosity which no doubt the dealer had expected to provoke. He pressed a spring. Suddenly the mahogany panel slid along a groove, fell silently away and revealed the canvas to the admiring eyes of the stranger. At the sight of this immortal creation he forgot the fantastic objects he had studied in the shop and the wayward visions he had seen in slumber. He became himself once more, saw that the old man was merely a creature of flesh and blood, fully alive and in no way phantasmagorical. He began to live again in the real world. The tender solicitude, the mild serenity of our Lord's countenance exerted an immediate influence on him. A fragrance shed from Heaven dispelled the infernal tortures which were burning the marrow of his bones. The head of the Saviour of mankind seemed to stand out from the darkness of the background; a halo of light glittered brightly round his hair, from which this light had its source; in the brow and flesh-tones there was an eloquent conviction which issued from every feature in penetrating waves. The vermilion lips had just given utterance to the word of life, and the spectator was straining to recapture the sacred echoes of it in the air, beseeching the silence to repeat its entrancing parables, listening for it through future centuries and finding it again in the teachings of the past. The whole Gospel was contained in the calm simplicity of those eyes which called for adoration and offered refuge to the heavy-laden. Indeed the Catholic religion in its entirety could be read in the sublime and tender smile, expressive of the precept which sums it up: *Love one another!* It was a painting that inspired prayer, enjoined forgiveness, stifled selfishness and awakened every dormant virtue. Sharing the enchanting power of music, Raphael's work put the spectator under the imperious spell of his own memories. Its triumph was so complete that the painter himself was forgotten. The light which played on this masterpiece enhanced its beauty: there were moments when the Saviour's head, far removed, seemed to be stirring in the centre of a luminous haze.

'I covered that canvas with gold pieces,' said the dealer coolly.

'So then, death is the only way!' the young man exclaimed as he emerged from his daydream. It had ended in a thought which had put him back on the way towards the destiny awaiting him: step by step, imperceptibly, it had brought him down from the pinnacle of hope to which he had been clinging.[14]

'Ha! Ha! I was right then to suspect you!' replied the old man, grasping the other's hands and squeezing them in one of his with a vice-like grip.

The stranger smiled sadly at this misunderstanding, and said in a soft voice:

'Have no fear, sir. It's my own death and not yours I am talking about. – Why should I not admit an innocent piece of deceit?' he went on, after taking a look at the anxious old man. 'I was waiting for nightfall in order to drown myself without fuss. I came in to have a look at your treasures. Would not anyone pardon a man of science and poetry for indulging in this last pleasure?'

The mistrustful dealer sagaciously scrutinized the gloomy countenance of his pretended customer as he listened to his words. Being soon reassured by his doleful tone of voice, or perhaps because he discerned in his pallid features the sinister destiny which not so long ago had appalled a roomful of gamblers, he released his hands. But, taught by the experience of a century at least, he retained enough suspicion to stretch one arm negligently towards a sideboard as if to lean on it, and said, as he took up a stiletto:

'Have you been a supernumerary at the Treasury for three years without being paid a bonus?'[15]

The stranger could not refrain from smiling as he shook his head.

'Has your father reproached you too cruelly for being born? Or have you lost your honour?'

'If I consented to sacrifice my honour, I could go on living.'

'Have you been hissed off the stage at the Funambules

14. The idea here seems to be that, for a moment, Valentin is inclined to yield to the Saviour's call, but that in a revulsion of feeling he rejects it.

15. The antiquary suggests a number of possible motives for suicide.

theatre? Or have you been forced to write ballads to pay for your mistress's funeral?[16] Or, more likely, you are suffering from shortage of gold? Or perhaps you are trying to get the better of boredom. Come now, what vulgar error is driving you to suicide?'

'Do not look for the motives for my death in the commonplace urges which lead to the majority of suicides. Sparing myself the trouble of revealing to you my unexampled sufferings, difficult to express in ordinary language, I will just state that I am in the most profound, the most ignominious, the most excruciating of all kinds of destitution. And,' he added in a tone of voice whose savage pride gave the lie to the words he had just uttered, 'I will beg neither for help nor for consolation.'

'Well, well, well!'

These three syllables which were all the old man first uttered by way of reply sounded like the squeak of a rattle. Then he began again thus:

'Without forcing you to beg, without causing you to blush, without giving you a French centime, a Levantine para, a Sicilian tarant, a German heller, a Russian kopek, a Scottish farthing, a single sestertium or obol of the ancient world or a piastre of the new world, without offering you anything whatsoever in gold, silver, bullion, banknotes or letters of credit, I propose to make you richer, more powerful and more respected than a king can be – in a constitutional monarchy.'

The young man, believing the old fellow to be in his dotage, sat still as if paralysed without venturing to reply.

'Turn round,' said the dealer, suddenly seizing the lamp in order to direct its light on to the wall opposite the picture. 'Look at that WILD ASS'S SKIN,' he added.

The young man stood up abruptly and showed some surprise as he espied above the seat on which he was sitting a piece of shagreen fastened to the wall, not exceeding the dimensions of a fox's pelt. But, thanks to a phenomenon which at first he could not explain, this skin projected, from amid the deep darkness which reigned in the shop, such luminous rays that you might

16. This is what happens, in *Lost Illusions*, Part II (1843), to the poet Lucien de Rubempre.

have thought they emanated from a small comet. Unable to believe his eyes, the young man walked up to the supposed talisman which, it appeared, was to preserve him from misfortune. Although ridiculing it in his own mind, he leaned forward, stimulated by understandable curiosity, in order to examine the skin from every possible angle, and soon discovered a natural explanation of its strange brilliance. The black grains of the hide were so carefully polished and burnished, its zig-zag stripes were so clear and clean that, like the facets of a garnet, every irregularity in the surface of this oriental leather formed a tiny focus which vividly reflected the light. He mathematically demonstrated the cause of this phenomenon to the old man, whose only response was a sly smile. This smile of superiority convinced the young scientist that he was being made just then the victim of a hoax of some kind. Disinclined to take to the grave with him yet another riddle, he swiftly turned the skin round like a child in a hurry to find out the secret of a new toy.

'Aha!' he exclaimed. 'Here is the impress of the seal that Orientals call the seal of Solomon.'

'So you recognize it?' asked the dealer, snorting twice or thrice in a way expressive of more ideas than the most vigorous words could have communicated.

'Is there any man in the world so simple-minded as to believe in such stories?' the young man exclaimed, irritated at this silent laughter, so full of bitter derision. 'Do you not know,' he added, 'that Eastern superstitions held sacred the mystic form and the mendacious characters of this emblem which represents a fabulous power? I don't believe I should be accused of any greater credulity in this circumstance than if I talked of sphinxes or gryphons, whose existence is admitted as a matter of mythology.'

'Since you are an orientalist,' the old man resumed, 'perhaps you can read this inscription?'

He brought the lamp close to the talisman which the young man was holding back to front, and drew his attention to characters encrusted in the cellular tissue of this extraordinary hide, as if they had been part of the animal whose skin it had once been.

'I confess,' the stranger exclaimed, 'that I can scarcely guess the process used to engrave those letters so deeply on a wild ass's skin.'

And, as he made a sharp turn towards the tables laden with curiosities, his eyes seemed to be looking for something.

'What do you want?' the old man asked.

'Some tool to cut into the shagreen, in order to see if the letters are stamped or inlaid in it.'

The old man presented his stiletto to the stranger, who took it and attempted to cut into the skin at the place where the words were inscribed; but when he had removed a thin layer of leather the letters still showed so clear and so identical with those which were printed on the surface that, for a moment, he had the impression that he had removed nothing.

'The industry of the Levant has secrets that belong to it alone!' he said as he looked at the talismanic writing in a somewhat anxious frame of mind.

'Yes indeed,' the old man replied. 'It is better to blame it on man than on God!'

This is how these mysterious words were arranged:

او ملكتـني ملكت الكل

و لكن عمرك ملكي

و اراد الله هكذا

اطلب و ستنال مطالبك

و لكن قس مطالبك على عمرك

وهي هاهنا

فدكل مرامك ستنزل ايامك

اتريد في

الله مجيبك

آمين

That is to say, in our tongue:

POSSESS ME AND THOU SHALT POSSESS ALL THINGS.
BUT THY LIFE IS FORFEIT TO ME. SO HATH
GOD WILLED IT. EXPRESS A DESIRE
AND THY DESIRE SHALL BE FULFILLED.
BUT LET THY WISHES BE MEASURED
AGAINST THY LIFE. HERE IT LIES.
EVERY WISH WILL DIMINISH ME
AND DIMINISH THY DAYS.
DOST THOU DESIRE ME?
TAKE AND GOD WILL
GRANT THY WISH.
AMEN.

'Ah! So you can read Sanskrit [17] with ease,' the old man said. 'Perhaps you have travelled in Persia or Bengal?'

'No, sir,' replied the young man, running his finger curiously over the symbolic skin, which was tough enough to be taken for a piece of foil.

The old dealer set the lamp back on the column from which he had taken it, throwing the young man a glance expressive of cold irony, one which seemed to be saying: 'Already he's no longer thinking of dying.'

'Is it a hoax? Is there some mystery behind it?' the young stranger asked.

The old man shook his head and gravely answered:

'That I cannot tell you. I have offered the terrible power this talisman gives to men endowed with more energy than you seem to possess; but, while mocking at the problematic influence it might exert over their future destinies, not one of them would take the risk of concluding this pact so fatefully proposed by I know not what force. I think as they do: I doubted, I abstained, and ...'

'And you have never even tried it?' the young man broke in.

'Tried it!' the old man replied. 'If you were on top of the

17. The supposed text of the original, given above, is in arabic translated for Balzac by the orientalist Baron von Hammer-Purgstall.

column in the Place Vendôme, would you *try* throwing yourself in the air? Can one stop a course once one has embarked on it? Has it ever been possible to juggle with death? Before you came into this cabinet you had resolved on suicide; but suddenly you are absorbed by a puzzle and distracted from the notion of dying. Child that you are, does not every one of your days pose an enigma to you which is more interesting than this one? Listen to me. I have seen life under the licentious court of the Regency.[18] As you are now, I was penniless then and begging for crusts of bread. Nevertheless, I have reached the age of one hundred and two and become a millionaire: misfortune brought me wealth, and ignorance gave me education. I am going to reveal to you, in a few words, one of the great mysteries of human life. Man exhausts himself by two acts, instinctively accomplished, which dry up the sources of his existence. Two words express all the forms that these two causes of death can assume: will and power.[19] Between these two terms of human action there is another formula which wise men cling to, and to it I owe my happiness and long life. The exercise of the *will* consumes us; the exercise of *power* destroys us; but the pursuit of *knowledge* leaves our infirm constitution in a state of perpetual calm. So desire or volition is dead in me, killed by thought. Movement, or power, has been dissolved by the natural play of my organs. In short, I have invested my life, not in the heart, so easily broken, nor in the senses which are so readily blunted, but in the brain which does not wear out and outlasts everything. No kind of excess has galled either my soul or my body. And yet I have encompassed the whole wide world. My feet have trodden on the highest mountains of Asia and America. I have learnt all human languages and lived under every kind of rule. I have lent my money to a Chinese and taken his father's body as a pledge. I have slept under the tent of the Arab in reliance on his word, I have signed contracts in every European capital, and without a qualm I have left my gold in Red Indian wigwams. In short I have had everything I wanted because I have learned to dispense with everything. My sole ambition has

18. 1715–23.
19. See Introduction, p. 10, note 6.

been to see. To see, is that not to gain knowledge? And in the gaining of knowledge, young man, is there not intuitive enjoyment? Is it not to discover the very substance of fact and take possession of its very essence? What remains of a material possession? Only an idea. So then, judge how magnificent must be the life of a man who, being able to imprint his mind with every reality, transports into his soul the sources of happiness and extracts from them a thousand ideal ecstasies free of all earthly defilement. Thought is the key to all treasures and confers the joys of a miser without the anxieties a miser is prey to. And so my spirit has soared over the whole world and my pleasures have always consisted in intellectual enjoyments. My revelry has been to contemplate oceans, forests, mountains, to study nations. I have seen all, but in tranquillity and without fatigue. I have never coveted, but waited for things to come my way. I have walked through the universe as if it were the garden of an estate which belonged to me. The things that men call disappointments – loves, ambitions, setbacks, sadness are for me ideas that I convert into reveries; instead of feeling them I express and translate them; instead of letting them consume my life I dramatize and develop them; they divert me as though they were works of fiction which I can read thanks to an inner vision. Never having overtaxed my organs, I continue to enjoy robust health. Since my mind has inherited all the forces which I have not misused, this head of mine is still better furnished than my showrooms are. Here,' he said, tapping his forehead, 'here are the riches that matter. I spend beatific days letting my intelligence dwell on the past; I can summon to mind whole countries, vistas of beauty, views of the ocean, the faces that history has transfigured. I have an imaginary seraglio in which I possess all the women I have never had. Often I mentally review your wars and revolutions and pass judgement on them. Oh! How could one prefer the febrile and frivolous admiration for flesh more or less rosy, for shapes more or less rounded, how could one prefer all the disasters of frustrated desires to the superb faculty of summoning the whole universe to the bar of one's mind, to the thrill of being able to move without being throttled by the thongs of time or the fetters of space, to the pleasure of embracing and seeing everything, of leaning over the edge of the world in order to interrogate the other spheres and listen to the voice of God? Here you have,' he said in resonant tones as he pointed to the wild ass's skin, '*power* and *will* united. Here are your social ideas, your inordinate desires, your intemperance, the joys which kill, the pains which make life too intense – perhaps evil is only a violent pleasure. Who can say at what point delight becomes a pang or a pang delight? Are not the most vivid lights of the ideal world soothing to the eyes, while the softest darkness of the physical world always wounds them? Are not wisdom and knowledge almost synonymous terms? And what is dementia other than power or willpower carried to excess?'

'Yes, yes indeed! Excess! I want to live to excess!' the stranger cried as he grasped the skin.

'Young man, take care!' cried the centenarian with incredible vehemence.

'I had decided to give my life to study and thought, but they have not even provided me with food,' the stranger replied. 'I don't want to be either the dupe of a sermon worthy of Sweden-borg, or of your eastern amulet, or of your charitable efforts to keep me in a world where henceforth it is impossible for me to live – Let's put it to the test!' he added, convulsively seizing the talisman, his eyes fixed on the old man. 'I wish for a dinner of royal splendour, a Bacchanalian feast worthy of the century in which, they say, every perfection has been achieved. Let my fellow-guests be young, witty, free from prejudice and gay to the point of folly! Let the wines follow one another, each sharper and more effervescent than the last, and heady enough to make us drunk for three days! Let the night be embellished with passionate women! My wish is that delirious, wild revelry shall sweep us away on its four-horse chariot beyond the ends of the earth and cast us on to unknown shores! Whether our souls soar up to heaven or dive into the mire, whether they reach upwards or plunge downwards, what matter to me? So then I command this sinister power to melt all joys into a single joy for me. Yes, my need is to enfold all the pleasures of heaven and earth in one last embrace and to die of it. And therefore my will is that libations be followed by licentious orgies worthy of ancient times. I call for songs to awaken the dead, threefold kisses, endless kisses echoing through Paris, wakening married couples and kindling them to a lust which shall take them back to their youth, even were they over seventy!'

A peal of laughter from the throat of the little old man rang in the ears of the young lunatic like a roar from hell's mouth and put an imperious stop to his ravings.

'Do you think,' the dealer asked him, 'that the floor here is going to open suddenly to make way for tables sumptuously laid out and guests from the other world? No, no, rash young fool. You have signed the pact, and there is no more to say. From now on, your desires will be scrupulously satisfied, but at the expense of your life. The circle of your days, represented by this skin, will shrink in accordance with the force and number of your desires, from the lightest to the most exorbitant. The brahmin to whom I owe this talisman once explained to me that there would be a mysterious conformity between the destiny and the wishes of its possessor. Your first desire is a vulgar one: I could bring it to pass myself, but I leave that to the chain of events in your new existence. After all, you were bent on dying: well, your suicide is merely postponed.'

The stranger, surprised and irritated at being continuously mocked at by this singular old man, the half-hearted nature of whose philanthropic intentions appeared to him to be clearly demonstrated by this last gibe, exclaimed:

'Well, sir, it will be easy to see if my luck changes during the time it will take me to cross the embankment. But, if you are not amusing yourself at the expense of an unhappy man, I wish, as repayment for so fatal a service, that you may fall in love with a ballet-dancer! You will then realize what happiness there is in a life of dissipation, and perhaps you will start spending lavishly all the wealth you have husbanded in so philosophic a spirit.'

He left without hearing the deep groan that the old man uttered, crossed the showrooms and walked down the staircase of the establishment, followed by the stout, chubby-faced attendant who tried in vain to light his way; he was running with the swiftness of a thief surprised red-handed. In the blindness which came from a kind of delirium, he did not even notice the incredible ductility of the wild ass's skin which, now as supple as a glove, rolled up in his frenzied fingers and easily went into the coat pocket in which he stowed it almost mechanically. As he dashed out from the door of the shop on to the roadway, he charged into three young men who were walking along with arms linked.

*

'Brute!'
'Idiot!'
Such were the first courtesies they exchanged. Then:
'Why! It's Raphael!'
'Well now, we were looking for you.'
'What! It's really you?'
These three friendly greetings took the place of insult as soon as the light from a street-lamp swinging in the wind fell on the faces of this astonished group.

'My dear fellow,' said the young man whom Raphael had nearly knocked over. 'You must come with us.'
'Why, what's afoot?'
'Come along with us and I'll tell you all about it.'
Willy-nilly, Raphael found himself surrounded with friends, and they, linking arms with him to keep him in their joyous band, bore him off towards the Pont des Arts.
'We have been hunting for you for the past week or so, dear chap,' continued the spokesman of the group. 'At your respectable Saint-Quentin abode, whose immovable sign, incidentally, still offers alternative black and red letters as in the time of Jean-Jacques Rousseau, your Léonarde[20] told us you had gone to the country. And yet we certainly didn't look like money-lenders, process-servers, creditors, bailiffs, etc. No matter! Rastignac had spotted you the evening before at the Bouffons,[21] so we plucked up courage and made it a point of honour to find out if you were roosting on the trees in the Champs-Elysées or spending the night on stretched ropes in one of those philanthropic establishments in which mendicants sleep at a penny a time; or if you

20. The cook in the robbers' cavern in Lesage's *Gil Blas*, I, iv.
21. Alternative name for the Théâtre des Italiens.

were better off than that and were camping out in some boudoir or other. But nowhere did we find you, nor was your name listed in either of the debtors' prisons. The ministries, the opera-house, the brothels, cafés, libraries, police registers, newspaper-offices, restaurants, theatre foyers, in short, all the orderly and disorderly houses in Paris having been systematically combed, we were mourning the loss of a man endowed with enough genius to make people search for him both at court or in prison. We were talking about canonizing you as a hero of the July Revolution! And upon my word we really were upset at losing you.'

At this moment, Raphael was crossing the Pont des Arts with his friends, and from there, without listening to them, he was looking at the Seine, whose roaring waters were reflecting the lights of Paris. As he passed over this river, into which he had been planning to throw himself not long since, he reflected that the old man's predictions had already come true: the hour of his death had inevitably been deferred.

'And we were really missing you!' his friend continued, still harping on the same theme. 'We have a scheme afoot in which you were to be included as a superior man, that is to say, as a man who can rise to any occasion. The dilapidation of the constitution by the royal conjurer is proceeding faster than ever today, my dear fellow.[22] The infamous monarchy which has been overthrown by popular heroism was a woman of loose life with whom one could banquet and make merry; but our country itself is a virtuous – not to say shrewish – spouse. We must, whether we will or not, put up with her frigid caresses. So here we are: political power has been transferred, as you know, from the Tuileries Palace to the newspaper offices, just as economic power has changed its address from the Faubourg Saint-Ger-main[23] to the Chaussée-d'Antin.[24] But here's something you perhaps don't know: the government, that is to say, the aristo-

22. This and what follows is a sally against the constitutional monarchy of Louis-Philippe which, by what Balzac calls a piece of juggling, replaced the 'infamous monarchy' of Charles X in July 1830.
23. The aristocratic quarter of Paris.
24. The financial and banking quarter.

cracy of bankers and barristers who today pay lip-service to patriotism as formerly the priests to monarchism, sees the need to hoodwink the good people of France with new words for old ideas, after the example of the philosophers of every school and the hard-headed men of all times. And so it's a question of inculcating in us a royally national point of view by proving to us that we are much happier paying twelve hundred millions and thirty-three centimes to the country, represented by Messrs So-and-So, than eleven hundred millions and nine centimes to a king who said *I* instead of *We*. In a word, a newspaper solidly backed by two or three hundred thousand francs has been founded with a view to creating an opposition party which will content the malcontents without doing any damage to the Citizen-King's national government. Now, since we don't give a damn whether it's freedom or tyranny, religion or irreligion; since our view is that our country is a stock of capital in which ideas are bartered and sold for so much a line, in which every day brings succulent dinners and theatre-shows galore; a place swarming with cunning whores, in which suppers last until dawn and a mistress is hired for the hour like a cab; since Paris will always be the most adorable of cities – the homeland of joy, liberty, wit, lovely women, bad men and good wine where the cudgel of the law will never fall too heavily on our shoulders because we are too close to those that wield it . . . we, the true votaries of our god Mephistopheles, have taken it upon us to whitewash public opinion, dress the actors in new costumes, nail new boards on the governmental fair-booth, administer physic to the *doctrinaires*,[25] rejuvenate the venerable republicans, smarten up the Bonapartists and revictual the centre party, on condition that we may be allowed to laugh up our sleeves at king and country, to change our opinions between morning and evening, to live a joyous life in the manner of Panurge or Turkish fashion, reclining on our downy cushions.

'We are hoping you will hold the rains of this burlesque, this macaronic empire; and so we are taking you off here and now to the dinner given by the founder of the aforesaid newspaper,

25. A middle political party whose principles the Orleanist Monarchy was more or less to apply.

a retired banker who, not knowing what to do with his gold, wishes to convert it into wit. You will be welcomed as a brother, we shall proclaim you king of those irreverent spirits whom nothing can daunt and whose perspicacity ferrets out the intentions of Austria, England or Russia before Russia, England or Austria have formed any intentions! Yes, we will crown you sovereign of those mighty intelligences who furnish the world with such people as Mirabeau, Talleyrand, Pitt and Metternich; in short all those clever rogues who gamble among themselves with the destinies of empires as common men play dominoes for a glass of kirsch. We have put you forward as the doughtiest wrestler who has ever tried a fall with debauchery, that marvellous monster with which every emancipated mind is impatient to come to grips; we have even gone so far as to affirm that it has not yet conquered you. I trust you will live up to expectations. Our host Taillefer has undertaken to go beyond the unimaginative saturnalia of our small-minded modern Luculluses. He's rich enough to put grandeur into pettiness, to instil grace into vice. Are you listening to me, Raphael?' the orator paused to ask.

'Yes,' the young man replied, less astonished at the accomplishment of his wishes than surprised at the natural way events were being linked together in a logical chain. Although he found it impossible to believe in the intervention of magic, he was lost in wonderment at the changes and chances of human destiny.

'But you say "yes" as if you were thinking about your grandfather's death,' one of his neighbours retorted.

'Ah!' Raphael replied with an accent of naïvety which amused these writers, the rising hope of France. 'I was thinking, my friends, that we are about to become very great scoundrels! Up to now we have merely been impious in our cups, we have evaluated life when drunk and allowed our digestive processes to dictate our judgement of men and things. Blameless in deeds, we have been bold in words. But now, branded with the red-hot iron of politics, we are about to enter the great convict-prison and there lose our illusions. Even if we no longer believe in the devil, we may still regret the Eden of our youth, that period of innocence when we used to extend our tongues devoutly to a good priest to receive the precious body of Our Lord Jesus Christ. Ah! My good friends, if we drew so much pleasure from committing our first sins, it was because they had remorse to embellish them, to give them spice and savour; whereas now . . .'

'Oh! Now,' the first speaker continued, 'What remains to us is . . .'

'What?' another asked.

'Crime . . .'

'That's a word which reaches as high as the gallows and as deep as the Seine,' retorted Raphael.

'But you don't understand me . . . I'm talking of *political* crimes. Since this morning, the only kind of life that appeals to me is that of a conspirator. As for tomorrow, I don't know if this whim of mine will last; but this evening the anæmic pallor of our civilization, as monotonous as a railway line, makes my stomach heave with disgust. I find myself responding with passion to the horrors of the retreat from Moscow, the excitements of *The Red Rover* [26] and the life of a smuggler. Since there are no more Carthusian monasteries in France, I would at least like to have a Botany Bay, a sort of work-house destined for the little Lord Byrons who, after crumpling up life as they would a table napkin after dinner, have no other resource than to set their country on fire, blow their brains out, conspire to establish a republic, or clamour for war . . .'

'Emile,' Raphael's neighbour remarked hotly to the last speaker, 'upon my word, had it not been for the July Revolution, I should have taken orders and gone to vegetate in the depths of the country, and . . .'

'And you would have read your breviary every day?'

'Yes.'

'How stupid!'

'Yet we read the papers every day!'

'Not bad for one who writes for them! But watch what you're saying, everybody reads the papers these days. Journalism, you see, is the religion of modern society, and that's a step forward!'

'How do you make that out?'

26. A novel of piracy by Fenimore Cooper, published in 1828.

'The high priests of journalism are not obliged to believe in this new religion they preach – nor are the common people . . .'

Chattering thus, like good fellows who had all studied Latin at school, they arrived at a mansion in the Rue Joubert.

Emile was a journalist who had acquired more reputation by doing nothing than others from a successful productive career. A bold, biting, spirited critic, he possessed all the qualities of his defects. Jovial and outspoken, he would blister a friend to his face with a thousand sarcasms but, behind his back, he would defend him with courage and loyalty. He made fun of everything, his own prospects included. Always short of money, he remained, like all men with a future before them, wallowing in inexpressible idleness, condensing a whole book into one epigram for the benefit of people who were incapable of putting one witticism into a whole book. Lavish of promises that he never kept, he had made his fortune and reputation into a cushion on which he slept, thus running the risk of coming to his senses, as an old man, in an almshouse. With all that, keeping faith with his friends to the point of death, a swaggering cynic and as simple-hearted as a child, he worked only by fits and starts or under the spur of necessity.

'If I may use the expression of Master Alcofribas,[27] we are about to enjoy a slice of good cheer,' he said to Raphael, pointing to the boxes of flowers which gave verdure and perfume to the staircase.

'I like entrance halls to be well-heated and furnished with rich carpets,' Raphael replied. 'Luxury from the threshold inwards is rare in France. Here I feel as if I were returning to life.'

'And, upstairs, we are going to drink and make merry once more, my poor Raphael . . . For that matter,' he continued, 'I hope that we shall win the contest and come out on top of all those people there.'

With a mocking gesture, he pointed to the guests as they entered a salon resplendent with gilding and illuminations, one in which they were instantly welcomed by the most outstanding young men in Paris.

27. Alcofribas Nasier, anagram for François Rabelais. The reference is to *Pantagruel* I, xxi.

One of them had just revealed original talent and with his first picture shown himself the equal of the most celebrated Empire painters. Another had very recently ventured to publish a book full of vitality, one which was stamped with a sort of literary disdain and disclosed new vistas to the modern school. Further on, a sculptor, whose rugged features marked him out as a man of vigorous genius, was chatting with one of those cold satirists who, as occasion demands, refuse at one moment to recognize superiority and at another discern it everywhere. Here the cleverest of our cartoonists, with an eye full of malice and an acid tongue, was listening for epigrams with a view to translating them into pencil sketches. There a young and daring critic, who excelled at distilling the essence of political thought or effortlessly condensing the ideas of a prolific writer, was in conversation with the poet whose works would excel all others of our time if he were as talented as he was malevolent. Both of them were endeavouring not to speak their minds and yet not to lie as they exchanged honeyed flatteries. A famous musician was mockingly consoling in a minor key a young politician who had recently had a fall in the Chamber which had not harmed him in the slightest. Young authors devoid of style stood beside young authors devoid of ideas, prose-writers full of poetry beside very prosy poets. Surveying these incomplete beings, a needy Saint-Simonian, simple enough to believe in his own doctrine, charitably coupled them together, no doubt hoping to transform them into devotees of his own sect.[28] Lastly, among those present were two or three learned men whose speciality it is to take all the sparkle out of conversation, and a few vaudeville-writers ready to throw into it a few of those ephemeral gleams which, like the glitter of a diamond, contribute neither warmth nor light. A few dispensers of paradoxes, laughing up their sleeves at the people who ape them in their admiration or their contempt for men and things, were already adopting the two-edged policy of conspiring against all parties without taking sides with any. The trenchant critic whose motto is *nil admirari*, who blows his

28. The Saint-Simonians were a prominent sect of socialists, the founders of a sort of religion, who did their best to enlist writers and artists in their cause by preaching the 'sacred mission' of art.

nose in the middle of a *cavatina* at the Théâtre des Italiens, starts clapping before everyone else and, when his opinion is forestalled, takes the opposite stand, was also there, watching for the opportunity to appropriate other people's witticisms.

Among these guests, five had a future before them, a dozen or so were to acquire a temporary reputation. As for the rest, they might well, like all mediocrities, have repeated to one another the famous, though fallacious, motto adopted by Louis XVIII: *Let us join forces and forget the past.* Their host's cheerfulness was mitigated by the anxiety proper to a man spending ten thousand francs. Every now and then his eyes impatiently turned towards the door of the salon in expectation of a late arrival. There soon appeared a short, stout man who was welcomed with a flattering buzz of voices: it was the notary who, that very morning, had carried through the legal formalities for the founding of the newspaper. A footman dressed in black then drew back the doors of a vast dining-room into which all the guests dived unceremoniously to find their places round an enormous table. Before leaving the salons, Raphael cast a final glance around him. His wish had certainly come completely true. Every room was tapestried in silk and gold. Rich sconces supporting innumerable candles lit up the slightest details of the gilded friezes, the delicate chasing of the bronzes and the luxuriant colourings of the furnishings. The rare blooms in a number of flower-stands, constructed artistically of bamboo, were dispensing sweet perfumes. Everything, including the draperies, was redolent of unpretentious elegance. In short, from everything he saw there emanated an indefinable poetic grace which was calculated to act like a charm on the imagination of a man in penury.

'An income of a hundred thousand francs provides a very pretty commentary on the catechism and gives us wonderful help for putting a stock-exchange valuation on moral principles!' he said with a sigh. 'Yes indeed, what virtue I have is averse from walking on foot. Vice for me means living in a garret, wearing threadbare clothes, a grey hat in winter and owing money to the concierge . . . Ah! let me wallow in luxury like this for a year – or six months, what matter? Then I will die

At least I shall have known, drained dry, devoured a thousand lives!'

'Oh!' said Emile, who was listening to him. 'You are taking a stockbroker's coupé as a symbol of happiness. Come now, you would soon be bored with wealth once you saw that it robbed you of the chance of posing as a superior man. Has an artist's choice ever wavered between the poor life the rich lead and the rich life the poor lead? Must not such people as you and I always have an uphill struggle? So now, get your stomach into working order. Lo and behold,' he said, pointing with a heroic gesture to the majestic, thrice holy and reassuring spectacle presented by the accommodating capitalist's banqueting-hall.

'That man,' he went on, 'took the trouble to amass a fortune solely in order that we should have the benefit. Is he not a sort of sponge left unclassified by such naturalists as study the order of polypi: all we need to do is squeeze them gently; their heirs will wring them dry in due course. Is there not style in the bas-reliefs decorating these walls? And what a feeling for luxury in the chandeliers and pictures! If we are to believe envious people and those who obstinately probe into the motives behind human action, this man, in Revolutionary times, murdered several persons, including, they say, his best friend (a German) and this friend's mother. Can you find room for criminality in the greying hair of this venerable Taillefer?[29] He looks like a very decent man. See how the silverware glitters. Could anyone imagine that each glint is a dagger that strikes him to the heart? Ridiculous! You might as well believe in Mahomet. If general rumour is correct, here we are: thirty men of courage and talent who are about to eat the entrails and drink the blood of a whole family; and the two of us, in our youthful candour and enthusiasm, would be accomplices in the crime! I've half a mind to ask our capitalist if he is an honest man ...'

'Don't ask him yet!' cried Raphael. 'Ask him when he's dead drunk. By then we shall have dined.'

29. The indentification of the Amphitryon of this feast, Taillefer, with the murderer of *The Red Inn* (1831) took place later, in accordance with Balzac's system of 'Reappearing Characters.' cf. below, p. 12 and p. 13.

The two friends sat down in laughing mood. First, with a glance more rapid than speech, every guest paid his tribute of admiration to the sumptuous spectacle presented by a long table, white as the driven snow, on which rose the napkins in symmetrical pyramids, each crowned with a little roll of white bread. The crystal glasses reflected iridescent, starry gleams, the candles set dancing infinite cross-gleams of spangled light, while the dishes placed under silver domes whetted appetite and curiosity. Few words were spoken. Each diner shot a glance at his neighbour. Madeira circulated. Then the first course appeared in all its glory. It would have done honour to the late, lamented Cambacères[30] and earned the plaudits of Brillat-Savarin.[31] Claret and burgundy, red and white, were served with regal munificence. This first part of the feast was comparable in every way to the opening scene of a five-act classical drama.

The second act became somewhat prolix. Every guest had drunk reasonably well, changing vintages according to his whim, with the result that, at the moment when the remnants of this magnificent course were being removed, tempestuous discussion had got under way. Some pallid foreheads were beginning to redden; several noses were taking on a purple tint. Faces were becoming flushed and eyes were sparkling. During this dawn of intoxication, speech was not overstepping the bounds of propriety but, bit by bit, banter and witticisms started flying. Then slander very unobstrusively raised its tiny serpent's head and spoke in its fluty voice; here and there a few souls listened attentively, still hoping to keep sober.

So then the second course found them in a very excited state of mind. They all ate as they talked, and talked as they ate. They drank without noticing how much they were drinking, so fine and fruity was their bouquet, and so contagious was the example set. Taillefer made a point of spurring on his guests, and brought forth the terrible Rhône wines, fiery tokay, and the heady old vintages of Roussillon. Like horses fresh from the staging-post,

30. One of the three Consuls appointed to govern France in 1799: a noted gourmet.

31. Author of a *Physiology of Taste or Meditations on Transcendent Gastronomy* (1826).

these guests, under the stimulus of champagne impatiently awaited but which was soon lavishly supplied, allowed their minds to gallop along through the waste land of arguments that no one heeds, telling the sort of story that no one listens to, breaking in repeatedly with the sort of interrogation which receives no response. Untrammelled orgy raised its mighty voice, compounded of innumerable clamours rising to a climax like Rossini's crescendos. Then came insidiously motivated toasts, boastful assertions and challenges. All and sundry exchanged the capacity of their intellects for the capacity of hogsheads, tuns, and casks. Every one of them seemed to speak with two voices. A moment came when the masters all talked at once and the servants waiting at table smiled. But this medley of words in which paradoxes of dubious lucidity and home truths in strange garb clashed amid shouts, prejudicial affirmations, flat assertions and foolish ones – just as on the battlefield cannon balls, bullets and grape-shot whizz past in all directions, – this rough-and-tumble would no doubt have intrigued a philosopher or surprised a politician on account of the strangeness of the ideas or the eccentricity of the proposals. It was at once a book to read and a picture to gaze at.

Philosophies, religions, ethical systems, so different in different latitudes, the various types of governments, in short all the great inventions of the human intellect fell under a scythe as long as that of Father Time, and you might have found it difficult to decide whether that scythe was being wielded by a god of wisdom the worse for drink or by a god of wine who had grown wise and clear-sighted. Carried away as it were in a whirlwind, the minds of these drinkers, like an angry sea dashing against cliffs, seemed intent on shattering all the laws between which civilizations go drifting along, thus unwittingly obeying the will of God, who leaves good and evil in nature while keeping to Himself the why and wherefore of this unending struggle. At once furious and ludicrous, the discussion was a sort of witches' sabbath of intelligent minds. Between the sour jests uttered by these children of the Revolution at the birth of a newspaper and the joyous utterances of topers at the birth of Gargantua, there yawned the vast gulf that divides the sixteenth from the nineteenth century. The former laughed as it prepared the way for destruction; our century stands laughing in the midst of ruins.

'What's the name of the young man down there?' the notary asked as he pointed to Raphael. 'I think I heard him called Valentin.'

'What do you mean with your plain, simple "Valentin"?' Emile exclaimed with a laugh. 'Raphael de Valentin, if you please! We bear *sable, an eagle or, crowned argent, beaked and taloned gules*, with a splendid motto: NON CECIDIT ANIMUS! We are not a foundling child, but the descendant of the Emperor Valens, head of the line of the Valentinois, founder of the cities of Valence in France and Valencia in Spain, legitimate heir of the eastern Empire. If we allow Mahmoud to reign in Constantinople, it's out of the sheer kindness of our heart – also for lack of money or troops.'

Emile drew in the air, with his fork, a coronet above Raphael's head. The notary pondered for a moment, and then started drinking again, permitting himself as he did so a meaningful shrug by which he seemed to confess that he found it impossible to gather into his professional net the towns of Valence and Constantinople, Sultan Mahmoud, the Emperor Valentius and the family of the Valentini.

'Might not the destruction of those ant-hills known as Baby-lon, Tyre, Carthage or Venice, which have been constantly crushed beneath the feet of any passing giant, be a warning given to man by some ironic power?' asked Claude Vignon, a sort of Grub Street hack hired by play the Bossuet at ten sous a line.

'Moses, Sulla, Louis XI, Richelieu, Robespierre and Napoleon are perhaps one and the same man reappearing from one civili-zation to another, like a comet in the sky!' a disciple of Ballanche replied.[32]

'Why probe into the workings of Providence?' asked Canalis, the ballad-maker.[33]

32. Pierre-Simon Ballanche (1776–1847), a semi-mystic philosopher who exerted g... influence on French idealist thought during this period.

33. A poet created by Balzac who had ... ...thing of Lamartine and Vigny in his make-up.

'Why drag in Providence?' the trenchant critic broke in. 'I know no term in the world which is more elastic.'

'But, my dear sir, Louis XIV caused the death of more men in the construction of the aqueducts at Maintenon than the National Convention in constructing an equitable tax-system, a uniform legal system, in uniting the country and in ensuring an equal division of inheritances,' said Massol, a young man who had taken to republicanism for lack of a syllable in front of his name.[34]

'Come, sir,' replied Moreau de l'Oise, a worthy landowner, 'you who would like to see blood flowing like wine, cannot you just for once leave every man's head on his shoulders?'

'To what end, sir? Are not the principles of social order worth a few sacrifices?'

'Hey, Bixiou,'[35] a young man said to his neighbour. 'What's-his-name the republican maintains that cutting off yonder landowner's head would be a sacrifice!'

'Men and events are nothing,' the republican was saying as he continued to punctuate his theory with hiccups. 'In politics and philosophy only principles and ideas count.'

'How horrible! You would execute your friends without compunction for the sake of an *if* . . .?'

'But don't you see, sir, the man who feels remorse is the real villain, for he has some idea of virtue; whereas Peter the Great and the Duke of Alba embodied systems, and the pirate Monbard[36] embodied an organization.'

'But cannot society do very well without your systems and organizations?' asked Canalis.

'Oh, granted!' the republican replied.

'Nonsense! Your stupid republic turns my stomach! If it were established, we couldn't even carve a chicken in peace without infringing the agrarian law.'

'Your principles are excellent, my little Brutus stuffed with

34. Presumably the supposedly aristocratic 'de', which Balzac himself, no Republican, had assumed.

35. Bixiou stands for the contemporary caricaturist Henry Monnier.

36. Known as 'the Exterminator' for his savagery against the Spaniards on the South American coast towards the end of the seventeenth century.

truffles! But you're like my valet: the fellow is so obsessed by the mania for cleanliness that if I let him brush my clothes to his heart's content I should have nothing to wear.'

'You are morons! You want to clean up a nation with tooth-picks,' the fanatical republican retorted. 'According to you, justice is more dangerous than thieves would be.'

'Come! Come!' the solicitor Desroches exclaimed.

'What bores they are with their politics!' said the notary Cardot. 'Close the door. There's no science or virtue that is worth a single drop of blood. If we were to call on truth to settle its accounts we should perhaps find it bankrupt.'

'Ah! It would no doubt have cost us less to enjoy ourselves doing evil than to quarrel about doing good. And so I myself would swap all the last forty years' speeches in Parliament for a tasty trout, a fairy-tale by Perrault or a sketch by Charlet.'

'You're absolutely right! . . . Pass me some asparagus . . . For, after all, liberty engenders anarchy, anarchy leads to despotism, and despotism brings us back to liberty. Millions of people have perished without being able to establish any of those systems. Is not that the vicious circle in which the moral world will always turn? When man thinks he has brought things to perfection, all he's done is to shuffle them around.'

'Oho!' exclaimed Cursy the vaudevillist. 'In that case, gentlemen, I propose a toast to Charles X, the father of liberty!'

'Why not?' said Emile. 'When despotism is embedded in the laws, then liberty is embodied in manners and customs, and *vice versa*.'

'Let us then drink to the imbecility of the people in power who are giving us so much power over imbeciles!' said the banker.

'Come now, my friend. At least Napoleon gave us a legacy of glory!' shouted a naval officer who had never gone farther than the port of Brest.

'Oh! Glory's a dreary commodity! It's expensive and doesn't last. Is not glory the egoism of the great, just as happiness is the egoism of fools?'

'Sir, you must be a very happy man!'

'The first individual to fence off a field was no doubt a rather feeble person, for organized society is of advantage only to puny people. Both the aborigine and the thinking man, placed as they are at the two extremes of the moral world, have an equal horror of property.'

'What a quaint idea!' cried Cardot. 'If property didn't exist, how could we draw up conveyances?'

'These green peas are fabulous!'

'And the next day the priest was found dead in bed . . .'

'Who's talking of death? That's no joking matter! I have an uncle.'

'No doubt you would bear his loss with fortitude.'

'No question of that.'

'Listen, gentlemen! . . . A METHOD OF KILLING ONE'S UNCLE. Hush (*Listen, listen!*) First take an uncle, stout and fat, at least seventy years old – they are the best kind (*Sensation*). On some pretext or other give him a *pâté de foie gras* to eat.'

'What a hope! My uncle is tall and thin, a miser and no trencherman.'

'Indeed? Uncles like that are monsters who live longer than they should.'

'And,' continued the expert on uncles, 'inform him, while he's digesting his food, that his banker is refusing payment.'

'Suppose that doesn't do the trick?'

'Set a pretty whore on him.'

'Suppose he is . . .' said the other, making a negative gesture.

'Then he's no true uncle . . . an uncle is essentially one for the girls.'

'Malibran's[37] voice has lost two of its notes.'

'Not true, sir.'

'Quite true, sir.'

'Aha! quite true, not true! Isn't that the history of every religious, political and literary dispute? Man is a clown walking the tight-rope over the void.'

'To listen to you, I'm an ass?'

'No, you're an ass not to listen to me.'

'Education! What stupidity! Monsieur Heineffettermach[38]

37. A great *prima donna* of that epoch.
38. An imaginary German scholar and statistician.

70

estimates the number of printed volumes at over a thousand million, and a man can't read more than a hundred and fifty thousand in a lifetime. Then explain to me what you mean by *education*. For some people education consists in knowing the names of Alexander's horse, and that of Berécillo, the mastiff belonging to the sixteenth century poet Tabourot; and in *not* knowing the name of the men who invented timber-floating or porcelain. For others, to be educated means being liked and respected as an honest man while destroying an inconvenient will, instead of stealing a watch after being cautioned, with every aggravating circumstance, and dying on the scaffold hated and dishonoured.'

'Will Nathan[39] last?'

'Why not? He has some very clever ghost-writers!'

'And Canalis?'

'He's a great man. Let's forget him.'

'You're drunk, both of you.'

'The immediate consequence of parliamentary democracy is a levelling-down of intelligence. Art, science, architecture, everything is corroded by that hideous vice, egoism, the leprosy of our day. Your 300 middle-class legislators will think only of planting poplar-trees. Despotism does great things illegally, whereas democracy does not even take the trouble to do small things legally.'

'Your mutual education system[40] turns out identical coins in flesh and blood,' interjected a royalist. 'Individuality disappears in a people reduced to one level by state schools.'

'And yet,' the Saint-Simonian asked, 'is it not the aim of society to provide well-being for all and sundry?'

'If you had 50,000 francs a year, you wouldn't bother about the welfare of the people. Are you filled with a fine philanthropic fervour? Go to Madagascar: there you will find a nice, new little nation, ready for Saint-Simonian treatment, ready to be classified and put into a chemist's show-bottle. But here everyone fits quite naturally into his honeycomb cell, like a peg in its hole.

39. One of Balzac's pseudo-Romantists with Byronic pretensions.
40. An experiment in education initiated in Imperial times – a system in which masters and pupils cooperated.

Porters are porters and idiots are stupid without needing to obtain a degree from a council of Fathers.[41] Ha! Ha!'

'You are a supporter of Charles X.'

'Why not? I love despotism, which proclaims a certain measure of contempt for the human race. I have no hatred for kings. They are so amusing! Isn't there something to be said for sitting enthroned in a chamber thirty million leagues away from the sun?'

'But let us sum up the broad conspectus of civilization,' the man of science was saying to the inattentive sculptor, for whose edification he had embarked upon a discussion about the beginnings of social life and about primitive races. 'When nations first came into being, force was in a sense material, unified, crude. Then, with the multiplication of centres of population, governments evolved by breaking down, more or less skilfully, the original authority into its constituent components. Thus, in remote antiquity, power resided in theocracy: the priest wielded both the sword and the censer. Later two priesthoods emerged: pontiff and king. Today, our society representing the culminating point of civilization, has spread power over a number of pressure-groups, and we find ourselves confronting the power of industry, the power of thought, the power of money, the power of speech. Power, having now lost its unity, is steadily moving towards a social dissolution against which there is no other barrier than self-interest. And so we lean neither on religion nor material force, but on intelligence. Is the pen as mighty as the sword? Is discussion as worth-while as action? That is the problem.'

'Intelligence has destroyed everything!' cried the legitimist. 'Face the fact: absolute liberty causes nations to commit suicide, like an English millionaire, bored because there are no fresh worlds to conquer.'

'What can you tell us that we don't already know? By now you have made a laughing-stock of every authority, and it's even normal to deny the existence of God! You no longer believe in

41. Further satirical reference to the ecclesiastical pretensions of the Saint-Simonian 'church', which created a sort of priesthood dependent on a 'Père Suprême' or Pope.

anything, and this century is like an aged sultan plunged into debauchery! It's ended with your Lord Byron, bringing poetry to the last pitch of despair, taking criminal passions as his theme.'

'Do you know,' answered Bianchon,[42] completely drunk, 'that a pinch of phosphorus more or less makes your man of genius or your scoundrel, your man of wit or your idiot, your virtuous man or your criminal?'

'Can one treat virtue so lightly?' exclaimed Cursy. 'Virtue, the theme of all plays, the climax of every drama, the basis of all courts of law . . .'

'Oh, hold your tongue, you ass! Your idea of virtue is Achilles without his heel,' said Bixiou.

'More wine!'

'Bet you I'll down a bottle of bubbly at one go!'

'Any chance it'll make your wit sparkle?' asked Bixiou.

'They're as drunk as waggoners,' said a young man who was solemnly pouring wine into his waistcoat.

'Yes, sir, government in these days is the art of giving effect to public opinion.'

'Public opinion? The most perverted of all trollops! According to you high-minded moralists and politicians, one ought always to set your laws above nature, and public opinion above one's conscience. It's true and it's untrue. Society may have given us down for our pillows, but it has made us pay for that advantage by giving us gout – just as it has invented legal wrangles in order to temper justice, and colds in the head as a sequel to cashmere shawls.'

'Monster!' said Emile, interrupting the misanthrope. 'How can you slander civilization in the presence of such delicious food and wine and with your feet in the trough? Get your teeth into this roebuck with gilded paws and horns, but not into the mother that feeds you . . .'

'Is it *my* fault if Catholicism manages to put a million gods into a sack of flour, if republicanism always ends up with some Napoleon or other, if monarchy rings the changes between the

---

42. The most prominent and most ubiquitous doctor in *The Human Comedy*.

assassination of Henri IV and the sentencing of Louis XVI, and if liberalism leads to La Fayette?'

'Did you embrace La Fayette last July?'[43]

'No.'

'Then hold your tongue, sceptic.'

'Sceptics are the most conscientious of men.'

'They have no consciences.'

'What a thing to say! They have at least two consciences.'

'Take out an insurance policy for heaven? Why, sir, that's an idea worthy of this commercial age. The religions of antiquity were merely a glorified extension of physical pleasure. But *we* have glorified the soul, *we* have extended hope; that's a decided step forward!'

'Well, my good friends, what can you expect of a century satiated with politics?' asked Nathan. 'Look how they've treated the *History of the King of Bohemia and his seven Castles*,[44] a most enchanting work!'

'That?' shouted the critic, his voice carrying from one end of the table to the other: 'phrases picked out haphazard from a hat, a work of lunacy!'

'You're a fool!'

'You're a scoundrel!'

'Oh! Oh!'

'Ha! Ha!'

'There'll be a duel.'

'No fear!'

'Tomorrow, sir.'

'This very instant,' Nathan replied.

'Come, come! You're a couple of blusterers!'

'You're another!' said the challenger.

'They can't even stand upright.'

43. Having fought with the North American colonists in their rebellion against England, La Fayette had become a figure-head representing the cause of freedom. Duped by the supporters of Louis-Philippe in July 1830, he had become a figure of fun for satirical republicans. To have embraced him in July 1830 was to have subscribed to the hypocrisy which accompanied the accession of Louis-Philippe,

44. A fantastic story published in 1830 by Charles Nodier, one of the initiators of French Romanticism.

'Oh! So I can't stand upright?' retorted the bellicose Nathan, pulling himself up like a fluttering kite.

He threw a vacant gaze round the table, and then, as if exhausted by this effort, he fell back on his chair, lowered his head and abstained from further speech.

'Wouldn't it be a joke,' said the critic to his neighbour, 'to fight a duel over a work I have never clapped eyes on?'

'Emile, mind your coat. The man next to you is turning pale,' said Bixiou.

'Kant, sir? Another balloon sent up to keep simpletons amused. Materialism and spiritualism are two pretty battledores with which charlatans in cap and gown knock the same shuttlecock to and fro. God is everywhere, says Spinoza. From God comes everything, says Saint Paul. Idiots both! Is it not one and the same movement to open or shut a door? Does the egg come from the hen or the hen from the egg? . . . I'd like a slice of that duck, if you please . . . That's what science amounts to.'

'Noodle!' the scientist shouted. 'The question you put is settled by a single fact.'

'What fact?'

'University chairs were not made for philosophy. Philosophy was made for the chairs. Put on your glasses and study the budget.'

'Thieves!'

'Imbeciles!'

'Knaves!'

'Dupes!'

'Where, except in Paris, would you find so sharp, so rapid an exchange of ideas!' Bixiou exclaimed, assuming a baritone voice.

'Come on, Bixiou, do us one of your parodies. Come now, give us a take-off.'[45]

'What do you want? Nineteenth century?'

'Listen!'

'Quiet!'

'Pipe down everybody.'

'Pipe down yourself, sailor-boy!'

'Fill his glass and shut the little idiot up!'

45. Bixiou, like Monnier, was gifted as a mimic

75

'Your health, Bixiou.'

The artiste buttoned his black coat up to his throat, fitted on his yellow gloves, pulled a face and squinted to mimic the *Revue des Deux Mondes*. But his voice was drowned in the hubbub, and it was impossible to take in one word of his satire. Perhaps he was not representative of the nineteenth century, but at any rate he was fully representative of the *Revue* because he had no notion what he was talking about.[46]

*

Dessert was served as if by magic. The table was graced by an enormous centrepiece in gilded bronze, a product of Thomire's workshops. Tall figures, endowed by a celebrated artist with the forms which Europe has accepted as types of ideal beauty, raised and held aloft baskets of strawberries, pineapples, fresh dates, green grapes, yellow peaches, oranges shipped express from Setubal, pomegranates, Chinese fruits, in short every surprise that luxury can afford: miracles of the confectioner's art, the sweetest of dainties and the daintiest of sweetmeats. The colours of these gastronomic masterpieces were set off by the sheen of the china, by shimmering lines of gold, by the glitter of the cut-glass vases. Graceful as the liquid fringes of the ocean, light green moss-mantled landscapes by Poussin translated into Sèvres porcelain. The whole territory of a German principality could not have paid for this arrogantly flaunted display.

Silver, mother of pearl, gold and crystal glass were once more set forth in new shapes. But torpid eyes and the wordy feverishness of intoxication scarcely allowed the guests even a hazy view of this fairyland worthy of an oriental tale. The dessert wines brought their bouquet and flame, penetrating philtres, enchanting vapours which give birth to a sort of intellectual mirage, bind the feet in potent bonds and load the hands with lead. The pyramids of fruit were pillaged, the noise of voices swelled, tumult increased. From then on no man's speech remained distinct, glasses were shattered, horrible bursts of laughter sounded

46. Buloz, editor of the *Revue des Deux Mondes*, the outstanding literary periodical of those times, refused contributions from Balzac. Hence these attacks. Later there was to be open war between them.

like rockets. Cursy seized a horn and began to sound a fanfare, which was as effective as a signal from the devil. The whole gathering howled in delirium, whistled, sang, shouted, roared, growled. You would have been amused to see people of gay temperament becoming as gloomy as the last act of a Crébillon tragedy or as pensive as sailors in a longboat. Men usually discreet were telling their secrets to gossips who were not listening. The melancholic wore the dimpling smiles of ballet pirouetting girls. Claude Vignon was swaying about like a bear in a cage. Close friends were picking fights with one another. The animal resemblances on human faces, as physiologists have demonstrated them so fascinatingly, became vaguely apparent in the bodily gesture and posture of the guests. In fact they provided a ready written book for a scientist such as Bichat,[47] had he been present to study them coolly and soberly. The master of the house, conscious that he himself was drunk, dared not stand up, but grinned fixedly in approval of the antics of his guests, while doing his best to maintain a becomingly hospitable expression. His broad face, now red, blue, almost purple and terrible to look upon, kept time with the wagging heads around him by movements resembling the rolling and pitching of a ship at sea.

'Did you murder them?' Emile asked Taillefer.[48]

'The death penalty, so they say,' Taillefer answered, 'is about to be abolished in honour of the July Revolution.'[49] He raised his eyebrows with an air of cunning mingled with stupidity.

'But don't you sometimes see them again in your dreams?' Raphael insisted.

'There's a statute of limitations!' the wealthy murderer replied.

'And on his grave,' cried Emile in a sardonic tone,' the stonemason will carve the words: "Passers-by, vouchsafe a tear to his memory!" . . . Oh!,' he continued, 'I wouldn't mind giving five francs to a mathematician who could prove to me the existence of hell by means of an algebraic equation.' He threw up a coin and shouted: 'Heads that God exists!'

47. Marie-François-Xavier Bichat, an anatomist who made a great mark, but died young (1771–1802)

48. See above, p. 64, not 29.   49. It never was.

'Don't look to see,' said Raphael, seizing the coin. 'How can one know? Chance is such a joker.'

'Alas!' Emile continued with a comically sad air. 'I don't know where to tread between the geometrical conclusions of the sceptic and the paternoster of the Pope. What matter? Let's fill up again. *Drink*! That, I believe, is the oracular pronouncement emitted by the divine bottle, and it serves as a conclusion to Rabelais's *Pantagruel*.'

'The paternoster? To it we owe,' Raphael replied, 'our art, our architecture, our sciences perhaps and – a greater benefit still! – our modern governments, in which a vast and productive society is marvellously represented by five hundred intelligent beings,[50] a society in which the forces opposed to one another cancel out and leave all power to CIVILIZATION, the great queen who replaces the ancient and terrible figure of the KING, a simulacrum of destiny which man has interposed between Heaven and himself. Faced with so many works accomplished by religion, atheism appears as a sterile skeleton. What do you say?'

'I think,' said Emile, coldly, 'of the rivers of blood shed by Catholicism. It has tapped our veins and hearts to make an imitation of the Flood. But no matter! Every thinking man must march under the banner of Christ. He alone consecrated the triumph of mind over matter. He alone gave us a poetic revelation of the intermediary world which separates us from God!'

'You believe that?' Raphael replied with the enigmatic smile of a drunken man. 'Well, in order not to commit ourselves, let us drink the famous toast: *Diis ignotis*.'[51]

They drained their goblets full of learning, carbonic acid, perfume, poetry and scepticism.

'If the gentlemen would like to move into the drawing-room, coffee will be served,' said the *maître d'hôtel*.

*

By now almost all the guests were whirling in that delightful

50. The allusion here is a little obscure, but Balzac may well be poking fun at the 'democracy' established under Louis-Philippe. The 'five hundred' may roughly refer to the members of the Chambre des Députés.

51. 'To the unknown gods.' A parody of the remark of St Paul, *Acts*, xvii, 23.

limbo in which the light of the mind is extinguished and the body, released from the tyranny of its master, gives itself up to the delirious joys of freedom. Some of them, having reached the highest point of intoxication, remained dejected and painfully concerned to snatch at any idea which would convince them of their own existence; others, sunk in a lethargy brought on by the sluggish process of digestion, renounced all movement. Some orators, undaunted, were still uttering vague remarks of whose meaning they themselves were uncertain. A few snatches of song echoed out like the tinkling of a musical box forced to grind out its artificial and soulless tune. Silence and rowdiness had become strange bedfellows.

None the less, on hearing the sonorous voice of the *maître d'hôtel* who was announcing fresh joys in his master's name, the guests rose to their feet and dragged, supported or even carried one another along. For a moment the whole troop stood stock still and spellbound on the threshold of the room. The immoderate pleasures of the banquet paled into insignificance before the spectacle prepared by their host to titillate the most voluptuous of their senses. Beneath the sparkling candles of a gold chandelier, around a table laden with silver gilt, a group of women suddenly appeared before the stupefied guests whose eyes began to gleam like so many diamonds. Rich were their adornments, but richer still was their dazzling beauty which far eclipsed all the marvels that this palace contained. These girls had fairy-like charms and passionate eyes, livelier and brighter than the torrents of light which brought out the satin sheen of the hangings, the brilliant whiteness of the marble statues and the delicate curves of the bronzes. The senses were set on fire at the sight of their tossing heads, the contrasts presented by their hair-styles and poses, so diverse in charm and character. It was like a hedge of flowers mingled with rubies, sapphires and coral; a girdle of black necklaces on snowy necks, with light sashes playing around them like the flames of beacons; haughty turbans and modestly provocative tunics.

This seraglio offered seductions for every eye and pleasures to suit every whim. Ravishingly posed, a dancer appeared to be nude under the wavy folds of her cashmere. There a diaphanous

79

gauze, here iridescent silk concealed or revealed mysterious perfections. Tiny, slender feet spoke of love while fresh and rosy lips were mute. Delicate and decorous-seeming girls, make-believe virgins whose pretty hair breathed out pious innocence, appeared as airy visions that a breath could dissipate. Then there came aristocratic beauties proud of glance but indolent; slim, willowy, graceful; bowing their heads as if they were still in the market for royal protection. An English girl, a white, chaste, ethereal figure wafted down from the clouds of an Ossianic landscape, looked like an angel of melancholy or repentance fleeing before crime. Nor was there lacking in this tempting assembly the woman of Paris, whose whole beauty resides in indescribable gracefulness, vain of her toilet and her wit, armed with her omnipotent fragility, pliant but unyielding, a siren without heart or passion, yet able by artifice to create the treasures of passion and simulate the accents of the heart. The eye was caught too by Italian girls, placid in appearance but conscientious in the felicities they dispense, by richly endowed and magnificently proportioned women from Normandy, and yet others from the south, with dark hair and almond-shaped eyes. Having spent the time since morning furbishing their charms, they reminded you of the beauties that Lebel[52] used to assemble at Versailles, and came on the scene like a bevy of eastern slave-girls awakened by the trader for departure at dawn.

They stood there shamefaced and shy, and pressed round the table like bees buzzing inside a hive. This timid embarassment, at once reproachful and coquettish, was either calculated or involuntary bashfulness. Perhaps a feeling which woman never completely lays aside enjoined on them to wrap themselves in a mantle of virtue in order to give greater charm and piquancy to the prodigalities of vice. Thus the plot hatched by old Taillefer seemed likely to fail, for to start with these men, normally uninhibited, were subjugated by the daunting power which invests a woman. A murmur of admiration ran through the room like the soft strains of music. Sexual desire had been damped by wine, and instead of being swept up in a whirlwind of passion,

52. Louis XV's *valet de chambre* and pander.

the guests, caught in a moment of weakness, gave themselves over to the delights of voluptuous ecstasy. The artists among them, at the dictate of the poetry which always holds artists in thrall, were content to contemplate the delicate nuances which distinguished these paragons from one another.

Stirred by a thought perhaps attributable to some emanation of carbonic acid from the champagne he had drunk, a man of philosophic bent shuddered as he imagined the misfortunes that had brought these women, once worthy perhaps of the purest of tributes, to this place. Not one of them, doubtless, but had some painful story to relate. Almost every one brought her own particular hell with her, trailing behind her the memory of some faithless lover, of promises betrayed, of joys which had been paid for with misery.

The guests approached them politely, and conversations started as varied as the characters involved. They split into groups. It might have been taken for the drawing-room of a respectable house in which young ladies move round offering guests who have dined the succour that coffee, liqueurs and sweets bring to gourmands who are enduring the discomfort of a recalcitrant digestion. But soon a few bursts of laughter were heard, the noise grew, voices were raised above it. The spirit of orgy, which for a moment had been quelled, made periodical bids to reassert itself. The alternating *pianissimo* and *fortissimo* bore a vague resemblance to a Beethoven symphony.

Sitting on a comfortable sofa, the two friends first of all saw approaching them a tall, well-proportioned girl of superb carriage, with rather irregular features but a striking and impetuous face, which awoke interest by the marked contrasts that characterized it. Her black hair with its wanton curls looked as if it had already been tousled in amorous sport, and fell lightly over her wide and gracefully attractive shoulders. Those long, dark tresses half concealed a queenly neck on which the light gleamed here and there, bringing into relief the delicacy and beauty of its curves. Against her white, matt skin the warm tones of her colouring stood out brightly. Her eyes, under long lashes, darted forth bold flames – sparks to enkindle love; her red, moist mouth, her parted lips invited kisses. She was of sturdy build but amorously lissom; her bosom and arms were amply developed, like those of Caracci's buxom figures; yet she gave an impression of litheness and suppleness, and her appearance of vigour suggested the agility of a panther, just as the cleanly-cut elegance of her limbs gave promise of tigerish voluptuousness.

No doubt laughter and wantoning came naturally to this young woman, but there was something frightening in her eyes and smile. Like a sibyl possessed by a demon, she was more likely to astonish than to please. Every variety of expression crowded with lightning rapidity over her mobile features. A bored libertine might have found her stimulating, but a young man would have recoiled in terror. She was like a more than life-size statue fallen from the portico of a Greek temple: sublime at a distance, but rough-hewn when seen close up. Nevertheless her beauty was startling enough to arouse the impotent, her voice might well calm deaf ears, a glance from her might well bring dry bones to life. And so Emile compared her – vaguely – to a tragedy by Shakespeare, to some wonderful arabesque in which joy itself is strident while love is unspeakably savage and faery grace and fiery bliss follow hard on bloody and tumultuous rages; to a monster who bites and fondles, who laughs like a demon or weeps like an angel, who is able in one single embrace to improvise every feminine seduction save the melancholy sighs and charming modesty of a virgin and then, one instant later, flies into a fury, lacerates her own breast, shatters her own passion and her lover with it: in short, destroys herself as does a revolutionary mob.

Dressed in a gown of crimson velvet, she was trampling heedlessly underfoot the flowers that had already fallen from some of her companions' heads, and disdainfully held out a silver tray to the two friends. Proud of her beauty, proud perhaps of her vices, she displayed a white arm vividly set off against the velvet. She reigned there like the queen of pleasure, like an image symbolizing human joy, the kind of joy that squanders riches amassed by three generations, stands laughing over corpses, mocks at ancestors, dissolves pearls and shatters thrones, turns young men into dotards and not infrequently dotards into young men; joy of the sort allowed only to those giants among men who are weary of power, ground down by thought, or for whom war has become a mere game.

'What's your name?' asked Raphael.

'Aquilina.'

'Aha! you're straight from *Venice preserved*!' cried Emile.

'Yes,' she answered. 'Just as Popes give themselves new names when elected to sovereignty over men. I took another name when I achieved sovereignty over all women.'

'So then,' Emile broke in excitedly, stimulated by this touch of poetry, 'you have, as your namesake had, a noble and redoubtable conspirator who loves you and is ready to die for you?'

'I did have such a one,' she replied, 'but I had the guillotine for a rival. Therefore I always put a few shreds of scarlet in my dress so that my joy shall stay always within bounds.'

'Oh! If you start her on the story of the four sergeants of La Rochelle,[53] she'll never finish. Say no more, Aquilina. Has not every woman a lover to weep for? But they haven't all of them, like you, luck enough to have lost him on the scaffold. Oh! I would much rather know that mine was buried in a grave at Clamart than in the bed of a rival.'

These words were uttered with a sweet and melodious voice by the most innocent-looking, the prettiest and gentlest little creature ever conjured out of a magic egg by a fairy wand. She had stepped forward silently, showing a delicate face, a slender figure, bewitchingly modest blue eyes and a fresh, pure forehead. An ingenuous naiad, escaping from her stream, could not be more timid, more fair, more artless than this girl, who seemed to be about sixteen years of age, to be ignorant of evil – of love also – to know nothing of life's storms, to have just emerged from a church where she had been beseeching the angels to obtain her recall to Heaven before her time. In Paris only can be found such seemingly guileless creatures who hide the foulest depravity and the sublest refinement of vice beneath a brow as mild and tender as a field of daisies.

Misled at first by the celestial promise contained in this girl's

53. Four republican conspirators executed for high treason in September 1822. One of them was, in Balzac's fiction, Aquilina's lover (*Melmoth réconcilié*, 1835).

sweetness and charm, Emile and Raphael accepted the coffee she poured out for them into cups presented by Aquilina, and they began to question her. Before the gaze of these two poets she succeeded in illuminating, by some sinister allegory, an unknown aspect of human life, as she exhibited, in contrast to the crude, passionate self-expression of her stately companion, a picture of cold, sadistic corruption, irresponsible enough to commit a crime and hard-headed enough to do it with a laugh; the picture of a heartless demon who punishes rich and tender souls for feeling the emotions to which she herself is insensible, who can always produce a smile of venal love, shed tears over the coffin of her victim and jump for joy the same evening at the reading of the will. A poet would have admired the beautiful Aquilina; the whole world would shrink away from the touching Euphrasie: one was the soul of vice, the other was soulless vice.

'I should love to know,' Emile asked this pretty creature, 'if you sometimes think of the future.'

'The future?' she replied with a laugh. 'What do you mean by the future? Why should I think of something that does not yet exist? I never look either behind or before me. Isn't it enough to cope with one day at a time? Besides, we know well what our future is: the poor-house.'

'How *can* you see the poor-house in front of you without trying to avoid it?' cried Raphael.

'What's so frightening about the poor-house?' asked Aquilina, 'when we are neither wives nor mothers, when old age puts black stockings on our legs and wrinkles on our foreheads, withers up everything feminine in us and wipes the joy from our clients' eyes, what could we be in need of? At that stage you see nothing in us, under our finery, but the elemental clay moving along on two legs, cold, wizened, decomposed, and giving forth the rustle of dead leaves. The prettiest dresses will be rags on us, the amber which perfumed the boudoir takes on the smell of death and stinks of the skeleton; then, if a heart still beats in the carcase, all of you jeer at it, not even allowing us the consolation of our memories. And so, whether at that period of our life we are living in a sumptuous mansion fussing over poodles, or sorting out rags in a poor-house, is not our existence just the same? Whether we hide our white hair under a red and blue checkered kerchief or a lace cap, whether we sweep the streets with a birch broom or the steps of the Tuileries with our satin gowns, whether we sit beside gilded hearths or warm our toes at the embers of an earthenware brazier, whether we get our kick from a public execution or sit in a box in the Opera House, does it really make much difference?'

'*Aquilina mia*, never, in the midst of your despair, have you reasoned so well,' Euphrasie continued. 'Yes, Cashmere, Alençon lace, perfume, gold, silk, luxury, all that glitters and all that delights is suitable only for youth. Time alone may requite us for our follies, but happiness absolves us. What I say amuses you,' she exclaimed with a venomous smile directed at the two friends: 'Am I not right? I would rather die of pleasure than of disease. I have neither a craving for perpetuity nor a great respect for mankind, seeing what God is making of it! Give me millions and I will squander them without keeping a single penny for next year. To live in order to give pleasure and reign: this is what each one of my heartbeats commands me. Society approves me: it is always giving me money to fling around. Why does God, every morning, provide me with the income for what I spend every evening? Why do you build alms-houses for us? Since He has not set us half-way between good and evil so that we should choose what injures or bores us, I should be a big fool if I didn't amuse myself.'

'What about other people?' asked Emile.

'Other people? They must look after themselves. I would rather laugh at their sufferings than be obliged to weep for my own. I defy any man to cause me the slightest pain.'

'What then have you suffered to think like this?' asked Raphael.

'I was jilted for the sake of an inheritance, I was!' she said, striking a pose that showed all her charms to advantage. 'And yet I had spent night and day working to keep my lover from starving! No more will I be the dupe of a smile, a promise. I claim the right to make my life one long round of pleasure.'

'But,' cried Raphael, 'is not happiness something spiritual?'

'Well,' Aquilina retorted. 'Is it nothing to see oneself admired and flattered, to triumph over all other women, even the most virtuous, to crush them beneath our beauty and riches? For that matter, we live more in one day than your simple housewife does in ten years. That just about settles it.'

'Isn't a woman odious without virtue?' Emile remarked to Raphael.

Euphrasie threw them a viperish glance and replied with an inimitably ironic accent:

'Virtue! We leave that to ugly and hunchbacked women. How would they manage without it, poor dears?'

'Come now, hold your tongue!' Emile cried out. 'Don't talk of what you know nothing about.'

'Oh! So I know nothing about it!' Euphrasie retorted. 'Devote your whole life to a man you detest, learn how to bring up children who abandon you and give them thanks when they break your heart. Those are the virtues you wish on women. And not content with that, to reward her for her self-denial, you come along and impose more suffering on her by trying to seduce her. If she resists, you compromise her. A lovely life! Better to stay free, love whoever you please and die young.'

'Aren't you afraid of having to pay for all that one day?'

'Look,' she replied, 'instead of having pleasure and pain mixed up, my life will be divided into two parts: a joyous youth I can be sure of and an indeterminate spell of old age during which I shall suffer at my ease.'

'She has never been in love,' said Aquilina in a deep tone of voice, 'she has never travelled hundreds of miles for the sake of a glance of denial, devoured with infinite delight. She has not let her life hang on a single hair, nor tried to stab one man after another to save her sovereign lord, her deity . . . All love has meant to her has been a handsome colonel.'

'Listen to *La Rochelle*![54] Euphrasie replied. 'Love is like the wind, it bloweth where it listeth, thou canst not tell whence it cometh. In any case, if you had ever been loved by a brute beast, you wouldn't ask for an intelligent lover.'

54. See above, p. 83, footnote. Euphrasie gives Aquilina this nickname to taunt her.

'Bestiality is forbidden by the Civil Code,' retorted the Juno-esque Aquilina ironically.

'I thought you had a softer spot for military men,' Euphrasie exclaimed with a laugh.

'Aren't they lucky, these girls, to be able to talk nonsense like this!' cried Raphael.

'Lucky?' said Aquilina, smiling in pity and terror as she cast a horrifying glance at the two friends. 'Oh! You have no idea what it means to be condemned to please one man when another, who is dead, lives on in your heart ...'

To contemplate these salons at that moment was to have a preview of Milton's Pandemonium. The blue flames of the punch gave an infernal tint to the faces of those who were still able to drink. Wild dances, spurred on by savage energy, were exciting laughter and shouts which cracked out like the detonations of fireworks. The boudoir and a smaller salon, strewn with people who had collapsed or were collapsing, gave the impression of a battlefield. The atmosphere was hot with wine, revelry and volubility. Drunkenness, delirium and obliviousness filled every heart, could be read on every face or deduced from a look at the floor, and were expressed in the very riotousness of the scene; everyone's eyes were covered with a filmy blur through which intoxicating vapours could be seen floating in the air. There had risen up, as in the luminous tracks of a sunbeam, a sheen of dust across which the most capricious shapes were flitting in the most grotesque of conflicts. Here and there were groups of entwined figures mingled confusedly with the noble masterpieces of white marble sculpture adorning the suites of rooms.

Although the two friends still retained in their ideas and organs a deceptive sort of lucidity, a last flicker, an imperfect semblance of awareness, they were quite unable to discern what was real in the strange fantasies or what was possible in the weird tableaux which kept sweeping past their wearied eyes. The oppressive sky which weighs on us in dreams, the fiery splendour of the faces we come upon in our visions, above all the indefinable sense of litheness laden with shackles which we experience, in short all the most abnormal phenomena of the state of sleep overcame them so utterly that they mistook the antics of this orgy for the caprices of a nightmare in which movement is noiseless and the ear hears no cries. At this moment the confidential manservant managed, not without difficulty, to draw his master into the antechamber and whispered to him:

'Sir, all our neighbours are at their windows and are complaining about the din.'

'If they're afraid of noise, let them put straw in front of their doors' Taillefer exclaimed.

Suddenly Raphael burst out laughing so unexpectedly that his friend asked him to explain.

'You would find it hard to understand me,' he replied. 'In the first place, I ought to confess that you stopped me on the Quai Voltaire at the moment when I was about to throw myself into the Seine and no doubt you would like to know the reasons for this suicide. But if I added this: thanks to an almost fabulous stroke of chance, the most poetic ruins of the material world had just then been summed up before my gaze in a symbolic representation of human wisdom; whereas at this present moment the debris of all the intellectual riches that we ransacked at table are summed up in these two women, the living images, the very replicas of human folly; and seeing that our profound indifference about men and things has served as a transition between two highly coloured pictures of two diametrically opposed systems of existence, would you be any the wiser? If you weren't drunk, you might discern a treatise of philosophy in all this.'

'If you hadn't got both feet planted on the ravishing Aquilina, whose snores have a certain analogy with the rumblings of an approaching storm,' replied Emile, who was curling and uncurling Euphrasie's hair without being too conscious of this innocent occupation, 'you would be ashamed of being so drunk and gabbling so much. The two systems you mention can be resumed in a single sentence and reduced to a single thought. A simple, mechanical mode of life brings us to a kind of bovine wisdom by stifling our intelligence under the weight of toil; whereas life spent in the vacuum of abstract thought or in the bottomless pit of the spiritual world leads to a kind of lunatic wisdom. In a word, stifle feeling in order to live long, or die young by accepting the martyrdom which passion brings: it's to that we are doomed. And yet this doom is at odds with the temperaments given us by the grim jester to whom we owe the mould in which all created beings are cast.'

'Imbecile!' Raphael broke in. 'If you go on abridging yourself like this, you'll run into volumes. If I had been pretentious enough to make a precise formulation of these two ideas, I would have told you that man is corrupted by the exercise of reason and purified by ignorance. And that is an indictment of human societies! But whether we prolong our lives with the wise or perish with fools, is not the result the same sooner or later? Did not the great abstractor of quintessences once express these two systems in two words: CARYMARY, CARY-MARA?'[55]

'You make me doubt the power of God, for you are more stupid than He is mighty,' Emile retorted. 'Our dear Rabelais summed up this philosophy in a still briefer formula: *perhaps*. From which Montaigne derived his *What do I know*? And even so these two ultimate words of moral science are scarcely different from the exclamation of Pyrrho, half-way between good and evil as Buridan's ass was between two measures of oats.[56] But let's give up this eternal discussion which today brings us down to a *yes* or a *no*. What experiment were you wanting to make by throwing yourself into the Seine? Were you envious of the hydraulic machine of the Pont Notre-Dame?'[57]

'Ah! If you knew the life I have led!'

'Ah!' Emile exclaimed. 'I didn't know you were so common-place. It's an outworn phrase. Don't you know that we all of us claim to have suffered more than anybody else?'

'Ah!' sighed Raphael.

'But you're a clown with your *Ahs*! Come now: does some malady of mind or body force you to draw back every morning,

55. Rabelais, *Gargantua*, xvii. Gibberish in quasi-magic formulas.

56. Pyrrho: a Greek sceptic, born 360 B.C. Buridan: a scholastic philo-sopher (fourteenth century) who, to exemplify a case of complete indecision, postulated a donkey, torn between hunger and thirst, confronted with a pail of water and a feed of oats.

57. A pumping-machine for distributing water to near-by districts in Paris.

by a contraction of your muscles, the horses which, in the evening, are to quarter you, as was the case with Damiens.[58] Have you had to eat your own dog uncooked and without salt, in your garret? Have you ever had children crying out to you: "I'm hungry?" Have you sold your mistress's hair for money to go gambling? Have you ever gone to a fictitious domicile to settle a fictitious note of hand drawn by a fictitious uncle and been afraid not to arrive in time? Come now, tell me. If you were going to drown yourself for a woman, for a protested bill, or just out of boredom, I give you up. Make your confession and tell no lies. I'm not asking you for historical memoirs. Above all, be as brief as your intoxication permits. I am as demanding as a reader and as near to falling asleep as a woman saying vespers by herself.'

'Poor idiot!' said Raphael. 'Since when is pain no longer proportionate with sensibility? When we reach that degree of scientific knowledge which will enable us to write the natural history of the human heart, to name and classify the various genera and subgenra, to divide it into families – crustaceans, fossils, saurians, microscopical species, etc. . . . – then, my good friend, it will be demonstrable that there exist tender hearts, hearts as delicate as flowers, hearts that can be broken as easily as flowers by slight bruisings which certain mineral kinds would not even feel . . .'

'For God's sake spare me the preface,' said Emile, half in amusement, half in sorrow, as he took Raphael by the hand.

58. Damiens was hanged, drawn and quartered in 1757 for stabbing Louis XV with a knife. The reference here is not clear. But Damiens's muscles resisted the quartering operation and had to be cut.

2. *The Woman without a Heart*

AFTER a moment's silence, Raphael said, with a careless gesture:

'I honestly don't know if I haven't the fumes of wine and punch to thank for the kind of lucidity that enables me at this instant to take in my whole life as one single picture; a picture in which forms and colours, light and shade and half-tones are faithfully rendered. This poetic play of my imagination would not astonish me were it not accompanied by a sort of disdain for my past joys and sorrows. Seen from a distance, my life is as it were contracted by some moral phenomenon. The protracted misery which has dragged on for ten years can be rendered today in a few sentences in which suffering will be no more than an idea and pleasure a philosophical reflection. I judge instead of feeling . . .'

'You're as boring as the preamble to a parliamentary amendment,' Emile exclaimed.

'That may be,' Raphael replied good-humouredly, 'Consequently, so as not to take excessive advantage of your indulgence, I will spare you the first seventeen years of my life. Up until then I lived, like you, like thousands of others, the school or college life whose imaginary troubles and real joys are our most cherished memories; a life whose Friday vegetables our worn-out palates crave for, though only so long as we do not actually have to taste them again; a delightful life, when we were made to do work that would seem a waste of time now – but when at least we were taught how to work.

'Can't you come to the point?' said Emile in a half-comic, half-plaintive tone.

'When I left school,' Raphael resumed, holding up his hand to assert his right to continue,' my father subjected me to a severe discipline. I had to sleep in a room adjoining his study, to go to bed at nine in the evening and get up at five in the morning. He wanted me to have a thorough grounding in the law,

91

and I went to lectures and worked in a solicitor's office simultaneously. But the rules of time and space were so rigorously applied to the walks I took and the work I did, my father asked at dinner for so strict an account of . . .'

Emile interrupted. 'What does that matter to me?' he asked.

'Oh! The devil take you!' Raphael replied. 'How can you enter into my feelings if I don't tell you the scarcely perceptible factors influencing my mind, shaping it to feel fear and keeping me for a long time in the primitive innocence of youth? Thus, until I was twenty-one, I had to submit to a discipline as cold as that of a monastic rule. To make you understand the dreariness of my life, it will perhaps suffice to describe my father to you: a tall, spare, austere man with a hatchet face and pale complexion; curt of speech, as cantankerous as an old maid and as fussy as a chief clerk in a government office. His paternity brooded over my mischievous and joyous fancies and clamped them down as it were under a dome of lead. If I ventured to display towards him any affectionate or tender feeling, he treated me like a child who is about to say something silly. I was more afraid of him than we used to be of our teachers at school, and for him I was always eight years old. I can still see him in my mind's eye. In his maroon frock-coat, in which he stood as straight as a paschal candle, he looked like a smoked herring wrapped in the reddish-brown paper used to cover pamphlets. And yet I was fond of my father; he was the soul of justice. Perhaps we can accept severity when it is justified by greatness of character, purity of morals and has in it a nice admixture of kindliness.

'Although my father never left me alone and although, before I was twenty, I never had ten francs to spend as I liked – ten wicked, rascally francs, a tremendous treasure for which I pined in vain, dreaming of the ineffable delights it would give me – he did at any rate try to provide a few distractions for me. After promising me a treat for several months, he would take me to the theatre, to a concert or a ball where I hoped to fall in with a mistress. A mistress! That would have spelt independence for me. But, being backward and shy, unskilled in the jargon of the salons and knowing no one in them, I returned as innocent and as tormented with desires as ever. Then, next morning, bridled by my father like a cavalry horse, I would return to my solicitor, the law school or the Law Courts. To deviate from the narrow path my father had traced out for me would have been to incur his wrath: he had threatened at my first misdeed to ship me off to the Antilles as a cabin-boy. And so I shivered with terror on the rare occasions when I dared to take an hour or two off to enjoy myself.

'Just think of me as I was: a roving imagination, a most susceptible heart, the tenderest of souls, the most poetic of minds, constantly in the presence of the most flinty, the moodiest and chilliest of temperaments. In short, marry a young girl to a skeleton and you'll have some idea of the kind of existence whose curious aspects I must only rapidly relate: plans for flight which evaporated at the mere sight of my father, moods of despair soothed by sleep, repressed desires, fits of sombre melancholy which music could dispel. I sighed out my misery in melody; Beethoven and Mozart were frequently my trusty confidants. I smile today at the memory of all the prejudices that troubled my conscience during that period of innocence and virtue: if I had set foot in a restaurant I should have thought myself lost; my imagination pictured a café as a den of iniquity in which men courted dishonour and ruin; as for risking money at gambling, I had none to risk. Oh! Even if it sends you to sleep, I must tell you about one of the most disturbing joys I ever experienced, one of those joys which as it were dig their claws into our hearts as the branding-iron bites into the convict's shoulder.

'It happened at a ball given by the Duc de Navarreins, a cousin of my father. But, so that you may perfectly understand my situation, let me tell you that I had on a threadbare coat, ill-fitting shoes, the sort of neckcloth a cabby would wear, and gloves that were anything but new. I tucked myself away in a corner where I could eat ices undisturbed and look at the belles of the ball. My father, seeing me there, for some reason I have never fathomed, so overcome was I by this token of confidence, gave me his purse and keys to look after. Ten feet away a card-game was in progress. I could hear the chink of gold. I was twenty and would have liked to spend a whole day sowing the wild oats appropriate to my years. This was a licentiousness of the mind totally different from the freakish sensuality of women of pleasure or the day dreams of green girls. For a whole year I had dreamed of riding in a carriage, dressed in fine clothes, with a beautiful woman beside me, playing the great lord, dining at Véry's, going every evening to the theatre, resolved not to return till morning to my father's house, and facing him with a story more complicated than the plot of *The Marriage of Figaro*, one which he would have found it impossible to unravel. I had reckoned the cost of these delights at 150 francs. Was I not still as charmingly innocent as a boy playing truant? So I stepped into an anteroom where I could be on my own and with trembling fingers and burning eyes I counted my father's money: 300 francs. The joys I anticipated from my escapade, conjured up by the sight of this sum, took shape before my eyes, capering like the witches in *Macbeth* around their cauldron, but they were alluring, quivering, delightful! I changed into a determined scoundrel! Without heeding the ringing in my ears or the quickened beat of my heart, I took out two twenty-franc pieces – I can see them to this day! The dates on them were worn off and Napoleon, stamped in effigy, seemed to grimace. Replacing the purse in my pocket, I approached a card-table clasping the two coins in my damp palm and prowled round the players like a hawk over a hen-coop. A prey to unspeakable anguish, I suddenly cast a keen glance around me. Certain of not being noticed by anyone who knew me. I placed my stake beside that of a fat, jolly little man, on whose head I heaped more prayers and vows than are offered up at sea during a succession of tempests. Then, with an instinct for villainy or machiavellianism which was surprising at my age, I went and stood near a door, gazing across the suite of rooms without seeing a thing. My eyes – my soul, too – were fluttering round the fatal green cloth.

'From that evening dates the first physiological observation to which I owe that kind of penetration which has enabled me to grasp some of the mysteries of our dual nature. I was standing with my back to the table on which my future happiness was being decided, a happiness the more profound perhaps for being criminal. Between the two players and myself there was a crowd of men, four or five rows of them standing talking. The buzz of voices made it impossible to distinguish the chink of gold coins which mingled with the strains of the orchestra; but, despite all these obstacles, thanks to a privilege accorded to the passions which gives them the power to annihilate space and time, I could distinctly hear what the two players were saying, I knew how the score stood and which of the two was going to turn up the king just as surely as if I had seen the cards, in short, though ten paces distant from the game, its vicissitudes turned me pale. My father suddenly went past in front of me, and then I understood the saying of the Scriptures: 'The spirit of God passed before his face!' I had won. I hurried towards the table, slipping through the crowd which was swirling round the players with the litheness of an eel escaping through a torn mesh in a fishing-net. My muscles had been tensed in agony; now they relaxed in joy. I felt like a condemned man who meets a royal procession on the way to the scaffold. It so chanced that a man with a string of medals on his chest claimed he was short by forty francs. Suspicious eyes were turned on me; I turned pale and beads of perspiration gathered on my brow – the crime of having robbed my father appeared truly avenged. Then the good little fat man said, in a decidedly angelic voice: "Every one of these gentlemen had placed his stake", and he paid the forty francs. I raised my head again and looked triumphantly round at the players. After restoring the gold I had taken from my father's purse, I left my winnings with the worthy and honest gentleman, and he continued to win. As soon as I found myself in possession of a hundred and sixty francs, I gathered them into my hand-kerchief in such a way that they could neither move nor jingle, and I left the game.

'"What were you doing in the card-room?" my father asked as we got into the cab.

'"Looking on," I replied, trembling.

'"But," my father rejoined, "there would have been nothing odd in your feeling yourself obliged, for appearance's sake, to put a little money on the cloth. People in society would judge you old enough to have the right to commit the occasional folly, and I should have overlooked it, Raphael, if you had used my purse."

'I made no answer. When we were home again, I returned keys and money to my father. Re-entering his room, he emptied his purse on to the mantelpiece, counted the gold, turned to me with quite a gracious air and said, leaving a more or less lengthy and significant pause between each sentence: "My son, you'll soon be twenty. You have given me satisfaction. You must have an allowance, if only so that you may learn to economize and realize the value of things. From tonight onwards I shall give you a hundred francs a month, and you'll spend it as you like. This will cover the first quarter of the year," he added, cradling the heap of gold with his hands as if to check the sum.

'I confess I felt like throwing myself at his feet, declaring that I was a thief, a rogue and, even worse, a liar! Shame held me back. I made as if to embrace him, but he gently repulsed me.

' "Now you are a man, *my child*," he said. "What I am doing is simple and right, and I deserve no thanks. If I have any right to gratitude from you, Raphael," he continued in mild but dignified tones, "it is for protecting your youth from the misfortunes that beset all young men in Paris. Henceforward we shall be just two friends. In a year from now you will take your law degree. You have acquired – not without having had to put up with a certain amount of vexation and certain privations – sound knowledge and a love of work, both of which are necessary to men called to handle affairs of state. It is time, Raphael, that you learn my plans. I want to make of you, not a barrister or a notary, but a statesman who may become the glory of an impoverished house . . . Until tomorrow!" he added, dismissing me with a mysterious gesture.

'From that day on my father told me of all his plans, keeping nothing back. I was an only son and had lost my mother ten years before. Long since, my father, the head of a historic family almost lost to memory in Auvergne, and not relishing the idea of ploughing his fields with a sword at his side, had come to Paris to wrest a fortune from the jaws of adversity. Endowed with the shrewdness which makes men from the south of France irresistible, provided they have energy as well, he had succeeded, in spite of having little backing, in attaining a position at the very centre of power. Then the Revolution came and shattered his prospects, but he had been foresighted enough to marry the heiress of a great house and, under the Empire, had believed himself to be on the point of reinstating our family in its former splendour. The Restoration gave back a substantial portion of her property to my mother, but ruined my father. Having formerly purchased several estates abroad which the Emperor had bestowed on his generals, he had for ten years been battling with liquidators and diplomats, in courts of justice in Prussia and Bavaria, in order to maintain a disputed title to these unlucky donations. My father introduced me into the inextricable maze of this vast lawsuit on which our future depended. It was quite possible that we might be condemned to refund the revenues from these estates as well as the proceeds from certain timber sales made between 1814 and 1817, in which case my mother's property would scarcely have sufficed to save the honour of our name. Thus, the very day when my father appeared to some extent to have emancipated me, I fell under the most odious of yokes. I had to fight as on a battlefield, working day and night, visiting politicians, trying to guess their allegiances, attempting to interest them in our suit, paying court to them, their wives, their servants, even their dogs, while putting an elegant front on this humiliating occupation and joking pleasantly about it. I now understood all the vexations which had left their searing mark on my father's face.

'So then, for about a year, I gave the impression of living the life of a man of the world; but behind this frivolity and my eagerness to make friends with well-placed people related to us or who could help us, lay a life of herculean toil. My amusements were in themselves a kind of counsel's pleas, and my conversations so many legal reports. So far I had been virtuous thanks to the sheer impossibility of indulging my youthful passions. But at that time fearful lest out of negligence I might cause my father's ruin or my own, I ruled myself with a rod of iron and went in fear of allowing myself any pleasure or expense. When we are young, when harsh contact with society has not yet robbed us of that delicate flowering of sentiment, that freshness of mind, that noble purity of conscience which never allows us to compromise with evil – it is then that we are acutely sensible of our duties. Our sense of honour speaks out loud and true. We say what we think frankly and unambiguously. That is how I was then. I wanted to justify the trust my father had placed in me. Not so long ago I would have been delighted to rob him of a paltry sum of money. But now that I bore with him the weight of business, helping him to defend his name and that of his house, I would have secretly made over to him all that I had and all I hoped to inherit, just as I sacrificed my pleasures and was happy to sacrifice them! And so, when M. de Villèle[1] exhumed, to our particular disadvantage, an imperial decree about forfeitures and brought us to ruin, I signed away all my property, reserving nothing but a valueless eyot in the middle of the Loire on which my mother was buried.

'Today perhaps I should be at no loss for arguments, sophistries, philosophical, philanthropical and political reasons to dispense me from committing what my solicitor called a quixotic folly; but, at twenty-one, as I said, we are filled with generosity, ardour and love. The tears I saw in my father's eyes on that occasion constituted for me the most splendid of inheritances, and the memory of those tears has often consoled me in poverty. Ten months after settling with his creditors, my father died of grief: he adored me and had ruined me, and the thought of it killed him. In 1826, being then twenty-two, towards the end of the autumn, as sole mourner, I followed to its grave the body of my father, my earliest friend. Few young people have ever found themselves alone with their thoughts behind a hearse, forlorn in Paris, penniless and with no future before them. Foundlings in state orphanages at least have a future on the battlefield; the government or the public attorney act as foster-father for them, they can look forward to an old folks' home. I had nothing at all. Three months later an official liquidator handed over to me eleven hundred and twelve francs, the net cash proceeds of my father's estate. Creditors had forced me to

1. Joseph, Comte de Villèle: an ultra-royalist statesman, prime minister from 1821 to 1828. The forfeiture in question is the loss of one's estates in consequence of a breach of engagement, etc.

sell our furniture. Having been accustomed from youth up to regard the objects of luxury with which I was surrounded as being of great value, I could not refrain from expressing some slight astonishment at this meagre product of the sale.

' "Oh!" said the liquidator. "All that was very rococo!"

'An appalling adjective! It defiled all I had held sacred in childhood, and robbed me of my early illusions, the dearest of all. My fortune consisted in a memorandum of sale, my future lay in a linen bag which contained eleven hundred and twelve francs, and society appeared before me in the person of an auction-room attendant who talked to me with his hat on. Jonathas, a family servant who was attached to me, to whom my mother had bequeathed on her death an annuity of four hundred francs, said to me as we left the house from which, as a boy, I had so often driven happily away in our carriage:

' "Make it last, Monsieur Raphael!"

The old fellow was in tears.

*

'Such, my dear Emile, are the events which determined my destiny and shaped my outlook, placing me when I was still only a youth in the falsest of all social situations,' said Raphael after a pause. 'I was connected by family ties – weak enough in all conscience – with a few wealthy houses which my pride would have forbidden to visit even if scorn and indifference had not already closed their doors to me. Although I was related to some very influential persons who were prodigal of their patronage to strangers, I had neither kinsfolk nor protectors. Always checked when I felt like being expansive, I had grown withdrawn. Although by nature I was frank and open-hearted, I was forced to appear cold and calculating. The tyranny exerted by my father had robbed me of all self-confidence. I was timid and awkward, unable to believe that my voice had any power to move or persuade; I was dissatisfied with myself, thought myself ugly, and was ashamed of my looks.

'Despite the inner voice which should sustain men of talent in their struggles and which cried out to me: "Take courage! Go forward!"; despite the sudden revelations I had in solitude of latent power within me; despite the hope which filled me as I compared recent works admired by the public with those which flitted across my mind, I had no more faith in myself than a child has. I was extremely ambitious; I thought myself destined to great things but felt that I was of no account. I needed my fellow-men but had not a single friend. I needed to make my way in the world, but I remained isolated, not so much afraid as ashamed. In the course of the year which at my father's behest I had spent in the vortex of high society, I had started with an innocent heart and fresh mind. Like all grown-up children I secretly aspired to a transcendent passion.

'Among the young men of my own age I came across a set of braggarts who went about with their heads held high, chatting idly to ladies who to me seemed quite unapproachable, paying them impertinent compliments, gnawing the pommels of their canes, striking attitudes, uttering ineptitudes, making light of the reputations of the fairest women, laying or claiming to have laid their heads on every pillow, giving the impression they could pick and choose their pleasures, reckoning all women, saints and prudes alike, ready prey, easily captured by a mere word, by the first insolent stare. I declare to you on my soul and conscience that the conquest of power or great literary renown appeared to me to be a triumph easier to carry off than to cut a dash with an intelligent, graceful young woman of rank. And so I found my beating heart, my emotions, my ideals at variance with the maxims of society. I had some boldness, but in my mind only and not in my outward behaviour. I came to know later on that women do not want to be sighed for. I have seen many that I adored from afar, to whom I was offering a staunchly loyal heart, a soul for them to rend, an energy which would not flinch from sacrifice or torture; but these women had given themselves to fools whom I would not have wanted even as porters. How many times, standing motionless and tongue-tied, have I not admired the woman of my dreams appearing before me in a ballroom; whereupon, mentally devoting my whole life to unending caresses, I would concentrate all my hopes in a single glance and ecstatically tender to her a love so naïve and youthful as almost to encourage betrayal. At certain moments I would have given my life for a single night of love.

'So then, having never found an ear into which to pour my impassioned words, a glance on which to rest my own or a heart to respond to my heart, I lived racked with all the torment of a self-devouring, impotent energy, either through lack of opportunity, or through timidity or inexperience. Perhaps I despaired of being able to convey my meaning or trembled at the thought of being too well understood. And yet there was a storm brewing within me at every polite glance that might be directed towards me. In spite of my readiness to interpret this glance – or any apparently affectionate words addressed to me – as tender advances, I never dared either to speak or hold my peace at the appropriate moment. So strongly did I feel, I could only make trivial remarks or maintain a stupid silence, I was no doubt too ingenuous for an artificial society that lives in the limelight and expresses all its thoughts in trite phrases or by formulae prescribed by fashion. Nor had I the art of speaking while saying nothing or saying nothing while speaking. In short, I had secret fires burning within me, a heart such as women love to encounter; I was a prey to the emotional fervour for which women long, and possessed the energy on which fools preen themselves – and yet every woman treated me with perfidious cruelty. And so I naïvely admired the salon heroes when they bragged of their triumphs; and I never suspected they might be lying. Probably I was at fault in looking for a frank and genuine love, in hoping I might find, in the heart of a light and frivolous woman, greedy for luxury, her head turned with vanity, the broad ocean of passion which raged tempestuously in my own breast. Oh! To feel oneself born to love, to make a woman truly happy, and to find no one, not even a brave and noble Marceline[2] or some elderly marquise! To carry treasures in one's wallet and not even to come across some unripe girl interested enough to wonder at them! I often felt like killing myself out of despair.'

'You're in a lovely tragic mood this evening!' cried Emile.

'Why not let me pass sentence on my life?' Raphael replied.

2. A middle aged woman in Beaumarchais's *Le Mariage de Figaro*. She is bent on marrying Figaro until she discovers that he is actually her son.

'If your friendship isn't strong enough for you to listen to my laments, if you're afraid to risk boredom for half an hour, go to sleep! But after that never call me to account for the suicide which is there waiting for me, like a wild beast, growling, rearing its head and roaring for me. I salute it. In order to judge a man you must at least enter into the secrets of his thought, his misfortunes, his emotions. If you only want to know about the material events in his life, you're merely asking for a chronological table: that's history as fools understand it.'

The bitter tone with which these words were uttered startled Emile into giving all his attention to Raphael while gazing at him in stupefaction.

'But now,' the narrator continued, 'the afterglow that lends colour to these incidents shows them in a new aspect. The order of things which I formerly considered as a misfortune may well have engendered the brilliant faculties which I prided myself on at a later stage. Might it not be that philosophical curiosity, the habit of excessive work and the love of reading which, from the age of seven until I made my entry into society, have kept me constantly occupied and endowed me with the ready talent I possess – if I am to believe what you say – for expressing my thoughts and covering more and more ground in the vast field of human knowledge? Do I not owe it to the solitude to which I was condemned, to the habit of suppressing my feelings and living the life of the mind, that I have acquired the power of comparison and meditation? And was not my sensibility, instead of being frittered away in the vexing trivialities of social life which wear down the finest minds and fray them to tatters, thereby so concentrated as to become the perfected organ of a will-power having higher aims than the whims of passion?

'Unappreciated by women, I recollect having observed them with the sagacity of love disdained. I can see now that the sincerity of my character must have counted against me. It may be that women like a little hypocrisy. In the course of a single hour I can be successively a child and an adult, a featherhead and a thinker, free from prejudice and riddled with superstitions, and indeed as feminine as women are; must they not have taken my ingenuousness for cynicism and regarded the very purity of my thought as the mask of a libertine? Intellectual conversation spelt boredom for them, and my womanish inertia was a sign of weakness. My excessively restless imagination, the curse of poets, no doubt made them look on me as a being incapable of love, inconstant in his ideas and devoid of energy. When I was tongue-tied they took me for an idiot. They were alarmed perhaps when I tried to be agreeable to them. So womankind condemned me, and in tears and mortification I submitted to this social verdict. But the penalty inflicted produced its result. I decided to avenge myself on society. I wanted to seize the imagination of every woman by achieving a dominant position in the world of the intellect, so that when my name was pronounced by a footman as I entered a salon all eyes would be turned in my direction. Even as a child I had decided to achieve greatness. I had tapped on my forehead, saying with André Chénier: "I have something here!"[3] I believed that there was in me a thought to express, a philosophical system to establish, a science to expound.

'O, my dear Emile! Today, now that I am only just twenty-six and sure to die unknown, without ever having been the lover of the woman I dreamed of possessing, let me tell you about my follies! Have we not all of us more or less taken our desires for realities? Indeed, I would not accept as a friend any young man who in his daydreams had not crowned himself with a laurel wreath, erected some pedestal or imagined himself embracing compliant mistresses. I myself have often been a general or an emperor. I have been a Byron, and then nothing at all. After disporting myself on the summit of human achievement, I perceived that all my mountains were still to be climbed and all obstacles still to be overcome.

'The overweening self-esteem which was bubbling inside me, the sublime faith in my destiny was what saved me. It may develop into genius provided one does not allow one's energy to be frittered away in contact with affairs as carelessly as a sheep leaves its wool on the thorns of the bushes through which it blunders. I wanted to cover myself in glory, working in silence

3. The gifted poet, guillotined in 1794, who is alleged to have said this as he laid his head on the block.

for the mistress I hoped to have one day. All women were summed up in one single one, and I believed I had found this woman in the first my eye fell upon. But, since I saw a queen in each one of them, I expected them, just as queens do who must necessarily make advances to their lovers, to meet me half-way, miserable, needy, timid as I was. Oh! I had so much gratitude as well as love stored in my heart for any one of them who might have pitied me, that I would have worshipped her for the whole of my life.

'Later on I learnt some cruel truths by dint of observation. In behaving this way, my dear Emile, I was running the risk of living eternally alone. Women are accustomed, thanks to some strange tendency of their nature, to notice only the flaws in a man of talent and only the good qualities in the character of a fool. They feel great sympathy for the qualities a fool possesses, since these exist as a perpetual flattery for their own defects, whereas a genius does not afford them enough enjoyment to compensate for his imperfections. Talent is an intermittent fever, and no woman is eager to share only the discomfort it brings; they all want to find in their lovers justification for satisfying their vanity. What they love in us is still themselves. Is not a man who is poor, proud, artistic, creative – is not such a man armed with an injurious egoism? He lives at the centre of a whirlwind of mental activity which embraces everything, even his mistress, who is forced to follow its twistings.

'Can a woman accustomed to flattery put her faith in the love of such a man? Will she search it out? Such a lover has not the leisure to loll beside a sofa and keep up the pretty pretence of sensibility by which women lay so great store, and at which insincere and unfeeling men are so expert. Since he has not time enough for his work, how could he waste it dressing up and cheapening himself? Ready as I was to give up my life at one stroke, I would not demean myself by frittering it away. In short, in the stratagems of a stockbroker who runs errands for some pale-faced, mincing woman, there is something shabby that sickens an artist. Love in the abstract is not enough for a man who is proud but great: he craves an absolute devotion. The little girls who spend their days trying on cashmere shawls or who turn themselves into display mannequins for the latest fashion can give no devotion: they merely demand it, and all they see in love is the pleasure of commanding, and not that of obeying. She who has become a true wife in body and soul follows obediently wherever he goes in whom she has placed her life, her strength, her glory and her happiness. Men of superior faculties need houris whose sole thought is the study of their needs, for to such men unhappiness lies in the discrepancy between their desires and the means of satisfying them. I thought myself a man of genius, and yet it was with mincing coquettes that I fell in love! Filled with such unconventional ideas, thinking I had no need of a ladder to climb up to the height of my ambition, possessing wealth that could buy me nothing, armed with an extensive knowledge which put too great a burden on my memory, which I had not yet classified and still less assimilated; without friends or relations, alone in the heart of the most frightful desert, a desert of paved streets, an animated, thinking, living desert, in which the climate is worse than hostile – it is indifferent to you: in such circumstances the decision I came to was natural though rash; it had an element of unfeasibility about it that gave me courage. It was as if I had made a wager with myself and were at once the player and the stake. This was my plan:

'My eleven hundred francs would have to last me three years, which was the period I reckoned would suffice to bring out a work which should draw public attention to me and make me a fortune or a name. I rejoiced to think that I was going to live on bread and milk like a hermit in the desert, plunged in the world of books and ideas, in an inaccessible sphere in the very midst of tumultuous Paris, a sphere of toil and silence in which, like a chrysalis, I was building a tomb around me in order to be reborn in brilliance and glory. I was going to risk dying so as to live. I calculated that by reducing existence to bare necessities, three hundred and sixty-five francs a year would suffice to keep me – in poverty. The fact is that this slender sum met my requirements so long as I was willing to submit to the claustrophobic discipline I had imposed upon myself.'

'Impossible!' Emile exclaimed.

'I lived like this for three years,' Raphael answered with a measure of pride. 'Let me work it out!' he continued. 'Three sous for bread,[4] two for milk, three for pork-butcher's meat kept my body and soul together and my mind in a state of singular lucidity. I have studied, as you know, the marvellous effects produced by diet on the imagination. My lodging cost me three sous a day; my lamp consumed three sous' worth of oil each night; I did my room myself. I wore flannel shirts to keep the laundry bill down to two sous a day. I used coal for heating and the price of that averaged out over the year never ran to more than two sous a day. I had clothes, linen and shoes to last three years, and I dressed up only to go to public lectures and libraries. All this amounted only to eighteen sous, and that left me two sous for emergencies. During that long period of study I don't remember ever crossing the Pont des Arts[5] or ever buying water, which I went to fetch every morning from the fountain in the Place Saint-Michel[6] at the corner of the Rue des Grecs. I assure you that I bore my poverty proudly. A man who anticipates a glorious future endures his life of penury like an innocent man being led to the scaffold: he feels no shame. I had refused to allow for possible illness. Like Aquilina, the prospects of a poor-house held no terrors for me. I never for a moment had any doubts about my good health. In any case, a poor man only retires to bed to die. I cut my hair myself until such time as an angel of love and goodness . . . But I must not anticipate.

'Let me just tell you this, dear friend: for lack of a mistress I lived with a great idea, a dream, a fiction of the kind we all start believing in sooner or later. Today I laugh at myself, at the *myself*, perhaps a saint, perhaps a poet, who no longer exists. The world and society, its manners and customs, seen from close quarters, have alerted me to the danger of my innocent faith and the unprofitableness of my arduous labours. Such stocking-up of provisions is useless to the ambitious man. If you go fortune-hunting you must travel light! The mistake of superior men

4. 1 sou = 5 centimes, 20 sous = 1 franc.

5. For which he would have had to pay a small toll (one sou).

6. This is not the present fountain, nor the present Place Saint-Michel, neither of which existed in Balzac's time.

lies in wasting their youth so as to make themselves worthy of favour. While these deluded people husband their strength and knowledge in order that they may bear without effort the weight of a power which evades them, the schemers, rich in words and empty of ideas, come and go, take advantage of the fools and establish themselves in the confidence of half-wits. On the one hand are those who study, on the other those who press on; the first are modest, the others audacious; the man of genius imposes silence on his pride, the schemer nails his flag to the mast and is sure to make good. The men in power are in such dire need to believe in ready-made merit, in talent that blows its own trumpet, that there is in the true man of science a certain childishness in hoping for the rewards of society. Believe me, I am not trying to paraphrase virtuous platitudes, that Song of Songs which unappreciated men of genius are eternally chanting: I merely wish to explain by due process of logic why mediocre men are so often successful.

'Alas! Study is so kind a mother that it is perhaps a crime to ask other rewards of her than the sweet and innocent joys she dispenses to her children. I remember how cheerfully I used to sit at the window with my bread and milk breathing in the fresh air and letting my gaze wander over a landscape of brown, grey or red roofs whose slates or tiles were covered with yellow or green mosses. If at first this view seemed monotonous to me, I soon discovered the singular beauties it contained. Sometimes, in the evening, light escaping from ill-closed shutters gave variety and animation to the black depths of this undiscovered country. Sometimes pale rays from the street-lamps down below cast yellowish gleams through the fog and brought into faint relief, along the streets, the undulations of these serried roofs which formed an ocean of motionless waves. And again, sometimes a few human shapes could be glimpsed in the midst of this cheerless wilderness: among the flowers of a hanging garden I might espy the hook-nosed, angular profile of an old woman watering her nasturtiums or, in the framework of a rotting dormer-window, a young girl thinking herself unobserved as she dressed her hair, and in fact I could not glimpse more than her bright forehead and her long tresses held up by one pretty white arm.

I admired the sparse and short-lived vegetation in the gutters, sorry weeds which a heavy shower would soon wash away! I studied the mosses whose colours had been refreshed by the rain and which the hot sun would change into dry, brown patches of velvet shot with varying hues. In short, the fleeting, poetic effects of the daylight, the melancholy of the fog, the sudden sparkle of sunshine, the silence and magic of the night, the mystery of dawn, the smoke rising from every chimney, all the details of that singular landscape, once I had become familiar with them, provided me with entertainment. I loved this prison of my own choosing. These Parisian savannahs consisting of roofs levelled out to form a plain, but covering abysses teeming with population sorted well with my mood and were in harmony with my ideas. It is tiring to re-enter suddenly into contact with the world when we descend from the celestial heights to which scientific speculations have transported us. And so I have always perfectly understood why monasteries are furnished so starkly.

*

'When I had firmly resolved to follow my new way of life, I looked for a lodging in the least busy districts of Paris. One evening as I returned from the Estrapade, I happened to pass through the Rue des Cordiers as I made my way home. At the corner of the Rue de Cluny I noticed a little girl of about fourteen playing at battledore and shuttlecock with one of her companions. Their laughter and frolics amused everyone around. It was a warm, fine evening and September was not yet out. In front of every door women were sitting and chatting as they might have done in a provincial town on a public holiday. I first of all studied the girl, whose features were delightfully expressive and whose body was a perfect model for a painter. A ravishing scene! I wondered how anything so idyllic was possible in the heart of Paris, and noticed that the street I was in led nowhere and therefore must be a quiet one. Remembering that Jean-Jacques Rousseau had lived hereabouts, I sought out a room in the *Hôtel de Saint-Quentin*.[7] I found it in so tumbledown a

7. An *hôtel garni*, i.e. a lodging-house in which furnished rooms are let.

state that it raised my hopes of finding cheap accommodation in it. So the fancy took me to look it over.

'Entering a low-ceilinged room, I saw the regulation copper candlesticks, each furnished with its tallow candle and standing in orderly fashion above each room-key. I was struck by the cleanliness which reigned in this hall – generally very ill-kept in most other lodging-houses, whereas this one was swept and garnished like a *genre* picture: the blue bed, the utensils, all the furniture were as pretty as if they were on display. The mistress of the house, a woman of some forty years, with a care-lined face and eyes dimmed as if with the tears she had shed, rose and came to me. I humbly told her how much rent I could afford, and then, showing no surprise, she picked out a particular key and led the way up to the attic where she showed me a room that looked out over the roofs and upon the courtyards of neighbouring houses from whose windows long poles protruded hung with clothes drying. Nothing could be more sordid than this attic with its dirty yellow walls which smelt of poverty and seemed to await a needy scholar. The roof followed a regular downward slope and the badly-fitting tiles gave glimpses of the sky. There was room for a bed, a table, one or two chairs, and I could fit my piano in under the eaves. Not having the wherewithal to furnish this cage, one worthy of the *Leads*[8] of Venice, the poor woman had never been able to let it. Since I had carefully excepted from the recent sale of my furniture such objects as were more or less my personal belongings, I soon came to terms with my landlady and on the following day I settled in.

'I lived in that aerial sepulchre for nearly three years, working day and night without remission and with so much pleasure that study seemed to me to be the noblest concern, the happiest way a man could spend his life. The tranquillity and silence necessary for the scholar have, like love, an element of sweetness and intoxication. The exercise of thought, the pursuit of ideas, the calm vistas of science lavish ineffable delights on us, indescribable like everything pertaining to the intelligence, whose phenomena are invisible to our grosser senses. That is why we

8. Venetian prisons in the roof-space of the Doge's palace: notorious for the horrible conditions in which prisoners were kept.

are always obliged to explain spiritual mysteries by similes drawn from the material world. The pleasure of swimming in the pure waters of a lake, in the midst of rocks, woods and flowers, alone and caressed by a warm breeze, would give to those who know nothing of such matters a very imperfect picture of the happiness I experienced when my soul was bathing in the glow of some mysterious illumination, when I listened to the awesome, confused voices of inspiration, when images from an unknown source streamed into my excited brain. To espy an idea dawning in the field of human abstractions and rising like the morning sun; or, better still, one which grows as visibly as a child, reaches puberty and slowly achieves virility, is a joy superior to all other terrestrial joys – or rather is a divine pleasure. Study endows everything around us with a kind of magic.

The shabby desk at which I wrote and the brown cloth that covered it, my piano, my bed, my armchair, the quaint designs of my wallpaper and the rest of my furniture came to life: I looked on them as humble friends, mute accomplices in the shaping of my future. How many times did I not communicate my thoughts to them as I looked at them! Often, as I let my eyes travel over a piece of warped moulding, I chanced on new developments, a striking proof of my argument, or words which I thought ideal for expressing thoughts almost impossible to formulate. By dint of contemplating the objects around me I found that each one of them had its distinctive appearance and character; they often spoke to me; and if, beyond the roofs, the setting sun cast some furtive gleam through my narrow window, they took on colour or became pale, brightened up, grew sad or merry, continually producing new and surprising effects. The slight incidents in the life of a recluse, to which the world, preoccupied with other things, pays no attention, are the consolation of prisoners. Was I not the captive of an idea, imprisoned in a system, but sustained by the prospect of my future fame? At every difficulty vanquished, I kissed the soft hands of the woman with starry eyes, elegant and rich, who one day was to stroke my hair as she tenderly murmured: "How much you must have suffered, dear angel!"

'I had undertaken two major works. In a small space of time a play was to bring me renown, a fortune and admission to the society in which I wanted to reappear enjoying the royal privileges of the man of genius. All of you looked upon this masterpiece as the earliest error of a young man fresh from college, a mere puerility. Your jests clipped the wings of fertile illusions which have never awoken to life again. You alone, my dear Emile, poured balm into the deep wound which other people had made in my heart! You alone admired my *Theory of the Will*, that voluminous work, to write which I had taught myself oriental languages, anatomy and physiology and to which I devoted the greater part of my time. This treatise, if I am not mistaken, will complete the researches of Mesmer, Lavater, Gall and Bichat[9] by blazing a new trail in human science. At that point the best part of my life comes to its close: the daily sacrifice, the silkworm's toil of which the world never knew and whose only reward perhaps lies in the toil itself. After reaching the age of reason, until the day when I finished my *Theory*, I observed, learned, read and wrote without relaxation, and my life was like one long schoolboy's imposition.

'Effeminate in my love of oriental indolence, enamoured of my dreams, a sensualist, I nevertheless went on working and refusing myself the pleasures which life in Paris could offer. I was fond of good cheer, but lived like an ascetic. I loved walking and the idea of sea voyages, wanted to visit various countries, and still enjoyed the childish pastime of making stones skim across water, but I stayed constantly at my desk, pen in hand. I was talkative by nature, but went to listen in silence to the professors who gave public lectures at the Bibliothèque Nationale and

9. Frederick Anthony Mesmer (1734–1815), a German, the theorist of 'animal magnetism'; he claimed to cure disease by using the magnetic influence he himself possessed (so did Balzac on occasions!): the founder in fact of 'mesmerism'. Jean Gaspard Lavater (1741–1801), a Swiss philosopher and theologian, founder of the alleged science of 'physiognomy', based on the theory that character is revealed in human features. Franz-Joseph Gall (1758–1828), a German, founder of the alleged science of 'phrenology', based on the theory that character is revealed in the conformation of the skull. Bichat (1771–1802), a brilliant French anatomist and physiologist. Balzac owed much to these four men for his own curious philosophical doctrine, and he put a great deal of himself into this aspect of Raphaël, as also into his 'alter ego', Louis Lambert, the hero of his novel of 1831–4.

the Museum. I slept on my lonely pallet like a Benedictine monk; and yet woman was my sole chimæra, a chimæra that I fondled but which constantly eluded me.[10] In short my life was one cruel antithesis, a perpetual falsehood. After that, do you still dare to pass judgement on mankind?

'Sometimes my natural appetites reawakened like long smouldering fires. Thanks to a sort of mirage or onset of delirium, deprived of all the women I lusted after, suffering every privation, and lodged in an artist's garret, I then saw myself surrounded with ravishing mistresses! I drove through the streets of Paris lolling on the soft cushions of a splendid carriage! I was eaten up with vice, I plunged headlong into debauchery, I derived and possessed all things; in fact I was drunk while I fasted, like Saint Anthony during his temptation. Fortunately sleep came in the end and dispelled these devouring visions; the next day science called me with a smile and I became its loyal votary once more. I imagine that supposedly virtuous women must often be buffeted by these wild storms of madness, desire and passion which rise up in us despite ourselves. Such dreams are not without their charm; do they not resemble the talk on winter evenings, when we are whisked off from our fireside to China? But what becomes of virtue during the delightful journeys we take when imagination overleaps every confining barrier?

'During my first ten months as a recluse I led the life of poverty and solitude I have described. Early in the morning and without being seen, I went and fetched in person my provisions for the day. I tidied my room, being at once both master and servant and taking unbelievable pride in playing Diogenes. But after a period during which the landlady and her daughter spied on my habits and way of life, studied my person and realized my poverty, perhaps because they themselves lived in very straitened circumstances, some ties were inevitably established between them and me. Pauline, the charming creature whose artless and unsophisticated grace had to some extent brought me there, did me several

10. Balzac here has in mind a Neapolitan fresco to which he several times alluded: *A Woman fondling her Chimæra*. Cf above p. 36, 'a Latin queen lovingly fondling her chimæra'. With Raphael woman herself becomes the chimæra!

services which it was impossible for me to refuse. All misfortunes are kin, speak the same language and show the same generosity, the generosity of those who, because they can call nothing their own, are prodigal of sympathy and lavish of their time and trouble.

'By imperceptible stages, Pauline took charge of my room and insisted on waiting on me; her mother made no objection. I saw the mother herself darning my linen and blushing to be caught at this labour of love. Having willy nilly become their protégé, I accepted their services. If one is to understand this curious relationship, one must make allowance for the extent a man living the life of the intellect can be swallowed up by his work, tyrannized by his ideas and can feel an instinctive abhorrence of the mechanical details of ordinary life. How could I resist the delicate attention with which Pauline approached me on tiptoe to bring me my frugal meal when she noticed that I had eaten nothing for seven or eight hours? With a woman's grace and the ingenuousness of childhood, she smiled at me with a gesture to indicate that I was to take no notice of her. She was another Ariel gliding into my cell like a sylph and anticipating my wants.

'One evening, with touching simplicity, Pauline told me her life story. Her father had commanded a squadron in the horse grenadiers of the Imperial Guard. At the passage of the Beresina[11] he had been taken prisoner by the Cossacks; later, when Napoleon proposed an exchange for him, the Russian authorities made an unsuccessful search for him in Siberia; to go by what the other prisoners said, he had escaped in the hope of reaching India. Since that time, Madame Gaudin, my landlady, had not been able to obtain any news of her husband. The disasters of 1814 and 1815 had found her alone, unprovided for and with no one to help her; so she had decided to let furnished lodgings in order to support her daughter. She still hoped that her husband would return. What grieved her most was that Pauline was growing up uneducated – her dear Pauline, a god-daughter of Princess Borghese, a girl who certainly would not have belied

1. A river in White Russia, the scene of an important rearguard action in the retreat of the French armies from Moscow in 1812.

the brilliant destiny her imperial patroness had planned for her. When Mme Gaudin told me of this bitter sorrow that was poisoning her life, when she said to me in heart-rending tones: "I would willingly give up both the scrap of paper that makes Gaudin a baron of the Empire and the claim we have to the estate of Wistchnau if only Pauline could be educated at Saint-Denis"[12] – suddenly I had an inspiration, and in recognition of the care these two women were lavishing upon me, the idea came to me of offering to finish Pauline's education. The simple-mindedness with which the two women accepted my proposal was equal to the ingenuousness which had inspired me to make it.

'I thus enjoyed many hours of recreation. The girl was most happily gifted by nature, and she learned with such ease that it was not long before she was a better pianist than I. As she accustomed herself to thinking out loud at my side, she displayed the thousand pretty ways of a young heart opening to life like the petals of a flower slowly unfolding in the sunlight; she listened to me with attentiveness and pleasure, fixing upon me her black, velvety, smiling eyes. She repeated her lessons with a soft, caressing accent and manifested a childish joy whenever I was pleased with her. Her mother, growing daily more anxious at having to preserve from all danger a girl who as she grew was developing to the full the promise of her graceful childhood, was relieved to see her stay indoors all day to study. My piano being the only one she could use, she took advantage of my absences in order to practise.

'I would return home and find Pauline in my room, in the most modest attire; but at her slightest movement, her supple waist and the charms of her person could be divined under the coarse material she wore. One could see that, like the heroine of *Peau d'Ane*,[13] she had a dainty foot shod in ugly shoes.

'But these pretty attractions, these maidenly charms, all this wealth of beauty were as good as lost on me. I had enjoined upon

12. A school founded for the education of daughters of holders of the Cross of the Legion of Honour.

13. A fairy-story by Charles Perrault (*Tales of Mother Goose*, 1691); a persecuted princess disguises herself under an ass's hide.

myself to see only a sister in Pauline and I should have been horrified to betray the confidence her mother showed in me. I admired this enchanting girl as if she were a picture, the portrait of a mistress who had died. In fact she was the child of my creation, a statue I had fashioned. Like a second Pygmalion, I tried to turn back into marble this living, warmly coloured, speaking and feeling virgin. I was quite stern with her, but the more overbearing a schoolmaster I showed myself, the gentler and more submissive she became.

'Although I was encouraged in my reserve and self-restraint by noble sentiments, yet I did not lack motives of a more legalistic kind. How one can be honest in money matters and dishonest in mind, is something I cannot understand. To deceive a woman or one's creditors has always been the same thing for me. To love a girl or let oneself be loved by her constitutes a real contract about whose terms one must be clear. We are free to abandon a woman who sells herself, but not a girl who gives herself, for she does not understand the extent of the sacrifice she is making. I could then have married Pauline, and it would have been folly to do so. Should I not have been exposing a gentle, virginal soul to frightful misfortunes? My poverty gave tongue, using egoistical arguments, and never failed to interpose its iron hand between this kind soul and myself. Also – I confess this to my shame – I cannot conceive of love in a garret. Perhaps that is a weakness in me traceable to that disease of mankind we call 'civilization', but a woman, be she as captivating as the fair Helen or Homer's Galatea,[14] has no hold upon my senses if there is mud on her shoes. Ah! let love be dressed in silk and satin, surrounded by all the marvels of that luxury which serves so wondrously to adorn it because love is itself perhaps a luxury. When I am moved by desire, I like to be able to crumple a stylish dress, to crush a flower, with wanton hand to demolish the elegant structure of a perfumed *coiffure*. Glowing eyes, hidden behind a veil of lace but with their sparkling looks visible through it as the flame through the cannon's smoke,

14. A nymph from Homer's *Odyssey*, beloved of the shepherd Acis, but who had the misfortune to be desired also by the giant Polyphemus.

these I find fantastically alluring. My kind of love demands silken ladders scaled in silence on a winter's night. What bliss to climb in, with snow on one's coat, and find in a chamber lit with scented tapers and hung with painted silks, a woman who, she too, is shaking snow from her shoulders. For what other name could be given to the voluptuous veils of muslin through which her form is vaguely outlined like an angel in a nimbus, and from which she will shortly burst free? Then again, my happiness is not complete without some fears, nor my confidence without a sense of risk. Last of all, I must see this mysterious woman again, but this time a dazzling social beauty, virtuous, bowed down to, wearing her lace and sparkling with diamonds, having all Paris at her feet, and on so lofty and imposing a pinnacle that no man dares avow his love for her. From the midst of her queenly court she steals a glance at me, one which gives the lie to all artifice, one which sacrifices all the world and all mankind to me!

'Truth to tell, I have a hundred times laughed at myself for falling in love with a few yards of blond lace, velvet or fine cambric; with the products of a hairdresser's skill, the magic of a blaze of candles, a carriage, a title, heraldic coronets painted by artists in stained glass or modelled by a silversmith, in short everything that is most artificial and least womanly in women; I have mocked at myself and reasoned with myself, but all in vain. A titled lady, with the aristocratic curl of her lips, the distinction of her manners and her self-respect, enchant me. When she sets up a barrier between herself and the world, she flatters all the vanities I cherish, and that brings me half-way to love. If she is envied by all, she seems to give more flavour to my joys. If my mistress does nothing that other women do, if she moves and lives on a different plane, if she is wrapped in a mantle that they cannot wear and is surrounded by her own special perfume, I feel that she belongs to me so much the more. The further she rises above the earth, even as regards the more earthy aspects of love, the more beautiful she appears to me. It's a fortunate thing for me that there has been no queen in France for twenty years: I should have been in love with the Queen herself!

'A woman must be rich to behave like a princess. How could

Pauline compete with my romantic fantasies? Could she sell me such nights as one would pay for with one's life? Could she offer me the love that kills, that brings every human faculty into play? [15] We are seldom ready to die for the love of a girl who has nothing to give but herself. I have never been able to stifle these feelings, these poetic imaginings. I was born for such love as cannot be consummated, and chance ruled that I should be served beyond my wishes. How often did I not dream of slipping satin shoes on Pauline's dainty feet, wrapping a gown of gauze round her body, as slender as a young poplar, throwing a light scarf about her breast and leading her down the carpeted stairs of her mansion to her elegant carriage! In these conditions, I would have adored her. I supposed in her a pride of which she was innocent. I stripped her of all her virtues, her simple grace, her charming ingenuousness and her winsome smile in order to plunge her into the Styx of our vices and make her heart incapable of feeling hurt; in order to raddle her with our crimes, make her the fancy doll of our salons, a slip of a woman who sleeps all the morning so as to waken in the evening in the false dawn of the candelabras. Pauline was all feeling. She was freshness itself. And I wanted her to be hard and cold!

'In the latest phases of my madness, memory has shown me Pauline as clearly as it repaints the scenes of our childhood. So many times have I sat enraptured, savouring delightful moments once again: sometimes I saw this adorable girl sitting by my desk, intent at her needlework, calm, silent and meditative as the weakening daylight from my dormer window touched her lovely black tresses with soft, silvery glints; or perhaps I heard the fresh ripple of her laughter or the rich tones with which she sang the graceful cantilenas which she composed so effortlessly. She was often transported, that dear Pauline of mine, when she made music, and then her face bore a striking resemblance to that noble head by which Carlo Dolci strove to represent Italy.[16] Cruelly, the memory of this girl was to haunt me like a pang of

15. There is (as often in Balzac) a kind of ironic forecast in these lines. This is exactly what Pauline will do in the end.

16. A Florentine painter (1616-86). Balzac probably owes his knowledge of this painting to the poet Alfred de Musset.

remorse, like an image of virtue, in the wilder moments of my existence. But let us leave the poor child to her destiny. However unhappy she may be, at least I sheltered her from a raging tempest by taking care not to drag her into my particular inferno.'

*

'Until last winter, I continued to lead the peaceful and studious life of which I have tried to give you some inadequate idea. In the early days of December 1829 I met Rastignac [17] who, in spite of my shabby costume, gave me his arm and inquired of my situation with truly fraternal interest. Captivated by his charm of manner, I briefly told him both about my life and my hopes. He began to laugh, told me I was a genius, but a fool at the same time. His Gascon volubility, his knowledge of the world, the flourishing state of his finances due to his cleverness in taking advantage of his position, all this acted on me irresistibly. Rastignac told me my fate was to die in an almshouse, unappreciated like a half-wit; he took charge of my funeral and buried me in a pauper's grave. He talked to me about charlatanism and indeed, with that delightfully ready tongue that makes him so fascinating, he showed me every genius in the light of a charlatan. He declared that I must be bereft of at least one sense – and that would be the death of me – if I went on living alone in the Rue des Cordiers. To hear him, I ought to go into society, get people used to pronouncing my name, and shed the humble *monsieur* which was unbecoming to a great man during his lifetime.

' "Fools call such activity *intriguing*," he exclaimed, "moralists proscribe it as being a *dissolute life*. But don't let's bother about men, let's look at results. You spend your life working: well, that will get you nowhere. Look at me: I'm fit for anything but good for nothing and bone idle. But I get everything I want. I jump the queue, and people make room for me. I brag, and they believe me. I run up debts and it's they who pay! Dissipation, my dear fellow, is a way of life. When a man spends his time squandering his fortune, he's very often on to a good

17. See above, Introduction, pp. 13–14.

thing: he is investing his capital in friends, pleasure, protectors and acquaintances. Take a merchant with a million in risk capital: for twenty years he neither sleeps, drinks nor has a good time; he worries about his million, sends it all round Europe; he frets and curses the day he was born; then someone goes bankrupt – I've seen it happen – and he's left without a penny, without a friend, with his reputation ruined. Whereas the spendthrift enjoys himself living to the full and enters his horses for the races. If he has the bad luck to lose his capital, he has the good luck to be appointed tax-collector, make a good marriage, become the secretary to a minister or an ambassador. He still has friends and reputation, and is never short of money. Knowing what levers to pull, he can work the system. Now then: isn't there method in my madness? Isn't this the moral of the comedy which is being played out every day in the world?"

' "Your treatise is finished," he added after a pause. "You have tremendous talent. Very well. You are coming up to the starting-line. Now you have to take charge personally of your success; it's the surest way. You must come to an understanding with the cliques and coteries and get the windbags on your side. As for me, I've a mind to take a hand in making a name for you. I will be the jeweller who sets the diamonds in your crown.

' "For a start, meet me here tomorrow evening. I will introduce you to a house to which all Paris flocks, our own particular Paris, the Paris of dandies, millionaires, all sorts of celebrities, in short the golden-mouthed men like Saint Crysostom. Once those people have taken up a book, that book becomes a best-seller. If it is really a good one, it means that they have awarded a certificate of genius without realizing what they're doing. If you've any sense, dear boy, you'll make your *Theory*'s fortune by acquiring a better understanding of the Theory of Fortune. Tomorrow evening you shall meet that lady of fashion, the beautiful Countess Fœdora."

' "I've never even heard of her." '

' "You're a Hottentot!" Rastignac retorted with a laugh. "You don't know Fœdora! A marriageable woman who has, near enough, an income of eighty thousand francs, who won't marry anyone or whom no one wants to marry. She's an enigma in

119

skirts: a half-Russian Parisian, a half-Parisian Russian! A woman in whose salon are published all the romantic productions which never see the light of day: the most beautiful, the most entrancing woman in Paris! You're not even a Hottentot. You're the missing link between the Hottentot and the lower creation. Good-bye until tomorrow."

'He spun round and disappeared without waiting for a reply from me, since he could not admit that any man in his right mind could refuse to be presented to Fœdora. How can one explain the fascination of a name? FŒDORA haunted me like an evil thought that one tries to compromise with. A voice told me: "You will visit Fœdora!" In vain did I argue with this voice and accuse it of lying: the name Fœdora crushed all my objections. In fact were not the woman and the name the symbol of all my desires and the theme-song of my life? This name evoked the artificial poetry of high society in Paris, its tinselly pomp and vanity. In my mind's eye I saw this woman as incarnating all the problems of passion that had driven me wild. But perhaps it was neither the woman nor the name, but rather all the worst side of my nature springing up within me to tempt me anew.

'Was not Countess Fœdora, rich and without a lover and standing firm against the seductions of Paris, the embodiment of my hopes and visions? I fashioned a woman for myself and pictured her in my thoughts, dreamed of her. During the night I could not sleep: I became her lover; into the space of a few hours I crammed a whole lifetime, a lifetime of love, and drank to the full the life-giving, burning draught of delight. The next morning, unable to endure the torture of waiting for evening to creep along, I went along to a lending-library, took out a novel and spent the day reading it, thus obviating the need to think or measure the passage of time. Whilst I read, the name of Fœdora echoed through my mind like a sound heard from afar, one that does not disturb but cannot be ignored. Fortunately I still possessed a black coat and white waistcoat, both in fair condition. Also, of my whole fortune, I still had about thirty francs which I had strewn about among my clothes and in my drawers in order to set between a five-franc piece and my whims the thorny hedge of a search and the hazards of a circumnavigation round my room. As I was dressing I pursued my hoard through a whole sea of papers. My meagre stock of cash will give you some idea of the hole which my gloves and the hire of a cab could make in my resources: they robbed me of bread for a whole month. Alas! we never lack money for superfluities but are always counting the cost of what is useful or necessary. We carelessly fling away our gold on dancing-girls but haggle with a workman whose starving family is waiting for an account to be paid. How many people have a coat that cost a hundred francs or a diamond set in the pommel of their cane but are forced to dine on twenty-five sous! It seems as if we can never pay dearly enough for the pleasures of vanity. Rastignac was punctual at our meeting-place, smiled at my metamorphosis and chaffed me about it. But, as we made our way to the countess's house, he gave me charitable advice on the way I should behave to her. He depicted her as avaricious, vain and distrustful; but her avarice went hand in hand with show, her vanity with simplicity, her distrustfulness with affability.

' "You know my commitments?" he said to me, "and you know how much I should lose by changing my mistress. When I studied Fœdora, I was disinterested and dispassionate: the observations I made are certainly accurate. When I had the idea of introducing you to her circle, I was thinking of your future. So be careful what you say to her. She has a wicked memory, she's clever enough to drive even a diplomat to despair, and can guess exactly when he begins to speak the truth. Between ourselves, I don't believe her marriage is recognized by the Tsar, for the Russian ambassador started laughing when I spoke of her to him. He does not receive her, and tips his hat very slightly when he meets her in the Bois de Boulogne. Nevertheless she is in Mme de Sérizy's social set and visits Mme de Nucingen and Mme de Restaud.[18] In France her reputation is intact; the Duchesse de Carigliano, the most strait-laced woman in the Bonapartist coterie, often goes and spends the summer with her on her

18. These last two are old Goriot's daughters in the novel of that name, in which Mme de Beauséant figures episodically; she plays an important part in *A Harlot High and Low*.

country estate. Many young fops, including the son of a peer of France, have offered her their name in exchange for her fortune; she politely rejected them all. Perhaps she's not interested in anyone below the rank of count! Well, you're a marquis. Go ahead if you find you like her! Now that's what I call giving useful information!"

'This pleasantry made me think that Rastignac was teasing me and trying to provoke my curiosity, with the result that my improvised passion had risen to a climax by the time we halted in front of a peristyle adorned with flowers. As we made our way up a wide carpeted staircase, where I noticed every refinement of English comfort, my heart beat faster. I blushed to think that I was belying my aristocratic birth, my feelings and my pride; I was becoming besottedly bourgeois. Alas! I had come from a garret, after three years of poverty. I had not yet learnt how superior to the trivia of life are the accumulated treasures, the enormous intellectual capital which enrich a man instantaneously when the burden of power falls on him without crushing him; for the habit of study has equipped him in advance for political strife.

'I saw before me a woman of about twenty-two, of medium build, in a white dress, with a circle of men around her, and holding a feather fan. As she saw Rastignac enter, she stood up, approached us, gave a gracious smile and, in a melodious voice, paid me a compliment which she had no doubt thought out beforehand. Our mutual friend had announced me as a man of talent; his adroitness and his Gascon grandiloquence ensured me a flattering welcome. She paid such particular attention to me that I felt embarrassed; but fortunately Rastignac had forewarned her of my modesty. In her salon I met scholars, men of letters, ex-ministers and peers of the realm. Conversation resumed shortly after my arrival had interrupted it, and, feeling that I had a reputation to sustain, I gathered confidence. Then, without abusing the privilege of speech once it was granted me, I endeavoured to sum up the points of discussion in a series of more or less incisive, profound or witty remarks. I made quite an impression. For the thousandth time in his life, Rastignac had shown himself an accurate prophet. When the company had grown to the point when each guest felt free to move about, my sponsor took my arm and led me through the suite of rooms.

' "Don't let her ladyship see that you are too much taken with her," he said. "She would too easily guess the motive of your visit."

'The salons were furnished with exquisite taste and contained a rare choice of pictures. Each room, as in the most opulent English houses, had its own special character; the silk hangings, the ornaments, the style of furniture, every decorative detail, were in harmony with a ruling idea. In a Gothic boudoir whose doors were concealed behind tapestry curtains, the bordering of the material, the clock, the patterns in the carpet were all Gothic. The ceiling, supported by its framework of dark, sculptured beams, exhibited a series of panels painted with grace and originality. The wainscoting was artistically carved. Nothing marred the total effect of the pretty ornamentation, least of all the casements with their panes of costly stained glass. I was surprised to come upon a small modern salon in which some artist had made full use of the resources of our decorative art, so delicate, so fresh, so soft and subdued in tone, so sober in its gilding. It was as tender and misty as a German ballad, a nest truly fit for lovers in 1827,[19] perfumed with baskets of rare flowers. Beyond this room I perceived a gilded salon in which the Louis XIV style had been revived; standing out against our present-day colour-schemes, it produced a quaint but agreeable contrast.

' "You'll be comfortably lodged here," said Rastignac with a slightly ironical smile. "Isn't it charming?" he added as he sat down.

'Suddenly he rose, took my hand, guided me to the bedroom and showed me, under a white canopy of muslin and watered silk, a sumptuous bed lighted by the soft rays of a lamp: the bed of a young fairy betrothed to a genie.

' "Is it not," he whispered, "the acme of immodesty, insolence and coquetry to allow us to gaze on that shrine of love? To allow no man into her bed, but permit any man to drop his visiting

19. At p. 110 above, we were in 1829! Balzac was often careless about chronology.

123

card on it? If I had no ties, I should love to see this woman reduced to submission and weeping at my door . . ."

' "But are you so certain of her virtue?"

' "The most audacious masters in the art of seduction admit having failed with her, still love her and have become her loyal friends. The woman is really an enigma!"

'These words brought me to a state of intoxication, and I was already jealous to the point of begrudging her past lovers. Thrilled with joy, I hurried back to the salon where I had left the countess, and found her in the Gothic boudoir. She stopped me with a smile, made me sit beside her, questioned me about my work and seemed to take a keen interest in it, particularly when I resorted to humorous explanations of my philosophical system instead of taking up a professorial tone and expounding it like a learned doctor. She seemed quite intrigued to learn that the human will was a material force similar to steam-power; that nothing in the moral world could resist it when a man trains himself to concentrate it, to control the sum of it and constantly to project that fluid mass upon other men's minds; and that he who had learned the technique could modify as he pleased everything relating to mankind, even the absolute laws of nature. Fœdora's objections showed that she possessed a certain subtlety of mind. I condescended to agree with her for a time in order to flatter her, then I refuted her feminine arguments in a single word by drawing her attention to a daily phenomenon – sleep, a seemingly commonplace phenomenon, but one which offers a host of insoluble problems to the scientist. The countess's curiosity was aroused. She remained silent for a moment as I told her that our ideas were complete, organic entities, inhabiting an invisible world and influencing our destinies, and in support of this I instanced the thoughts of Descartes, Diderot and Napoleon, which had guided, and still were guiding, a whole epoch. I had the honour of affording the lady a distraction. In taking leave of me she invited me to visit her: in court jargon, she granted me *les grandes entrées*.

'Whether it was because, in accordance with my usual laudable custom, I mistook mere politeness for genuine expressions of feeling, or because Fœdora saw in me a potential celebrity and was minded to enlarge her menagerie of egg-heads, I fancied I had made a good impression. I called to mind all my knowledge of physiology and my earlier studies of woman in order to spend the whole evening minutely examining this singular person and her behaviour. Hidden in a window-nook, I tried to guess her thoughts by seeking to deduce them from her bearing and by observing in her the stratagems of a hostess who comes and goes, sits down and chats, summons a man and questions him, leaning against the upright of a door to listen to him. In her way of walking I observed so gentle and languid a motion, such a graceful undulation in her dress, and such a power in her to excite desire that I began to wonder whether she was as chaste as she was said to be. Even if Fœdora would have nothing to do with love at present, she must have been extremely passionate in former times, for the experience of pleasure could be read in the very pose she assumed when talking to a man; she leaned against the panelling with a coquettish air, that of a woman about to succumb, but also ready to flee if too bold a glance alarmed her. With her arms lightly folded, she seemed to inhale the words addressed to her, listening indulgently with her very eyes, as though breathing sentiment with every fibre of her being. The fresh crimson of her lips stood out against her dazzlingly fair complexion. Her brown hair brought out rather well the orange tint of her eyes, which were veined like Florentine stone, and whose expression seemed to add a subtle meaning to the words she spoke. Finally the graceful swelling of her bosom was extremely attractive. Some jealous woman might have objected to the heaviness of her thick eyebrows, which seemed to meet, or might have criticized the fine down visible in the contours of her face. In all this I could see the imprint of passion. Love was inscribed on her Italian eyelids, her splendid shoulders, worthy of the Venus de Milo; it was written in her features, on her lower lip which was rather full and slightly shadowed. She was more than a woman: she was a romantic novel. Indeed, this wealth of feminine charm, the harmonious complex of lines and curves, the promise that this opulent frame gave to an adorer, were tempered by a constant show of reserve and extraordinary modesty which contradicted the impression given by her whole person. Only so keen an observer as I could discern the signs of a pleasure-loving destiny in this woman's temperament. Let me try to clarify this idea: there were in Fœdora two personalities, separated let us say, at the level of the bust. Below she seemed frigid, only the head betrayed amorous longings. Before bringing her eyes to rest on a man, she would prepare her expression, as though something indescribably mysterious were going on within her, as it might be a sort of convulsion reflected in those shining eyes. To conclude, either my knowledge was limited and I still had much to discover in the realm of psychology; or else the countess really did possess a wonderful personality, with emotions and waves of sympathy which communicated to her features the charm that enslaves and fascinates men by a purely spiritual process which is the more potent in that it harmonizes with the impulses of desire.

'I left the house enraptured, seduced by this woman, intoxicated by her display of luxury, every instinct in me aroused, the good and the bad, the sublime and the depraved. Feeling so transported, so much alive, so lifted above myself, I understood what it was that drew to her side artists, diplomats, successful politicians and financiers with souls as steel-lined as their strong-boxes: no doubt they came to her so that they might experience the same delirious excitement that caused every chord of my being to vibrate, made my blood tingle in every vein, set every nerve quivering and threw my brain into a turmoil. She had given herself to none of them in order to keep them all at her beck and call. Until a woman falls in love she remains a coquette.

' "Besides that," I said to Rastignac, "she may well have been married or sold herself to an old man, and the memory of her wedding night may have made her conceive a horror for love."

'I returned on foot from the Faubourg Saint-Honoré where Fœdora lived. Almost the entire length of Paris stretches between her mansion and the Rue des Cordiers; even though it was a raw night, it seemed a short way to me. What a crazy idea! To set out to conquer Fœdora, in winter – a hard one – when my worldly possessions amounted to less than thirty francs, when the distance between us was so great! Only a destitute young man knows how expensive a passion can be: carriages, gloves, clean linen and the rest! If love stays too long on a platonic basis it leads to ruin. In truth there is many a Lauzun[20] in the Law Schools who cannot hope to court a woman in a first-floor apartment.[21] Here was I, far from strong, undernourished, plainly dressed, pale and gaunt like an artist recovering from a recent bout of creativity, how could I compete with handsome, curly-headed young dandies, so exquisitely cravated as to put the Croats themselves[22] to shame, rich enough to have their own tilburys and wearing the cloak of insolence?

'"Bah! Fœdora or death!" I shouted as I crossed the Seine. "On Fœdora my fortune depends!"

'The handsome Gothic boudoir and the Louis Quatorze salon swept in front of my eyes. I had a fresh vision of the countess in her white dress with its ample, graceful sleeves, with her seductive walk and her alluring bosom. Back in my cold, bare garret, as untidy as a naturalist's wig, I was still obsessed with the images of luxury in Fœdora's house. Contrast was an evil counsellor – it is thus that crime is born – and, shaking with anger, I cursed my decent, honest poverty and the attic which had proved so excellent a forcing-bed for the production of ideas. I called God, the devil, the social set-up, my father, the whole universe to account for my destiny, for my misery. I went to bed as hungry as a hunter and muttering ridiculous imprecations: but I was firmly resolved to seduce Fœdora. This woman's heart was the final lottery ticket on which my fortune depended. I will spare you the tale of the first calls I made on her, in order to come quickly to the dramatic turn that events took.

'All the while striving to touch this womans' heart, I tried to conquer her intelligence and get her vanity on my side. So that I might be the more surely loved, I offered her countless occasions to increase her self-love. Never did I leave her in a state of

20. A dashing young noble of the age of Louis XIV. His love affair with Mademoiselle de Montpensier, a cousin of the King, had many vicissitudes.

21. Many of the large mansions of Paris were already divided into flats. The higher the storey, the less affluent were the occupants.

22. Cravats were originally an item in the uniform of Croatian soldiers which Louis XIV borrowed for one of his regiments. They had long since passed into civilian use and become a status symbol.

indifference: women must have emotion at all cost, and I lavished emotion on her. I would have made her angry with me rather than let her be unconcerned about me. But though at first, spurred on by firmness of will and the desire to make her love me, I acquired some ascendancy over her, my passion quickly grew and got the better of me; I was trapped into being truthful, lost my self-control and fell head over heels in love. I do not rightly know what it is we call, in poetry or conversation, *love*; but the emotion which suddenly developed in my dual nature I have never seen depicted anywhere, either in the rhetorical and affected phraseology of Jean-Jacques Rousseau, whose very lodging I was perhaps then occupying, or in the cold conceptions of our two centuries of literature, or even in Italian paintings. The view of the Lake of Bienne;[23] a few themes from Rossini; Murillo's *Assumption* possessed by Marshal Soult,[24] the letters of Marie-Catherine Lescombat,[25] certain desultory phrases in collections of anecdotes, and above all the prayers of ecstatics and a few passages from the *fabliaux*,[26] – these things, and only these, have the power to summon up anew the celestial landscapes of my first experience of love.

'Nothing in any human language, no translation of human thought made by the medium of paintings, statues, words or sounds, could ever reproduce the vigour, the authenticity, the completeness, the suddenness with which passion takes possession of the soul. Indeed, art is but fiction. Love passes through an infinity of mutations before mingling for ever with our life and staining it through and through with its indelible colour of flame. The secret of this imperceptible infusion escapes the analysis of the artist. True passion expresses itself in the cries and sighs which a dispassionate man finds boring. As one reads *Clarissa*, if one is to participate in Lovelace's rages one must be genuinely in love oneself. Love is a pellucid spring bubbling up from its bed of watercress, flowers and gravel which, swelling

23. It was to an island on this Swiss lake that Rousseau retired in 1765–6.

24. In command of the French forces in Spain during the Peninsular War, Soult looted quite a number of Spanish masterpieces.

25. Passionate letters written by this criminal to her lover, whom she instigated to murder her husband. They were hanged.

26. Popular tales in verse of the twelfth and thirteenth centuries.

into a stream, then into a mighty river, changes its nature and appearance as it floods along, before hurling itself into the immeasurable ocean in which unformed minds see only monotony, and in which noble souls find matter for profound and endless contemplation. How can one presume to describe those transitory shades of feeling, those scraps which command so high a price, those words whose intonation exhausts the treasures of language, those looks more meaningful than the most intricate poems? At each of those mystic stages by which we insensibly fall in love with a woman, an abyss opens before us, vast enough to engulf all the poetry of mankind. How indeed could we provide explanatory glosses of those vivid mysterious perturbations of the soul, when words fail us even to depict the visible mysteries of beauty? What bewitching moments! How many hours did I spend plunged in the indescribable ecstasy of merely *seeing* her! And I was happy! For what reason? I cannot say. At such moments, if her face were bathed in light, some strange phenomenon took place which made it resplendent: the barely perceptible down that gave a golden tinge to her fine and delicate skin softly defined her features with the grace which we admire in the distant sky-line when it merges with the sunshine. It seemed to me the daylight caressed her as though it became one with her, and that from her radiant countenance there emanated a light more brilliant than light itself. Then, if any cloud passed over her sweet face, the changing tints it produced gave diversity to her expression. Often a thought seemed to portray itself in her smooth white brow; her eye appeared to redden, her eyelids fluttered and she broke into a gentle smile; the sensitive coral of her lips grew animated, they parted and then closed again; certain glints in her hair cast a brown tone on the brightness of her temples; each of these changes spoke to me, each variation in her beauty brought new delight to my eyes and revealed in her new graces which my heart had not yet discovered. I looked for some expression of feeling, some hope for me, in every play of her features. These unspoken communications passed from soul to soul like sound lingering through its echo and were prodigal of fleeting joys which survived in the deep impression they made. Her voice threw me into a delirium which I could scarcely contain. Imitating some prince of Lorraine whose name I forget, I could have held a glowing coal in the hollow of my hand and never felt it while she caressingly ran her fingers through my hair.[27] I had passed beyond admiration and desire: I was under a spell, a victim of fate. Often, back in my room under the eaves, I had a vague vision of Fœdora in her home and led a wraithlike existence by her side; if she was unwell, I felt ill, and told her next morning:

' "You have not been well?"

'How many times did she not come to me in the silent watches of the night, called forth by the ferment of my ecstasy! Sometimes, appearing as suddenly as a shaft of light, she would strike the pen from my hand: startled, the studious muse fled in sorrow; Fœdora compelled me to renew my admiration by resuming the seductive pose I had seen only a few hours before. At other times I made my own way to her in the spectral world, greeted her like the spirit of hope and adjured her to let me hear the silvery tones of her voice. Then I woke up in tears.

'One day, after promising to go to the theatre with me, she suddenly and capriciously refused to leave her house and begged me to leave her alone. In despair at this wilfulness which robbed me of a day's work – and, shall I confess, my last gold coin – I went to the theatre to which she should have gone, wishing to see the play she had expressed a desire to see. Scarcely had I taken my seat when I felt a sort of electric shock and a voice told me "She is here!" I turned round and caught sight of the countess at the back of her box in the stalls, hidden in the shadows. I knew instinctively where to look: my eyes found her straight away with a preternatural keenness of vision and my soul had flown to what gave it life as a bee flies to a flower. By what means had my senses been thus alerted? Such quickenings of the soul may astonish superficial minds, but these effects resulting from our inner nature are as simple as the everyday phenomena of our external vision; so I was not so much surprised as vexed. The study I had made of the workings of our moral faculties, an almost virgin field, allowed me at least to

27. This feat – or something very like it – was actually performed by the hero of Balzac's *Chouans*, published two years before *The Wild Ass's Skin*.

discover in my passion some tangible proofs of my theory. This alliance between the scholar and the lover, between true idolatry and the love of science, had a bizarre quality about it. The scientist in me was often pleased with what reduced the lover to despair, and the lover, when he thought his affairs were prospering, was happy to throw science to the four winds.

'Fœdora saw me and her brow became clouded: my presence embarrassed her. At the first interval I went and joined her. She was alone, and I stayed. Although we had never spoken of love, I felt that the time for broaching the subject was near. I had not yet spoken of my secret to her, and yet a state of expectancy existed between us. She used to inform me of her plans for future amusements and would ask me each evening, with a kind of friendly anxiety, if I should be calling the following day. She used to throw me a quizzical glance when she made some humorous sally, as if she had intended it for my exclusive pleasure. If I was withdrawn, she would coax me out of my depression. If she pretended to be angry, I had the privilege, up to a point, of asking her what was wrong. If I were guilty of some gaffe she made me plead for a long time before forgiving me. These were lovers' quarrels, and we enjoyed them as such. She entered into them with such grace and coquetry, and I took such pleasure in them! But at this particular moment our intimacy was suspended completely, and we confronted one another as strangers. The countess's manner was icy; as for me, I apprehended a calamity.

' "Please take me home," she said when the play was over.

'The weather had suddenly changed. When we came outside it was sleeting. Fœdora's carriage could not get across to the door of the theatre. A commissionaire, when he saw a well-dressed lady obliged to cross the street, held his umbrella open over our heads and, when we were in the carriage, stood waiting for a tip. I had no money, and would at that moment have signed away ten years of my life for a couple of pennies. My manhood, and the countless vanities that make up a man, were beaten down by an infernal humiliation. The words: "I have no change, my good man" were spoken in a harsh tone which seemed to be dictated by my thwarted passion – spoken by me, this man's brother; by me, no stranger to poverty; by me, who had once calmly given away seven hundred thousand francs! The footman pushed the commissionaire out of the way and the horses galloped away. As we drove back to her house Fœdora, absorbed in thought or pretending to be so, answered my questions with disdainful monosyllables. I relapsed into silence. It was an excruciating moment. On our return, we took our seats by the chimney-piece. When the manservant had withdrawn after poking up the fire, the countess turned to me with an indefinable air and said in somewhat solemn tones:

' "Since my return to France, my fortune has tempted a number of young men. I have received enough declarations of love to satisfy my pride. I have met men whose attachment was so sincere and profound that they would still have married me even if they had only found in me the penniless girl I used to be. In short, you must realize, Monsieur de Valentin, that I have been offered an accretion of riches and additional titles; but you should know too I have never again received persons so ill-advised as to speak to me of love. If my affection for you were superficial, I should not be giving you a warning in which there is more concern for you than pride in me. A woman runs the risk of receiving a rebuff when, supposing herself loved, she refuses in advance a proposal which is always flattering. I know the comic scenes in which Arsinoé and Araminte appear,[28] and so I am familiar with the way I might be answered in such circumstances. But I hope I shall not be judged badly this evening by a man of superior merit for having been candid with him."

'She expressed herself with the calm of a solicitor or a notary explaining to clients the procedure in a law-suit or the terms of a contract. The light, seductive tones of her voice betrayed not the slightest emotion; but her face and bearing, which were always dignified and decorous, seemed to me to have become as cold and reserved as those of a diplomat. She had no doubt prepared her speech and mapped out this scene. Oh! My dear friend, when women of a certain type find pleasure in rending

---

28. Arsinoé is the prude in Molière's *Misanthrope* whose advances to Alceste are brutally snubbed. Araminte is the heroine of Marivaux's *Fausses Confidences*: she confesses her love to her steward Dorante.

our heart, when they have made up their minds to plunge a dagger into it and to twist it round in the wound, are not such women adorable? They must be in love, or they want to be loved. One day they will make it up to us for causing these sufferings, just as God, so it is said, is sure to reward us for our good deeds. They will repay us a hundred-fold in pleasure for the pain they have inflicted on us, knowing how violent it has been. Is not their cruelty dictated by passion? But to be put on the rack by a woman whose indifference is death to us – that is the most horrible of torments. At that moment, without knowing it, Fœdora was trampling on all my hopes, shattering my life and destroying my future with the cold unconcern and innocent cruelty of a child who, out of curiosity, tears the wings off a butterfly.

'"Later on," Fœdora continued, "you will, I hope, realize what warm affection I offer my friends. For them I shall always be found kind and devoted. I could give my life for them, but you would despise me if I submitted to their love without sharing it. I need say no more. You are the only man to whom I have spoken words like these."

'At first I could not utter a sound; my efforts were all devoted to controlling the storm that was rising within me. But shortly I thrust down my anger into the depths of my soul and began to smile.

'"If I tell you I love you," I replied, "you will banish me. If I allege indifference you will punish me for that. Priests, magistrates and women never divest themselves of their robes completely. Silence is sometimes the best policy: allow me then, madame, to remain silent. To have thought to warn me in so fraternal a fashion, you must surely have feared you might lose me, and that idea might well satisfy my pride. But let us steer clear of personalities. You are perhaps the only woman with whom I can as a philosopher argue about a resolution so contrary to the laws of nature. Compared with the other specimens of your kind, you are a sport. Well, let us put our heads together and try in good faith to discover the cause of this psychological anomaly. Does there exist in you, as in many women who are proud of themselves and enamoured of their own perfections, a feeling of refined egoism which makes you horrified at the idea of belonging to a man, of abdicating your freedom and submitting to a conventional superiority which you find insulting? In that case you would seem a thousand times more beautiful to me. Or were you brutally initiated to love? Or perhaps the value you no doubt attach to the elegance of your waist-line, to the delightful firmness of your bosom, makes you afraid of the havoc that maternity can cause: would you not secretly find that the best of reasons for rejecting too ardent a lover? Or have you certain imperfections which make you virtuous in spite of yourself? . . . Do not get angry; I am just discussing, studying the question, at a thousand leagues' distance from passion. Nature, which causes children to be born blind, can surely create women who are deaf, dumb and blind to love. Honestly, you would be a gift for a medical investigator! You just don't know your own worth. You may legitimately feel disgusted with men. I agree with you, I too think them all ugly and hateful. But you are right," I added as I felt my heart swelling within me, "you must despise us: the man does not exist who is worthy of you!"

'I will not tell you all the sarcasms I hurled at her, laughing all the while. Well, neither the most cutting remark nor the sharpest irony drew from her either a start or a gesture of resentment. She listened with her habitual smile on her lips and in her eyes, the smile which she wore like a garment, always the same, for her friends, for mere acquaintances and strangers, too.

' "Isn't it kind of me to allow myself to be laid out like this on the dissecting-table?" she asked, snatching a moment when I was looking at her in silence. "You can see," she continued with a laugh, "that no silly touchiness interferes with the friendship I am offering you. Many women would punish you for your impertinence by shutting their doors to you."

' "You can tell me to stop coming here without being obliged to state the reason for your severity." As I said that, I felt ready to kill her if she had indeed shown me the door.

' "You are out of your mind," she exclaimed with a smile.

' "Have you ever considered," I retorted, "what violent love can lead to? A man driven to despair has murdered his mistress before now."

' "Better to be dead than unhappy," she coldly replied. "A man as passionate as that is bound, one day, to desert his wife and leave her in destitution after squandering her fortune."

'Such arithmetical logic dumbfounded me. It was clear there was a gulf between this woman and myself. We should never be able to understand each other.

' "Good-bye," I said to her, coldly.

' "Good-bye," she replied, with a friendly inclination of the head. "Until tomorrow."

'I gazed at her for a moment, and all the love I was renouncing shone from my eyes. She was standing, smiling at me with the conventional, hateful smile of a marble statue, expressing a frigid mockery of love. Can you easily conceive, my dear friend, all the painful thoughts that assailed me as I returned home through the rain and the snow, trudging along over the slush of the quays for two or three miles, having lost everything?

'Oh! the idea that she was not even thinking of my povetry and believed that, like her, I was rich and kept a comfortable carriage! My hopes were in ruins around me! It was no longer money that was at stake, but all my spiritual solvency. I wandered about, turning over in my mind every part of that strange conversation, and going so far astray in the constructions I put upon it that I ended up by doubting the literal value of the words and ideas expressed. And yet I was still in love. I still loved that cold woman whose heart demanded to be reconquered every successive moment and who, by always annulling the promises she had made the evening before, presented herself anew the next day as a mistress yet to be won. As I was turning through the wicket-gates of the Institute, I was seized with a feverish impulse. I remembered that I was starving. I did not possess a penny. Worst of all, the rain was ruining my hat. How after this could I address an elegant woman and present myself at her salon without a decent top-hat? So far, by taking extreme care of it, whilst cursing the absurd and stupid fashion which condemns us to hold our hats constantly in our hands and exhibit the lining, I had kept mine in a passable condition. Without being either brand new or decrepit, very silky or devoid of its nap, it might well pass for the hat of a careful man. But its artificially prolonged life was reaching its end, it was bruised, crippled, done for – a mere tatter, a worthy representative of its owner. For lack of thirty sous to pay for a cab I was losing my laboriously preserved elegance.

'Ah! How many unknown sacrifices had I not made to Fœdora during the last three months! I had often spent the money that should have bought me bread for a week in order to pay her a short visit. Leaving my work and going without food was nothing! But crossing the streets of Paris without getting splashed, hurrying along to get out of the rain so as to arrive at Fœdora's house as presentable as the fops who surrounded her, ah! that task presented innumerable difficulties for a preoccupied and amorous poet! My happiness and my love depended on a spatter of dirt on my one and only white waistcoat. To have to give up all idea of seeing her if my clothes were muddied or if I got wet! To be without five sous to pay a shoeblack to remove the smallest spot of mud on my boot! My passion had increased with all these unsuspected tortures, which to an irritable man were tremendous. Those who live in penury make sacrifices of which they cannot speak to women living in a sphere of luxury and elegance, who see the world through a prism which imparts a golden tinge to both men and objects. These women, optimists out of selfishness, heartless because it is good form to be so, let their own enjoyment exempt them from reflection; and the round of pleasures they pursue absolves them from the sin of indifference to other people's misfortune. For them a penny is never a million, but a million seems like a penny to them. If love has to further its cause by making great sacrifices, it must also put a light veil over these sacrifices and shroud them in silence; on the other hand wealthy men, when they are prodigal of life and fortune, when they devote themselves, take advantage of the social prejudices which always direct a searchlight on to their amorous follies. For them silence speaks loud and any veil gives added grace, whereas my frightful penury condemned me to appalling suffering without my being permitted to say: "I love you!" or "I am dying!" But was this after all real self-devotion? Was I not richly rewarded by the pleasure I felt in sacrificing everything for her? The countess had caused me to attach extreme value and find excess of pleasure in the most trivial incidents in my life. Formerly careless about what I wore, I now respected my clothes as if they were my second self. Between receiving a sword-thrust and tearing my frock-coat I would not have hesitated! You must then put yourself in my place in order to understand my raging thoughts and the mounting frenzy which possessed me as I walked along and which the very fact of walking perhaps intensified! I experienced a kind of infernal glee at finding myself at the very peak of misery. I tried to discern some presage of good fortune in this latest crisis, but evil has an inexhaustible fund of resources.

'The door of my lodging-house was ajar. Light was shining out into the street through the apertures in the shutters. Pauline and her mother were chatting as they waited for me. I heard my name spoken, and I listened.

' "Raphael," Pauline was saying, "is much better-looking than the student in Number 7. He has such lovely fair hair! Don't you think there's something in his voice – I don't know what – something that stirs your heart? And besides, although he seems rather proud, he's so kind and has such distinguished manners! Oh! He really is quite a gentleman! I'm sure that all the women are mad about him."

' "You speak as if you were in love with him yourself," Madame Gaudin remarked.

' "Oh, I love him like a brother," she replied laughingly. "I certainly should be ungrateful if I did not feel friendly towards him! Has he not taught me music, drawing, grammar, in fact all I know? You don't take much notice of the progress I'm making, dear Mamma; but I'm becoming so learned that before very long I shall be ready to give lessons myself, and then we shall be able to keep a servant."

'I quietly retreated. Then, making a certain amount of noise, I entered the hall to pick up my lamp, which Pauline insisted on lighting. The poor child had applied a soothing balm to my wounds, and the praise she had innocently bestowed on my person gave me heart. I needed to recover faith in myself and to hear an impartial judgement on the true value of the gifts I possessed. My hopes, thus revived, perhaps cast their sheen on

137

things as I saw them. Perhaps, too, I had not paid serious attention to the scene, often enough displayed before me, of these two women in the middle of this room; but now I was able to admire a most delightful, a most lifelike representation of a quiet interior, so artlessly reproduced by the Flemish painters. The mother, sitting by an almost burnt-out fire, was knitting stockings, with an indulgent smile hovering on her lips. Pauline was painting screens; her colours and her brushes, spread out on a small table, spoke to the eye with piquant effect. But when she rose from her seat and stood lighting my lamp, its rays fell fully on her white skin and one had to be under the domination of a really terrible passion not to admire her rosy, transparent hands, the ideal pose of her head and her maidenly stance. Night-time and the silence lent their charm also to this late fire-side activity, this peaceful interior. Their constant labour, cheerfully endured, bore witness to a pious resignation inspired by lofty sentiments. There existed an indefinable harmony between the two women and the objects around them. The luxury in which Fœdora lived had something arid about it, and awoke evil thoughts in me, whereas this humble poverty and kindness of disposition was a cool draught to the soul. Perhaps I felt humiliated in the presence of luxury; near these two women, in the centre of this brown room in which a simpler kind of life found a haven in the emotions of the heart, I perhaps became reconciled with myself by finding a pretext for giving rein to the protective instinct which men are so proud to exercise. As I stood next to Pauline, she gave me an almost maternal look and exclaimed, her hands termbling as she set the lamp down hard:

'"Goodness! How pale you are! Why, he's soaking wet! My mother will wipe you down . . . Monsieur Raphael," she continued after a short pause, "you are fond of milk. We had some cream this evening. Wouldn't you like a taste?"

'She sprang like a kitten to a china bowl full of milk and so impulsively offered it to me, so prettily raised it to my lips that I felt hesitant.

'"You won't refuse me?" she said, with disappointment in her voice.

'Our two prides understood each other: Pauline seemed to be

suffering from her poverty and to be reproaching me for being haughty. I was touched. That cream might have been intended for her breakfast; however I accepted it. The poor girl tried to hide her joy, but it sparkled in her eyes.

' "I needed it badly," I said as I sat down. An anxious expression flitted over her brow. "Do you remember, Pauline, the passage in Bossuet where he shows God rewarding a man more richly for giving a glass of water than for winning a victory?"

' "Yes," she answered, and her breast rose and fell like that of a baby robin in the hands of a child.

' "Well, as we shall soon be parting," I added in a faltering voice, "allow me to express my gratitude for all the kind care you and your mother have taken of me."

' "Oh! don't let's start casting up accounts," she said with a laugh. But this laugh covered an emotion which I found painful.

' "My piano," I resumed, without appearing to have heard her remark, "is one of Erard's best instruments.[29] Accept it from me. Don't hesitate to do so, for I really could not take it with me on the journey I am proposing to make."

'Alerted perhaps by the melancholy tone with which I uttered these words, the two women seemed to have understood me and looked at me with a mixture of curiosity and fright. So then the affection I had been looking for in the chilly regions of high society was there at hand: genuine, unpretentious, but soothing and perhaps lasting.

' "You must not take things so much to heart," said the mother. "Stay with us. My husband is even now on his way home," she continued "This evening I read the Gospel of Saint John whilst Pauline held our door-key suspended from a Bible, and the key turned. It is a sign that Gaudin is well and prospering. Pauline did the same for you and for the young man in No. 7, but the key turned for you alone. We shall all be rich. Gaudin will come home a millionaire. I saw him in a dream on a ship full of snakes; luckily the water was rough, which signifies gold and precious stones from overseas."

'The empty but affectionate words, similar to the meaningless

29. Sébastien Frard (1752–1831), a famous maker of musical instruments. Thanks to him the piano superseded the harpsichord.

songs with which a mother lulls her invalid child to sleep, restored me to something like calm. The good woman's tone and look were expressive of that kindliness and gentleness which cannot banish grief, but does assuage it, soothe and soften it. More perspicacious than her mother, Pauline studied me with anxiety; her intelligent scrutiny seemed to read my present life and my future. I nodded my thanks to mother and daughter; then I took my leave, fearing that I might break down. Once alone in my garret, I got into bed, brooding on my predicament. My fatal imagination conceived a thousand baseless projects and prescribed many impossible resolutions. When a man is dragging his way through the ruins of his hopes, he may yet find something to build on; but I was at rock bottom. Ah! My friend, it is too easy to blame the poor. Those who suffer from the most active of all social dissolvents deserve our indulgence. Where poverty reigns, one cannot talk of shame, crime, virtue or intelligence. I was, at that juncture, devoid of ideas and bereft of strength, like a young maiden on her knees before a tiger. A man who is ruined and is not in love can dispose of himself, but a wretch in love is not his own master any more and cannot do away with himself. Love makes our own persons sacred, after a fashion: we respect in ourselves the life of another person. Love then becomes the direst of misfortunes, a misfortune which still clings to a hope, a hope that makes you willing to endure torture. I fell asleep having decided to find Rastignac in the morning and tell him about Fœdora's singular determination.

*

'Seeing me walk in on him at the early hour of nine, Rastignac cried: "Aha! I know what brings you here. Fœdora must have sent you packing. A few kindly spirits, jealous of your ascendancy over the countess, have announced your forthcoming marriage. God alone knows what follies your rivals have credited you with and what slanders they have put upon you!"

' "That explains everything!" I exclaimed.

'I recalled all the impertinent things I had said, and decided the countess had been sublime. I condemned myself as an infamous wretch who had not yet suffered enough; I now saw nothing more in the indulgence she had shown me than the patient charity of love.

*

' "Don't go too fast," the shrewd Gascon advised me. Fœdora posseses the penetration natural to women who are profoundly selfish, and perhaps she made up her mind about you when you were still dazzled by her wealth and luxury; you weren't clever enough to prevent her from reading your mind. She herself is dissembling enough not to forgive dissimulation in others. I believe," he added, "that I put you on the wrong track. In spite of her subtle intelligence and manners, she seems to me to be an imperious creature, like all women for whom pleasure is a thing of the head, not of the heart. For her, happiness consists entirely in enjoying the good things in life, in social pleasures; sentiment in her is merely play-acting; you would be unhappy with her and she would turn you into her head footman . . ."

'Rastignac's words fell on deaf ears. I interrupted him with a mock-cheerful account of my financial situation.

' "Yesterday evening," he answered, "a run of bad luck stripped me of all my liquid assets. If it hadn't been for that commonplace misfortune I would willingly have shared my purse with you. But let us go and breakfast at the tavern: perhaps a dozen oysters will bring us good counsel."

'He dressed and had his tilbury brought round. We walked into the Café de Paris as if we were a couple of millionaires with the impertinent manner of brazen speculators living on imaginary capital. The diabolical Gascon confounded me by his ease of manner and his imperturbable self-assurance. Just as we were taking our coffee to round off a most succulent and well-ordered meal, Rastignac, who was nodding right and left to various young men as distinguished for their personal grace as for the elegance of their dress, said to me as one of these dandies entered: "Here's your man." And he beckoned to a gentleman with a stylish cravat, who seemed to be looking for a suitable table, to come over to us.

' "This fellow," Rastignac whispered to me, "has received the Cross of the Legion of Honour for publishing works that he doesn't understand. He's a chemist, a historian, a novelist and publicist. He owns quarter, third, half shares in quite a number of plays, and he's as ignorant as Dom Miguel's mule. He's not a man but a name, a well-publicized label. And so you will never see him entering one of those offices that advertise facilities for writing.[30] He's astute enough to make fools of a whole congress of learned professors. In a word, he's a half-breed in the moral sense – neither wholly honest nor a complete knave. But not a word against him! He has already fought a duel. Society asks no more and says of him, "He's a respectable man."

' "Well, my excellent friend, my honourable friend, how goes it with Your Intelligence?" Rastignac asked the stranger as he sat down at the next table.

' "Oh, so-so. I'm snowed under with work. I've laid hands on all the material needed for writing some quite curious historical memoirs, but I don't know to whom I can attribute them. It's very tiresome. I have to make haste, because memoirs are going out of fashion."

' "Are they contemporary or pre-revolutionary memoirs about Court life. Or what?"

' "They concern the affair of the Queen's Necklace."[31]

' "Now isn't that a miracle?" Rastignac said to me with a laugh. Then turning again to the literary speculator, he continued, pointing to me: 'Monsieur de Valentin is one of my friends, whom I present to you as one of our future literary celebrities. He had an aunt once who was a prominent figure at Court, a *marquise*. And he has been working at a royalist history of the Revolution for the past two years."

'Then, leaning over towards this singular businessman he whispered in his ear: "He's a man of talent, but he's also a nincompoop who will write your memoirs for you, attributing them to his aunt, at 500 francs a volume."

' "It's a deal," the other man replied, tightening up his cravat. – "Waiter, my oysters! Hurry!"

30. The reference here seems to be to public reading-rooms for which one paid a small entrance-fee.

31. A well-known scandal involving Queen Marie Antoinette and Cardinal de Rohan.

' "Yes, but you'll give me twenty-five louis by way of commission, and you'll pay him for one volume in advance."

' "Oh no! I'll make a 50 per cent advance to make sure he meets the deadline."

'Rastignac repeated the tenor of this transaction to me in a low voice. Then, without consulting me, he replied to the man: "Done. When can we call on you to settle the affair?"

' "Well now, come and dine here tomorrow evening at seven."

'We rose from table. Rastignac tossed some change to the waiter, put the bill in his pocket, and we left. I was stupefied at the light-hearted recklessness with which he had sold my respectable aunt, the Marquise de Montbauron.

' "I'd as soon take ship for Brazil and teach algebra, about which I know nothing, to the Indians as tarnish the name of my family."

'Rastignac interrupted me with a burst of laughter. "What a ninny you are! Just take the two hundred and fifty francs and write the memoirs. Once they're finished, you ass, you'll refuse to let them be published under your aunt's name! Madame de Montbauron, who died on the scaffold, her panniers, the respect she was held in, her beauty, her face-powder and her slippers are worth far more than six hundred francs. If when it comes to it the publisher won't pay your aunt's full value, he'll have to get some elderly knight living on his wits or some shop-soiled countess to sign the memoirs."

' "Oh!" I cried. "Why did I ever leave my virtuous garret? As soon as one looks below the surface, society shows itself in a very dirty and shabby light!"

' "Why now," Rastignac replied, "you're talking poetry, and we have to talk business. You're a child . . . Listen: it will be for the public to judge the memoirs; as for our literary pander, has he not spent eight years of his life dealing with publishers and undergone cruel mortifications to establish relations with them? Your share in the work on this book is unequal to his, but, financially speaking aren't you getting the better bargain? Twenty-five louis for you are a much greater sum than a thousand francs for him. Come then! You can't object to writing historical memoirs, a work calling for art if ever there was one, when you consider that Diderot wrote six sermons for three hundred francs."

'"Anyway," I said to him with much emotion, "beggars can't be choosers. And so, my good friend, I owe you thanks. Twenty-five louis will make me quite rich . . ."

'"Richer than you think," he replied with a laugh. "If Finot gives me a commission on this deal, haven't you guessed that it will be for you? – Now let us go to the Bois de Boulogne. We shall see the countess there, and I will show you the pretty little widow I am to marry, a charming person, a plump little partridge from Alsace. She reads Kant, Schiller, Jean-Paul and God knows how many tear-jerkers. Her weakness is that she always wants to know what I think about them: I have to look as if I understand German sentimentality and know a stack of ballads – all of them the kind of medicine which my doctor forbids me to take. I still haven't succeeded in moderating her enthusiasm for this literature: she weeps bucketfuls when she reads Goethe and I too am constrained to weep a bit, just to oblige, for she has fifty thousand francs a year, my dear chap, and the daintiest little foot, and the daintiest little hand in the world! Indeed, if it weren't for that abominable Alsatian accent of hers she would be a most accomplished woman."

'We saw the countess, cutting a brilliant figure in a brilliant turn-out. The coquettish creature greeted us very affectionately, throwing me a smile which struck me at that moment as divinely loving. How happy I was! I believed she loved me, I had money in my pocket and all the treasures of passion: poverty was a thing of the past! Light-hearted as I was, merry, pleased with everything, I thought my friend's mistress charming. The trees, the air, the skies, the whole of nature seemed to reflect Fœdora's smile. On our way back from the Champs-Elysées we called on Rastignac's hatter and tailor. Thanks to the Affair of the Queen's Necklace I needed no longer to remain pusillanimously on the defensive, but could pass to a formidable war-footing. From now on I need fear no comparison, for grace and elegance, with the young men who swarmed around Fœdora. I returned home, locked myself in and remained in apparent tranquillity at my attic window; but I was bidding an eternal farewell to my sea of roofs, composing a dramatic masterpiece of my future life, anticipating love and all its joys. How tempestuous existence can become between the four walls of a garret! The soul of man is a sort of fairy, able to turn straw into diamonds; under its magic wand enchanted palaces spring up like the flowers of the fields under the warm breath of the sun. The following day, at about noon. Pauline knocked gently at my door and brought me – can you guess? – a letter from Fœdora. In it the countess asked me to meet her at the Luxembourg so that from there we could visit the Museum and the Botanical Gardens.

' "The messenger is waiting for your reply," Pauline said, after a moment's silence.

'I quickly scribbled a letter of thanks which Pauline took away. I got dressed. Just at the moment when, very pleased with myself, I was putting the finishing touches to my toilette, a sudden thought sent a cold shudder through me: "Has Fœdora come in her carriage or on foot? Will the weather be wet or fine? . . . In any case," I reflected, "whether she comes in a carriage or on foot, can one ever be sure of a woman's whims? She'll have no money and will want to give five francs to some little chimney-sweep because he looks picturesque in his rags."

'I had not a farthing and could expect no money before evening. How deeply, in such crises of youth, does a poet suffer for that powerful imagination which he owes to his habits of work and sobriety! In one instant a thousand excruciating thoughts stung me like a shower of arrows. I looked out through my window and saw that the weather was very unsettled. If the worst came to the worst I might well hire a carriage for the day, but should I not be trembling every moment, in the midst of my happiness, for fear of not meeting with Finot that evening? I did not feel I had the strength to cope with so many fears in the midst of my joy. Although certain to find nothing, I undertook a searching exploration through my room; I delved deep into my mattress looking for crown pieces, rummaged everywhere and even shook out my old boots. In a fever of neurotic anxiety, I stared wild-eyed at every piece of furniture after turning it upside down. Imagine the delirious joy I felt when, after opening for the seventh time the drawer of my writing desk which

I was inspecting with the sort of lethargy induced by despair, I discovered, sticking against one side of it, slyly lurking but clean, bright and shining as a rising star, a fine, noble five-franc piece! Without reproaching it either for its silence or for its cruelty in hiding away like that, I kissed it like a friend faithful in misfortune and hailed it with a shout that roused an echo. I turned round abruptly and saw Pauline, her face as white as a sheet.

' "I thought," she said in a voice quivering with emotion, "that you had hurt yourself! The messenger . . . (she broke off as if she were choking) . . . But my mother paid him," she added. Then she ran off, with an elfin and childlike grace. Poor little girl! I wished her all the happiness I felt. At that moment, I felt my heart held the sum-total of pleasure in the world, and would have liked to restore to the unfortunate their share, of which I imagined I was robbing them.

'We are nearly always right in our forebodings of calamity. The countess had sent her carriage home, preferring, in accordance with one of those whims that pretty women cannot always account for even to themselves, to go to the Botanical Gardens by way of the boulevards and on foot.

' "But it's going to rain," I said.

'It pleased her to contradict me. By chance, it remained fine during the whole time it took us to cross the Luxembourg. When we came out of the gardens, noting anxiously a heavy cloud blow up and let fall a few drops of rain, I stopped a cab. When we had reached the boulevards it stopped raining and the sky cleared again. Arriving at the Museum, I wanted to get rid of the cab, but she asked me to keep it. What torture I felt! But to chat with her while repressing the secret ecstasy which no doubt expressed itself in my features by a fixed, idiotic smile; to wander through the Botanical Gardens, to stroll along the shrub-lined avenues and to feel her arm pressing on mine: there was something indescribably fantastic about all this, as if I were dreaming in broad daylight! Yet her movements, whether we were walking or standing still, had nothing affectionate or tender about them, in spite of their apparent wantonness. When I tried to fall in so to speak with her vital rhythm, I detected an underlying secret petulance in her, and received an impression of a strangely uneven tempo. Soulless women have nothing soft in their gestures. And so neither our minds nor our bodily motions were in unison. There is no describing this material discord between two beings, for we have not yet acquired the habit of discerning thought in movement. This phenomenon of our nature is instinctively felt but cannot be expressed.

'During these violent paroxysms of my passion,' Raphael continued after a moment's silence as if answering some objection he had formulated in his own mind, 'I did not dissect my sensations, analyse the pleasure I felt, or count the beatings of my heart, as a miser inspects and weighs his gold pieces. Not in the least! Today experience casts its wan light on these past events and it is memory that brings back these images to me, as when in fine weather the waves pile up on the seashore, bit by bit, the fragments of a wreck.

' "You are in a position to render me an important service," the countess said to me, giving me an embarrassed look. "Now that I have told you the secret of my antipathy to love, I feel freer to ask for your assistance in the name of friendship. Will you not," she added with a laugh, "be much more meritorious in obliging me today?"

'I looked at her with pain in my heart. Feeling nothing for me, she was wheedling but not affectionate; she appeared to me to be playing her part like a consummate actress. Then suddenly her tone of voice, a look or a word from her revived my hopes. But if then my new-born love shone in my eyes, she sustained their glow without any softening of the brilliance of her own gaze, for, like a tiger's eyes, hers seemed to be lined with a lamina of steel. At such times I detested her.

' "The Duc de Navarreins's protection," she continued, putting a wealth of cajolery into her voice, "would be very useful to me for dealing with a certain person who is all-powerful in Russia, one who can intervene on my behalf to secure justice for me in a matter which concerns both my fortune and my social status – the recognition by the Tsar of my marriage. Is not the Duc de Navarreins your cousin? A letter from him would decide the issue."

' "I am entirely yours," I replied. "Command me."

' "You are very kind," she answered, giving me her hand, "Come and dine with me. I will make you my confessor."

'So then this woman, so suspicious, so secretive, whom no one had ever heard utter a word about her own interests, was going to ask my advice. "Oh! How much I now appreciate the silence you have enjoined!" I cried. "All the same, I would rather you had set me a more difficult task."

'At this moment she responded to my ecstatic gaze and did not reject my admiration: so she *did* love me? We arrived at her house. Luckily, the money I had was just enough to satisfy the coachman. I spent a delightful day alone with her in her boudoir: it was the first time I had been able to see her thus. Until that day her guests, her embarrassing politeness and her frigid manner had always kept us apart, even during her sumptuous dinners; but that evening I was as much at home with her as if I actually lived under her roof: she was mine, so to speak. My roving imagination was bursting its bonds, arranging the events of life as I wanted them to be and plunging me into the delights of satisfied love. Feeling as if I were her husband, I admired her as she busied herself with homely details, and it even made me happy to see her taking off her hat and shawl. She left me alone for a moment and returned looking charming with her hair tidied up. Her pretty toilet had been made for me! During dinner she lavished attentions on me and displayed infinite grace in the thousand little things which seem to be trifles but are really the half of what life contains. When we were both of us in front of a crackling fire, sitting on silk cushions, surrounded by the most desirable creations of a truly oriental luxury, when I saw by my side this woman famed for a beauty which made so many hearts beat faster, this woman so hard to win, talking to me, making me the target of all her coquetry, my rapturous joy was almost painful. Unfortunately for me I remembered the important piece of business I needed to conclude and rose to keep the appointment I had agreed on the previous day.

' "What! Already?" she said as she saw me pick up my hat.

'She loved me! So I believed at any rate, as I heard her utter these two words in a caressing voice. To prolong my felicity I would then willingly have bartered two years of my life for every hour she was willing to vouchsafe me. My happiness increased as I thought of all the money I was losing. It was midnight when she dismissed me.

'Nevertheless, next morning, I bitterly regretted my heroism, fearing I might have missed my opportunity in the affair of the memoirs, which was of such capital importance to me. I hurried to pick up Rastignac and we went and surprised the titular author of my future works just as he was getting out of bed. Finot read out to me an agreement in which there was no mention at all of my aunt; after we had signed it he paid out to me one hundred and fifty francs. All three of us lunched together. When I had paid for my new hat, sixty dining vouchers at six sous each and the money I owed, I had only thirty francs left. Still, all my troubles were over for a few days. If I had been ready to listen to Rastignac, I could have had riches galore by unashamedly adopting the "English system". He pressed me to let him open accounts for me, so that I could run up debts on the pretext that borrowing is the best way of sustaining credit. In his view, future expectations constituted the most secure and solid capital of all. Mortgaging my debts in this way on contingencies yet to materialize, he bestowed my custom on his own tailor, an artist who understood the "young men about town" and was willing to leave me in peace until I got married.'

*

'From then on I broke with the monastic and studious life I had led over the past three years. I visited Fœdora assiduously and tried to outdo in showiness the fops and boudoir heroes who frequented her. Believing I had escaped the jaws of poverty for good, I recovered my nimbleness of mind, outshone my rivals and acquired the reputation of being fascinating, brilliant, irresistible. And yet people of discernment said of me: "A clever fellow like that must let his mind rule his heart." They were charitable enough to vaunt my wit at the expense of my capacity to feel. "Lucky man not to be in love!" they exclaimed. "If he loved her, would he be so gay, so full of verve?" And yet in

Fœdora's presence I was as stupid as a lovesick man can be. When I was alone with her I had nothing to say. Or, if I did speak, I decried love. I paraded a sort of melancholy gaiety, like a courtier trying to conceal a cruel mortification.

'To put the case in a nutshell, I tried to make myself indispensable to her life, her happiness, her vanity: waiting on her day after day I was a slave at her beck and call, a plaything always within reach. Having thus frittered my day away, I went back home and spent my nights working, and slept no more than two or three hours of the morning. But since I had not Rastignac's experience of "the English system", I soon became penniless. Henceforth, my dear friend, being a lady's man without any ladies, an impecunious dandy, a love-lorn lover, I relapsed into my precarious existence, the cold, profound misery which is sedulously concealed beneath a deceptive show of luxury. I underwent the same sufferings as previously, though they seemed less bitter, no doubt because I had become inured to their terrible paroxysms. Often enough the tea and cakes so parsimoniously offered in the salons were my sole nourishment. Sometimes the countess's sumptuous dinners kept me going for two days. All my time, efforts and skill in observation were employed in trying to penetrate further into Fœdora's impenetrable character. Up to now, my opinion had been influenced by hope or despair. I saw her turn by turn as the most loving woman or the most unfeeling member of her sex. However, these alternating moods of joy and sorrow became intolerable to me: I tried to bring this cruel conflict to an end and kill my love. Occasionally sinister insight illuminated the gulf that lay between us. The countess's attitude justified all my fears: I had never yet espied a tear in her eyes; at the theatre she smiled coldly at the most pathetic scene. She kept all sensitivity of feeling for herself and had no inkling of happiness or unhappiness in others. In short she had made me her dupe! Ready to go to any length for her, I almost demeaned myself for her sake in calling on my kinsman the Duc de Navarreins, a self-centred man who blushed for my poverty and had done me too great wrong not to hate me. So he received me with the chilly politeness which makes gestures and words appear like so many insults. The troubled look he gave me made me feel sorry for him. I felt ashamed of him for his pettiness in the midst of so much grandeur, for his meanness in the midst of so much luxury. He talked to me of the considerable losses he had incurred in the fall of 3% government stock. I then told him the object of my visit. His change of manner from icy hostility to gradual warmth disgusted me. Well, my friend, he came to the countess's house and put me completely in the shade. For him Fœdora conjured up all her charm and displayed a new power of fascination. She bewitched him and, ignoring me, she negotiated her mysterious piece of business, about which I learnt never a word: I had merely been a means to an end! ... When my cousin was with her on other occasions she appeared to be unaware of my presence and received me with less pleasure perhaps than on the day I had been introduced to her. One evening she humiliated me in front of the duke by the kind of gesture and glance which no words can describe. I left in tears, devising innumerable plans for vengeance, plotting fearful rapes . . .

'I often took her to the Bouffons, and there, sitting by her side, lost in adoration, I gazed at her as I gave myself to the charm of listening to the music, spiritually ravished by the double delight of loving and finding my transports faithfully rendered in the composer's melodious phrases. The passion I felt was in the air, on the stage, triumphant everywhere except in my mistress's heart. I used to take her hand, study her features and her eyes, longing for our hearts to meet, for one of those sudden chords which, resounding in the orchestra, causes two souls to vibrate in unison; but her hand gave no response and her eyes remained inexpressive. Whenever the ardour of my emotions, shining in my face, breathed too fiery a breath on her cheek, she favoured me with the forced smile, the affected simper which hovers on the lips of every fashionable exhibition portrait. She paid no heed to the music. The divine scores of Rossini, Cimarosa and Zingarelli recalled no emotion and evoked no poetic memory in her: her soul was a waterless desert. At the theatre Fœdora displayed herself as a play within a play. Her opera-glass scanned one box after another; uneasy, though superficially tranquil, she was a slave to fashion: her box, her headgear, her carriage and her personal appearance meant everything to her. One sometimes meets people of herculean stature who hide a tender and affectionate heart under a bronze exterior; but Fœdora concealed a heart of bronze beneath her frail and graceful envelope. The deadly knowledge I had gained of human psychology stripped away many of her veils. If aristocracy of mind consists in forgetting oneself for the sake of others, in maintaining a constant gentleness of voice and gesture, in pleasing others by making them pleased with themselves, Fœdora, in spite of her acuteness, had not eliminated every trace of her plebeian origin; with her, self-forgetfulness was a pretence; her manners, instead of being instinctive, had been laboriously acquired; in short, her politeness smacked of servility. Nonetheless her honeyed words were regarded by her favourites as the expression of her kindliness and her pretentious exaggeration passed for noble enthusiasm. I alone had studied her airs and grimaces, I had stripped her inner being of the thin crust that satisfies society, and I was no longer taken in by her affectations; I knew that deep down in her there dwelt the soul of a cat. When some ninny or other complimented and extolled her, I was ashamed for her sake.

'And yet I was still enamoured! I still hoped to melt the ice in her by enfolding her in the wings of a poet's love. If I could once open her heart to feminine tenderness and initiate her into the sublimity of devotion, I should then see her as a perfect, an angelic creature! I loved her as a man, a lover, an artist, whereas in order to obtain her I ought not to have loved her at all. A supercilious fop or a coldly calculating man might perhaps have brought her to heel. Vain and artificial as she was, she might well have responded to the langauge of vanity and let herself get entangled in the snares of an intrigue: a cold and insensible man might have mastered her. I suffered the most horrible pangs, in the very depths of my soul, whenever, in her naïvety, she revealed her egoism. I was grief-stricken to think of her alone in the world, knowing no one to whom she could hold out her hand, with no friendly gaze to meet hers. One evening I summoned up courage to paint for her, in vivid colours, the sort of old age she could look forward to – abandoned, empty, dreary. Confronted with the spectacle of this frightful act of vengeance on the part of cheated nature, she made a shocking retort: "I shall always have a good income. Gold will always purchase whatever feelings we need for our comfort."

'I left her house dumbfounded by the line of logic taken by this woman, her luxury and her social class, at the same time as I reproached myself for my folly in idolizing her. I did not love Pauline because she was poor, therefore Fœdora, being rich, had every right to refuse Raphael. Our conscience is an infallible judge so long as we have not yet murdered it. "Fœdora," a sophistical voice was crying in my ear, "neither loves nor refuses anyone. She is free, but once upon a time she sold herself for gold. Whether he was her lover or her husband, her Russian count had possessed her. Surely she will be assailed by temptation once in her life. Wait for that moment!" Neither chaste nor promiscuous, this woman was living remote from humanity in her own particular sphere, whether an inferno or a paradise. Yet this enigmatic female robed in cashmere and embroidered fabrics set every human sentiment astir in my heart: pride, ambition, love, curiosity . . .

'A trick of fashion, or else that love of seeming singular which everyone is subject to, had brought into noisy popularity a particular show running at a cheap boulevard theatre. The countess expressed the wish to see the floury face of an actor who was all the rage with some people of intelligence, and I obtained the honour of taking her to the first performance of some paltry farce or other. The price of a box there was something under five francs, but I did not possess a brass farthing. Still having a half-volume of memoirs to write up, I dared not go and negotiate an advance from Finot, and Rastignac, my universal provider, was away. This constant shortage of ready cash was the bane of my life. To give an earlier instance: one evening, as we came out of the Bouffons when rain was pelting down, Fœdora had hailed a cab for me without my being able to evade her obliging show of solicitude: she would not hear of any excuse, either that I enjoyed rain or that I wanted to go to a gambling-house. Nothing would make her understand that my pockets were empty – neither my embarrassed demeanour nor the rueful jests I uttered. There was shame in my very glances, but could she interpret

153

glances? A young man's life is at the mercy of such odd whims! On the journey home, every turn of the wheels sent frantic thoughts whirling in my brain. I tried to pull out a plank from the floor of the cab, hoping that I could slip through it on to the roadway, but, meeting with insuperable obstacles, I gave way to convulsive laughter and relapsed into sullen calmness, as stupefied as a man in the stocks. When I reached the house, Pauline interrupted the first sentence I stammered with the question: "Are you short of change perhaps?" These words sounded sweeter in my ears than any of Rossini's music.

'But let me get back to the Funambules. To be in a position to take the countess to the performance in question, I had the idea of pawning the gold frame in which my mother's portrait was set. Although the pawnshop had always figured in my mind as a gateway to prison, even so it would be better to carry my bed and bedding there and pledge them than to beg for alms. The look on the face of a man you ask for money is so distressing! Certain loans granted cost us our honour, just as certain words of refusal spoken by a friend can cost us our last illusion.

'Pauline was working. Her mother had gone to bed. Casting a furtive glance at the bed, whose curtains were drawn back a little, I supposed that Madame Gaudin was sound asleep when I perceived her calm and sallow profile leaving its imprint on the pillow in a patch of shadow.

'"Is something worrying you?" Pauline asked me, laying down her brush on her work-table.

'"My poor girl, you can do me a great service," I replied.

'She looked at me with such an air of happiness that I was startled. Can it be that she's in love with me? I asked myself.

'"Pauline," I continued. And I sat down beside her in order to study her closely. She divined my thoughts, so interrogative was my tone of voice. She lowered her eyes, and I examined her intently, feeling that I could read as clearly in her heart as in my own, so pure, so candid were her features.

'"Do you love me?" I asked her.

'A little . . . madly . . not at all!" she cried.

'I concluded that she did not love me. Her mocking tone and pretty gesture meant no more than the frolicsome gratitude of a girl. And so I confessed to her the plight I was in and my embarrassing circumstances; I begged her to come to my help.

' "What, Monsieur Raphael?" she asked. "You are ashamed to go to the pawnshop, but you don't mind sending me there."

'I flushed, for a child's logic had confounded me. Thereupon she took my hand as if she wanted by an affectionate caress to make up for the harsh truth of her outburst.

' "Of course I would go," she said. "But there's no need. This morning I found two five-franc pieces behind the piano: they must have fallen behind the back, without your noticing. I put them on your table."

'Her good mother showed her head between the bed-curtains. "Monsieur Raphael, you are soon about to come into money. I am well able to lend you a small sum while you are waiting."

' "Oh Pauline!" I exclaimed as I clasped her hand. "If only I were rich!"

' "What need for that?" she asked with a pert little pout. Her hand was pulsating in time to my heart-beats. She withdrew it sharply and studied my palm.

' "You will marry a rich woman," she said. "But she will cause you much worry . . . Heavens above! She will kill you! . . . I am sure of it."

'Her cry showed that she espoused, up to a point, the irrational superstitions of her mother.

' "You are very credulous, Pauline!"

' "But it's certain!" she said, looking at me in terror. "The woman you will love will cause your death!"

'She took up her brush again, dipped it in the paint with every sign of agitation, and turned her eyes away from me. At that moment I would gladly have subscribed to her fantasies. No man who is superstitious can be a prey to complete misery for superstition often brings hope. Back in my room, I did in fact find the two splendid silver pieces whose presence there I could not account for. My thoughts wandering as sleep stole over me, I tried to work out what I had spent in the effort to explain this unexpected bonus. I fell asleep, deeply immersed in ineffectual calculations. Next day Pauline come up to see me when I was setting out to book a box at the theatre.

' "Perhaps ten francs are not enough," she said with a blush. "My mother asked me to let you have this money. Take it, do."

'The kind, delightful girl put fifteen francs on my table and tried to run away; but I caught her. Admiration dried the tears which were swimming in my eyes.

' "Pauline," I said, "you are an angel! The loan you offer me touches me much less than the delicacy of feeling with which you offer it to me. I was hoping for a rich and elegant titled woman. Now, alas, I wish I owned millions and could meet a girl as poor as you, with a heart as rich as yours. I would renounce the deadly passion which you say – and rightly perhaps – will kill me.

' "Hush! don't say it," she said, and ran off. The fresh trills of her nightingale's voice echoed along the staircase.

' "Happy girl, to be ignorant still of love", I thought, remembering the torments I had suffered over the past months.

'Pauline's fifteen francs stood me in good stead. Fœdora, mindful of the sweaty odour of the working-class audience in this hall in which we would have to sit for several hours, regretted not having a nosegay. I went in search of flowers for her, and returned to lay my life and fortune in her lap. I felt both remorse and pleasure in giving her a bouquet the price of which gave me a clear idea of the extravagant wastefulness of the surface gallantry practised in society. It was not long before she complained of the strong scent of a Mexican jasmine. Surveying the audience, and finding herself sitting on a hard bench, she was filled with nausea and blamed me for having brought her there! Though sitting beside me, she would not stay, she insisted on leaving.

'Having endured sleepless nights and wasted two months of my life, I still had not softened her. Never had this diabolical creature been more lovely, nor more unfeeling. During our return home, seated close to her in a narrow coupé, I breathed the same air as she, I touched her scented glove, I feasted my eyes on the treasures of her beauty, I could smell the gentle perfume of iris. Nothing could be more feminine, nothing less womanly. At that moment a ray of light enabled me to plumb the depths of her incomprehensible way of life. I suddenly remembered a book recently published by a poet, a truly artistic conception inspired by the statue of Polycles.[32] I thought I saw before me the monstrous creature who, as an officer, tames a spirited horse; and as a young girl, sits at her toilet-table and reduces her admirers to despair, while again, as a lover, he breaks the heart of a gentle and modest girl. Finding no other way of solving the problem of Fœdora, I told her the gist of that fantastic story; but no point of resemblance was apparent between herself and this poetry of the impossible. She was genuinely amused by it, as a child might be at a fable taken from the *Thousand and One Nights*.

'"To withstand the love of a man of my age," I mused as I returned home, "to be proof against the communicative warmth of that fine spiritual contagion, there must be some mysterious power shielding Fœdora. Perhaps, like Lady Delacour,[33] she is consumed with a cancer. Perhaps she is kept alive by artificial means."

This thought chilled me. Then I formed the most extravagant and yet the most rational project a lover could ever conceive. In order to make a physical examination of the woman in the same way as I had studied her intellectually, in order to complete my knowledge of her, I resolved to spend a night in her bedroom secretly; and this is how I carried out the enterprise, one which obsessed my mind as the lust for vengeance devours the heart of a Corsican monk.[34] The days she held court, Fœdora entertained too large a number of people for it to be possible to keep a strict account of exits and entrances. Feeling certain that I could remain in the house without causing a scandal, I impatiently

32. Balzac was thinking of Henry de Latouche's *Fragoletta*, 1829, a novel of which the hero/heroine is courted by a young man whose sister he is courting. The statue referred to is *The Hermaphrodite*, attributed to the ancient Greek sculptor Polycles, of which a copy existed in the Louvre.

33. The translator has been unable to trace this reference, no doubt to some contemporary fashionable novel.

34. It was asserted by Amédée Pichot, editor of the *Revue de Paris*, that the ensuing bedroom-scene had had its counterpart in real life, that Balzac in fact concealed himself one night in the bedroom of the courtesan and salon hostess Olympe Pélissier, who later became the mistress, then the wife of Balzac's friend the composer Rossini.

waited for the next *soirée* the countess was due to give. Whilst dressing I slipped into my waistcoat pocket a small English penknife to serve as a dagger in need. Had it been found on my person, such a paper-knife could arouse no suspicion, but since I had no idea where my romantic venture might lead me, I thought it well to carry some weapon.

'As the reception rooms began to be thronged, I went and reconnoitred the bedroom, and my first stroke of luck was that the shutters and blinds were closed. And since the chambermaid might come in to let down the curtains at the windows, I undid the loops to draw the folds across. I was taking a big risk in venturing to perform this domestic function in advance, but I was reconciled to the dangers of a situation which I had coolly calculated. About midnight I went and hid in the embrasure of a window. So that my feet should be invisible, I tried to climb on to the plinth of the wainscoting, leaned my back against the wall and grasped the handle of the window-frame. After ascertaining that I could balance myself, selecting my points of purchase and gauging the space which separated me from the curtains, I succeeded in acquainting myself with the difficulties of my position so that I might remain there undiscovered, provided that I was not troubled with cramps, coughs and sneezes. So as to avoid useless fatigue, I stood upright while awaiting the critical moment when I should have to stay suspended like a spider in its web. The white watered silk and muslin of the curtains hung before me in ample folds like organ pipes and I cut slits in them with my knife so as to be able to see everything through these peep-holes. I could hear the muffled sounds of conversation in the salons, the laughter punctuating the talk, voices occasionally raised. Then little by little this cloudy tumult, this dimly heard bustle diminished. Some of the men came to retrieve their hats which had been left near where I stood, on the countess's chest of drawers. When they brushed against the curtains I shuddered as I thought of the absent-minded, haphazard way people in a hurry to depart ferret about in all directions as they search for their belongings. Since no calamity occurred I augured well for the success of my enterprise. The last hat to be taken away was that of one of Fœdora's long-standing admirers who, believing himself to be alone, looked at her bed and heaved a great sigh followed by some kind of forceful exclamation. The countess, finding herself left with no more than half-a-dozen close acquaintances, suggested they take tea together in the boudoir adjoining her bedroom. Calumnies, one of the few things modern society still attaches belief to, mingled with epigrams, witty judgements and the clatter of cups and spoons. Devoid of pity for my rivals, Rastignac was provoking bursts of laughter with his mordant sallies.

'"Monsieur de Rastignac is not the sort of man to pick a quarrel with," said the countess with a laugh.

'"True enough," he replied ingenuously. "I have always been rational in my hatreds . . . In my friendships too," he added. "It may be that my enemies are as useful to me as my friends. I have made quite a special study of the modern idiom and the natural artifices which are used in any kind of attack or defence. Ministerial eloquence is an added social perfection. If one of your friends lacks wit, you talk of his honesty and candour. If another man's book is dull, you recommend it for the thoroughness of its research. If it's badly written, you praise the ideas it contains. Such and such a man is perfidious, inconstant, and eludes you at every turn: why then, you pronounce him charming, delightful, fascinating! But where your enemies are concerned, you bombard them with both the living and the dead. For their benefit you reverse the terms of your vocabulary, and you are as perspicacious in discovering their defects as you were skilful in bringing out the good qualities of your friends. This way of turning the eyeglass on to the proper moral points is the secret of our conversations and comprises all the art of the courtier. To forswear its use is to fight with bare hands against men armed to the teeth like medieval knights. I make full use of it. Sometimes I go too far, but it makes people respect me, me and my friends, for my sword gives as good as my tongue." One of Foedora's most fervent admirers, a young man whose impertinence had won him a certain celebrity, and even helped him to make his way in the world, took up the gauntlet so disdainfully thrown down by Rastignac. He began to talk of me and spoke in exaggerated terms of my talents and person: a method of backbiting which Rastignac had left out of account! This sardonic eulogy was misunderstood by the countess, who tore my reputation to tatters mercilessly: to amuse her friends she exposed the secret aspirations and hopes I had confided to her.

' "He's a man with a great future," said Rastignac. "the type to take savage revenge one day, perhaps. His talents are at least equal to his courage, and so I regard people who attack him as very rash, for he has a long memory..."

'... "and also writes memoirs," the countess added, showing some displeasure at the deep silence which followed Rastignac's remark.

' "Memoirs of a pseudo-countess, Madame," Rastignac retorted. "To write such things one needs a different sort of courage."

' "I don't think he can be lacking in courage," she replied: "he's faithful to me."

'I was sorely tempted to show myself suddenly in the midst of these scoffers, like the ghost of Banquo in *Macbeth*. I was losing a mistress but my friend had proved himself one. However, love all at once suggested to me one of those subtle and cowardly paradoxes which it invents to soothe all our sufferings. "If Fœdora loves me," I thought, "is she not forced to disguise her affection behind mischievous pleasantries? How often has a woman's heart not contradicted the falsehoods that fall from her lips?"

'At last my impertinent rival, the only one left with the countess, rose to depart.

' "What, already!" she said to him in cajoling accents which made my heart flutter. "Can you not give me a few more minutes? Have you nothing more to say to me? Will you not give up a few of your diversions for my sake?"

'He departed.

' "Oh!" she cried with a yawn, "what a lot of bores they are!" She tugged at a bell-rope, and the sound of the bell rang through the apartments.

'She entered her bedroom humming a phrase of the *Pria che spunti*.[35] No one had ever heard her sing, and this circumstance

35. An aria from Cimarosa's *Il Matrimonio Segreto*.

had given rise to strange conjectures. It was said that she had promised her first lover, bewitched by her talents and jealous about her from beyond the grave, to allow no one a pleasure which he wanted to be the sole person to have enjoyed. I strained every faculty in order to drink in these sounds. From note to note they soared up: she seemed to become inspired, the rich tones filled the room and the melody took on a truly divine quality. The countess's voice had a liquid clearness, an accuracy of pitch, a harmonious and vibrant timbre which pierced the listener's heart, stirred and excited him. Musical women are almost always amorous by nature. Surely one who could sing like that must know how to love? And so the beauty of her voice was one more element of mystery in this pre-eminently mysterious woman. I saw her then as I see you now: she appeared to be listening to herself, to be feeling a sensual delight which was all her own; it was as if she were enjoying all the thrills of love. She stood before the fireplace as she was finishing the leading motif of the *rondo*; but once she stopped singing her expression changed, her mouth drooped and every feature betrayed fatigue. She had dropped the mask; her role as actress was ended. And yet the ravage wrought on her beauty by her artistic exertions, or by the weariness of the hostess, was not without its charm.

' "There is the real woman!" I said to myself.

'She set one foot, as if to warm herself, on the bronze rail over the fender, removed her gloves, unfastened her bracelets and pulled off from over her head a gold chain at one end of which hung her perfume-box studded with gems. It gave me ineffable pleasure to watch her movements, as delicate and graceful as those of a cat grooming itself in a sunny nook. She looked at herself in the mirror and said out loud, as though crossly:

' "I wasn't looking my best this evening . . . My complexion is fading so fast, it's frightening . . . Perhaps I ought to go to bed earlier and give up this dissipated life . . . But where's Justine? What's she playing at?"

'She rang again, and her chambermaid hurried in. Where was her room? I had no idea. She came in by a secret staircase. I was curious and wanted to take stock of her. Carried away by my poet's imagination, I had more than once had misgivings about this invisible servant, a tall, dark, well-built girl.

' "You rang, madam?"

' "Twice!" Fœdora replied. "Are you going deaf?"

' "I was preparing your ladyship's milk of almonds."

'Justine knelt down and took off her mistress's shoes and stockings. Fœdora was nonchalantly reclining on an easy-chair by the fireside, yawning and scratching her head. There was nothing in any one of her movements that was not natural, nor did I discern any symptom of the secret suffering or the passions with which I had credited her.

' "Georges is in love," she said. "I shall dismiss him. Has he still not drawn the curtains this evening? What is he thinking about?"

'At this remark, all my blood rushed back to my heart. But the question of the curtains was dropped.

' "Life is very empty," the countess continued. "Take care now not to scratch me as you did yesterday. Look," she said, showing the maid her small, smooth-skinned knee, "I still bear the mark of your claws."

'She slid her bare feet into velvet slippers lined with swansdown and let her dress slip down while Justine started to comb out her hair.

' "You should get married, madam, and have children."

' "Children? That would be the end!" she exclaimed. "A husband! Where is the man to whom I could . . .? – Was my hair well arranged this evening?"

' "Not too well."

' "You're a fool!"

' "Nothing suits you less than to crimp your hair too much," Justine replied. "Big, smooth curls look much better on you."

' "You think so?"

' "Certainly, Madame. Short crimped hair only looks well on blondes."

' ". . . Get married? No! No! Marriage isn't the kind of trade I was born to."

'What a fearful scene for a lover! This lonely woman, without friends or relations, an atheist in the temple of love, a total sceptic where emotions were concerned – this woman, in order to satisfy the natural human need, however undeveloped it might be in her, to open her heart to a fellow-creature, was reduced to chatting with her chambermaid, and stringing together banal or meaningless phrases. I felt sorry for her. Justine unlaced her. I watched her with curiosity as the last veil was removed. I was dazzled by the sight of her virginal bosom. Through her chemise her pink and white body gleamed in the candle-light like a silver statue shining through a wrapping of gauze. Certainly there was no imperfection to make her dread the furtive glances of love.

'Alas! A lovely body will always triumph over the most martial resolutions! Justine's mistress sat down before the fire, mute and pensive, while her maid lit the alabaster lamp hanging in front of the bed. Justine went to fetch a warming-pan, got the bed ready and helped her mistress into it. Then, after spending a fair amount of time performing the meticulous services which clearly revealed the deep veneration in which Fœdora held herself, the maid departed. The countess turned over several times. She was disturbed in mind and she sighed. Her lips let out a not quite inaudible sound betraying a mood of impatience. She stretched out her hand towards the table, took from it a phial and before drinking her milk poured into it four or five drops of a brown liquid. And then, after uttering a few sad sighs, she exclaimed: "My God!"

'I found this exclamation – and more particularly the tone with which she uttered it – heart-breaking. Little by little she relapsed into total stillness. This frightened me; but soon there came to my ears the deep, steady breathing of the sleeper. I pushed aside the rustling silk of the curtains, stepped forward and stood at the foot of her bed, gazing upon her with feelings difficult to describe. Seen thus, she was ravishing. She had one arm flung over her head, like a child; her pretty face, in repose, with a fringe of lace around it, expressed a sweetness that set my heart on fire. I had relied too much on my self-control and had not realized what torture I was to suffer: to be so close to her, and yet so far away! It was a punishment I had brought upon myself and was obliged to endure. My God! That fragment of an unfathomable thought, the only glimmer I had of Fœdora's state of mind, had suddenly changed the idea I had of her.

That exclamation – was it trivial or profound, devoid of substance or fraught with meaning? – might as easily indicate contentment or dissatisfaction, bodily pain or mental suffering. Was it a blasphemy or a prayer? regret for the remembered past or dread of what the future held? In that single word a whole lifetime was summed up, one of poverty or wealth; there was even room in it for a crime! The enigma concealed behind this fair semblance of a woman was born anew: so many explanations of Fœdora were possible that nothing was finally explained. The varying rhythm of her breath as it issued from her lips, now weakly, now strongly, now heavy, now light, composed a kind of language which I translated into thoughts and feelings. I shared her dream, I hoped to enter her secret life by making my way into her sleep, I wavered between a thousand conflicting decisions, a thousand different judgements of her character. As I looked on her lovely countenance, so peaceful and so pure, I found it impossible to maintain this woman had no heart. I decided to make one more attempt. By telling her all about my life, my love for her, the sacrifices I had made for her, I might perhaps awaken pity in her, surprise a tear in the eye of this woman who had never wept. I had come to the point of staking all my hopes on this supreme test, when street noises announced the coming of day.

'For a moment I imagined Fœdora waking up in my arms. Why should I not slip into her bed and take her in my arms? I was so sorely obsessed with this idea that, to banish it, I made my escape into the salon without taking the precaution to move quietly; but fortunately I happened upon a private door opening on to a narrow staircase. As I had expected, the key was in the lock. I jerked the door open, ran boldly into the courtyard and, without looking round to see if I was being observed, I reached the street in three bounds.'

*

'Two days later, it had been arranged that a playwright should read a newly-written comedy to a gathering in her salon. I went to it intending to stay behind afterwards in order to make her a somewhat singular petition, which was to consecrate the whole of the following evening to me alone, admitting no one else across her threshold. But when I found myself alone with her my heart failed me. Every tick of the clock made me quake. The time was a quarter to twelve.

'"If I don't broach this matter with her," I told msyelf, "I'll dash my brains out on the corner of the mantelpiece."

'I gave myself three minutes' grace. The three minutes passed by, and I did not dash my brains out on the marble mantelpiece. My heart had become as sodden as a sponge in water.

'"You are extremely entertaining," she said.

'"Ah, Madame!" I replied. "If only you could understand me!"

'"What is wrong with you?" she asked. "You are turning quite pale."

'"I am trying to bring myself to ask a favour of you."

'She gave me an encouraging gesture and I made my request for the private meeting.

'"But of course," she said. "But why can you not speak to me here and now?"

'"I have no wish to mislead you. I must warn you how much you are committing yourself to. I want to spend this evening with you as a brother with a sister. Don't be afraid, I know there are things you cannot stand. You have come to know me well enough to be certain that I would ask nothing of you that might displease you; besides which, a bold man would not proceed in that way. You have extended to me the hand of friendship, you are kind and indulgent. Well, let me tell you that tomorrow I must bid you farewell . . . Don't take back your promise!" I exclaimed as I saw that she was about to speak.

'I left her.

'One evening last May, at about eight o'clock, I found myself alone with Fœdora in her Gothic boudoir. My nerves were steady, I was convinced that happiness would be mine: either I would win her, or else I would seek refuge in the arms of death. I had passed sentence on the timid lover I had been. A man who has confessed his weakness is wrong indeed. Wearing

165

a blue cashmere dress, the countess was reclining on a divan with her feet on a cushion. A beret of Eastern style, such as painters attribute to the early Hebrews, added a strange piquancy to her seductiveness. Her face was touched with a fugitive charm which seemed to prove that from one moment to another we are changed into new, unique beings, having no similarity with what we were in the past and what we shall be in the future. I had never seen her so dazzlingly beautiful.

' "Do you know," she said with a laugh, "that you have stung me to curiosity?"

' "I will not disappoint you," I replied calmly, sitting down beside her and taking her hand, which she did not withhold. "You have a very lovely voice."

' "But you have never heard me sing," she exclaimed, unable to suppress a start of surprise.

' "I will prove that I have when the time comes. Can it be that your superb singing voice is yet another mystery? Have no fear, I will not try to fathom this one."

'We spent about an hour in familiar conversation. Although I adopted the tone, manners and gestures of a man to whom Fœdora could refuse nothing, I also showed all the respect appropriate to a suitor. By these tactics I obtained the privilege of kissing her hand. She so daintily slipped off her glove, and in consequence I was so pleasurably steeped in the illusion I wished to cherish that my soul melted and overflowed in that kiss. With incredible self-abandon Fœdora allowed me to stroke and caress her. But don't imagine that I was fooled: if I had taken one step beyond these chaste fondlings, the cat would have unsheathed her claws. For about ten minutes we remained plunged in deep silence, I admired her and credited her with charms she did not possess. At that moment she was mine, all mine. I possessed this ravishing creature in the only way it was possible to possess her: intuitively. I wrapped her round in my desire, held her and clasped her, and in imagination I made her my bride. I owed my triumph over the countess to the power of magnetic attraction, and have always regretted that I did not completely subjugate this woman.

But just then I was not concerned with carnal love, I

aspired to her life and soul, I was lost in that glorious dream of ideal and complete happiness which we never believe in for long.

'At length, feeling that the last hour of my rapture had struck, I said to her: "Listen. I love you, as you well know, since I have told you so a thousand times. You ought to have understood me. You have failed to do so because I would not clothe my love in the pretty speeches of a fop or the protestations of a simpleton. What miseries I have suffered for your sake, and yet you are innocent of them. But in a few minutes' time you shall be my judge. There are two kinds of poverty. One is the kind which walks the streets flaunting its rags, unwittingly reincarnating Diogenes, eating scraps and reducing life to its simplest terms; happier perhaps than the wealthy, in any case carefree, it accepts the world at the point at which men of power would rather relinquish it. The second kind is the poverty of luxury, the poverty of the Spanish grandee, beggared but still proud of his title; wearing a haughty look and a feather in his hat, white waistcoat and yellow gloves, owning a carriage and losing a fortune for lack of a centime. The former is the destitution of the commoner, the latter is that of crooks, monarchs and men of talent. I am neither a commoner nor a king nor a cook, and maybe I have no talent – I am an exception. The name I bear enjoins me to die rather than beg . . . Never fear, Madame, I am rich today, I have title to as much of the earth as I need," I added as I saw her assume the cold expression of one taken unawares by a request to contribute to charity made by a lady of rank.

' "Do you recall the day when you wanted to go to the Gymnase[36] without me, believing that I should not be there?"

'She nodded.

' "I had spent my few last francs in order to meet you there . . . Do you remember the walk we took through the Botanical Gardens? The carriage we hired cost me all I had."

'I told her of all my sacrifices and depicted my life, not as I am depicting it to you now, in the intoxication of wine, but in the noble intoxication of the heart. My passion spilled over in ardent

36. A fashionable theatre of the period which owed its reputation to the fact that Eugène Scribe's popular vaudevilles could be seen there.

expressions, in emotional appeals now forgotten and which neither art nor memory could reproduce. It was not the tepid narration of a love which I had come to loathe: the love I bore her, in the strength and beauty of the hope I still felt, inspired me with such words as throw a whole life into relief by reiterating the cries of a lacerated soul. My accents were those of the last prayers uttered by a dying man on the battlefield. She wept. I stopped short. Great God! *That* was what caused her tears to flow: the sham emotion which can be bought for five francs at a theatre box-office: like a good actor, I had brought the house down!

' "Had I but known . . ." she said.

' "Say no more," I cried. "I still love you enough at this moment to kill you . . ."

'She raised her arm to seize the bell-rope. I burst into laughter.

' "There's no need to summon help," I continued. "You shall live out your life in peace. To kill you would be to show a poor understanding of hatred. Fear no violence from me: I spent a whole night at the foot of your bed, without . . ."

' "Sir, really!" she exclaimed, blushing. But after that first expostulation prompted by the modesty any woman, even the most insensitive, must possess, she threw a contemptuous look at me and added:

' "You must have felt very cold!"

' "Madame, do you believe that your beauty is so precious to me?" I replied, guessing what thoughts were troubling her. "I see in your face the promise of a soul even more beautiful than your body. Nay, Madame, men who see only the woman in a woman can every night purchase beauties worthy of a seraglio and buy themselves happiness at cut rates . . . But *I* was ambitious: I wanted your heart to beat in unison with mine, not realizing, as I do now, that you have no heart. If there were a man to whom you were destined, I would murder him . . . On second thoughts, no! You might be in love with him, and his death might perhaps cause you pain . . . Oh, how I suffer!" I burst out.

' "If it consoles you at all," she said gaily, "I can assure you that I shall belong to no one."

' "Very well," I broke in. "You blaspheme the Almighty, and you will be punished for it. Some day you will be lying on your divan, unable to endure either light or sound, condemned to live in a kind of tomb, suffering unheard-of ills. Then, when you seek to know the cause of that slow, avenging torture, be mindful of the unhappiness you have so recklessly inflicted as you passed on your way. Having everywhere sown imprecation, you will reap a harvest of hatred. We pronounce judgement on ourselves, and ourselves execute such judgement, in accordance with a law operative in this world; one that ranks higher than human justice, lower than divine justice."

' "Ah !" she laughed. "No doubt it's very criminal of me not to love you. Is it my fault? No, I do not love you : you're a man, that's reason enough. I am happy living alone, why should I subject my life, selfish as you may think it, to the whims of a master? Marriage is a sacrament by virtue of which we only take on someone else's troubles in exchange for our own. In any case, I find children tiresome. I was honest enough in warning you of my character. Why could you not have been satisfied with my friendship? I would like to be able to offer you some compensation for whatever pain I caused you in failing to guess your little financial worries. I appreciate the extent of your sacrifices, but only love could requite you for your devotion and your delicate attentions; and I love you so little that I find this scene rather upsetting."

' "I realize I am being ridiculous, forgive me," I said in mild tones, unable to restrain my tears. "I love you enough," I went on, "to listen with delight even to the cruel words you utter. Oh ! would that I could write my love in all my heart's blood !"

' "All men make more or less the same classical declaration," she replied, still laughing. "But it appears that they find it very difficult to expire at our feet, for I am always coming across these walking dead . . . It is midnight, permit me to retire."

' "And in two hours' time you will exclaim *My God* !"

' "Ah yes ! The night before last ! I was thinking of my broker. I had forgotten to tell him to sell my 5% bonds and buy 3% which had gone down a few points in the course of the day."

'I gazed at her in fury. Ah, there are times when a crime

would be the execution of poetic justice! Being used to listening to the most impassioned declarations, no doubt she had already forgotten my words and tears.

' "Would you marry a peer of France?" I asked her, coldly.

' "Perhaps – if he were a duke as well."

'I took my hat and gave a farewell bow.

' "Allow me to accompany you to the door of my apartments," she said, and there was sharp irony in her gesture, the tilt of her head and her tone of voice.

' "Madame . . ."

' "Monsieur?"

' "I shall never see you again."

' "Indeed I hope not," she replied, bowing her head with an impertinent expression.

' "You wish to be a duchess?" I continued, fired with a sort of frenzy provoked by her attitude. "Is it titles and honours that you covet? Very well, suffer me to love you, command my pen to write and my voice to resound only for you. Be the secret principle of my life, be my guiding star! Then accept me for your husband only when I have become a minister, a peer of France, a duke . . . I will make myself everything you wish me to be!"

' "You certainly made quite good use of your time," she said with a smile, "in your solicitor's office. You know how to put passion into your pleas."

' "The present belongs to you, wretched woman," I cried, "but the future belongs to me. All I lose is a wife. You lose a name and a family. Time will bring forth my vengeance: it will rob you of your beauty and bring you to a lonely death, but it will give me fame!"

' "Thank you for the peroration," she said, stifling a yawn and making it plain by her attitude that she wanted to be rid of me.

'Her final remark reduced me to silence. I concentrated all my hatred in the look I gave her and rushed away. I simply had to forget Fœdora, cure myself of my madness, return to my studious solitude, or die. To this end I undertook a programme of intensive work, hoping to finish my manuscript. I did not leave my attic for a fortnight and grew haggard, spending all my nights in study. But for all my determination and the spur administered by despair, I worked painfully, in fits and starts. Inspiration had deserted me. I could not banish from my mind the bright, mocking phantom of Fœdora. Under each of my thoughts there brooded another thought, a morbid one, an obscure desire, as terrible as remorse. Like the monks of the Thebaid, though without praying as they did, I lived in the desert and delved deep into my soul instead of delving into the rocky ground. I would have been prepared if necessary to lash a spiked girdle tight about my loins, if by physical pain I could have deadened my spiritual anguish.'

*

'One evening Pauline came into my room.

' "You are killing yourself," she said in a voice of supplication. "You ought to go out and visit your friends . . ."

' "Ah! Pauline, your prophecy was right. Fœdora is killing me. I want to die. Life is intolerable to me."

' "Is there then only one woman in the world?" she asked with a smile. "Why do you bring infinite anguish into so short a life?"

'I looked at Pauline with stupefaction. Then she left me alone. I had not noticed that she had gone, and had heard her voice without taking in what she was saying. Before long I was obliged to take the manuscript of my memoirs to my editor. Preoccupied with my passion, I had no idea how I had managed to live without money. I only knew that the four hundred and fifty francs due to me would suffice to pay my debts. So I went to draw my wages, and I met Rastignac, who commented on my altered appearance and my thinness.

' "What hospital have you been in?" he asked.

' "That woman is killing me," I retorted. "I can neither despise nor forget her."

' "Better kill her, then you'd give up thinking about her," he exclaimed, laughing.

' "I have certainly thought of that," I replied. "But though I occasionally feel some relief at the idea of a crime – rape or murder or both – I find myself incapable of committing it in reality. The countess is a nine days' wonder – she would beg for mercy, and not everybody can be an Othello!"

' "She's like all the women we can't have," Rastignac broke in.

' "I'm going mad!" I cried. "From one moment to another I feel the howl of insanity inside my head. My thoughts are like phantoms that dance before my eyes and elude my attempts to grasp them. I prefer death to this kind of life. So I am earnestly looking for the best way to end the struggle. There's no longer question of the living Fœdora, the Fœdora of the Faubourg Saint-Honoré, but of my private Fœdora, the one who is here!" I cried, smiting my forehead. "What do you think of opium?"

' "Oh no! Extremely painful!" Rastignac replied.

' "Charcoal fumes?"

' "Too vulgar!"

' "The Seine?"

' "The drag-nets and the Morgue are very filthy."

' "A pistol-shot?'

' "Suppose you miss? You're disfigured for life. Listen," he added. "Like all young men I have wondered about suicide. Which of us has not thought of killing himself two or three times before reaching his thirtieth birthday? The best solution I've found is to wear oneself to death by living for pleasure. Sink deep into dissipation and either you will drown your passion . . . or yourself. Intemperance, my boy, is the most royal of deaths. It has lightning apoplexy at its command. Apoplexy is a pistol-shot that does not miss. Orgies lavish all the physical pleasures on us: are they not opium sold retail? By forcing us to drink to excess, debauchery challenges wine to mortal combat. Does not the Duke of Clarence's butt of Malmsey taste better than Seine mud?[37] Each time we nobly roll under the table, is that not the equivalent of a minor stroke? If the police patrol picks us up, do we not, as we lie on the cold mattresses in the lock-up, enjoy the pleasures of the Morgue minus the swollen bellies and the

37. Found guilty of conspiring against his brother, King Edward IV, this Duke of Clarence was allowed to choose the manner of his death, and elected to be drowned in a butt of Malmsey wine.

decomposing green and blue flesh, plus the knowledge of what we are going through? Indeed," he continued, "this slow suicide is far different from the death of a bankrupt grocer. Tradesmen have brought the river into disrepute by throwing themselves in so as to soften their creditors' hearts. If I were you I would try to die elegantly. If you are willing to invent a novel mode of death by fighting that kind of duel with life, I will be your second. I am bored; I have suffered a disappointment. The Alsatian widow they wanted me to marry has six toes on her left foot. I can't live with a six-toed woman! The story would get around and cover me with ridicule. And then, she hasn't above eighteen thousand francs a year: her fortune is dwindling and she's growing more toes. Devil take her! . . . Let's lead a wild life, chance might bring us happiness!"

'Rastignac swept me off my feet. This brilliant plan held out too strong an attraction and revived too many hopes; in short, it had too poetic a colouring not to seduce a poet.

' "But how about money?" I asked him.

' "You've got four hundred and fifty francs?"

' "Yes, but I owe my tailor and my landlady . . ."

' "Pay your tailor? You're hopeless, you'll never even manage a seat in the cabinet."

' "But what can we do with twenty louis?"

' "Stake them."

'I shuddered.

' "Ah!" he continued, noticing how I recoiled. "You want to launch out into what I call the *Rake's System*, and you're afraid of a piece of green baize!"

' "Listen," I replied. "I promised my father never to set foot in a gambling-house. Not only is this promise sacred, but I am overcome with horror just walking past the doors of such an establishment. Here are 300 francs. Take them and go without me. While you are risking our fortune I'll go and settle my bills and then I'll wait for you at your place."

'And that, my friend, is how I came to perdition. It's enough for a young man to meet a woman who doesn't love him, or even one who loves him too much, for his whole life to be upset. Good fortune saps our strength as misfortune extinguishes our

173

virtues. Back in my Saint-Quentin lodgings, I gazed around at the garret in which I had led the blameless life of a scholar, a life which could perhaps have been honourable and long-lasting, one which I ought never to have abandoned in order to take up the life of the passions which was dragging me down into the abyss.

'Pauline found me in this melancholy mood. "Why, what's the matter?" she asked.

'I rose to my feet in silence and counted out the money I owed her mother, adding an advance of six months' rent. She scrutinized me with a sort of terror.

' "I am leaving you, dear Pauline."

' "I guessed as much!" she cried.

' "Listen, dear child, I might well come back here. Keep my cell vacant for half a year. If I am not back by November 15th or thereabouts, you will be my heiress. That sealed manuscript," I said, showing her a packet of papers, "is the fair copy of my major work on *The Will*. You will deposit it at the Royal Library. As for everything else I leave here, it is yours to do with as you wish."

'Pauline gave me a look that weighed heavy on my heart. She stood there like the incarnation of conscience.

' "I shall have no more lessons?" she asked, pointing to the piano. I made no answer.

' "Will you write to me?"

' "Good-bye, Pauline." I drew her gently towards me, and then, upon her brow made for love, but as pure as the snow which has not yet touched the soil, I set a brother's kiss, an old man's kiss. She ran out. I did not want to see Madame Gaudin. I put my key in its usual place and walked away. As I left the Rue de Cluny, I heard a girl's light footsteps behind me.

' "I had embroidered this purse for you, will you refuse that too?" Pauline asked.

'I thought I could see, in the light of the street-lamp, a tear in Pauline's eyes, and I sighed. Reacting, both of us perhaps, to the same thought, we separated with the haste of people fleeing from the plague.

'The life of dissipation I was now embracing seemed to be

oddly manifested by the room in which I awaited Rastignac's return with serene indifference. In the middle of the chimney-piece there stood a clock surmounted by a Venus sitting on her tortoise and holding in her arms a half-smoked cigar. Elegant pieces of furniture, presents from this or that mistress, were scattered about. A luxurious divan was strewn with discarded socks. The comfortable, well-sprung armchair in which I had sunk was covered with scars like a veteran soldier: its arms were scored and its back encrusted with the pomade and stale hair-oil deposited by the heads of all his friends in succession. Wealth and poverty were unashamedly coupled on the bed, on the walls, everywhere. It put one in mind of Neapolitan palaces, those palaces in Naples with beggars squatting on the steps. It was the bedroom of a gambler or a profligate whose luxury is entirely personal, who lives on sensations and cares little for harmonious surroundings. Moreover the total picture was not lacking in poetic effect. There stood life with its spangles and tatters, disconcerting and incomplete as it is in reality, but vivid and unpredictable as in a deserted camp-site where marauders have pillaged everything that has taken their fancy. A volume of Byron, with many of its pages missing, had served as kindling in the grate of the young man, typical of his kind in that he risks a thousand francs at the gaming table and has no fuel for a fire, who dashes about in a tilbury and yet owns not one clean, unmended shirt. Tomorrow a countess, an actress or a game of écarté will provide him with a right royal wardrobe. Here a candle was stuck in the green case of a tinderbox, there lay a woman's portrait despoiled of its frame of chased gold. How could a young man naturally avid for emotion renounce the attractions of a life so rich in contrasts, one which affords him the thrills of war in time of peace?

'I had almost dozed off when Rastignac kicked the door open and shouted out: "Victory! Now we can die in comfort . . ."

'He showed me his hat heaped up with gold, placed it on the table, and we danced around it like a couple of cannibals round the stewpot, howling, skipping, leaping, punching each other with blows fit to kill a rhinoceros and singing at the prospect of every pleasure in the world stored up for us in that hat.

' "Twenty-seven thousand francs," Rastignac kept on saying as he added a number of banknotes to the pile of gold. "Other people would find this money enough to live on, but will it suffice for us to die on? Oh certainly! We will expire in a bath of gold . . . Hurrah!"

'And we started capering again. We shared out like co-heirs, coin by coin, beginning with the double napoleons, passing from the big pieces to the little ones and spinning out our joy with a long succession of cries: "Yours!" . . . "Mine!"

' "We won't sleep tonight," Rastignac cried. "Joseph, some punch!" He threw some gold to his faithful manservant.

' "There's your share," he said. "That should see you underground!" '

*

'The next day I bought some furniture at Lesage's. I rented the flat where you got to know me in the Rue Taitbout and hired the best upholsterer in Paris to decorate it. I bought some horses. I flung myself into a whirlpool of pleasures which were hollow and real at one and the same time. I gambled, alternately winning and losing enormous sums – but only in the ballroom, in our friends' houses and never in gambling-dens, which I continued to hold in pious horror as always. Little by little I acquired friends. I won their attachment thanks to affairs of honour or else to the trustful facility with which we confide secrets to boon-companions; or it may well be that all firm friendships between men are due to shared vices. I ventured on a few literary compositions which earned me some compliments. The prominent figures in commercial literature, realizing they had nothing to fear from my competition, praised me, more through a desire to mortify their rivals than in recognition of my own achievements. I became a *viveur*, to use the picture-esque word which the langauge of orgy has consecrated. I made it a point of honour to burn myself up as fast as possible, to outdo the merriest rakes in verve and vigour. I was always fresh and elegant. I passed for a wit. Nothing in me betrayed the appalling mode of existence which turns a man either into a funnel for liquor, a digestive apparatus or a stud-horse.

'But soon debauchery appeared before me in all the majesty of its horror, and I understood its real nature. In very truth, sage men of orderly conduct who stick labels on bottles for their heirs can scarcely conceive either the theory of that lavish way of living or its normal condition: how to reveal its poetry to provincials who still regard tea and opium, those two delightful stimulants, as being intended for medicinal use only? Even in Paris, the metropolis of thought, does one not come upon half-hearted sybarites? Incapable of supporting an excess of pleasure, do they not return home exhausted after an orgy, just like those worthy bourgeois who, after hearing a new opera by Rossini, complain that music gives them a headache? Do they not reject that way of life as an abstemious man refuses to eat any more Ruffec pasties because the first one disagreed with him? To be intemperate requires as much skill as to write poetry, and in addition demands some fortitude of spirit. In order to grasp the mysteries of the dissolute life and savour its beauties, a man must to some extent apply himself to it as a subject for serious study. Like all sciences, it is rebarbative at first and bristles with difficulties. Tremendous obstacles hedge round a man's greatest pleasures – not his enjoyments taken one by one, but the various disciplines that reduce the rarest sensations to a matter of habit, formularize them and make them productive by creating for him a dramatic life within his life, by necessitating a prompt and exhorbitant dissipation of his vital forces.

'The conduct of war, the government of men and the practice of the arts represent principles of corruption which are placed as much out of reach for most men as is debauchery; all involve hidden secrets hard to uncover. But once a man has grappled with these great mysteries he finds himself bestriding a new world. Generals, ministers and artists are all under some pressure to plunge into dissipation by the need to find violent distraction from their ordinary way of life, so much at variance with the norm. War is after all debauchery in the expenditure of blood, as politics are a debauchery in the exploitation of interests. All unnesses are of one family. They are social monstrosities which have the magnetic pull of the abyss and draw us towards it as Saint Helena beckoned to Napoleon: its fascination makes us dizzy, and we desire to plumb its depths without knowing why. The idea of infinity perhaps resides in these great deeps, and they hold perhaps a strong and flattering appeal for man, who brings everything into the orbit of his experience. As a foil to the paradise of his studious hours and the joys of conception, the tired artist asks either for the sabbath-day rest like God himself – or, like Satan, infernal pleasures to oppose the activity of the senses to the activity of his faculties. Lord Byron could not have relaxed over the chatter of the whist-table which charms the leisure hours of retired tradesmen. Being a poet, he had to play a game of hazard with Sultan Mahmoud in which Greece was the stake.[38] In war does not man become a destroying angel, a kind of executioner, but on a gigantic scale? Do we not need abnormally powerful enchantments to make us accept the atrocious pains, so destructive of our frail envelope, which encircle the passions like a hedge of thorns? If a smoker writhes in convulsions and suffers something like agony after over-indulgence in tobacco, has he not nevertheless partaken of magic feasts in unknown fairylands? Without staying to wipe her feet, blood-soaked to the ankles, has not Europe returned to war over and over again? Is not mankind in general subject to fits of intoxication, as nature to paroxysms of rut? For the private citizen, for the Mirabeau who vegetates under a peaceful reign while dreaming of storms to come, debauchery takes in everything; it embraces lastingly life in every aspect, or rather it is a duel with an unknown power, with a monster: at first the monster strikes fear into you, you must seize him by the horns, at the cost of incredible exertions. Nature may have given you a constricted or sluggish stomach; you subdue it, expand it and teach it to carry its wine; you tame your intoxication, spend whole nights without sleep, in short you make yourself as hard-boiled as a cavalry officer by creating yourself a second time as if in mocking defiance of the Deity. When a man has changed his own nature in this way, when the raw recruit has disciplined himself to face the cannon and the fatigues of the march, without as yet being

38. Byron joined the Greeks in rebellion against the Turks, and died at Missolonghi in 1824.

enslaved to the monster, but without either of them yet knowing which will be the master, they roll over each other in the dust, now victorious, now vanquished, in a sphere in which everything is marvellous, in which the sorrows of the spirit are lulled to sleep, in which only the ghosts of ideas live on. Already the grim struggle has become a necessity.

'Materializing the fabulous heroes of legend who have sold their souls to the devil in order to obtain from him the power to do evil, the rake has bargained his death for all the pleasures of life multiplied and made fertile. Life, instead of flowing interminably between two dreary river banks, behind a merchant's counter or in a lawyer's office, races and bubbles along like a mountain torrent. In a word, debauchery is to the body what mystic joys are no doubt to the soul. Drunkenness plunges you into dreams whose phantasmagoria are as intriguing as those of ecstasy can be. It brings hours as delightful as a girl's caprices, spent in captivating conversation with friends, finding phrases which paint a whole existence, it gives you unalloyed, unrepining joys, allows you to travel untiringly and to utter whole poems in a few short sentences.

'The brutish satisfaction of the beast, into which science has probed in the search for a soul, is succeeded by the enchanting torpors yearned for by men tired of mental activity. Do they not all feel the need for complete repose, and is not debauchery a sort of tax levied on genius by the forces of evil?

Consider all great men: if they are not voluptuaries, it is because nature has denied them a robust constitution. Whether in mockery or through jealousy, some power vitiates their minds or their bodies in order to neutralize the achievements of their talents. During the hours spent drinking, men and women appear before you dressed up in the livery you have chosen for them, you are king of creation, and can refashion it nearer to the heart's desire. While you are in this perpetual delirium, the excitement of the gaming-table, if you so wish, will pour its molten lead into your veins. The day comes when you belong to the monster: you awake, as I did, in a fury; impotence is seated at your bedside. Were you a warrior? Consumption is devouring you. A diplomat? A cardiac flutter makes your life to hang by a thread. As for me, perhaps an infection of the lungs will tell me it is time to depart, as of old it told Raphael of Urbini, killed by too much loving. That is how I lived! I came to social life either too early or too late; it may be that I should have wreaked some havoc in it if I had not blunted my powers in this way. Was not the universe cured of Alexander by the cup of Hercules at the end of an orgy?[39] To conclude, there are certain thwarted destinies for which awaits either Heaven or Hell, debauchery or Saint Bernard's monastery.

'An hour or so since, I could not find the courage to show these two creatures the error of their ways,' he said, pointing to Euphrasie and Aquilina. 'In fact they were personifications of my own history, an image of my life! I could not accuse them, they appeared before me as my judges. However, in the middle of this living poem, as I was reeling under the onset of this disease, I encountered two crises productive of many a bitter pang. In the first place, a few days after I had hurled myself like Sardanapalus, on to my funeral pyre, I met Fœdora under the colonnade of the Bouffons. We were waiting for our carriages.

' "Ah! So you are still in the land of the living!"

'This remark translates the smile she gave to her attendant admirer as she no doubt told him my story and passed judgement on my love as being nothing out of the ordinary. She was congratulating herself mistakenly on her perspicacity. Oh! That I should still be dying for her, still adoring her, still seeing her in my excesses, in my bouts of drunkenness, in the beds of harlots, and should feel that I was a target for her sarcasms! If only I could have plunged my hand into my bosom, wrenched from it my love and cast it at her feet!

'In the second place, I easily exhausted my stock of money. But three years' austerity of diet had made me extraordinarily robust and, when I again became penniless, I was in a flourishing state of health. In order to continue the process by which I hoped to encompass my death, I signed short-term notes of hand, of which the day of settlement eventually arrived. What cruel

39. A gold goblet which, a myth relates, the god Helios gave to Hercules. Also the name given to large two-handled goblets. Legend has it that Alexander the Great died after emptying one at a draught.

emotions, and how acutely a young man feels them! I was not yet due for old age; I was still young, tenacious of life and fresh in spirit. My first debt revived all my virtues, which approached me with mournful steps and desolate demeanour. I was able to come to terms with them, as one does with an old aunt who scolds us to begin with but ends by shedding tears and handing us money. But my imagination was less indulgent: it showed me my name travelling from city to city wherever there are discount houses in Europe. As Eusebius Salverte has said,[40] "Our name is what we are." After much wandering, it would return, like a German *doppelgänger*, to the house I myself had never quitted, to wake me up with a start.

'Those bank officials, those incarnations of the commercial conscience, clad in grey and wearing the silver badge which is their masters' livery, had once been objects of indifference to me when I saw them walking through the streets of Paris; but now I hated them even before they hove in sight. One fine morning one of them was certain to call me to account for the eleven bills of exchange which had my signature scrawled on them. This same signature had been worth 3,000 francs, more than I was worth myself! The bailiffs, looking unmoved on every kind of despair, and even on death itself, rose up before me like the hangman saying to a condemned man: "It is striking half past three." Their clerks had the right to apprehend my person, to scribble down my name, to defile and make a joke of it. I WAS IN DEBT! To be in debt means that one no longer belongs to oneself. Other men could call me to account for my life. Why had I eaten *pudding à la chipolata*? Why did I drink chilled wines? Why did I sleep, walk, go about thinking and amusing myself and not pay them? In the middle of a poem, in the throes of an idea, at lunch with friends, everywhere jollity and good-humoured jesting, I might see an individual in a brown coat come in, with a shabby hat in his hands. This individual would be the debt I owed, my bill of exchange, a spectre who would blight my joy, force me to leave my table in order to talk to him, rob me of my gaiety, oblige me to give up my mistress,

40. Author, in 1824, of *A Historical and Philosophical Essay on the names of men, peoples and places.*

all I had, even the bed I lay on. Remorse for a crime is more bearable: it does not fling us into the street or a debtors' prison, it does not plunge us into such execrable sinks of vice; it merely brings us to the scaffold, where the executioner confers on it a sort of nobility. At the moment when our head falls, everybody believes we are innocent; whereas society allows not a single virtue to the penniless rake. And then, those two-legged debts dressed in green cloth, wearing blue spectacles or carrying multi-coloured umbrellas, those debts incarnate with which we find ourselves face to face at a street corner at a time when we were feeling cheerful,[41] these creatures were going to have the disgusting privilege of saying: "Monsieur de Valentin owes me money and won't pay. I've got him now. He had better not scowl at me!" We must bow and be gracious to our creditors. "When will you pay me?" they ask. And we find ourselves obliged to tell lies, to beg money of another man, cringe before a blockhead sitting on his cash-box, put up with his cold looks, his blood-sucker's stare which is worse than a blow on the face; we have to tolerate his ready-reckoner's homilies and his crass ignorance. A debt is a work of the imagination which such people do not comprehend. Often a borrower is swept along in the clutch of a noble impulse, while no great or generous motive ever informs or directs those who live in the world of money and know of nothing but money. I myself held money in horror.

'And then again, a bill of exchange may be metamorphosed into an old man with a family to feed and wearing the breast-plate of righteousness. I could perhaps find myself in debt to a *tableau vivant* by Greuze, a paralytic with a swarm of children, or a soldier's widow, all of them holding out their hands to me in supplication: fearsome creditors with whom one has to shed tears and to whom, even after we have paid them, we still owe charity. The night before the bills fell due I had gone to bed in the deceptively calm frame of mind of a prisoner awaiting execution or a man on the eve of a duel: such people always allow themselves to be lulled to sleep by some fallacious gleam of hope. But when I woke up in the morning and collected my

41. Throughout most of his life Balzac was obliged to go warily in public because of the danger of being arrested for debt.

wits, when I felt that my soul was imprisoned in a banker's wallet, set down in red ink on a statement of accounts, my debts began hopping about like locusts. I could see them inside my clock, on my chairs or encrusted in my favourite pieces of furniture. Delivered in bondage to the law-court harpies, those gentle inanimate household slaves, were to be carted off by bailiffs' men and flung brutally into the street. Ah! My worldly belongings were still flesh of my flesh. My door-bell rang not only in my flat, but also in my heart: it hit me where kings should be hit – on the head.[42] I suffered real martyrdom, with no heaven for recompense. Indeed, for a generous-hearted man, to be in debt is to be in hell, a hell inhabited by worse than demons, by brokers and bailiffs. An unpaid debt spells degradation; it is a first step in knavery and, worse still, a lie: it is a blueprint for crime, it knocks together the planks for the scaffold.

'My notes of hand were protested. Three days later I paid them, and this is how: a speculator proposed that I should sell him the island I possessed in the Loire in which my mother lay buried. I accepted. As I signed the contract in the office of the purchaser's notary, I sensed in the depths of this dark room the kind of chill one feels in a vault. I shivered as I recognized the same sort of damp cold as had gripped me as I stood on the edge of my father's grave. I took this chance event as an evil omen. I seemed to hear my mother's voice and see her ghost; some uncanny agency caused my name to resound in my ears in muffled tones amid the tolling of bells! The price I received for the island left me two thousand francs after the settlement of all my debts. I could certainly have resumed the peaceful existence of a scholar, returned to my garret after the experience I had gained of life, my head filled with an immense store of observations, and already having made something of a reputation for myself. But Fœdora had not relinquished her prey. We had often met in society. I ensured that my name should constantly sound in her ears, repeated by her suitors, who marvelled at my wit, my horses, my carriages, my success. She remained cold and in-

42. A reminiscence of a remark made by Cromwell when he had resolved on Charles the First's trial and execution: 'Princes must be knocked on the head.'

sensible to eveything, even to Rastignac's shocking remark: "He is killing himself for you!"

'I enlisted the whole world in my vengeance, but I was far from happy! In diving as I had down to the miry bedrock of my life, I had always and ever more keenly apprehended the delights of a shared love; I pursued it as a will-o'-the-wisp through chance encounters made at orgies. My misfortune was to be cheated in my noblest beliefs; I was punished for my virtuous acts by ingratitude, while my wickedness was rewarded by countless pleasures. A sinister morality, but wholly applicable to the debauchee! In short Fœdora had passed on to me the leprosy of her vanity. I looked deep into my soul and saw it to be gangrened and rotten. The devil had put the stamp of his cloven foot on my brow. Henceforth I could not dispense with the continual trepidations of a life put at risk every moment, or with the detestable refinements which riches accustom us to. Had I owned millions I should still have gone on gambling, gourmandizing, womanizing. I could no longer bear to be by myself. I needed harlots, boon-companions, wine and rich food to keep me in a perpetual daze. The bonds which tie a man to his family had snapped for ever in me. A galley-slave of pleasure, I had no choice but to carry out my predestined suicide. During the last days of my dwindling fortune, I plunged each night into incredible excesses; and yet each new morning flung me back into life. Like a man living on a life annuity, I could have walked through fire unperturbed. In the end I found myself left with a twenty-franc piece. Then I remembered Rastignac's stroke of luck . . .'

'But look here!' cried Raphael, suddenly remembering his talisman and pulling it out of his pocket.

Whether because, exhausted by the trials of that long day and the deep draughts of wine and punch, he was no longer in control of his senses; or because, exasperated by the vision he had conjured up of his past life, he had by degrees become intoxicated with the torrent of his own words, Raphael had worked himself up to a pitch of excitement like a maniac in a frenzy.

'To the devil with death!' he cried, brandishing the skin. 'I am for life now! I am rich and have all the virtues. Nothing can stand against me. Who would not be good-hearted when he is all-powerful? Aha! Ho ho! I have wished for two hundred thousand francs a year, and that's what I'll have! Bow down before me, you swine wallowing on this carpet as if it were a dungheap! I own you – though it's not a possession to boast about. I am rich. I can buy the lot of you, even that snoring deputy yonder. Come, you rabble of high society, on your knees! I'm your Pope.'

At that moment Raphael's vociferations, until then smothered by the *basso continuo* of snoring men, became suddenly audible. The majority of the sleepers woke up shouting, saw the disturber of the peace tottering about among them and blasted his drunken rowdiness with a chorus of curses.

'Hold your tongues!' Raphael shouted back. 'To your kennels, dogs! – Emile, I'm rolling in wealth. You shall have genuine Havanas.'

'I follow you,' the poet replied. '*Fœdora or death!* Go ahead. The sugar-sweet Fœdora has taken you in. All women are daughters of Eve. There's nothing dramatic in your story.'

'Ah! So you were asleep, you sly dog?'

'No, no . . . Fœdora or death. I take your meaning.'

'Wake up!' cried Raphael, striking Emile with the wild ass's skin as if he hoped to draw electric sparks from him.

'Death and damnation!' cried Emile, staggering to his feet and seizing Raphael round the waist. 'Come, my friend, remember that you are in the company of lost women.'

'I'm a millionaire!'

'Millionaire or not, you're certainly drunk.'

'Drunk with power. I'm able to kill you. Silence, I'm Nero! I'm Nebuchadnezzar!'

'Look, Raphael, we're not in respectable company. You ought to keep quiet for the sake of your own dignity.'

'I've kept quiet all through my life. Now I'm going to take vengeance on the whole world. I shan't waste my time squandering squalid money, I shall follow the example of the times, and epitomize the modern age, by consuming human lives, intellects and souls. That's no cheese-paring luxury, is it? – the opulence of the plague. I'll exterminate them all with yellow fever, blue, green fever, with armies, with scaffolds. Fœdora can be mine now . . . But no, I don't want Fœdora. She's my disease, I'm dying of Fœdora! I want to forget Fœdora.'

'If you go on shouting, I shall pick you up and carry you into the dining-room.'

'Do you see this skin? It's Solomon's testament. He's my property, that little pedant of a king. I own Arabia, Petraea, too! The universe is mine. You are mine if I wish it. Ah! if I wish it, beware! I can buy up all your editorial board, you'll be my valet. You shall write couplets and run my paper for me. Valet! *valet* means "He's in good health, because he doesn't do any thinking."'

At this, Emile dragged Raphael off into the dining-room.

'Yes, of course, my friend, I'm your valet. But you are going to be a newspaper editor. Quieten down! Behave yourself out of consideration for me! You like me, don't you?'

'Do I like you! You'll have Havana cigars with this skin. I come back to the skin, the skin is sovereign. A sovereign remedy too: I can cure corns. Have you any corns? I'll remove them.'

'I've never seen you in such a stupid mood.'

'Stupid, my friend? No. This skin shrinks whenever I express a desire . . . it's an antiphrasis. The brahmin – there's a brahmin in the woodpile – the brahmin was a joker because, you see, desires ought to stretch . . .'

'True enough.'

'I tell you . . .'

'Yes, that's very true. I agree with you. Desires stretch . . .'

'I tell you, the skin . . .'

'Yes.'

'You don't believe me. I know you, my friend, you tell as many lies as a new-crowned king.'[43]

'How can you expect me to agree with your drunken ravings?'

'Will you bet on it? I'll prove it to you. Let's measure it up.'

'God help us!' cried Emile as he saw Raphael busily ferreting about in the dining-room. 'He'll never go to sleep.'

Valentin, inspired with the cunning of a monkey thanks to the singular lucidity which occasionally contrasts in drinkers with

43. A side-hit at Louis-Philippe.

the obtuse hallucinations of intoxication, managed to find an inkstand and a napkin as he went on muttering: 'Let's measure it, let's measure it.'

'All right,' said Emile. 'Let's measure it.'

The two friends stretched out the napkin and superimposed the shagreen skin upon it. Emile, whose hand seemed steadier than Raphael's, used a quill to draw an ink line round the edges of the talisman, while his friend was saying:

'I wished for an income of two hundred thousand francs, did I not? Well, when I have it, you will see that all my shagreen[44] has diminished.'

'Yes . . . Now go to sleep. Shall I settle you on this sofa? There, are you all right?'

'Yes, thank you, my nursling of the Press. You shall keep me amused, you shall whisk the flies away from me. A friend in need has the right to be the friend of the man in power. And I *will* give you Hav . . . ana . . . ci . . . gars.'

'Come then, sleep off your gold, millionaire.'

'And you, sleep off your articles. Goodnight. Say goodnight then to Nebuchadnezzar! . . . Love! Let's drink! To France. Glory and rich . . . riches.'

Soon the two friends added their snores to the music that echoed through the various rooms. A concert without an audience! The candles burned down one by one and shattered their crystal sockets as they went out. Night wrapped its black crêpe around the long orgy in which Raphael's tale had been as it were a verbal orgy, an orgy of words without matter, or matter too often left unexpressed.

*

The next day, towards noon, the lovely Aquilina arose yawning, still tired, bearing on her cheeks the marks of the painted velvet stool upon which her head had rested. Euphrasie, awakened by her companion's movements, suddenly started up with a hoarse cry; her pretty face, so fair and fresh the night before, was as yellow and pale as that of a prostitute on her way to the almshouse. One by one the guests bestirred themselves, uttering harsh groans as they felt the stiffness in their arms and legs and

11 A word-play on *shagreen* and *chagrin*.

the thousand different forms that exhaustion took as it smote them on their wakening. A footman opened the blinds and windows of the salons. Everyone was now up, recalled to life by the warm sunbeams glistening on the heads of the late slumbering company. The women's elegantly dressed hair had become dishevelled as they tossed and turned in their sleep, and their costume had lost its freshness, so that they presented a hideous spectacle in the bright light of day: their hair hung down untidily, the expression on their faces had changed, their eyes, once sparkling, were dull with lassitude. Complexions that had been so radiant in artificial light now looked horribly bilious; lymphatic faces, so soft and lily-white, in repose, had turned green, while lips, deliciously rosy a short time since, but now parched and pallid, bore the shameful stigmata of drunkenness.

The men disowned their mistresses of the night before on seeing them so robbed of colour, so cadaverous, like flowers crushed underfoot after a procession has passed along the street. But these disdainful men were even more disgusting to look at. You would have shuddered to see those human masks – with sunken, red-rimmed eyes too blurred, apparently, to take anything in – torpid with wine, dulled by troubled slumbers which far from refreshing them, had left them more tired than before. Those haggard faces, exhibiting unblushingly the grosser appetites with no spark of the poetry with which we imaginatively clothe them, gave an unspeakable impression of ferocity and cold bestiality. This awakening of vice naked and unadorned, this skeleton of evil stripped to the bone, cold, empty, unenhanced by the sophistries of intelligence and the enchantments of luxury, horrified even those intrepid athletes most accustomed to wrestling with debauchery. Artists and courtesans were dumb as they gazed wild-eyed at the disorder reigning in the suite of rooms, laid waste and ravaged by the fires of passion.

Suddenly satanic laughter resounded when Taillefer, hearing the muffled groans of his guests, attempted to salute them with a forced smile. His blood-red, sweaty, bloated face presided over this infernal scene like the very picture of unrepentant crime (See *The Red Inn*)[45]. The picture was complete: life at its

45. See footnotes pp. 13 and 64.

most sordid in the midst of luxury, a horrible medley of ostentation and destitution, the awakening of vice after it had squeezed all the fruits of life in its fierce grasp, leaving nothing around it but defilement and wreckage and falsehoods, in which it no longer believes. It was like Death grinning in the midst of a family stricken by the plague: gone are the perfumes and the dazzling lights; gone the cheerful jests and all ardent desire. All that remains is the sickening odour of disgust and the poignant moral it preaches; but also the morning sun, as bright as truth, the fresh air as pure as virtue, in contrast to the over-heated atmosphere laden with the vapours of an orgy!

Hardened though they were to vice, not a few of the girls present called to mind how when younger they would awake from sleep, pure and innocent, with the vision, glimpsed through cottage casements, twined round with roses and honeysuckle, of a lush landscape ringing with the lark's joyous trills, lit by a misty sunrise and decked with the whimsical arabesques of the dew. Others called up the vision of the family partaking of the morning repast: a scene of indefinable charm, parents and children gathered round a table, the innocent laughter, the food as simple as the hearts of those who shared it. An artist was thinking of the calm of his studio, the chaste lines of the statue he was working on and the graceful model who was awaiting him. A young man, remembering the lawsuit in which the fate of a family was involved, turned his thought to the important conference which required his presence. The scholar yearned for his study and the noble work he was engaged in writing. Hardly one but reproached himself for time ill-spent.

It was then that Emile, as fresh and pink-faced as the smartest salesman in a fashionable shop, made his appearance, a smile on his face.

'You're all uglier than debt-collectors!' he cried. 'You'll not be doing a stroke of work now, the day's wasted. I'm for having lunch.'

'Hearing this, Taillefer left the room to give some orders. The women languidly departed in search of mirrors to repair the disorder of their toilet. Each guest pulled himself together. Those most sunk in vice lectured the novices. The courtesans derided those revellers who seemed to lack the stomach to prolong this exhausting banquet. In a moment the spectres came to life again, gathered into groups and smilingly questioned one another. A few footmen, deft and quick-footed, rapidly moved the furniture and other pieces back to their proper places. A splendid breakfast was served, and the guests crowded back into the dining-room. And there, although the ineffaceable imprint of the night's excesses persisted, at any rate there were some traces left of life and thought, as in the last convulsions of a dying man. As in a Shrovetide procession, the saturnalian revelries were interred by mummers wearied with dancing, surfeited with drunkenness and prepared to accuse pleasure itself of lacking savour rather than admit their own inability to savour it. No sooner had this dauntless assembly gathered round the capitalist's table when Cardot who, the previous evening, had prudently vanished after dinner to finish his orgy in the marital bed, was observed, a gentle smile hovering over his judicious features. He seemed to have had a presentiment of some legacy to pore over, to divide, inventory and engross, some inheritance fraught with deeds to be drawn up, big with fees, as juicy as the quivering tenderloin into which the host was even then plunging his knife.

'Oh ho! We're going to take breakfast with a notary duly present!' de Cursy exclaimed.

'You are just in time to assess and endorse all these documents,' the banker said to him, pointing to the dishes on the table.

'There's no will to be drawn up here. As for marriage contracts, perhaps yes!' said the man of science, who for the first time within a year had enjoyed a first-class sleeping partner.

'Oh! Ho!'

'Ha! Ha!'

'One moment please,' said Cardot, deafened by this chorus of bad jokes. 'I am here on serious business. I am bringing six millions to one of you.' A deep silence ensued. Then, turning to Raphael who at that moment was casually mopping his eyes with a corner of his napkin, 'Sir,' he said, 'your mother's maiden name, was it not O'Flaherty?'

'Yes,' Raphael replied automatically. 'Barbara Maria.'

'Have you in your possession your birth certificate and that of Madame de Valentin?'

'I think so.'

'Well, sir,' Cardot continued, 'you would appear to be the sole heir of Major O'Flaherty, late of Calcutta, who died in August 1828.'

'Why, it's an *incalcuttable* fortune!' cried the trenchant critic.

'The major having made several bequests in favour of various public bodies, the French government entered a claim for his estate with the East India Company,' the notary resumed. 'As of now it is in realizable assets. For the last fortnight I had been vainly seeking for the heirs and assigns of the said Barbara Maria O'Flaherty when yesterday, at the dinner-table . . .'

Just then Raphael suddenly stood up with the spasmodic movement of a man who receives a knife-thrust. There was a kind of silent acclamation. The guests' first reaction was prompted by unexpressed envy – all eyes were turned on him like so many bright lights. Then a murmur, such as one hears among a discontented audience in the stalls, a noise like that of a distant riot started up and swelled in volume: every man present had something to say about the tremendous fortune which the notary had announced. Completely restored to his senses by this prompt act of obedience on the part of fate, Raphael quickly spread out on the table the napkin with which, not long since, he had measured the dimensions of the wild ass's skin. Paying no attention to the hubbub, he laid the talisman down on it, and gave an involuntary shiver as he perceived that a narrow margin separated the skin from the outline traced on the linen cloth.

'Why now, what's the matter with him?' Taillefer exclaimed. 'He's made an easy fortune.'

'Support him, Châtillon!'[46] said Bixiou to Emile. 'Joy is killing him.'

A fearful pallor brought out every muscle in the drawn face of the newly-designated heir. His features shrank, the skin over

---

46. A garbled quotation from Voltaire's tragedy *Zaïre*.

his bones turned white and the hollows in his cheeks grew dark. The mask was livid and the eyes were fixed in a stare. He was looking upon DEATH. The millionaire banker surrounded with faded courtesans and surfeited faces, this spectacle of joy on its death-bed, was the living image of his life. Raphael looked three times at the talisman which had room and to spare within the inexorable lines penned on the napkin. His attempts to doubt his eyes were frustrated by a clear presentiment. The world was his, he could do what he wished but wished to do nothing henceforth. Like a traveller lost in the desert, he had a small quantity of water to slake his thirst and had to measure his life by the number of draughts he took. He could reckon up the days every wish must cost him. He now believed in the magic skin. He listened to his own breathing. He already felt ill and was asking himself: 'Am I not consumptive? Did not my mother die of tuberculosis?'

'Ha! Ha! Raphael,' said Aquilina. 'You're going to have a really good time. What are you going to give me?'

'Let's drink to the death of his uncle, Major O'Flaherty! There's a man for you!'

'Raphael will be a peer of France.'

'Bah! What's a peer of France since the Revolution of July!' asked the trenchant critic.[47]

'Will you take a box at the Bouffons?'

'I hope you'll stand us all treat,' said Bixiou.

'Raphael's the fellow to do things on a grand scale,' said Emile.

The cheers and laughter of his fellow guests resounded in Valentin's ears, but not a word did he take in. He was vaguely thinking of the routine, apathetic life of a Breton peasant, over-burdened with children, ploughing his field, living on buck-wheat bread, drinking his cider straight from the jug, believing in the Blessed Virgin and His Majesty the King, making his Easter communion, dancing on Sundays on the village green, and listening to the priest's sermon without understanding a word of it. At this moment the spectacle before him – the gilded

47. The Monarchy of July had abolished the hereditary principle and cut down the powers of the new peerage.

wainscots, the courtesans, the food, the luxury – all seized him by the throat and set him coughing.

'Do you want some asparagus?' the banker called out to him.

'*I want nothing*!' Raphael answered in thundering tones.

'Bravo!' Taillefer retorted. 'You understand what wealth is: the freedom to be impertinent. You belong to us! Gentlemen, let us drink to the potency of gold. Monsieur de Valentin, now a millionaire six times over, has come into power. He's a king; he can do anything, he's above everything, like all rich men. Henceforth, the statement: ALL FRENCHMEN ARE EQUAL BEFORE THE LAW, in the first clause of the Charter, has no application to him.[48] He will not obey the laws, the laws will obey him. There are no scaffolds or hangmen for millionaires.

'No,' replied Raphael, 'they are their own executioners.'

'Another vulgar error!' the banker shouted.

'Let's drink!' said Raphael, stuffing his talisman into his pocket.

'What are you up to?' Emile asked him, catching at his hand. 'Gentlemen,' he continued addressing the company who were more than a little taken aback by Raphael's reactions, 'there is something you must know. Our friend de Valentin – I mean MONSIEUR LE MARQUIS DE VALENTIN – possesses a secret for making a fortune. His wishes come true at the very moment he utters them. Unless he wants us to think of him as a heartless lackey, he's going to make us all rich.'

'Ah! darling Raphael, I'll tell you what I want: a pearl necklace,' cried Euphrasie.

'If he has any gratitude he'll give me two carriages, each of them harnessed with lovely fast horses!' said Aquilina.

'Wish me an income of a hundred thousand francs!'

'I want some cashmere shawls.'

'I want my debts paid!'

'Wish an apoplexy on my uncle, the old skinflint!'

'Raphael, I'll settle for ten thousand francs' income.'

48. The Charter of French liberties, 'granted' in 1814 and amended in 1830. There is no need to emphasize Balzac's cynical rejection of the principles it was supposed to embody.

'What a lot of donations seem to be required!' the notary said.

'The least he could do would be to cure my gout!'

'Bring down the price of the funds!' cried the banker.

All these requests exploded like the shower of rockets which terminates a firework display. And those who besought him so frantically spoke perhaps more in earnest than in jest.

'My dear friend,' said Emile in a grave tone, 'I'll be satisfied with two hundred thousand francs a year. Come now, do your job like a good fellow!'

'Emile,' said Raphael, 'don't you know what that would cost me?'

'No excuses!' the poet exclaimed. 'Ought we not to make sacrifices for our friends?'

'I've a good mind to wish for the death of every one of you!' Valentin replied, casting a sombre and searching look on all the guests.

'Dying men are devastatingly cruel,' laughed Emile. Then he added seriously: 'You're rich now. Well, I won't give you two months to become stinkingly selfish. You're already stupid and can't take a joke. All you need now is actually to believe in your magic skin . . .'

Raphael, for fear of being made the butt of his fellow diners' jests, relapsed into silence and drank himself into momentary forgetfulness of his fatal power.

3. The Death-Agony

In the early days of December, an old man past seventy was walking along the Rue de Varenne regardless of the rain, and peering up at every front door he passed, looking for the address of Marquis Raphael de Valentin with the simplicity of a child and the absorbed air of a philosopher. On his face, fringed with long, untidy grey hair and withered like an old parchment shrivelling in the fire, could be read the signs of a violent sorrow struggling with an authoritarian nature. If a painter had come upon this singular individual, dressed in black, thin and bony, undoubtedly, once back in his studio, he would have consigned him to his album and written underneath the portrait: *A Classical Poet in search of a rhyme.* Having checked the number which had been given him, this living replica of Rollin[1] knocked timidly at the door of a magnificent mansion.

'Is Monsieur Raphael at home?' the worthy man asked of the liveried doorkeeper.

'Monsieur le Marquis receives no one,' the servant replied, gulping down a large sop of bread which he was spooning out of an ample bowl of coffee.

'But his carriage is there,' replied the unknown caller, and pointed to a smart equipage standing under a canopy of wood fashioned like a canvas awning which extended over the flight of steps to keep the rain off. 'He will be coming out. I'll wait for him.'

'Oh no, old chap! You might be here till tomorrow morning,' the porter replied. 'There's always a carriage waiting for the master. But please go away. I should lose an annuity of six hundred francs if I only once allowed inside, without orders to the contrary, any person not belonging to the house.'

At that moment a tall old man whose costume was very like that of an usher in a civil service department emerged from the

1. A professor of the Collège de France (1661–1741), the author of a treatise on education; his pedantry was almost proverbial.

entrance hall and hurried down the steps as he scanned the dumbfounded old petitioner.

'Anyway, here's Monsieur Jonathas,' said the porter, 'Ask him.'

The two old men, drawn to each other by sympathy or mutual curiosity, met in the centre of the vast circular courtyard in which tufts of grass were growing between the paving-stones. A chilling silence reigned in this house. Merely to see Jonathas was to feel curious about the mystery written on his features and hinted at by every aspect of this gloomy residence.

*

Raphael's first care on entering into possession of the immense fortune his uncle had left him, had been to track down the devoted old servant on whose affection he could count. Jonathas wept for joy on seeing his young master again, for he believed he had said good-bye to him for ever. But his happiness was unbounded when the marquis promoted him to the exalted post of steward. Old Jonathas became an intermediary power between Raphael and the rest of the world. Put in supreme control of his master's fortune, the blind agent of his undivulged intentions, he served as a sixth sense by means of which the emotions of life filtered through to Raphael.

'Pardon me, sir, but I would like to speak to Monsieur Raphael,' the old man said to Jonathas, walking a little way up the flight of steps in order to shelter from the rain.

'Speak to Monsieur le Marquis?' the steward exclaimed. 'He scarcely ever speaks a word even to me, who've been as good as a foster-father to him.'

'But I too am his foster-father,' the old man cried. 'If your wife once fed him at her breast, I myself laid him at the breast of the Muses. He is my nursling, my child, my *carus alumnus*! I shaped his intelligence, cultivated his understanding, developed his genius – to my own honour and glory, if I dare say so. Is he not one of the most remarkable men of our time? I had him under me in the sixth and third classes and in rhetoric.[2] I was his teacher.'

2. The top classics form in French schools, where seniority rises from VI to I, not the reverse as in English schools.

'Ah! You are Monsieur Porriquet?'

'I am indeed. But, sir . . .'

'Hush hush!' said Jonathas to two kitchen-boys whose voices were breaking the claustrophobic silence in which the house was wrapped.

'But, sir,' the schoolmaster continued. 'Is Monsieur le Marquis ill?'

'Why, sir,' Jonathas replied, 'the good Lord alone knows what's wrong with my master. See here; the whole of Paris doesn't contain two houses like this one. Do you hear? Not two houses. No, indeed. Monsieur le Marquis acquired this house from a duke and peer, and has spent three hundred thousand francs furnishing it. Look now: that's quite a sum, three hundred thousand francs! But every room in the house is a real miracle. "Good! I said to myself when I saw all this splendour, it's going to be the same as with his late grandfather: the young marquis is going to hold open house!" Nothing of the sort: my master has refused to see anyone. He leads a very peculiar life, Monsieur Porriquet, you follow me, an *inconciliable*[3] life! He gets up every day at the same time. I alone, mark you, I alone am allowed to go into his room. I wake him at seven o'clock, winter and summer alike. An odd arrangement, eh? Once in, I say to him:

' "Monsieur le Marquis, it's time to wake up and get dressed."

'He wakes up and gets dressed. I have to hand him his dressing-gown, which is always cut in the same style and in the same material. It's my job to replace it when it's no longer serviceable, merely to save him the trouble of asking for a new one. Could you credit it? The fact is he has a thousand francs a day to spend and he does what he pleases, the dear lad. What's more, I'm so fond of him that if he fetched me a cuff on the right cheek I'd turn him the left one! If he told me to do much more difficult things than he does, I'd still do them, you know. As it is, he gives me so many fiddling little things to do that it takes me all my time. He wants to read the papers, right? Well, I'm ordered to put them in the same place on the same table. I also come to shave him every day at the same time, and my hand mustn't

3. Jonathas is given to malapropisms. This is one for 'inconceivable'.

tremble. The chef would lose the three thousand francs' annuity waiting for him after Monsieur's death if lunch wasn't served *inconciliably* every morning at ten, and dinner exactly at five. The menu for every day in the year is drawn up in advance. Monsieur le Marquis has nothing to wish for. He has strawberries when strawberries can be got, and mackerel as soon as the first delivery reaches Paris. The bill of fare is printed: he knows by heart in the morning what his dinner will be. Also he dresses at the same time, in the same clothes, the same linen, always put out by me, d'you see, on the same chair. I also have to take care that his clothes are always made of the same cloth; and when necessary, supposing his frock-coat shows signs of wear, I have to put out another in its place without a word. If it's fine day, I go in and say to my master:

'"Should you not take the air, sir?"'

'He answers yes or no. If he's thinking of going out for a drive he doesn't have to wait for his horses, they're always in the shafts: the coachman's *inconciliably* there, whip in hand, as you see him now. In the evenings, after dinner, Monsieur goes one day to the Opéra and another day to the Ital . . . but no, he hasn't been to the Italians yet. I only managed to get a box for him yesterday. Then he comes in at exactly eleven o'clock and goes to bed. Any time of the day he's doing nothing, he reads; he reads and reads, that's his fancy. I have to go through the *Journal de la Librairie*[4] before he does so as to buy new books, so that he can find them on his mantelpiece the day they come out. It's my job to go to his room every hour to look after the fire and everything else and to see that he has everything he could want. I tell you, sir, he gave me a little note-book to learn by heart, with all my jobs written down in it: a regular catechism! In summer I must lay in stocks of ice to keep the temperature at the same degree of coolness, and at all seasons I have to put fresh flowers everywhere around. And he's so rich! He can spend a thousand francs a day and satisfy every whim. He had to make do with the bare necessities of life long enough, poor boy! He doesn't bother anyone. He's as good as good can be, he

4. This was the official list, which had been appearing since 1811, of all the new publications printed in France.

never complains but, mind you, there mustn't be the slightest sound in the house nor in the garden! In short, my master hasn't to state a single wish; everything goes by clockwork and by the book. And he's right: if you don't keep the servants under your thumb, everything is soon at sixes and sevens. I tell him everything he's due to do, and he listens. You wouldn't believe how far he's carried all this. His rooms are all . . . how would you say? . . . laid out in a row. It's like this: suppose he opens the door of his bedroom or study. Click! All the other doors spring open – it's some mechanism that does it. That way he can go from one end of the house to the other without having to open a single door. It's nice and handy, and makes things easy for us servants. And that cost a fortune, I can tell you! Well, to put it in a nutshell, Monsieur Porriquet, he said to me:

' "Jonathas, you'll look after me like a baby in his swaddling clothes." Yes, sir, that's how he put it: in his swaddling clothes! "You'll have to see to all my wants for me."

'I'm the master, you understand? And it's almost as if he were the servant. But why? You may well ask. That's what nobody knows, except him and the good Lord above. It's *inconciliable*!'

'He must be writing a poem,' said the professor.

'You think he's writing a poem, sir? It must be a hard grind then! But I don't think so, you know. He often tells me he wants to live like a piece of *vergetation*, he wants to *vergetate*. Why, it was only yesterday, Monsieur Porriquet, he was looking at a tulip and while he was dressing he said:

' "That's my life . . . I'm *vergetating*, my good Jonathas!" Now they say he's become a *manymoniac*. It's *inconciliable*.'

'Everything points to the fact, Jonathas,' the schoolmaster resumed with an air of grave authority which profoundly impressed the old manservant, 'that your master is engaged on some important project. He is immersed in far-reaching meditations and doesn't want to be distracted by the preoccupations of daily life. Lost in his intellectual labours, a man of genius forgets everything else. One day the celebrated Newton . . .'

'Newton, you say?' said Jonathas, 'I don't think I know him.'

'Newton, a great mathematician,' Porriquet continued, 'spent twenty-four hours leaning his elbow on a table; when he came out of his reverie the next day, he still thought it was the day before, just as if he had been sleeping . . . I'll go and see your master, the dear young man. Perhaps I could be of some use to him.'

'Not so fast!' Jonathas exclaimed. 'Even if you were the King of France – the real one, I mean[5] – you wouldn't get in unless you broke the doors down and walked in over my dead body. But, Monsieur Porriquet, I'll run and tell him you're here and I'll ask straight out: "Shall I show him up?" He'll answer yes or no. Never do I say to him: *Do you wish? Do you want? Does Monsieur desire?* "Those words are ruled out of the conversation. I let slip one of them once. "Do you want to be the death of me?" he asked, in a proper rage.

Jonathas left the old schoolmaster in the hall signalling to him to remain there; but he was back shortly with a favourable answer and led the retired teacher through a suite of sumptuous rooms which all had their doors open. Porriquet espied his pupil from afar sitting by the fireplace. Wrapped in a dressing-gown of large patterned material and sunk deep in a well-sprung armchair, Raphael was reading the newspaper. The extreme melancholy to which he appeared a prey was evident in the unhealthy posture of his slumped body, it was painted on his brow and on his face which was as pallid as a withered flower. There was about him that kind of effeminate grace which distinguishes wealthy invalids, not to mention certain peculiar details. His hands, like those of a pretty woman, were of a soft and delicate whiteness. His fair hair, which had worn thin, was curled round his temples with studied coquetry. A Greek cap, pulled awry by a tassel which was too heavy for the light cashmere of which it was made, drooped over one side of his head He had dropped at his feet the malachite paper-knife set with gold which he had been using to cut the pages of a book. On his knees was the amber mouthpiece of a magnificent Indian hookah whose enamelled spirals lay across the carpet like a snake and whose fragrant perfume he was forgetting to

5. That is, Charles X, who had abdicated in 1830. Jonathas, an old-fashioned loyalist, evidently regards the present king, Louis-Philippe, as a usurper.

inhale. And yet the young man's general air of physical debility was belied by a pair of blue eyes into which it seemed as if all life had withdrawn and which shone with an intensity of feeling which immediately attracted attention. It was a painful gaze to meet.

Some men might have read despair in it, others an inner struggle as terrible as remorse. It was the searching gaze of the impotent man who chokes his desires back into the innermost recesses of his heart, or that of a miser allowing his fancy to play with the thought of all the pleasures that his money might procure him but refusing to indulge in them so as not to make inroads on his hoard; or the gaze of Prometheus in chains, of the fallen Napoleon when he learned at the Elysée Palace in 1815 of the error in strategy committed by his enemies, asked for command of the army for another twenty-four hours, and was refused it. Such a gaze as is seen only in the eyes of a conqueror who is also a damned soul! Such a gaze, too, as Raphael had cast, a few months earlier, on the Seine and on his last gold coin as he staked it on the gaming-table. He was subjecting his will, his intelligence to the gross common sense of an old peasant scarcely civilized by fifty years of domestic service. Glad almost to become a sort of automaton, he was abdicating life for the sake of living and plucking all the poetry of desire from his soul. In order the better to contend with the cruel power whose challenge he had accepted, he had attained chastity in somewhat the same manner as Origen,[6] by castrating his imagination.

The day after he had been suddenly enriched by a legacy, and had seen the shrinkage of the wild ass's skin, he was dining with his notary, and over dessert heard a rather fashionable physician telling the story of how a Swiss consumptive had cured himself of his disease. This man had not spoken one word for ten years, and had trained himself to breathe only six times a minute in the dense atmosphere of a cow-house while following an extremely light system of dieting. 'I model myself on that man!' thought Raphael, who was determined to live at any price. In the lap of luxury, he led as mechanical a life as a steam-engine.

6. In order to avoid succumbing to the sin of lust, Origen, a third-century Christian fanatic, is said to have emasculated himself.

As the old schoolmaster contemplated this mummified youth, he shuddered: in this slight and sickly body everything seemed artificial. Looking at the marquis whose eyes were burning and whose brow was heavy with thought, he could no longer recognize the schoolboy with the fresh, rosy complexion and agile young limbs whom he remembered. If the worthy classicist – a sagacious critic and champion of good taste in literature – had ever read Lord Byron, it would have occurred to him that he was looking at Manfred when he had hoped to see Childe Harold.

'Good-day, Papa Porriquet,' Raphael said to his former teacher as he pressed the old man's icy fingers in his moist and fevered hand. 'How are you keeping?'

'I'm keeping very well, thank you,' replied the old man, frightened by the touch of that clammy hand. 'And yourself?'

'Oh, I hope to stay in good health.'

'You are no doubt busy on some splendid work of literature?'

'No,' Raphael replied. '*Exegi monumentum*, Papa Porriquet. I made one important contribution to science and now I have done with it for ever. I scarcely know where my manuscript is.'

'It's written in a pure style, I trust?' the old teacher asked. 'I hope you won't have adopted the barbarous jargon of that new school which thinks it is performing miracles by re-inventing Ronsard!'[7]

'My work is devoted solely to physiology.'

'Well, that's different,' the schoolmaster observed. 'Grammar has to adapt itself to new scientific advances. Nevertheless, my boy, a clear, harmonious style, the language of Massillon, Monsieur de Buffon and the great Racine, a classical style in short, never does any harm. But, my friend,' he broke off and added: 'I was forgetting the purpose of my visit. It's not a disinterested one.'

Remembering too late the verbose and flowery eloquence to which long years in the classroom had accustomed his former teacher, Raphael almost repented of having admitted him. But,

7. The 'new school' is the Romantic one. In 1828 the rising critic, Sainte-Beuve, published a work on sixteenth-century poetry and drama which traced the affinity of this 'new school' with Ronsard and his contemporary poets.

just when he was on the point of wishing he were outside, he swiftly repressed his secret desire, casting a furtive glance at the wild ass's skin, which was hung up where he could see it, pinned out on a piece of white material on which its fateful outlines were carefully traced by a red line exactly enclosing it. Since the fatal orgy Raphael was stifling every lightest whim and had been living in such a way as not to cause the slightest tremor in the terrible talisman. The skin was like a tiger with which he had to live without awakening its ferocity. So he listened patiently to the old teacher's long-winded discourse. It took old Porriquet an hour to tell of the persecutions to which he had been subjected since the Revolution of July. The worthy man, being in favour of a strong government, had expressed the patriotic desire that grocers should remain behind their counters, that statesmen should be left to conduct affairs of state, that barristers should confine their activities to the law-courts and peers of the realm to the Luxembourg,[8] but one of the Citizen-King's popular ministers had had him dismissed from his post on the grounds of his Carlism.[9] So the old man was out of a job, with nowhere to live and no means of subsistence. He had a penniless nephew who depended on him for his maintenance fees at the Seminary of Saint-Sulpice; and it was less for himself than for his adopted child that he had come to beg his former pupil to appeal to the new minister, not for his reappointment, but for the post of principal in a provincial college. Raphael was about to succumb to an invincible drowsiness when the petitioner's droning voice at last ceased to rumble in his ears. Compelled by sheer politeness to look into the colourless, fixed eyes of the old man and listen to his slow, emphatic delivery, he had been reduced to a state of torper, mesmerized by an inexplicable inertial force.

'Well, my good old Porriquet,' he replied without knowing for sure what question he was answering, 'I can do nothing, nothing at all. But *I most heartily wish* that you may succeed.'

At that moment, without observing what effect this conventional phrase, dictated by egoism and indifference, had on the

8. The palace at which the French peerage assembled.
9. Loyalty to the ex-king Charles X.

old man with his sallow, wrinkled forehead, Raphael leapt up like a startled roe. He saw a thin white space appear between the edge of the dark skin and the red ink outline. He let forth so terrible a roar that the poor schoolmaster was scared out of his wits.

'Begone, you old fool!' he cried. 'You'll get your appointment! Couldn't you have asked me to settle an annuity of three thousand francs on you rather than to utter a suicidal wish? Your visit in that case would not have cost me anything. There are a hundred thousand jobs available in France, but I've only one life! The life of one man is worth more than all the jobs in the world ... Jonathas!'

Jonathas appeared.

'See what you've done, you infernal idiot! Why did you propose that I should see this gentleman?' he asked, pointing to the petrified old man. 'Did I put my soul in your keeping so that you should tear it to shreds? You have just shortened my life by ten years. One more mistake like that, and you'll be following me to the grave as I followed my father. Would it not have been preferable to possess the lovely Fœdora rather than to give this old carcass, this shred and tatter of humanity, what he wanted? I've money enough for such as him. Besides, let all the Porriquets in the world die of hunger, what do I care?'

Raphael was white with anger; a thin line of foam showed between his quivering lips and there was a bloodthirsty expression in his eyes. At the sight of him, the two old men were seized with convulsive shudders, like two children discovering an adder. The young man sank back into his armchair. Then a sort of mental reaction set in and tears streamed from his burning eyes.

'Oh! My life! My lovely life! ...' he said. 'There must be no more charitable thoughts! No more love! Nothing more!'

He turned to the old teacher.

'The harm is done, old friend,' he continued in a gentle voice, I shall have amply rewarded you for the care you gave me, and the thing that harms me will at least have done some good to a worthy and honest man.'

These almost unintelligible words were spoken in so desolate a tone that the two old men wept as one weeps when one hears a moving air sung in a foreign language.

'He must be epileptic!' Porriquet whispered.

'You are as kind as ever, good friend,' Raphael continued in mild tones. 'You are trying to excuse me. Infirmity cannot be blamed on a man, whereas inhumanity counts as a vice. Leave me now,' he added. 'Tomorrow or the day after, perhaps even this evening, you will receive notice of your appointment, for *resistance* has triumphed over *movement*.[10] Good-bye.'

The old man withdrew, horror-stricken and a prey to lively anxiety about the state of Valentin's mental health. For him this scene had had a vaguely supernatural flavour. He doubted the evidence of his senses and was wondering if he had not just awakened from a painful dream.

'Listen to me, Jonathas,' the young man said to his old servant. 'Try to understand the mission I have entrusted to you.'

'Yes, Monsieur le Marquis.'

'It is as though I were a man not subject to the laws commonly governing humanity.'

'Yes, Monsieur le Marquis.'

'All the pleasures of life disport themselves around my death-bed like so many alluring ballet-dancers: if I beckon to them, I die. Death dogs me always! You must be a wall between the world and me.'

'Yes, Monsieur le Marquis,' the old manservant replied, wiping his lined forehead which was bathed in sweat. 'But if you don't want to see ballet-dancers, how will you manage this evening at the Italians? An English family returning to London has sold me their season-ticket, which gives you a wonderful box, oh, a superb box! on the first tier.'

Raphael had fallen into a brown study and was no longer listening.

*

10. Under the Monarchy of July 1830 two rival policies were struggling for mastery: conservatism (*resistance*) and liberalism (*movement*). Porriquet's appointment to a headmastership will mark a triumph for the former policy, since he himself is a conservative. However, Raphael's enigmatic remark refers also to his private predicament, the life-force (*movement*) having lost yet another battle in the struggle against the force of death (*resistance*).

Do you see that magnificent carriage? From outside it looks like a simple brown brougham, but its panels are resplendent with the coat of arms of an ancient and noble family. As it sweeps along, the shop-girls stare in admiration and with longing at the yellow satin, the Savonnerie carpet, the braid trimmings which are as fresh as rice-straw, the downy cushions and the sound-proof plate-glass. Two footmen in livery ride behind this aristocratic coach; but inside, the silk upholstery supports a fevered head with dark rings round the eyes, the head of Raphael, sad and pensive. The fatal image of wealth! He is speeding through Paris like an arrow and arrives before the doors of the Théâtre Favart;[11] the carriage steps are let down, the two valets support him, and an envious crowd stares at him.

'What's he done, that chap, that he should be so rich?' asked a down-at-heel law student who, for lack of a few francs, was denied the chance of listening to Rossini's magic harmonies.

Raphael walked slowly along the aisles of the auditorium, promising himself no enjoyment of the pleasures he had envied so much in former times. While waiting for the second act of *Semiramis*, he walked about in the foyer and wandered through the galleries, not bothering about his box, which he had not yet entered. Already, pride of ownership had died away in his heart. Like any invalid, all he could think of was the disease that afflicted him. Leaning against the mantel of the fireplace in the foyer, crowded with fops young and old, past and present ministers, peers without peerages and peerages without peers as created by the Revolution of July, a whole nation, in short, of speculators and journalists, Raphael noticed, a few feet away, one face that stood out from all the others as strange and other worldly. He pushed forward, with insolently narrowed eyes, to examine this peculiar creature more closely. 'What an admirable painting that would make!' he said to himself. The eyebrows, the hair, the Mazarin-style twirl of beard which the stranger sported with a touch of vanity, were dyed black; but the cosmetic, applied to hair which no doubt had turned too white, had turned it an unnatural, purplish colour which changed according to the brightness of the candlelight. The wrinkles on his

11. The Opéra-Comique.

flat, angular face were filled in with thick layers of red and white paint, and expressed slyness and anxiety at one and the same time. This heavy make-up had come away in patches, a circumstance which strangely accentuated his decrepitude and the natural greyness of his complexion. It was hard to keep from smiling at the sight of this face with its pointed chin and bulging forehead, rather similar to the grotesque wooden faces carved by German shepherds in their leisure hours.

Had anyone observed Raphael and this aged Adonis one after the other, he would have judged the marquis to have a young man's eyes set in an old man's mask, while the stranger had the dull eyes of an old man under a young man's mask. Valentin tried to remember when and where he had seen this little old man before – wizened, fashionably cravated, booted like a man in the prime of life, clinking his spurs and crossing his arms as if he had all the bubbling energy of youth pent up in his breast. There was nothing strained or artificial about his demeanour. His elegant evening coat, carefully buttoned up, covered a sturdy though worn frame and gave him the appearance of an old dandy still clinging to fashion. This kind of animated puppet afforded Raphael all the charm of an apparition and he contemplated it as he might have contemplated an old smoke-begrimed Rembrandt recently restored, varnished and reframed. In mentally making this comparison he succeeded in tracking down the truth amid the chaos of his memories: he recognized the antique-dealer, the man who was responsible for his present misfortunes. At that moment the bloodless lips of this fantastic creature, kept on the stretch by false dentures, parted in a soundless chuckle, which suggested to Raphael's vivid imagination a striking analogy with the hypothetical face of Goethe's Mephistopheles, as painters have portrayed it.

Raphael's sceptical mind was assailed by innumerable superstitious terrors; he was ready to believe in the power of the devil and in all the demonic spells related in medieval legends and embroidered on by poets. Recoiling in dread from the prospect of meeting the fate of Faust, he impulsively invoked Heaven, for like all dying men he believed fervently in God and the Blessed Virgin. A pure and radiant light showed him the heaven of Michelangelo and Sanzio Urbino: clouds, a white-bearded old man, winged heads and a beautiful woman sitting in an aureole. He understood now and could make his own those all but human fantasies which suggested an explanation of what had befallen him and still allowed him to hope. But when he brought his eyes back to the theatre foyer, he no longer saw the Blessed Virgin, but a ravishing harlot: the detestable Euphrasie, the light and supple-bodied dancer in a dazzling dress studded with oriental pearls, who presented herself, flushed with impatience at her equally impatient old escort, and displayed herself to this gathering of envious speculators, smiling insolently, casting her sparkling eyes boldly around, calling on them to bear witness to the bottomless purse of the merchant whose treasures she was squandering. Raphael then remembered the sardonic wish he had uttered in return for the old man's fateful present, and tasted all the delights of vengeance as he saw how complete had been the overthrow of that sublime wisdom which had originally seemed so impregnably grounded. The centenarian's mirthless grimace had been directed to Euphrasie, who replied with a word of love. He offered her his withered arm, took two or three turns round the foyer, and gave delighted welcome to the passionate glances and compliments addressed to his mistress by members of the crowd; but he was oblivious of the disdainful laughter and the sarcastic jibes of which he was himself the target.

'From what graveyard did this young ghoul disinter that corpse?' cried the most sprucely turned out of all the romantic poets present. Euphrasie smiled back. The jester was a slim young man with bright blue eyes and a moustache; his frock-coat was cut short, his hat worn at an angle; he was quick at repartee and slick with the current jargon.

'How many old men,' thought Raphael, 'crown a life of honest toil and virtue with an act of folly! This man has one foot in the grave and wants to lead a life of dalliance! . . .' Valentin, ogling Euphrasie, buttonholed the merchant: 'How now, good sir,' he cried, 'have you forgotten the austere maxims you used to profess?'

'Ah!' the antique dealer replied in a voice already cracked. 'I am now as happy as a young man. My values were all topsy-turvey. A whole lifetime can be contained in an hour of love.'

At this moment the bell rang for the second act and the spectators returned to their seats. Raphael took his leave of the old man and entered his box. As he did so, his eyes fell on Fœdora, sitting directly opposite him on the other side of the auditorium. The countess, who had evidently just arrived, was throwing back her scarf, uncovering her neck and performing the indescribable little movements of a coquette arranging herself: all eyes were fixed on her. She held out her hand for her opera glasses which she had given her escort to carry. By her gesture and the way she looked at this new beau, a young peer of the realm, Raphael divined the tyranny to which his successor was subjected. The young man, no doubt caught in the same snare as had entrapped him formerly, a dupe like himself and like himself struggling with all the power of a genuine love against this woman's coolly calculating nature, must have been suffering all the tortures from which Valentin had happily escaped.

Fœdora's face shone with inexpressible joy when, having directed her glass at all the other boxes and conducted a rapid examination of the women's dresses, she felt assured that she outshone the prettiest and most elegant ladies present by the beauty and the splendour of her costume. She laughed to show off the whiteness of her teeth and tossed her flower-bedecked head to attract attention. Her glance travelled from box to box as she ridiculed the clumsily poised toque worn by a Russian princess or an ill-chosen hat which sat horribly badly on the head of a banker's daughter. Then she suddenly turned pale as she met Raphael's steady gaze; the lover she had discarded withered her with an intolerable glance of contempt. No other among her erstwhile admirers challenged her authority; in all the world only Valentin was proof against her charms. Any power that can be defied with impunity is on the verge of ruin: this maxim is more deeply engraved in a woman's heart than in the councils of kings. Thus Fœdora realized that Raphael spelled the doom of her prestige and triumph as a coquette. A remark he had made the day before at the Opéra had already gone the round of the Paris salons; the keen edge of this terrible epigram had inflicted an incurable wound on the countess. In France we have learned how to cauterize a flesh-wound, but we have not yet discovered a salve for the hurt caused by an idle quip.

At that moment, when every woman in the theatre was looking alternately at the marquis and the countess, Fœdora would have cheerfully consigned Raphael to a dungeon deep in some fortress; all her skill in dissimulation could not prevent her rivals from guessing what she was suffering. To cap it all, even that ultimate consolation – the delightful thought: 'I am the fairest of them all!' – that phrase which never lost its power to soothe her ruffled vanity – even that solace was denied her. As the overture to the second act began, a woman entered the box next to Raphael's which had remained empty up to then. From the whole pit rose a murmur of admiration. A vast wind whipped up the waves of that sea of human faces: all eyes were fastened on the newcomer. Young and old made such a prolonged tumult that, as the curtain rose, the players in the orchestra turned round to ask for silence; but then they too joined in the applause and increased the vague swell of voices. Lively conversations broke out in every box. The women had armed themselves with their opera-glasses and old men, galvanized into youth, rubbed up the lenses of their monocles with their doeskin gloves. Then by degrees the enthusiasm subsided, the opera-singers gave voice, and order was restored. The cultured audience, ashamed at having yielded to a natural impulse, assumed once more the aristocratic coolness of good manners. The rich take pride in the fact that nothing can astonish them, and consider themselves bound to discover the defect in any masterpiece which will dispense them from showing admiration, as ordinary people might.

None the less, several men sat as still as statues, heedless of the music, frankly entranced in their contemplation of the girl placed near to Raphael. Valentin noticed in a box in the pit, close to Aquilina, the florid, ignoble face of Taillefer, who greeted him with an approving grimace. Then he observed Emile standing in the stalls and signalling to him as if to say: 'Have you no eyes for the beautiful creature beside you?' Lastly there was Rastignac, squiring Madame de Nucingen[12] and her daughter,

12. See above, p. 144. Rastignac eventually transferred his interest from mother to daughter, Auguste de Nucingen, who later became his wife.

who was twisting his gloves like a man in despair at being chained where he was, with no chance of joining the divine stranger.

Raphael's life hung on a yet unbroken pact he had made with himself: he had promised himself he would never look closely at any woman, and in order to shield himself from temptation he carried a monocle whose microscopic lens, skilfully inserted, destroyed the harmony of the loveliest features and gave them a hideous aspect. Still a prey to the terror which had gripped him that morning when, at a wish expressed out of mere politeness, the talisman had been so prompt to shrink, Raphael was firmly resolved not to look round at his neighbour. Seated as duchesses sit, at the corner of the box with their backs to the audience, he was boorishly blocking the stranger's view of one half of the stage, giving the impression that he scorned her, and even that he was not aware a pretty woman was sitting behind him; while she was leaning her elbow on the rail of the box, in exact imitation of Valentin's posture, with her head held at three-quarter profile as she watched the singers, just as if she were posing for a painter. The two of them looked like two lovers having a tiff, turning their backs on each other but ready to make it up with a kiss at the first tender word. Every now and then the light marabou feather decking her hair, or a wisp of the hair itself, brushed against Raphael's head and gave him a pleasant little thrill which he courageously resisted. Presently he felt the soft touch of the frills of lace with which her dress was trimmed, while the folds of the dress itself rustled with a soft feminine enchantment quivering on the air. Then the imperceptible movement imparted by the act of breathing to the breast, the neck and clothing of this dainty beauty, all her gentle living presence was suddenly communicated to Raphael as by an electric spark; the tulle and the lace faithfully transmitted to his shoulder the delicious, tantalizing warmth of that bare, white back. Thanks to a chance freak of nature these two things, sundered by the conventions, separated by the abyss of death, were breathing in unison and perhaps thinking of each other. The penetrating scent of sandalwood completed Raphael's intoxication. His imagination, like a horse rearing up at an obstacle and maddened by the ropes that were hobbling it, rapidly traced in fiery brush-strokes a portrait of a woman. He abruptly turned round. Shocked no doubt at finding herself in contact with an unknown man, she too made a similar movement: they confronted one another, the same thought illuminating their two faces.

'Pauline!'

'Monsieur Raphael!'

Both petrified, they gazed at each other for an instant in silence. Raphael saw that Pauline was dressed simply and with good taste. Through the gauze that chastely veiled her bosom, perceptive eyes might see a lily-white skin and guess at the shapeliness of a bosom that any woman would have admired. And she had lost nothing of her maidenly modesty, her heavenly candour, her graceful pose. Her quivering sleeve betrayed the trembling of her body and the rapid beating of her heart.

'Oh! Come tomorrow,' she said, 'come to the Hôtel Saint-Quentin to take away your papers. I will be there at midday. Be punctual.'

She got up hastily and disappeared. Raphael made as if to follow her, but fearing to compromise her, he stayed behind, glanced at Fœdora and found her ugly. But, not being able to take in a single note of the music, finding the atmosphere stifling, with swelling heart he left the theatre and went home.

'Jonathas,' he said to his old servant as soon as he got into bed, 'give me half a drop of laudanum on a lump of sugar and tomorrow do not wake me until twenty minutes to twelve.'

'I wish to be loved by Pauline!' he cried next morning, looking at the talisman with unspeakable anguish. The skin made no movement. It seemed to have lost its contractile power – no doubt it could not gratify a desire which was already fulfilled.

'Ah!' Raphael exclaimed, feeling as if some leaden cloak, worn by him from the day he had been given the talisman, had slipped from off his shoulders: 'You lie, you do not obey me, the pact is broken! I am free and shall live! Was it all nothing but a cruel practical joke?'

Even while he spoke these words he dared not believe in what he was thinking. He dressed as simply as he used to in times past and decided to walk to his former lodging. He tried to revert mentally to the happy days when he could yield without danger to the impetuosity of his desires, and when he had not yet passed judgement on all human joys. He walked along, no longer seeing the Pauline of the Hôtel Saint-Quentin, but the Pauline of the previous evening, the ideal mistress so often dreamed of; a girl of intelligence, affectionate, artistic, appreciative of poets and poetry and living in the lap of luxury; in a word Fœdora endowed with a soul, or Pauline a countess and twice a millionaire as Fœdora was. When he found himself on the broken step, the worn flags under the door where so often he had been visited by despairing thoughts, an old woman came out and said to him:

'Are you not Monsieur Raphael de Valentin?'

'Yes, my good woman,' he answered.

'You can find your way to the room you once occupied?' she continued. 'You are awaited there.'

'Is this house still kept by Madame Gaudin?' Raphael asked.

'Oh no, sir. Madame Gaudin is now a baroness. She lives in a fine house of her own on the other side of the river. Her husband has returned. My goodness, he's rolling in money. They say she could buy up the whole of the Saint-Jacques quarter if she wished. She gave me her business and the balance of her lease as a gift. Ah! She's a very good woman, there's no mistaking. She's no more stuck-up today than she was yesterday.'

Raphael ran lightly up to his garret, and as he reached the top of the stairs he heard sounds coming from the piano. Pauline was there, modestly clad in a cambric dress; but the cut of it, her gloves, her hat and the shawl she had tossed on the bed, everything showed that she had come into a fortune.

'Ah! Here you are at last!' Pauline cried, turning round and rising to her feet in unfeigned delight.

Raphael went and sat down beside her, with flushed face, shy and happy. He gazed at her in silence.

'Why did you leave us?' she continued, lowering her eyes as a blush suffused her cheeks. 'What became of you?'

'Ah! Pauline, I have been, and still am, very unhappy.'

'There now!' she cried, very moved. 'I guessed how things

were when I saw you yesterday evening, well dressed and apparently rich, but is the truth, Monsieur Raphael, still as it always was?'

Valentin could not hold back the tears that filled his eyes, and he stammered: 'Pauline, I . . .' He could not finish, but love shone in his eyes and his heart overflowed in the look he gave her.

'Oh! He loves me! He loves me!' cried Pauline.

Raphael could only nod in assent, for he felt incapable of uttering a single word. At the gesture he made the girl took his hand, pressed it and said, half smiling, half sobbing:

'We're rich, we're rich, rich and happy! Your Pauline is rich . . . But I ought to be very poor today, for I have sworn a thousand times that I would give up all the treasures of the earth just to hear you say: *I love you*! Oh Raphael, my beloved! I possess millions. You love luxury, you can have everything you want. But you must want my heart too – there is so much love in it for you! Had you not heard? My father has returned. I am a wealthy heiress. My mother and he are leaving me free to decide my own future; free, you understand?'

Raphael held Pauline's hands in a kind of delirium and was kissing them so ardently, so avidly that his kiss resembled a sort of convulsion. Pauline freed her hands, placed them on Raphael's shoulders and squeezed them. In perfect understanding they embraced each other with that sweet, sacred fervour, in total forgetfulness of self, which colours that first, unique kiss by which two souls take possession of each other.

'Ah!' Pauline cried as she fell back on her chair. 'I will never leave you again!' Then she continued with a blush: 'I don't know what makes me so brazen!'

'Brazen, my Pauline? Have no fear. It is love, true love, profound and eternal as mine is. Is it not so?'

'Oh, speak, speak, speak,' she urged him. 'It's so long since I heard words from your mouth . . .'

'You loved me then in the days before?'

'Dear God, did I love you? How many times have I wept – there, look – as I swept out your room, grieving for your poverty and my own. I would have sold myself to the demon to relieve you of a single care. Today, Raphael my dearest one – for you are truly my own – mine that handsome head, mine your heart, yes indeed, your heart above all, my eternal treasure! . . . Where was I?' she went on after a pause. 'Ah! I remember. Well, we have three, four or five millions, I believe. If I were poor, I should perhaps be anxious to bear your name and be called your wife; but now, I would willingly sacrifice the whole world for you. I would wish to become your servant again, now and for ever. Be sure, Raphael, that in offering my heart, my person, my fortune, I shall not be giving you anything more today than the day when I put there – she pointed to the table drawer – a certain five-franc piece. Ah! How your joy hurt me on that occasion!'

'Why are you rich?' Raphael exclaimed. 'Why have you no worldly vanity? There's nothing I can do for you!' And he wrung his hands out of happiness, despair and love.

'When you are Madame la Marquise de Valentin – I know you, angelic soul – the title and my fortune won't be worth . . .'

'. . . a single hair of your head!' she cried.

'I too have millions. But what does wealth matter to us now? Oh! I have my life. I can offer you that. Take it.'

'Ah, Raphael, your love is worth the whole world. Can it be that even your thoughts are for me? I'm the happiest woman alive.'

'Hush, we'll be heard,' said Raphael.

'Not possible! There's no one in the house,' she replied with a pout.

'Come to me then!' cried Valentin, holding his arms out to her. She leapt on to his knees and joined her hands round Raphael's neck.

'Kiss me,' she said, 'for all the sorrow you gave me, to wipe away the anguish I felt when you were out enjoying yourself, for all the nights I spent painting my screens.'

'Your screens?'

'Since we are rich, my precious one, I can tell you everything. Child that you are! How easy it is to make a fool of a clever man! Do you imagine that you could have had white waistcoats and clean shirts twice a week which you were paying three francs a month for laundry? Why, even your milk cost twice what you paid for it. I took you in over every single thing: fuel, oil, and money too! O my Raphael, don't take me for your wife,' she said, laughing. 'I'm far too deceitful!'

'But how did you do it?'

'I worked till two in the morning. I gave my mother half what I got for the screens, and you the other half.'

They gazed at each other for a moment, both of them dazed with joy and love.

'Oh!' Raphael exclaimed. 'I'm sure we shall have to pay one day for this happiness with some terrible sorrow.'

'You're not married, are you?' cried Pauline. 'Oh! I'll not let any other woman have you.'

'I am free, my beloved.'

'Free!' she repeated. 'Free, and you belong to me!' She sank to her knees, clasped her hands together and looked at Raphael with ardent devotion.

'I'm afraid of going mad! How handsome you are!' she continued, passing her hand through his fair hair. 'What a goose your Countess Fœdora is! I can't tell you what pleasure it gave me yesterday to see all those men looking towards me! *She* never had a tribute like that! Listen, dearest, when my back touched your arm, I heard some mysterious inner voice telling me: "He's there!" I turned round, and there you were! Oh! I simply had to run away – I was longing to fling my arms round your neck in front of everybody.'

'How lucky you are that you can talk about it!' Raphael exclaimed. 'I can't, my heart is bursting, I'd like to cry but I can't. Don't take your hand away. I believe I could stay here all my life looking at you like this, happy and contented.'

'Oh! Say that again, my love!'

'Ah! What good are words?' Valentin replied, letting a hot tear fall on Pauline's hand. 'Later I will try to describe my love to you; at present I can only feel it.'

'Ah!' she exclaimed. 'The noble soul, that splendid genius, that heart I know so well, they are all mine now, as I am all yours.'

'For ever, sweetest girl,' said Raphael in a voice vibrant with emotion. 'You will be my wife, my good genius. Your presence has always dispelled my sorrows and brought solace to my soul. At this moment I feel as it were purified by your angelic smile, ready to begin a new life. The cruel past and my sad follies seem now to be no more than bad dreams. By your side I am pure, I breathe the air of happiness. Oh! Be for ever with me,' he added, pressing her reverently against his throbbing heart.

'Let death come when it will,' Pauline cried ecstatically. 'I have lived.'

Happy the man who can divine the joys that filled them, for if he can, he must have known them once himself.

Two hours later, Pauline broke the silence. 'Oh my Raphael,' she said; 'I don't want anyone henceforth to enter this dear garret!'

'We must wall up the door, put bars at the window and purchase the house,' the marquis replied.

'So we will,' she said. And then, an instant later:

'We have quite forgotten to look for your manuscripts!'

They both burst into merry, innocent laughter.

'Bah!' Raphael cried. 'What do I care for any of the sciences!'

'Indeed, good sir? But what about the quest for glory?'

'You are my sole glory.'

'How unhappy you were when you were doing all this tiny writing,' she said as she flicked over the sheets of the manuscript.

'My Pauline...'

'Oh yes, I am your Pauline... So then?'

'Where are you living now?'

'In the Rue Saint Lazare, and you?'

'In the Rue de Varenne.'

'We shall be a long way from one another, until...'

She made a pause, looking at her lover with a coquettish and mischievous air.

'But we have at the very most only a fortnight to remain in separation,' Raphael replied.

'Really? Shall we be married in a fortnight's time?' She jumped up and down like a child.

'Oh, I'm an undutiful daughter', she went on 'I've forgotten all about my father and mother and everything else. You don't know, dear heart, how ill my father is. He has returned from India in very poor health. He almost died at Le Havre, where we went to meet him – Oh heavens!' she exclaimed, looking at her watch. 'It's already three! I must be there when he wakes up at four. I am the mistress of the house. My mother does everything I wish. My father worships me, but I don't want to take advantage of their kindness. That would be too bad! Poor father, it was he who sent me to the *Italians* yesterday evening . . . You'll come and see him tomorrow, won't you?'

'Will Madame la Marquise de Valentin do me the honour of taking my arm?'

'I'm going to take the key of this room with me,' she continued. 'Is it not a palace, this treasure of ours?'

'Pauline, one more kiss.'

'As many as you wish. Dear God,' she said, gazing at Raphael. 'Will it be always like this? It's like being in a dream.'

They slowly descended the staircase. Then, arm in arm, keeping step together, both of them trembling under the weight of the same happiness, pressing against each other like a pair of doves, they came to the Place de la Sorbonne, where Pauline's carriage was waiting.

'I want to visit you in your home,' she exclaimed. 'I want to see your bedroom and your study and to sit at the desk at which you work. It will be like old times' – this she said with a blush . . . 'Joseph,' she said to a footman, 'I am going to the Rue de Varenne before returning home. It's a quarter past three, and I must be back by four. Georges will have to whip up the horses.'

The two lovers were very quickly conveyed to Valentin's mansion.

'Oh! How pleased I am to have seen all this,' Pauline exclaimed as she fingered the silk of the curtains which draped Raphael's bed. 'When I fall asleep I shall think I'm here. I shall picture your dear head on this pillow. Tell me, Raphael, did you ask anyone's advice about the furnishing of your house?'

'No one's.'

'Is that true? It wasn't a woman who...'

'Pauline!'

'Oh, I feel terribly jealous! But you have perfect taste. To-morrow I shall buy a bed just like yours.'

His head swimming with happiness, Raphael took Pauline in his arms.

'Oh! My father... my father!'

'I'll take you back then, I'll not be parted from you for longer than I need.'

'How loving you are! I didn't dare ask you to...'

'Are you not my whole life?'

It would be tiresome to transcribe in detail all the adorable chatter of these lovers, since it is only the tone in which the words were uttered, the looks and indescribable gestures which accompanied them, that give them value. Raphael escorted Pauline home, and returned with as much joy in his heart as any man can feel in this world without succumbing. When he was back in his armchair by his fireside, thinking of the sudden and complete realization of all his hopes, a chilling thought transfixed him like the blade of a dagger driven into the victim's breast: he looked at the wild ass's skin and saw that it had shrunk a little more. He uttered the great French oath, though without the jesuitical reticences of the Abbesse des Andouillettes,[13] leaned his head on the back of his chair and remained still, his eyes staring at a Grecian vase without seeing it.

'Good God!' he exclaimed. 'What! all my desires, all of them!... Poor Pauline!'...

He took a pair of compasses and measured the skin to see how much life that morning had cost him.

'I haven't enough left for a couple of months!' he said.

He was bathed in a cold sweat. Then suddenly he gave way to an indescribable burst of rage. He seized the skin, crying: 'What a fool I am!' He left the house, ran across the gardens

13. *Tristram Shandy*, Book VII, chapters xxi–xxv. The abbess and a novice are travelling with mules which will only walk uphill if they are sworn at. The 'reticence' consists in dividing the swear-word into two: the Abbess pronounces the first half, her novice the second; they thus reduce the sin of swearing to practically nothing.

and threw the talisman down a well, saying: *'Che serà, serà!*
The devil take all this nonsense!'

*

So then Raphael gave himself up to the happiness of loving
and living with Pauline in the closest intimacy. Their wedding,
delayed by difficulties which there is no point in explaining, was
to be celebrated in the early days of March. They had tested
their love, had no doubts about each other, and since the happiness both felt revealed all the power of their affection, never
had two souls, two temperaments been so perfectly united in
passion as they were. The more they studied each other, the
more they loved: the one showed as much delicacy as the other
modesty, and both were plunged in the same ecstasies – the
sweetest of all, those that the angels enjoy. There were no clouds
in their sky: by turns the desires of one were a law to the other.
Being both of them rich, they could satisfy every fancy, and for
that reason had no fancies. Exquisite taste, a feeling for all that
is beautiful and a true sense of poetry filled the bride's soul. Dis-
daining the trinkets most women love, she prized her lover's
smile higher than all the pearls of the orient; she chose her
richest adornment in muslin and flowers. In any case, Pauline
and Raphael avoided society, finding each other's company so
delightfully fulfilling. Theatre-goers saw this charming, illicit
couple every evening regularly at the Italians or the Opéra. If at
first some slanderous remarks enlivened salon talk, soon the torrent of events sweeping over Paris caused this pair of harmless
lovers to be forgotten. Besides, the prudes were satisfied up to a
point by the announcement of their forthcoming wedding, and
by good luck their servants held their tongues. Consequently no
particularly spiteful remark was made to penalize them for their
happiness.

Towards the end of February, at a period when a number of
fine days brought the promise of springtime joys, Pauline and
Raphael were breakfasting together one morning in a small conservatory, a kind of salon filled with flowers, opening straight on
to the garden. At that hour the mild, pale winter sun, whose rays
filtered through the rare shrubs, was warming the air, and the

eye was delighted by the strong contrasts of colour between the various kinds of foliage, the clusters of flowers and all the play of light and shadow. While the rest of Paris was still huddling for warmth in front of its cheerless hearths, the young couple were laughing together in a bower of camellias, lilac and heather. Their joyous heads rose above the narcissus, lilies of the valley and Bengal roses.

The floor of this delightful, richly-stocked conservatory was covered by a African rush mat which had all the colouring of a carpet. The walls covered with green drill showed not the slightest trace of damp. The furniture was made of seemingly rough wood, but its polished bark shone with cleanliness. On the table, attracted by the smell of milk, a kitten was crouching, letting Pauline dab its fur with coffee; she was teasing it, holding the cream away, just letting it sniff it enough to try the animal's patience and drive it wild; she burst into laughter at each of its antics and made one comical remark after another on purpose to prevent Raphael from reading the newspaper which he had already lowered a dozen times. The gaiety of this early morning scene would defy description, as does everything that is natural and unaffected. Raphael was still pretending to read his paper, but secretly watching Pauline's tussles with the kitten: *his* Pauline wrapped in a long dressing-gown which did not entirely conceal her figure, *his* Pauline with her hair still tousled and showing one tiny blue-veined white foot in its black velvet slipper. Charming to look at in a negligée, as delicious as the whimsical figures of Westhall,[14] she gave the impression of being both girl and grown woman although, being more of a girl than a woman perhaps, the happiness she felt was unclouded, for she knew nothing of love but its joyful beginnings. At the moment when, completely absorbed in this sweet reverie, Raphael had forgotten his newspaper, Pauline seized it, crumpled it into a ball and threw it into the garden; and the kitten chased after the leading article, driven by every wind that blew, after the usual fashion of leading articles. When Raphael, his attention distracted by this childish scene, tried to resume his reading, and

14. An English water-colourist (1765–1836), a very successful illustrator of books.

bent down to pick up the news-sheet he had dropped, peals of laughter rang out, merry and unrestrained, one born of another like the trills of a bird's song.

'I'm jealous of your newspaper,' she said as she wiped away the tears her childlike laughter had brought to her eyes. 'Is it not a crime,' she continued, suddenly becoming a woman once more, 'to read about Russian foreign policy in my presence, and to prefer Tsar Nicholas's prose to the speech and looks of love?'

'I wasn't reading, sweet angel, I was watching you.'

At that instant the heavy step of the gardener, his hobnailed boots crunching on the gravel of the paths, was heard approaching the conservatory.

'Excuse me, Monsieur le Marquis, if I interrupt – and you too, Madame. But I'm bringing you the most curious thing I have ever seen. I was just drawing a bucket of well-water, if I make so bold, and there was this strange sort of seaweed in it. Look at it! Say what you will, it must be very much at home in water, for it wasn't either wet or damp. Dry as a plank and not a bit swollen. Well, Monsieur le Marquis knows more about such things than me, for sure, and I thought I'd better bring it to him, as a curio, like.'

And the gardener showed Raphael the inexorable wild ass's skin, whose surface was reduced in area now to a mere six square inches.

'Thanks, Vanière,' said Raphael. 'Certainly very interesting.'

'What is wrong, my angel? You're losing your colour,' Pauline cried.

'Leave us, Vanière.'

'I'm frightened,' the girl went on; 'your voice – it's quite different . . . What's the matter? Are you in pain? Where do you feel it? You're ill. – A doctor!' she cried. 'Help, Jonathas, help!'

'Pauline, my dear, be quiet,' exclaimed Raphael, who had got a hold on himself again. 'Let's go into the house. There must be some flower here whose scent is upsetting me. That verbena, perhaps.'

Pauline pounced on the inoffensive shrub, pulled it up by the stem and threw it into the garden.

'My angel!' she cried, clasping Raphael in as strong an embrace as the love that bound them together, and with languorous coquetry giving him her red lips to kiss. 'When I saw you turn pale, it came to me that I could never outlive you; my life is your life. Raphael, my own, run your hand over my back. I still feel death creeping across it, making me shiver with cold. Your lips are burning. And your hand . . . is icy.'

'Foolish girl!' Raphael exclaimed.

'Why that tear? Let me drink it.'

'O Pauline, Pauline, you love me too much!'

'There's something extraordinary going on inside you, Raphael. Don't hide it from me, it won't take me long to guess your secret. – Give me that,' she said, snatching up the wild ass's skin.

'You are my executioner!' the young man shouted, throwing a look of horror at the talisman.

'How your voice has changed!' said Pauline, letting the fatal symbol of destiny fall to the ground.

'Do you love me?' he asked her.

'Do I love you! What a question!'

'Very well, go, leave me alone.'

The poor child did as she was bid.

'What!' Raphael exclaimed once he was alone. 'It a century of enlightenment in which we have learnt that diamonds are carbon crystals, in an age when there is an explanation for everything, when the police would haul a new Messiah before the courts and refer his miracles to the Academy of Sciences, at a time when we require a notary's initials before trusting anything, why should I alone believe in a sort of *Mene, Mene, Tekel, Upharsin?* In God's name, no! I will not believe that the Supreme Being can take pleasure in tormenting one of his inoffensive creatures. Let us consult the scientists.'

*

A short time later he was standing in front of a little pond half-way between the Wine Market, an immense storehouse of hogsheads, and the Salpêtrière, an immense seminary of alcoholics – where several rare species of duck were disporting themselves; the iridescent colours of the bird's plumage were sparkling in the sunlight like stained-glass windows in a cathedral. Every kind of duck in the world was there, quacking, paddling, thronging together and constituting a sort of duck parliament summoned against its will, but luckily without either written constitution or political principles and, secure from the sportsman's gun, living peacefully under the eye of the occasional naturalist who chanced to examine them.

'There is Monsieur Lavrille,' one of the keepers said to Raphael, who had asked to speak to this great zoological authority.

The marquis beheld a little man deep in learned cogitation before a couple of ducks. This middle-aged professor had a mild face, made milder still by an obliging air. But his obsession with science affected his whole appearance. His wig, which he was for ever scratching and pushing into fantastic positions, showed a fringe of white hair and revealed the single-minded search for truth which, like all passions when they dominate us, makes men quite oblivious of worldly matters, to the point where they lose all sense of personal identity. Raphael, though himself a studious devotee of science, looked in admiration at this naturalist, whose nightly vigils were devoted to the advancement of human knowledge and who added to the reputation of French science even in the errors he made. It is true that a lady of fashion might have smiled at the gap between the scientist's breeches and his striped waistcoat, a gap chastely bridged by the linen of a shirt which he had worked into puckers by dint of alternate kneelings and risings in the process of making his zoological observations.

After a few polite preliminaries, Raphael thought it advisable to pay Monsieur Lavrille a conventional compliment on his ducks.

'Oh! We're not short of ducks,' the naturalist replied. 'This genus is, as you no doubt know, the most numerous of the order of palmipeds. It begins with the swan and ends with the *zinzin* duck, and includes one hundred and thirty-seven varieties of quite distinct individual species, each differently named, with quite separate habits and habitats and distinctive appearance, so that you could no more mistake one for another than you could take a negro for a man of Caucasian race. Indeed, sir, when we eat duck for dinner, most of the time we have no notion of the extent . . .'

He broke off at the sight of a pretty little duck which was waddling up the sloping edge of the pond.

'There you see the cravated swan, an orphan from Canada, who has come a great distance to show us his brown and grey plumage and his little black cravat! Look, he's having a scratch . . . And there's the famous down goose or eider duck, under whose down our fashionable ladies sleep. Isn't it pretty? Who could fail to admire its little reddish-white belly and green beak? I must tell you, sir, I have just been observing a mating which I had quite given up hope of bringing off. The marriage was very successfully consummated and I am quite impatient to see the fruits. I am hoping to obtain a new species – that will bring the number up to 138 – and possibly they will name it after me. There are the newly-weds' – he pointed to a pair of ducks. 'The bride is a laughing goose – *anas albifrons* – and the bridegroom the great whistling duck – Buffon's *anas ruffina*. For a long time I couldn't decide between the laughing duck, the white-browed duck, and the spoonbill duck (*anas clypeata*): look, there's the spoonbill, that big, dark brown rascal with the green-tinted neck so coquettishly iridescent. But, sir, the whistling duck was crested, and that decided me, as you can imagine. The only variety we lack here is the variegated black-capped duck. Some of my colleagues maintain that this duck is the double of the crooked-billed teal. But I take a different view . . .'

He gave an admirable gesture, equally expressive of the modesty and the pride of the scientist, a pride full of obstinacy, a modesty without an ounce of self-deprecation.

'I think they are wrong,' he added. 'You can see, my dear sir, that we don't waste our time here. At present I am writing a monograph of the genus duck . . . But I am at your disposal.'

As they walked towards a pretty little house in the Rue Buffon, Raphael submitted the wild ass's skin to Monsieur Lavrille's inspection.

'I know this product,' said the scientist at last, after bringing his magnifying glass to bear on the talisman. 'It must have been used as a covering for some sort of box. The shagreen is of great antiquity. Nowadays, casemakers prefer to work with shark-skin, so called, which as I'm sure you know, is the skin of the *raja sephen*, a fish found in the Red Sea.'

'But as regards this skin, you were saying, sir, if I understood you rightly . . .'

'This,' the scientist broke in,' is quite another matter. Between sharkskin and shagreen there is the same difference as between the ocean and dry land, between a fish and a quadruped. How-ever, the fish skin is harder than the skin of the land animal. This' – he pointed to the talisman – 'is, as you no doubt know, one of the most interesting products of zoology.'

'Is that so?'

'Sir,' the scientist went on, dropping into his armchair, 'this is the skin of an ass.'

'That I know,' said the young man.

'There exists in Persia an extremely rare donkey, the onager of antiquity, *equus asinus*, the *koulan* of the Tartars. Pallas[15] went there to observe it, and he was the first to make a scientific study of it. In actual fact, this animal was for a long time taken for a fabulous beast. It is, as you know, well-famed in Holy Scripture. Moses issued an interdict against yoking it with related species. But the onager is still more famous for the prostitutions of which it has been the object, about which Biblical prophets often speak. Pallas, as you no doubt know, declares, in the second volume of his *Act. Petrop*, that these strange practices are still piously believed in by the Persians and the Nogaïs as a sovereign remedy against kidney disease and sciatica. That's a thing we never suspected, we ignorant Pari-sians!

'The Museum does not possess an onager. A superb animal! Its eye is equipped with a sort of reflecting film, to which orient-als attribute the power to fascinate. Its coat is shinier and smoother than that of our finest horses; it is marked with more or less tawny stripes and is very like that of a zebra. Its wool is

15. A German naturalist (1741–1811), author of *Travels in various Provinces of the Russian Empire and Southern Asia*. There is a French translation in 5 vols., 1788–93. It describes the 'koulan' and gives a picture.

soft, wavy and silky to the touch. Its eyesight is as keen and accurate as that of a man. It is rather bigger than even our finest domestic asses, and displays an extraordinary courage. If it happens to be ambushed, it defends itself with remarkable tenacity against the most ferocious animals. When running, the speed it reaches can only be compared with the flight of a bird. In a race between an onager and the best Arab or Persian horses, the latter would die of exhaustion.

'According to the father of the learned Dr Niebuhr,[16] whose death we were mourning recently, as you no doubt know, the average speed of these admirable creatures is seven thousand geometric paces per hour. Our degenerate asses of today give no idea whatsoever of this proud and indomitable beast, with its alert, spirited carriage, its shrewd and intelligent appearance, its graceful head and charming movements. In the East, the onager is the king of the beasts. Turkish and Persian superstition even credit it with a mysterious origin, and the name of Solomon is brought into the tales recited by story-tellers of Tibet and Tartary about the prowess attributed to these noble animals. Finally, a tame onager is worth enormous sums; it is almost impossible to catch one in mountainous districts, where it bounds like a chamois and seems to fly like a bird. The fable of winged horses – our Pegasus – was no doubt born in these regions, where shepherds would frequently catch sight of an onager jumping from rock to rock. The saddle asses produced in Persia by the mating of a she-ass with a tamed onager are dyed red in accordance with immemorial tradition, and this usage has perhaps given rise to our proverb: "as vicious as a red donkey". At a period when natural history was very much neglected in France, some traveller or other, I think, must have brought here one of those curious animals which never take kindly to domesticity. Hence the saying I have quoted.

'The skin you are showing me,' the naturalist continued, 'is certainly the skin of an onager. There are arguments about the derivation of the name. Some maintain that *chagri* is a Turkish word, others that Chagri is the town where the hide of this

16. Berthold Georg Niebuhr, the historian, died in 1831. His father, Carsten Niebuhr, was the author of books on travels in Arabia

animal undergoes a chemical treatment quite well described by Pallas, whence comes the particular grain for which we admire it. I have a communication from Martellens, in which he informs me that *Châagri* is a brook . . .'

'My dear sir, I must thank you for providing me with material enough to furnish Dom Calmet with one of his admirable footnotes if the order of Benedictines still existed.[17] But I have had the honour of pointing out to you that this fragment was originally of a dimension equal to . . . that map' – Raphael pointed to an open atlas. 'Now during the last three months it has very perceptibly shrunk . . .'

'I see,' answered the scholar. 'Well, sir, the skins of any creature that was once alive are subject to a natural shrinking process, easily accounted for, the rapidity of which depends on atmospheric conditions. Even metals expand or contract to a perceptible degree, for engineers have observed quite wide gaps developing between blocks of masonry originally held together by iron clamps. Science is vast and human life is very short. That is why we cannot claim to know all the phenomena of nature.'

'Sir,' Raphael interjected, with slight embarrassment. 'Forgive me for asking this, but are you quite sure that this skin is subject to the normal laws of zoology? Can it be stretched?'

'Oh, certainly ! . . . A plague on it !' said Monsieur Lavrille as he tried to distend the talisman by pulling it out. 'Anyway, sir, if you go and see Planchette, the famous professor of mechanics, he will surely discover some way of acting on this skin, to soften and distend it.'

'Thank you, sir, you are saving my life !'

Raphael took his leave of the learned naturalist and hurried away to find Planchette, leaving the worthy Lavrille in the middle of his study filled with jars and dried plants. Without knowing it, he had gained from this visit the sum total of human science: a nomenclature ! The good Lavrille was rather like Sancho Panza telling Don Quixote the story of the goats: he spent his time counting the animals and giving each a number. Lavrille, with one foot in the grave, had barely knowledge of more than a tiny fraction of the infinite quantity of creatures

17. The Order was not restored in France until 1837.

which God has cast into the ocean of the worlds for a purpose of which we are ignorant. But Raphael was pleased. 'I can bridle my ass now!' he cried.

Sterne had said long before him: 'Spare your ass if you would live to be old.' But the beast in question takes so much humoring!

Planchette was a tall, spare man, a genuine poet lost in perpetual contemplation, always looking into a bottomless abyss: MOTION. They are often regarded as mad by lesser spirits, these sublime and misunderstood thinkers, who deserve rather to be admired for the way they live, despising comfort and social life, spending whole days smoking an unlighted cigar, or who enter a drawing-room without having always applied their coat-buttons to the right buttonholes. One day, after spending months calculating the dimensions of space or tracing parabolas on graph paper, they turn out to have analysed a fundamental law of nature and broken it down to its simplest principles. Suddenly the crowd is confronted with some wonderful new engine or some vehicle whose simple lines astonish and confound everyone. The modest scientist smiles as he asks his admirers: 'What have I created? Nothing at all. Man doesn't invent a force, he directs it; all science does is to imitate nature.'

Raphael came upon the expert in mechanics as he stood planted on his two legs like a hanged man dropped straight from the gallows. Planchette was studying an agate marble rolling round a sun-dial and waiting for it to stop. The poor man had neither pension nor decoration, for he knew nothing of the art of gilding his calculations. Happy to live in the hope of making discoveries, he thought neither of fame, the world, nor himself: his life was devoted to science for science's sake.

'Impossible to define that!' he cried. 'Good day, sir,' he continued on catching sight of Raphael. 'I'm at your service. How is your Mamma? ... Step indoors and see my wife.'

'What was there to stop me living such a life?' Raphael thought, as he drew the scientist from his abstraction by asking him for a means of treating the talisman which he showed him.

'Even if you were to laugh at my credulity, sir,' said the marquis as he concluded, 'I will hide nothing from you. This skin seems to me to possess a power of resistance that nothing can overcome.'

'Sir,' said Planchette, 'men of the world always treat science rather cavalierly, they all talk to us more or less like the dandy at the end of the last century, who visited Lalande[18] with a group of ladies after an eclipse and asked him: "Would you be so kind as to do it again?" What effect do you wish to produce? The aim of mechanics is either to use or to neutralize the laws of motion. As regards motion itself, I tell you in all humility that we cannot say what it is. Beyond that, we have observed a certain number of recurrent phenomena which govern the action of solids and fluids. By reproducing the generative causes of these phenomena we can transport bodies, transmit to them a locomotive force within a ratio of determined speed, project them, divide them simply or *ad infinitum*, either by breaking or pulverizing them; then we can twist them, impose on them a rotatory movement, modify, compress, dilate and expand them. This science, sir, rests on a single fact. You see that marble. It's at this point on the stone. Now it's at that point. By what name shall we call this act, so natural physically speaking but so extraordinary as soon as one thinks about it? Movement, locomotion, change of place: what tremendous vanity is concealed under words! Does it really solve anything, to give a thing a name? And yet all science is there. Our machines take advantage of or adapt that act, that fact. This trivial phenomenon applied to great masses will suffice to blow Paris to pieces. We can increase velocity at the cost of energy, we can increase energy at the cost of velocity. But what is energy? What is velocity? Our science is as powerless to tell us as it is to create movement. Motion, whatever it is, is a tremendous power, and man cannot invent power of any sort. Power is one, like movement, which is the very essence of power. Everything is movement. Thought is a form of movement. Nature is founded on movement. Death is a movement towards an objective hidden from us. If God is eternal, be sure that He is eternally in motion. Perhaps God *is* movement. That could be why movement is as inexplicable as He is; profound as He is, limitless, incomprehensible, intangible. Who

18. An illustrious astronomer, 1732–1807.

has ever touched, encompassed, measured movement? We feel its effects without seeing them. We may even deny them as we deny God. Where is He? Where is He not? Whence comes He? Where is the principle from which He proceeds? Where is the end towards which He is moving? He wraps us round, presses on us but eludes us. He is evident as a fact, obscure as an abstraction, effect and cause simultaneously. Like us. He must have space: but what is space? Movement alone reveals it to us; without movement space is no more than a word devoid of meaning. Being an insoluble problem, similar in that respect to the problem of the vacuum, to creation itself, to the infinite, movement confounds human thought, and the only certainty man can have is that he will never be able to conceive it. In between each one of one points successively occupied in space by that marble,' the scientist went on, 'human reason finds an abyss, an abyss into which Pascal fell.

'In order to act upon an unknown substance which you wish to subject to an unknown force, we must first of all study that substance. According to its nature it will either shatter to pieces under a blow, or it will withstand it; but if it spits and this is not what you want to happen, we shall not attain the proposed result. If you want to compress it, it will be necessary to subject every particle of the substance to an equal pressure so as to diminish uniformly the spaces between them. If you want to stretch it, we must try to bring to bear on each molecule an equal centrifugal force; for, unless we adopt this procedure exactly, we shall produce rents and tears. You see, sir, there exist in movement an infinity of modes, an unlimited number of combinations. What effect do you wish to produce?'

'Sir,' Raphael explained impatiently, 'I wish for some sort of pressure strong enough to expand this skin indefinitely.'

'Substance being finite,' the mathematician replied, 'cannot be indefinitely distended, but compression will necessarily increase its surface area at the expense of its thickness; it will grow thinner and thinner until the material fails . . .'

'Obtain this result, Monsieur, and you will have earned millions.'

'I should be robbing you,' the professor replied with the

phlegm of a Dutchman. 'I will briefly demonstrate to you the working principles of a machine under which God himself would be squashed like a fly. It would reduce a man to the state of blotting-paper: a man in boots and spurs, cravat, hat, with his money, jewels, everything . . .'

'What a horrifying machine!'

'Instead of drowning their children, the Chinese ought to put them to this sort of use,' the scientist replied, without a thought for the respect man owes to his progeny.

Absorbed in his project, Planchette took an empty flowerpot with a hole in the bottom, and placed it on the slab of the sun-dial; then he went and fetched a lump of clay from a corner of the garden. Raphael remained entranced like a child listening to his nurse telling him a fairy-story. After placing the clay on the slab, Planchette drew a pruning-knife from his pocket, cut two pieces of elder and proceeded to hollow out the inside, whistling as if Raphael had not been there.

'Those are the elements of the machine,' he said. He fastened one of the elder tubes to the bottom of the pot by a piece of bent clay piping, so that the mouth of the tube was fitted to the hole in the pot. It looked like an enormous tobacco pipe. On the surface of the sundial he spread a layer of clay which he moulded into the shape of a shovel, settled the flowerpot in the broadest part and fixed the branch of elder on to the portion representing the handle of the shovel. Finally he put a blob of clay on the extremity of the elder tube and stuck the other hollowed branch upright in it, shaping another piece of piping to join it to the horizontal branch, in such a way that the air, or any other given fluid, could circulate through the improvised machine and flow from the mouth of the vertical tube, through the intermediate canal, right into the empty flowerpot.

'Sir,' he said to Raphael with the gravity of an Academician delivering his inaugural speech, 'this apparatus constitutes one of the immortal Pascal's greatest claims to our admiration.'

'I don't follow you.'

The scientist smiled. He went and detached from a fruit-tree a little bottle in which his local chemist had provided him with a solution for catching ants. He broke off the bottom in order to turn it into a funnel, fitted it carefully into the mouth of the hollow branch that he had stood up vertically in the clay, exactly opposite to the large reservoir represented by the flower-pot. Then, with a watering-can, he poured into it a sufficient quantity of water for it to be exactly level both in the big vase and the little round opening of the elder tube . . . Raphael was still thinking of his wild ass's skin.

'Water,' said the physicist, 'is even now generally considered to be an inelastic substance. Do not forget that fundamental principle. Nevertheless it *can* be compressed, but so slightly that we can safely discount its contractile property. You see the surface presented by the water which has risen to the top of the flower-pot?'

'Yes.'

'Well, suppose that surface to be a thousand times greater than the orifice in the elder-branch through which I have poured the liquid. Now note, I take away the funnel . . .'

'Yes, I see.'

'Well, sir, if by some means or other I increase the volume of this mass by introducing yet more water through the orifice of the little tube, the fluid, forced down it, will rise in the reservoir represented by the flowerpot until the liquid reaches the same level in both.'

'Clear enough,' Raphael exclaimed.

'But there is this difference,' the scientist continued. 'If the slender column of water poured into the little vertical tube exerts a pressure say of one pound, since this pressure will be infallibly transmitted to the liquid mass and will react on all points of the surface presented by it in the flowerpot, there will be a thousand columns of water which, tending each one of them to rise as if they were pushed upwards by a force equal to that which pushes the liquid down in the vertical tube, will necessarily produce here' – Planchette pointed to the top of the flower-pot – 'a power one thousand times greater than the power introduced there' – he pointed now to the wooden tube stuck upright in the clay.

'That is simple enough,' said Raphael.

Planchette smiled. 'In other words,' he went on with the remorseless logic typical of mathematicians, 'if we want to prevent the water flooding in, we need to exert on each section of the larger surface, a pressure equal to that in the vertical conduit; but we must allow for one difference, namely that if the liquid column is one foot high, the thousand small columns in the wide surface will be of very slight elevation. Now,' said Planchette, flicking away his tubes, 'let us replace this absurd little apparatus by metallic tubes of suitable force and dimensions; if you cover with a strong mobile plate the fluid surface of the large reservoir, and fix above it another plate tough and resilient enough to withstand any strain, and if further you grant me the power of continuously adding water to the liquid mass via the little vertical tube, the object caught between the two solid planes must necessarily cave in under the huge pressure bearing constantly down on it. To cause water to flow indefinitely into the small tube is child's play in hydraulics, and so is the device for transmitting the force of the liquid mass to a plate. Two pistons and a few valves are all that is needed. You can therefore imagine, my dear sir,' he said, taking Valentin by the arm, 'that there is scarcely any substance which, placed between these two clamps of unlimited power, will not be squeezed out flat.'

'What!' Raphael cried, 'the author of the *Provincial Letters* invented . . .'

'Quite unaided, sir. The science of mechanics knows nothing more simple or more beautiful. The contrary principle, the power of water to expand, gave us the steam engine. But the expansionary factor in water is finite, whereas its inelasticity, being so to speak a negative force, is necessarily infinite.'

'If this skin can be stretched,' said Raphael, 'I promise you I will raise a colossal statue to Blaise Pascal, found a prize of one hundred thousand francs to be awarded every ten years for the solving of the most outstanding problem in mechanics, present all your female relatives to the first and second degree with marriage dowries and lastly build an asylum for mathematicians who lose their reason or their money.'

'That would be very useful,' Planchette replied. 'Now sir,' he continued with the placidity of a man living on an entirely intellectual plane, 'tomorrow we will go and see Spieghalter. That

234

distinguished engineer has just constructed and perfected, from plans of mine, a machine by means of which a child could compress a thousand bundles of hay into his hat.'

'We shall meet tomorrow, sir.'

'At your service.'

'Talk of mechanics!' Raphael exclaimed, 'is it not the finest of sciences? The other man with his wild asses, his classifications, his ducks, his genera and his jars full of foetuses, is fit only to mark the score in a public billiard-hall!'

The next day Raphael, full of optimism picked up Planchette, and they made their way together to the Rue de la Santé, the Street of Good Health, a name of good omen. The young man was introduced into Spieghalter's work-sheds, a vast building in which he could observe a multitude of red-hot, roaring forges. Fire rained down, nails covered the ground, there was an ocean of pistons, screws, levers, girders, files, nuts and bolts, a sea of castings, beams, valves and steel bars. Iron filings caught in your throat. Iron was in that hot air, the men were coated in iron, the whole place reeked of iron, iron which was alive, organic, flowing, walking, thinking, taking every shape, obedient to every chance command. Through the roaring of bellows, the crescendo of hammers, the whistle of the lathes that made the iron groan, Raphael wended his way to a large machine-room, clean and airy, where he had leisure to examine the tremendous press of which Planchette had spoken. He gazed in wonder at what one might call the joists of iron and the twin iron side-pieces held firm by indestructible mouldings.

'If you were to turn that crank smartly seven times,' Spieghalter told him, pointing to a handle of polished iron, 'you would shatter a plate of steel into thousands of flying splinters which would shoot into your limbs like needles.'

'The devil!' cried Raphael.

Planchette personally slid the shagreen skin between the twin plates of the master-press and, full of the self-confidence that accompanies scientific conviction, he rotated the lever at speed.

'Flat on the ground, everyone, if you value your lives,' yelled Spieghalter in stentorian tones as he flung himself down.

A horrible screech resounded through the workshop. The water in the hydraulic press burst the castings, spurted forth in a jet of immeasurable force and – fortunately – shot off in the direction of an old forge which it tipped up, knocked over and twisted out of shape as a water-spout snakes round a house and whirls it away.

'Oh!' said Planchette, calmly enough. 'The shagreen is as sound as a bell. Master Spieghalter, there must have been a flaw in your casting, or a crack in the main tube . . .'

'Impossible. I'm sure of my casting. This gentleman can take his contrivance away with him. It must have the devil himself inside it.'

The German seized a blacksmith's hammer, threw the skin on to an anvil and, with all the strength anger can give, dealt the talisman the most savage blow that ever rang through his workshops.

'Not a sign of any damage,' Planchette exclaimed as he ran his fingers over the recalcitrant hide.

The workmen ran up. The foreman took the skin and plunged it into the hot coals of a forge. Everybody, forming a half-circle round the fire, impatiently waited for an enormous pair of bellows to take its effect. Raphael, Spieghalter and Professor Planchette formed the centre of this begrimed and attentive crowd. Seeing all those pale eyes, those heads of hair powdered with iron dust, the shiny black clothes and the hairy chests of the workmen, Raphael imagined himself transported to the fantastic nocturnal landscape evoked in German ballads. After leaving the skin in the heart of the fire for ten minutes, the foreman gripped it with a pair of tongs.

'Give it back to me,' said Raphael.

Jokingly, the foreman held it out to Raphael, who took it and ran it easily through his fingers, finding it cold and pliable. There rose a cry of horror and the workmen dashed out, leaving Valentin alone with Planchette in the deserted workshop.

'Decidedly there's something devilish in this!' Raphael exclaimed in despair. 'Is there then no power on earth that can lengthen my life by one day?'

'The mistake was mine, sir,' the mathematician said with an

236

air of contrition. 'We should have subjected this strange skin to the action of a rolling-mill. I wasn't using my eyes when I suggested hydraulic pressure.'

'But it was I who asked you to do it,' Raphael answered.

The scientist breathed a sigh of relief like a prisoner at the bar acquitted by twelve jurymen. Nevertheless, interested in the strange problem presented by the skin, he pondered a moment and said:

'This mysterious substance must be treated with reagents. Let's go and see Japhet. It may be that chemistry can provide the answer better than mechanics.'

Valentin drove off at a fast trot in the hope of finding the famous chemist, Japhet, in his laboratory.

'Well now, old friend,' said Planchette as he saw Japhet seated in an armchair and contemplating a precipitate. 'How goes it with Dame Chemistry?'

'She's dozing. Nothing new. All the same the Academy has acknowledged the existence of salicine. But salicine, asparagine, strychnine and digitaline are no new discoveries.'

'For want of new compounds to invent,' said Raphael, 'it appears that you are reduced to inventing names.'

'You're absolutely right, young man!'

'Here,' said Professor Planchette to the chemist, 'try and analyse this substance for us. If you succeed in isolating whatever compound it contains, I name it *diaboline* in advance, for when we tried to compress it, just now, we smashed a hydraulic press!'

'Let's have a look at it!' the chemist exclaimed in glee. 'Maybe it's some new undiscovered element.'

'No, sir,' said Raphael, 'it is quite simply a bit of an ass's hide.'

'Sir!' protested the celebrated chemist with dignity.

'I'm not joking,' the marquis assured him, handing over the skin.

Baron Japhet applied to the skin the papillae of his tongue, so expert in detecting the tastes of salts, acids, alkalis and gases. After a few trials he declared:

'It has no taste! Come now, let's give it a little drink of fluorine.'

Subjected to the action of this solvent which has so rapid an effect on animal tissues, the skin remained unaffected.

'This is not shagreen!' the chemist cried. 'We will treat this mysterious substance as a mineral and give it a nasty shock by dropping it into an infusible crucible in which I happen to have some red potassium.'

Japhet went out and shortly returned.

'I beg you, sir,' he said to Raphael. 'Allow me to detach a small portion of this singular substance. It's so unusual . . .'

'A small portion?' cried Raphael. 'Not the thinnest shaving. In any case, just try!' he added, half in jest, half in sad earnest.

The chemist broke a razor in his efforts to cut the skin. He tried to disintegrate it with a powerful electric discharge, then he subjected it to the action of a voltaic battery: all the thunderbolts of his particular science were useless against the terrible talisman. It was seven in the evening. Planchette, Japhet and Raphael, oblivious of the passage of time, awaited the result of a final experiment. The shagreen emerged unscathed from the fearful assault of a controlled charge of nitrogen chloride.

'I am lost!' Raphael exclaimed. 'The hand of God is in this. I must die . . .'

He left the two scientists dumbfounded.

'We must take care not to talk about this in the Academy: our colleagues would make fun of us,' said Planchette to the chemist after a long pause during which they eyed each other without daring to communicate their thoughts.

These two scientists were like Christians emerging from their graves and discovering that God was not in his heaven. Science? powerless! Acids? mere water. Red potash? in disgrace! The voltaic pile and electric discharges? Just a game of cup-and-ball!

'A hydraulic press cracked like an egg-shell!' Planchette added.

'I believe in the devil,' said Baron Japhet after a moment of silence.

'I believe in God,' Planchette replied.

Each of them was true to his vocation. For a physicist, the universe is a machine which needs someone to work it. For chemistry, that science invented by some demon intent on decomposing everything, the universe is but a cloud of eddying gas.

'Bah! It must have been to console us that our friends the doctrinaires propounded that somewhat nebulous axiom: *facts are stupid.*'

'It seems to me,' the chemist retorted, 'that your axiom is at least as stupid as any fact.'

They started to laugh and went in to dinner, reassured at having reduced a miracle to a mere phenomenon.

*

Valentin returned home in a cold rage. There was nothing he believed in any more, his brain was in a turmoil, his ideas were whirling and wavering like those of any man confronted with an unacceptable fact. He had been ready to believe that there was a hidden flaw in Spieghalter's machine. The failure of science did not astonish him, nor the fact that the skin was fireproof; but its suppleness when he handled it and its resistance to all the means of destruction at man's disposition – this appalled him. This was the incontrovertible fact that made his head swim.

'I must be mad,' he thought. 'Though I have eaten nothing since morning, I am neither hungry nor thirsty, and I have a burning feeling in my chest...'

He put the wild ass's skin back in the frame which had formerly held it and, after tracing a line of red ink round the present outline of the talisman, he sat down in his armchair.

'Eight o'clock already!' he exclaimed. 'The day has sped away like a dream.'

He leaned his elbow on the arm of the chair, rested his head on his left hand and sat there, steeped in gloomy meditation, revolving such destructive thoughts as criminals carry, locked up in their hearts, to the scaffold.

'Ah! Pauline,' he cried. 'Poor child! There are chasms which love cannot cross, strong though its wings may be.'

At that moment he very distinctly heard a stifled sigh and

by virtue of one of the many touching privileges of passion, recognized the breathing as none other than Pauline's.

'Oh!' he said to himself, 'that is my fate. If she were here, I would wish to die in her arms.'

A gay outburst of unconstrained laughter caused him to turn his head towards his bed, and he saw, through the diaphanous curtains, Pauline's face smiling like a child delighted at having brought off a piece of mischief. Her lovely hair fell on her shoulders in a cascade of ringlets; she lay there like a Bengal rose placed on a bed of white roses.

'I cajoled Jonathas into letting me in,' she said. 'Does not this bed belong to me, since I belong to you? Don't scold me, darling, I only wanted to sleep near you and take you by surprise. Forgive me my foolishness.'

She scrambled out of bed with the agility of a kitten, radiant in muslin, and perched herself on Raphael's knee.

'What chasms were you talking about, my love?' she asked, and a cloud of anxiety gathered on her brow.

'The chasm of death.'

'You hurt me when you talk like that,' she replied. 'There are certain ideas on which we poor women cannot let our minds dwell. They kill us – is it due to the strength of our love or our lack of courage? I don't know. I'm not afraid of death,' she went on with a laugh. 'To die with you, tomorrow morning, joined in a last kiss, would be happiness. It would still seem to me I had lived a hundred years or more. What does the number of days matter if, in a night, in an hour, we have run through a whole life of peace and love?'

'You are right. Heaven is speaking through your lovely lips. Let me kiss them and let us die.'

'Let us die, then,' she replied, laughing.

About nine o'clock next morning, daylight was filtering through the chinks in the Venetian blinds. Though it was screened by the muslin curtains, even so it brightened the rich colours of the carpet and the silken furnishings of the bedroom where the lovers lay side by side. Gilt ornaments glinted here and there. A sunbeam had just faded out on the soft eiderdown that the night's love-play had caused to slip to the floor. Pauline's dress, hanging from a large swing-mirror, could be made out as a filmy apparition. Her dainty shoes had been dropped at a distance from the bed. A nightingale came and perched on the window-sill; its repeated warblings and the flutter of its wings as it suddenly unfolded them in flight, awakened Raphael.

'If I am to die,' he said, forming a conclusion to the thought he had begun in a dream,' it must be that my organism, this structure of flesh and bone animated by my will and which makes an individual of me, gives evidence of some detectable lesion. The symptoms of impaired vitality must be known to the medical profession; a physician should be able to tell me if I am in a state of health or sickness.'

He gazed at his sleeping sweetheart who had her arms round his neck, thus expressing even during sleep the tender solicitude of love. Lying gracefully like a child, with her face turned to him, Pauline seemed still to be looking at him and offering him her lovely mouth, with lips parted by her pure and regular breathing. Her small white teeth brought out the scarlet freshness of her lips on which a smile was hovering. The roses on her cheeks were at this moment of a brighter red, and the lilies in it of a purer white than during the most amorous hours of daytime. Her attitude of graceful self-abandon, so trustful, blended with the charm of love the adorable attractions of sleeping childhood. Even the most ingenuous of women still comply, during their waking hours, with certain social conventions which place limits on the free expression of their souls; but sleep seems to restore in them the spontaneity that adds so much beauty to childhood. Like one of those sweet creatures straight from heaven whom the faculty of reason has not yet taught to curb their gestures, nor the faculty of thought to veil their gaze with secret bashfulness, Pauline just now was incapable of blushing at anything. Her profile showed in clear relief against the fine cambric of her pillows, and the wide frills of lace mingling with her dishevelled hair gave her a slight air of roguishness. But she had fallen asleep in the midst of pleasure and her long lashes lay on her cheek as if to protect her eyes from too strong a light or to assist the concentration necessary to preserve a perfect but short-lived bliss. Her tiny pink-and-white ear, framed within a wisp of hair and outlined in a shell of Mechlin lace, might have driven an artist, a painter – or an old man – mad with love; or even perhaps restored a madman to his senses. To watch your mistress as she sleeps, smiling in a peaceful dream as you mount guard over her, loving you even as she dreams, at a time when she seems not to exist as a sensate being, offering you silently her lips which in sleep speak to you of the last kiss; to see a confiding woman, half-naked, but wrapped in love as in a cloak, and chaste in the very midst of disorder; to look at her scattered garments, a silk stocking tossed aside at your instance the night before, a girdle untied in evidence of utter trust in you : such joys have surely no name? The girdle is a poem in itself : the woman it defended no longer exists, she belongs to you, she has become *you* : henceforth, to betray her is to injure yourself. In tender mood, Raphael let his eyes rove over the room with its atmosphere laden with love and charged with memories, where the daylight itself had taken on voluptuous tones. Then his gaze returned to this woman, so pure and youthful of form, still loving him, whose every feeling was for him alone. He wanted to live for ever. As soon as his eyes rested on Pauline, she opened hers as if a sunbeam had lit on her.

'Good morning, darling,' she said, smiling. 'How handsome you are, wicked boy !'

Their two heads, endowed with a grace born of love and youth, in the half-light and silence around them, formed one of those divine scenes whose ephemeral magic belongs only to the early days of passion, just as artlessness and guilelessness are attributes of childhood. Alas ! These springtide joys of love, like the laughter of our young days, are destined to take flight, surviving only in our memories, and serving either to reduce us to despair or to waft a consoling breath of perfume to us, according to whichever bent our secret meditations chance to take.

'Why did you wake up?' asked Raphael. 'I had so much pleasure watching you sleep that tears came to my eyes.'

'I too,' she replied, 'wept last night as I watched you in your sleep – but not for joy. Listen to me, my Raphael, listen. When you are asleep, you do not breathe freely, there's something that rattles in your chest that alarms me. As you sleep you give little dry coughs, just like my father who is dying of consumption. I could recognize in the noise your lungs made some of the strange symptoms of that disease. What is more, you had a temperature, I am sure; your hand was hot and moist . . . Darling, you are young,' she added, shivering. 'You could yet be cured, if by some mischance . . . But no!' she exclaimed joyously, 'what am I worrying about, it's catching, the doctors say.'

She wrapped her two arms round Raphael, and drew in his breath in the kind of kiss in which souls communicate.

'I've no wish to die old,' she said. 'Let's both die young and go to Heaven with our hands full of flowers.'

'One always forms plans like that when one's in good health,' Raphael answered as he plunged his hands into Pauline's hair.

But he was immediately seized by a terrible fit of coughing: the deep and hollow coughs which have a churchyard ring about them, which make the foreheads of the sufferers turn pale, and leave them trembling and bathed in sweat after shattering their nerves, making their ribs ache, jarring their spine and filling their veins with a strange sense of heaviness. Raphael, white-faced, overcome, sank slowly down in the state of collapse of a man who has squandered all his energy in a final effort. Pauline watched him fixedly, her eyes widened by fear; she remained motionless, white and speechless.

'We must start being sensible, my love,' she said, trying to conceal from Raphael the dreadful forebodings that filled her heart.

She buried her face in her hands, to blot out the vision of the hideous spectre of DEATH. Raphael's face had become livid and as cavernous as a skull exhumed from some deep grave to further the investigations of an anatomist. Pauline recalled the exclamation which had escaped Valentin's lips the evening before, and said to herself: 'Yes, there are chasms which love itself cannot cross. It must let itself be engulfed in them.'

A few days after this depressing scene, Raphael found himself, one March morning, sitting in an armchair surrounded by four doctors who had placed him in a good light in front of his bed-room window and were alternately feeling his pulse, tapping his chest and questioning him with some show of interest. The sick man was trying to read their thoughts while interpreting their gestures and the slightest lift of their eyebrows. He had placed his last hopes in this medical examination. These sovereign judges were to pronounce a sentence of life or death. Hence, wishing the advice of the most advanced men of science, Valentin had summoned to his bedside the oracles of modern medicine. He owed it to his vast fortune and aristocratic name that the leading representatives of the three systems of treatment currently in vogue were attending him in person. Three of the doctors present embraced the whole of medical philosophy, personifying as they did the conflict engaged between Idealism, Positivism, and a certain sceptical Eclecticism. The fourth doctor was Horace Bianchon, a man in the forefront of science with a great future ahead of him; Bianchon, perhaps the most distinguished of the new type of physician, a sage and modest representative of that studious younger generation, waiting to come into its inheritance and put to use the knowledge amassed by the School of Paris over the past fifty years, that generation which will perhaps build the monument for whose construction the preceding centuries have assembled so much varied material.[19] A friend of the marquis and of Rastignac, he had been in attendance on Raphael for several days previously, and was there to help him answer the questions of these three professors, to whom he explained every now and then, with a certain insistence, the symptoms which, so he thought, pointed to pulmonary consumption.

'You no doubt have indulged in many excesses and led a dissipated life? You have devoted yourself to strenuous intellectual pursuits too, I daresay?' asked one of the three famous doctors, who to judge by his square head, broad countenance and vigorous constitution seemed to be gifted with a genius superior to that of his two rivals.

'I tried to kill myself by debauchery after toiling for three years at a vast work which one day perhaps will command your attention.'

The tall doctor gave a satisfied nod as if saying to himself:

19. On Bianchon, see above, Introduction p. 13.

'It's just as I thought!' This doctor was the illustrious Brisset, who headed the so-called *organic* school, sprung from the teaching of such men as Cabanis and Bichat; he was the positivist, the materialist, seeing in man an autonomous being, subject exclusively to the laws of his organization, whose normal state and morbid affections can be explained by tangible causes.

Hearing this reply, Brisset looked in silence at a man of average height whose florid face and fiery eyes seemed to belong to some satyr of antiquity and who, leaning his back against the corner of the window-recess, was attentively contemplating Raphael without uttering a word.

This was Dr Caméristus, a man of exalted mind and faith, the leader of the 'vitalists', the enthusiastic champion of the abstract doctrines of van Helmont;[20] he saw in human life a lofty, mysterious principle, an inexplicable phenomenon which defies scalpels, baffles surgery, eludes the action of pharmaceutical drugs, algebraical formulae and anatomical demonstrations, and mocks at all our efforts: a kind of intangible, invisible flame governed by some divine law, and which often remains active inside bodies condemned by our pronouncements, even as it occasionally forsakes organizations which seem perfectly sound.

A sardonic smile hovered over the lips of the third physician. Dr Maugredie,[21] a man of distinguished, but sceptical and satirical turn of mind, who trusted only in the surgeon's knife, agreed with Brisset that a man might die while in perfect health and recognized, with Caméristus, that a man might well go on living after his death. He found some value in all theories, adopted none of them, claimed that the best way to proceed in medical matters was to do without theory and stick to the facts. This Panurge[22] of the School of Medicine, with his phenomenal

20. J. B. van Helmont (1577–1644), born in Brussels. A physician, chemist and mystic.

21. The three names invented by Balzac for his fictitious doctors are recognizably derived from those of three well-known practitioners of his day: Brousset, Récamier, and Magendie.

22. One of the main characters of Rabelais's *Pantagruel*, conspicuous for his scepticism.

powers of observation, this great explorer, this great scoffer, this champion of desperate expedients, was examining the wild ass's skin.

'I should like to have ocular evidence of the coincidence between your desires and the shrinking of the skin,' he said to the marquis.

'For what purpose?' Brisset exclaimed.

'For what purpose?' Caméristus repeated.

'Ah! You are in agreement!' Maugredie replied.

'Such a contraction is quite simple,' Brisset asserted.

'It is supernatural,' said Caméristus.

'Quite right,' Maugredie retorted, putting on an expression of gravity as he returned the skin to Raphael, 'the shrivelling of cutaneous tissue is an inexplicable and yet natural phenomenon which from the beginning of time has caused despair among doctors and pretty women.'

A close examination of the three doctors made it clear to Valentin that none of them felt any sympathy for his sufferings. All three of them, silent at each answer he gave, looked him up and down with indifference and questioned him without showing themselves in the least sorry for him. Their lack of concern was barely disguised by the politeness of their manners. Whether because they were so sure of themselves, or else because they were deliberating within themselves, the words they uttered were so few and so perfunctory that at times Raphael thought their minds were elsewhere. Every now and then Brisset alone murmured: 'Good! Ah yes!' on hearing of all the desperately worrying symptoms vouched for by Bianchon. Caméristus remained profoundly abstracted; Maugredie looked like a writer of comedy studying two quaint figures with the idea of reproducing them faithfully on the stage. Horace Bianchon's deep distress and melting grief showed in his face. He had been in practice for too short a time to remain unmoved at the sight of suffering or impassive at a deathbed; he had not learned the art of checking those compassionate tears which blur the vision and may prevent a man from grasping the right moment to intervene, like an army commander who snatches victory without listening to the cries of the dying. After they had been there for about half an hour and so to speak taken the measure of both disease and patient, as a tailor measures a young man for his wedding-suit, they uttered a few commonplace remarks and even broached political topics. Then they proposed to pass into Raphael's study in order to exchange ideas and reach their verdict.

'Gentlemen,' Valentin asked, 'please may I be present during your discussion?'

At this request, Brisset and Maugredie protested vigorously and, despite the patient's insistence, refused to deliberate in his presence. Raphael bowed to usage, thinking that he might slip into a corridor and easily eavesdrop on the medical arguments the three professors were about to embark on.

'Gentlemen,' said Brisset on entering, 'allow me to give you my opinion without delay. I do not wish either to impose it on you or to have an argument about it. In the first place it is clear and precise, and results from a complete similitude between one of my patients and the *subject* we have been summoned to examine; besides that, I have an appointment at my clinic, and the importance of the circumstance which demands my presence there will be my excuse for being the first to speak. The *subject* in question is suffering from mental exhaustion just as much as . . . What has he been writing, Horace?' he asked of the young practitioner.

'A *Theory of the Will*.'

'The devil he has! That's a vast subject . . . He's exhausted, as I said, by mental strain, by irregularities of diet and the repeated use of over-powerful stimulants. The violence done to the cerebral and physiological faculties has thus undermined the functioning of the whole organism. Anyone can recognize, gentlemen, by the facial and somatic symptoms, a prodigious irritation of the stomach, inflammation of the sympathetic nerve, hypersensitivity of the epigastrium and contraction of the hypochondriac area. You have noticed the enlargement and protrusion of the liver. Finally, Bianchon here has taken regular note of his patient's digestive processes and told us that they were difficult and laborious. Strictly speaking, he has no stomach left: the *man* has disappeared. The intellect is atrophied because digestion is no longer operative. The progressive deterioration of the epigastrium, the very centre of life, has vitiated the entire system.[23] Hence the constant and flagrant irradiations: the disorder has reached the brain via the nervous plexus, hence the excessive irritability of that organ. Monomania has set in. The patient is a prey to his obsession. For him this wild ass's skin really does shrink; whereas it has possibly always been exactly as we saw it. But whether it contracts or not, this piece of shagreen is like the fly that a certain grand vizier could not brush off his nose. Apply leeches to the epigastrium without delay, calm the irritation of that organ which controls all the vital functions, keep the patient on a diet and the monomania will cease. I need say no more to Dr Bianchon: that will be enough for him to understand the broad outline and the details of the treatment. It is possible that complications will arise; perhaps the respiratory passages are irritated also; but I believe the treatment of the intestinal organs to be more important, more necessary and more urgent than that of the lungs. The concentrated attention he has given to the study of an abstract science, and certain violent passions, have produced grave disturbances in that vital mechanism. However, there is still time to respring it, there is nothing here that has been damaged beyond repair. So then you can easily save your friend's life,' he concluded, addressing Bianchon.

'Our learned colleague is confusing cause and effect,' Camér-istus began. 'Certainly, he has correctly observed the deterioration that has taken place in the patient's organs. However, it is not true to say that the stomach has gradually projected irradiations into the organism as a whole and into the brain, as you see the cracks radiating outwards from a hole in a pane of glass. A blow was needed to make that hole: who or what dealt that blow? How can we know? Have we made sufficient observation of the patient? Have we been told all the incidents in his life? Gentlemen, the principle of life, van Helmont's *archaea*, is impaired in him, the vital force is attacked in its very essence; the divine spark, the transitory intelligence which, one might say, coordinates all the parts of the machine and is responsible

23. The epigastrium, this bone of contention between Brisset and Caméristus, is defined as 'that part of the abdomen which is immediately over the stomach'.

for the activity of the will, the ability to function as a living organism – this has ceased to regulate the day-to-day working of the machine and of its separate organs: hence the disorders so well diagnosed by my learned colleague. The movement has not been from the epigastrium to the brain, but from the brain in the direction of the epigastrium. No!' he said, striking his breast forcefully, 'No! I am not a mere walking stomach! No! That is not the be-all and the end-all. I can't find it in me to declare that, if my epigastrium is in good working order, nothing else matters.'

He went on in a quieter voice: 'We cannot possibly attribute to a single physical cause, and prescribe in consequence a single, uniform treatment for, the grave disorders which arise in different subjects who are attacked to a more or less serious extent. No one man resembles another. We each of us have our special organs, differently affected, differently nourished, equipped to perform different functions and to develop themes necessary for the accomplishment of an order of things beyond our comprehension. That portion of the great ALL which, moved by a lofty will, produces and sustains in us the phenomenon of animation, works according to a distinctive formula in every man and makes of him a being in appearance autonomous, but linked at one point to a transcendent cause. It is therefore incumbent on us to study each subject separately, to examine him in detail and discover what is the constituent element and the motive power in his life.

'Between the softness of a wet sponge and the hardness of pumice stone, there are infinite gradations. The human species embraces a similar spectrum. Between the spongy organisms of lymphatics and the iron strength in the muscles of a limited number of men destined to a long life, how many errors would be committed by the application of a single, implacable therapeutic system which relies on crushing, weakening those vital sources of recuperative strength in man which you always claim are in a state of irritation? In the case we are considering I would advise purely psychological treatment, an analysis in depth of the psyche. Let us seek the cause of the ill in the deep recesses of the mind, not in the entrails of the body! A physician must proceed by intuition, being a man endowed with special gifts to whom God grants the power to interpret the movement of the vital spirits, just as He gives eyes to the prophet to gaze into the future, to the poet the faculty of evoking nature, to the musician the ability to arrange sounds in a harmonious order of which the pattern is perhaps stored up on high! . . .'

'Always the same medicine,' Brisset muttered, 'absolutists, monarchical, religious!'

'Gentlemen,' Maugredie broke in, hastily covering up Brisset's outburst. 'Let us not forget our patient.'

'So that's what science amounts to!' was Raphael's sad exclamation. 'They can't decide whether to cure me with a string of beads or a string of leeches; it's the lancet of Dupuytren[24] versus the prayers of the Prince of Hohenlohe![25] On the border-line between facts and words, between mind and matter, stands Maugredie, a doubting Thomas. I find it everywhere the same, men's hesitation between assent and denial, what Rabelais called *Carymary, Carymara*: either my disease is spiritual, carymary! or material, carymara! Can they say if I shall live? No. At least Planchette was more honest when he said: "I don't know." '

Then Valentin heard Dr Maugredie speaking:

'The patient is a monomaniac, you say. Very well, we grant that!' he exclaimed. 'But he has 200,000 francs a year: such monomaniacs are very scarce, and we owe them at least an opinion. As for knowing if his epigastrium has reacted on his brain or *vice versa*, we might be able to settle that after he's dead. To sum up then: he's ill, there's no denying that. He needs some sort of treatment. Never mind theories. Give him leeches to calm the intestinal irritation and the nervous disorder we can all see he's suffering from, and then let's send him to the waters. That way we shall be following both systems. If it's lung trouble, we have little hope of saving him, and so . . .'

Raphael slipped back from the corridor and resumed his seat

24. Guillaume Dupuytren, 1777–1835. A brilliant surgeon, the archetype for Balzac's 'Human Comedy' surgeon, Despleins.

25. 1794–1850. He took orders and became a Jesuit, later a bishop; he was renowned for the cures he effected on the basis of prayer.

in his armchair. Before long the four doctors emerged from the study. Horace became the spokesman and said:

'These gentlemen have unanimously recognized the necessity of an immediate application of leeches to your stomach, and the urgency of a treatment which will act on your morale as well as your physical condition. In the first place, a diet to calm the irritation of your organs . . .' Brisset nodded. 'Secondly, a course of hygienic treatment to revive your morale. This means that we unanimously advise you to take the waters at Aix in Savoy, or Mont Dore in Auvergne, whichever you prefer. The air and scenery of Savoy are more pleasant than those of Le Cantal – but you will take your choice.'

This time it was Caméristus's turn to nod.

'These gentlemen,' Bianchon continued, 'having detected certain lesions in your respiratory organs, have confirmed the correctness of the prescriptions I have been making up till now. They are satisfied you will make a good recovery, provided you follow sensibly these various regimes in succession . . . And . . .'

'And that's the reason for your daughter's dumbness!'[26] said Raphael with a smile as he drew Horace into his study to remit him the fees for this futile consultation.

'They keep to their own logic,' the young doctor replied. 'Caméristus feels, Brisset examines, Maugredie doubts. Man is compounded, is he not, of a soul, a body, and a reasoning mind? In each individual, one or other of these three primary causes is predominant, and there will always be the human element in human sciences. Believe me, Raphael, we don't effect cures, we help cures on. Between medicine as practised by Brisset and that practised by Caméristus, there's something else: wait-and-see medicine. But, in order to practise this with success, one must have studied one's patient for ten years. There's a negative element deep down in medicine, as in all the sciences. So try and live sensibly. Try a journey to Savoy. The best plan is and always will be to put one's trust in nature.'

*

26. A quotation from Molière's *Reluctant Doctor*. The peasant bumpkin Sganarelle, bullied into pretending to be a doctor, makes a ludicrous diagnosis explaining why a rebellious girl, feigning dumbness for amorous reasons, happens to be dumb.

One month later, having returned from their walk one lovely summer evening, a few of the people who had come to take the Aix waters met together in the club rooms. Seated near the window with his back turned to the others, Raphael remained a long time alone, plunged in one of those indeterminate reveries during which one thought gives rise to another and then fades away without ever taking definite shape, passing through our consciousness like diaphanous, almost colourless, clouds. At such moments sadness is sweet, joy is wrapped in a haze and the soul is near to sleep. Yielding to this sensuous life, Valentin was drowsing in the warm evening air, breathing the pure sweet-scented breezes that blew from the mountains; relieved at being delivered from pain and at having at last reduced the menace of his shagreen skin to naught. At the moment when the scarlet hues of the setting sun died out on the peaks, it grew chilly and he left his seat, pushing the window shut.

'Pardon me, sir,' an old lady said to him, 'would you be kind enough not to shut the window? It is stifling here . . .'

This request jarred on Raphael's ear-drum with a singularly sharp resonance. It was like an imprudent remark escaping from a man in whose friendship we had been anxious to believe, one which dispels some sweet illusion of sympathy by revealing unsuspected depths of egoism. The marquis gave the old woman the icy glance of an impassive diplomat, summoned a waiter and curtly told him : 'Open that window !'

At these words, lively surprise was visible on every face. The company began to whisper, giving the invalid more or less meaningful looks as if he had committed some unpardonable solecism. Raphael, who had not entirely shed his original shyness, felt momentarily ashamed of himself. But he threw off his torpor, recovered his energy and tried to account for this strange scene. Suddenly he had a flash of illumination, in which the past appeared to him in a distinct vision; the reasons for the antipathy he inspired became suddenly apparent like the network of veins in a corpse which anatomists, by the injection of some chemical colouring, cause to spring into relief. He recognized himself in this fleeting vision, followed his own existence in it day by day and thought by thought. He realized – not without surprise –

that he cut a sombre and distraught figure in this cheerful society; always brooding over his destiny, preoccupied with his illness, refusing to engage in the most trifling conversation, shunning those short-lived intimacies which spring up the more readily between people who meet on the road because they never expect to meet again; indifferent to everyone else, like one of those rocks at sea, in short, which respond neither to the lapping of the wavelets nor to the fury of the storm.

Then, in a rare, privileged burst of intuition, he read the minds of them all. As the gleam of a sconce showed him an old man's yellow cranium and sardonic profile, he remembered that he had won at cards with him without offering him a return game. Further away he recognized a pretty woman whose flirtatious advances he had rebuffed. In every reproachful face he read some grievance, of a kind hard to put into words but which arises essentially from some secret hurt done to another's self-esteem. Involuntarily he had wounded the petty vanities of every man and woman he had been in contact with. Guests at the parties he had given or those to whom he had offered the loan of his horses had resented his display of wealth. Surprised at their ingratitude, he had avoided offering them that sort of humiliation; as a result, they supposed he despised them and accused him of arrogance. Looking into their hearts in this way, he was able to decipher their most secret thoughts. He conceived a horror for society and its superficial good manners. Being rich and more intelligent, he was envied and hated. His silence thwarted curiosity and his modesty struck those small-minded social butterflies as haughtiness. He guessed what secret, unforgivable crime he was guilty of in their eyes: that of rising above the jurisdiction of their mediocrity. Unamenable to their inquisitorial despotism, he could do without them. To revenge themselves for this clandestine assumption of sovereignty on his part, they had instinctively banded together in order to show him their power, subject him to a measure of ostracism, and teach him that they also could do without him.

Moved to pity, originally, by this insight into society, after a moment he shuddered as he thought of the subtle power he possessed to strip away the veil of flesh in which man's moral nature lies buried. He closed his eyes as if to shut out the vision. A dark curtain was suddenly lowered over this sinister but truthful peep-show, but he found himself in the horrible state of isolation reserved for the great ones of this earth. Just then, he was taken with a violent fit of coughing. Far from hearing a single one of the conventional, indifferent murmurs which at least simulate a kind of polite compassion among persons of breeding whom chance has thrown together, he caught the sounds of hostile protests and complaints whispered in low voices. Society refused even to put on a show of sympathy for him, perhaps because it sensed he could see through the show.

'His disease is contagious . . .'

'The club secretary ought to forbid him access to the rooms.'

'In decent society it is positively forbidden to cough like that.'

'When a man is as ill as that he should not come to watering-places . . .'

'He'll drive me away.'

Raphael rose in order to escape from the general reprobation and wandered round the rooms. He wanted to find someone who would take his part and walked up to a young woman sitting alone, thinking of paying her a few flattering compliments; but at his approach she turned her back on him and pretended to be watching the dancers. Raphael was afraid he might already, in the course of that evening, have availed himself of his talisman; lacking both the will and the courage to engage in conversation, he left the salon and took refuge in the billiard-room. There nobody spoke to him, greeted him or gave him the slightest kindly look. In his current reflective mood he had an intuitive revelation of the general, rational cause for the aversion he had aroused. This small society was, unwittingly perhaps, obeying the great law which rules high society, whose implacable ethic became plain in its entirety to Raphael. Retrospective consideration showed him that it was completely typified in the person of Fœdora. He could not expect to meet here with any greater sympathy for his physical sufferings than had been extended to his moral sufferings in her salon. Elegant society expels from its midst those that are wretched, as a man in vigorous health expels morbid humours from his body. Society abhors pain and misfortune, is as terrified of them as of contagion, and its choice is soon made between contagion and vice: vice is a sign of affluence. However dignified misfortune may be, society understands how to belittle and ridicule it with an epigram. It draws caricatures in order to throw in the faces of dethroned kings the insults it thinks it has received from them; like the young Roman matrons in the Circus, it never shows mercy to the fallen gladiator; it lives on gold and ridicule . . . *Death to the weak!* That is the watchword of what we might call the equestian order established in every nation of the earth, for there is a wealthy class in every country, and that death-sentence is deeply engraved on the heart of every nobleman or millionaire. Take any collection of children in a school: this microcosm of society, reflecting it all the more accurately because it does so frankly and ingenuously, always contains specimens of the poor helots, creatures made for sorrow and suffering, subject always either to pity or to contempt: the Kingdom of Heaven is theirs, say the Scriptures. Take a few steps farther down the ladder of creation: if a barnyard fowl falls sick, the other hens hunt it around, attack it, scratch out its feathers and peck it to death.

Faithful to this law of egoism, society exerts all its rigours to punish those bold enough to spoil its feasts, or sour its pleasures, by exhibiting their wretchedness. Whosoever suffers in body or soul, whoever is poor or weak, is a pariah. Let him stay in his wilderness! If he steps beyond it, he finds winter everywhere: cold looks, cold manners, cold words, cold hearts; he can count himself fortunate if he does not reap insults where he might have hoped to find the fruits of consolation! You who are dying, stay where you are on your lonely beds! Old men, crouch alone by your cold hearths! Poor girls, if you are dowerless, freeze or burn in your solitary garrets! If the world tolerates any particular misfortune, this is only because it sees a way of adapting it to its own use and profit, putting a saddle and saddle-cloth on its back and a bit in its mouth, and riding about on it for the pleasure it can give. Pinched and crabbed ladies' companions, put a gay face on things, endure the vapours of your supposed benefactress; carry her lap-dogs, they are your rivals for her affections; amuse her, anticipate her whims but keep a watch on your tongues! And you, king of unliveried valets, shameless parasite, leave your true self at home, digest as your host digests, weep with his tears, laugh when he laughs, fall into convulsions over his witticisms – but no backbiting until he's down. That is how the world honours misfortune: it kills it or drives it away, vilifies it or castrates it.

These reflections welled up in Raphael's heart with the spontaneity of poetic inspiration. He looked round him and felt the sinister chill which society distils in order to fend off misery and which grips the soul more cruelly than the winter blast freezes the body. He folded his arms, stood leaning against the wall and subsided into deep melancholy. He thought how little happiness this dreadful palace police really procures for society. What does it gain by it? Distractions devoid of pleasure, joyless mirth, revels without gaiety, frenzy without ecstasy, in short the charred wood and ashes on the hearth without a flicker of flame. When he raised his head again, he was alone, for the billiard-players had vanished.

'All I would need to do,' he told himself, 'to make my coughing sound like music in their ears, would be to exert my powers!' And at that thought he armed himself with contempt, as with a shield between himself and the world.

The next day, the spa doctor came to visit him and, with a show of kindly solicitude, inquired about his health. Raphael felt a tremor of joy when he heard the friendly words addressed him. The doctor's face was all gentleness and kindness: the curls of his blond wig were redolent of the love of mankind; the square cut of his coat, the creases in his trousers, his shoes as broad as a quaker's, everything about him, including the semi-circle of powder on his slightly bent shoulders deposited there by his little pigtail – everything denoted apostolic benevolence, Christian charity and the self-devotion of a man who, out of zealous concern for his patients, had taught himself to play whist and backgammon skilfully enough always to win their money.

'Monsieur le Marquis,' he said after a long chat with Raphael, 'I think I know how to dispel your melancholy. By now I know enough about your constitution to affirm that the doctors of Paris, for all their ability of which I am well aware, are in error about the nature of your illness. Short of accidents, Monsieur le Marquis, you may live as long as Methuselah. Your lungs are as strong as a blacksmith's bellows and your stomach would put that of an ostrich to shame. But if you go on living at a high altitude you run the risk of being promptly and expertly laid in consecrated ground. Monsieur le Marquis will understand if I explain this succinctly. Chemistry has proved that respiration in man constitutes a real process of combustion whose lesser or greater degree of intensity depends on the richer or rarer supply of the phlogistic elements amassed by the organism peculiar to each individual. In your case, there is no lack of phlogiston; you are, if I may so express myself, over-oxygenated by the ardent temperament of men of your passionate stamp. By breathing the keen, pure air which quickens the pace of life in men of phlegmatic fibre, you give further stimulus to a combustion which is already too rapid. So then one of the conditions of your survival is the dense atmosphere of byres and valleys. Yes, the vital air for a man consumed by his genius is to be found in the lush pastures of Germany, at Baden-Baden or at Toplitz. If you can steel yourself to live in England, its foggy atmosphere will calm your fever. But the waters here, one thousand feet above the Mediterranean sea-level, could be deadly to you. That is my opinion,' said he with a modest shrug of the shoulders. 'It is against my interests to give it, since, if you act upon it, we shall have the misfortune to lose your company.'

Had it not been for his closing words, Raphael would have been persuaded by the sham benevolence of the honey-tongued doctor. But he was too acute an observer not to divine, by the tone, gesture and look which accompanied that mildly ironical phrase, the mission this little man had been entrusted with by the rest of his pleasure-loving patients. And so these rubicund idlers, these bored old women, these English tourists, these ladies of fashion who had escaped from their husbands and had been conducted to the waters by their lovers, were taking it upon themselves to drive away a poor, weak, ailing invalid who hardly seemed capable of withstanding the daily persecution to which he was subjected! Raphael accepted the challenge, anticipating some amusement in this intrigue.

'Since my departure would distress you,' he told the doctor, 'I shall try to take advantage of your good advice, even while staying here. Starting tomorrow I will have a house built in which we will modify the air in accordance with your prescriptions.'

Accurately interpreting the sardonic smile which played over Raphael's lips, the doctor thought it best merely to bow, and left him without a further word.

The lake of Bourget is a vast cup, enclosed by jagged mountain peaks, at the bottom of which there gleams, at an altitude of seven or eight hundred feet above the Mediterranean, a splash of water which is bluer than any other water in the world. Seen from the top of the Dent-du-Chat this lake looks like a turquoise dropped there by accident. This lovely sheet of water is nine leagues in circumference and, in certain places, nearly five hundred feet deep. To glide in a boat over the surface of the lake with a clear sky overhead, to hear nothing but the splash of the oars, to see a horizon bounded only by cloud-capped mountains, to admire the sparkling snow of the French Maurienne; to drift past blocks of granite wearing the velvet of bracken or dwarf shrubbery, then past rich mountain pasturage; here a patch of wilderness, there a fertile tract, like a pauper looking on at a feast: such harmonies and such discordances go to make up a spectacle in which everything is great and everything diminutive. Looking out over mountains changes the conditions of optics and perspective: a fir-tree one hundred feet high seems no taller than a reed, wide valleys appear to be as narrow as mountain tracks. This lake is the only one where heart may speak to heart. There one may meditate or let one's thoughts turn to love. Nowhere else could one find a lovelier accord between water and firmament, mountain and plain. There you will find a balm for all life's vexations. It is a place which will keep one's sorrowful secrets, offering consolation and alleviation of their pangs; into love it infuses a certain gravity, a certain introspection which purifies and deepens passion. A kiss has a larger import here. But above all it is the lake of memories; it enhances their charms by tinging them with the colour of its waves; it is a mirror in which past and present are reflected.

Raphael felt his burden bearable only when he was in the midst of this lovely scenery; here he could remain indolent, meditative, free from desire. After the doctor's visit he went for a row and got the boatman to land him near the lonely foreland of a pretty hill on which the village of Saint-Innocent is perched. From this kind of promontory the eye takes in the Mont de Bugey, at the feet of which flows the Rhône, and the lower waters of the lake. But from that point Raphael loved to gaze across at a building on the opposite bank, the melancholy Abbey of Haute-Combe, the burial-place of the kings of Sardinia, who lie there at the foot of the hills, prostrate like pilgrims who have reached their journey's end. The even, rhythmical dip of oars broke the silence of this scene and gave it a voice as monotonous as the chanting of monks. Surprised at seeing visitors in this part of the lake, where no one ordinarily came, the marquis, without emerging from his reverie, looked to see who was sitting in the boat and recognized in the stern the old lady who had so harshly addressed him the evening before. As the boat passed before Raphael, the only person to greet him was the old lady's companion, an impoverished gentlewoman whom he did not recollect having seen before.

The party were soon lost to view behind the foreland and after a few minutes Raphael had already dismissed them from his mind, when he heard near by the swish of a dress and the sound of light footsteps. Turning round, he recognized the lady's companion; guessing by her air of constraint that she wanted to speak to him, he walked back to her. She appeared to be in her mid-thirties, tall, thin, bony, with frigid manners; and, like any old maid, she seemed embarrassed to be looking him in the eye, an initiative which accorded ill with her hesitant, self-conscious, inelastic steps. Old and young at once, she expressed by means of a certain stiffness of bearing the exorbitant value she placed on her treasures and perfections. She had, moreover, the discreet, nun-like gestures of women accustomed to cherish themselves, in obedience, probably, to the inescapable compulsion women are under to be comlicome.

'Sir, your life is in danger, you must not return to the club,' she said to Raphael, retreating a little as she spoke as though her virtue were already compromised.

'But Mademoiselle,' Valentin replied with a smile, 'I beg you to explain yourself more clearly, since you have deigned to come here...'

'Ah!' she returned. 'It needed a powerful motive to bring me here, otherwise I would not have risked incurring the displeasure of Madame la Comtesse, for if she ever knew that I informed you...'

'But who would tell her, Mademoiselle?' Valentin exclaimed.

'You are right,' the old maid replied, blinking at him like an owl exposed to strong sunlight. 'But be wary. Several young men who want to force you to leave the Spa have formed a pact to insult you and compel you to fight a duel.'

The voice of the old countess rang out in the distance.

'Mademoiselle,' said the marquis, 'my gratitude...'

His would-be saviour had already run away on hearing her mistress, whose shrill voice was raised once more from behind the rocks.

'Poor woman! The persecuted always band together to help one another,' thought Raphael as he sat down under a tree.

The key to all knowledge is, beyond dispute, the mark of interrogation: we owe most of our greatest discoveries to the question *How?* and wisdom throughout life perhaps consists in for ever asking oneself *Why?* But on the other hand such habits of trained inquiry destroy our illusions. Thus it was then that Valentin, having taken the old maid's good deed, without any intention of philosophizing about it, as a text for his wandering thoughts, decided that it was dripping with gall.

'There's nothing extraordinary,' he thought, 'in a lady's companion falling in love with me, since I am only twenty-seven, have a title and an income of two hundred thousand francs! But that her mistress, who's as hydrophobic as any cat could be, should have taken her out in a boat and deposited her near me, that surely is a strange and wonderful thing! Here are a couple of women who have come to Savoy to sleep all day, and who never know at noon if it's not still night: can they have risen before eight today to make it seem sheer chance that they should come across me here?'

Before long he had decided that this old maid and her middle-aged innocence were merely a new manifestation of that devious, mischief-making watering-place society, a contemptible trap, a clumsy plot, the shifty ruse of a priest or a woman. Was the duel in question a mere fabrication, or were they simply trying to frighten him? Persistent and pestering as flies, these pin-headed creatures had succeeded in pricking his vanity, awakening his pride and exciting his curiosity. Not wishing either to be their dupe or to pass as a coward, and even a little amused by this petty drama, he went to the Club that same evening. He remained standing quietly with his back to the marble chimney-piece of the principal salon, taking care not to give them any cause for comment or criticism. But he kept their faces under scrutiny and seemed to be issuing a kind of challenge to the company by his guarded behaviour. A mastiff that knows his own strength awaits the attack on his home ground and does not engage in useless barking. Towards the end of the evening he strolled into the casino, walking across from the entrance door to the door leading into the billiard room, where from time to time he took a glance at the young men who were busy at their game. After he had taken a few turns he heard his name mentioned. Although they were speaking quietly, Raphael had no difficulty in guessing that he was the subject of an argument; in the end he overheard a few remarks uttered aloud:

'You?'

'Yes, I!'

'I dare you!'

'Shall we bet on it?'

'Oh! We'll send him off all right.'

Just as Valentin, in his curiosity to know what the bet was about, moved forward to listen closely to the conversation, a young man, tall, strong, with a healthy colour, and the steady, impertinent stare of men of solid substance, stepped out of the billiard room.

'Sir,' he said to Raphael, addressing him in even tones, 'I have taken it upon me to tell you something that you don't seem to know: everyone here, and I myself in particular, feel a strong aversion to your face . . . You are too civil not to sacrifice yourself to the general good, and I beg you not to come any more to the Club.'

'This pleasantry, sir,' replied Raphael coolly, 'which used to be current under the Empire in various garrison towns, is considered very bad form today.'

'It is no pleasantry,' the young man retorted. 'I must say it again. Your health would be very much the worse if you remained here: the warmth, the bright lights, the atmosphere of the salon and the company are bad for the complaint you suffer from.'

'Where did you study medicine?' Raphael asked.

'I graduated, sir, at the shooting-school of Lepage in Paris. I took my doctor's degree from Cérisier, the King of the rapier.'

'You still have one degree to take,' Valentin retorted. 'Study the code of polite behaviour and you will be a perfect gentleman.'

At this point the young men in the billiard-room came out to join them. Some were smiling, some silent. The card-players, their attention aroused, abandoned their game in order to give ear to this dispute which stirred their passions. Standing alone in this hostile world, Raphael tried to keep cool and avoid putting himself in the wrong in any way; but, hearing his opponent permit himself a sarcasm in which insolence was wrapped in an eminently incisive and witty form, he made a grave reply:

'Sir, polite usage no longer tolerates striking a man on the cheek, but I cannot find words to brand such cowardly conduct as yours.'

'That's enough, now, that's enough! You will settle this matter tomorrow,' cried several young men, interposing themselves and separating the two antagonists.

Raphael left the salon, having been adjudged the challenger and having agreed to a rendezvous close to the château of Bordeaux, in a small sloping meadow not far from a recently constructed road which the victor could use to reach Lyons. Raphael would either have to nurse his wound or leave the spa. In either case society would win. Next morning, at about eight, Raphael's adversary, accompanied by his two seconds and a surgeon, was the first to arrive at the duelling-ground.

'This is an ideal spot,' he said cheerfully. 'And what marvellous weather for an exchange of shots,' he added, looking up at the blue vault of heaven, the waters of the lake, and the cliffs, without any misgiving born of doubt or the prospect of death. 'If I send a ball through his shoulder,' he continued, 'he'll be laid up for a month, I take it, doctor?'

'A month at least,' the surgeon replied. 'But stop twisting that willow-branch. If you tire the muscles of your wrist you won't be able to aim straight. You might kill the man instead of wounding him.'

The rattle of an approaching carriage was heard.

'Here he comes,' said the seconds. And soon they saw advancing along the road a barouche drawn by four horses with two postilions as outriders.

'What an odd notion,' exclaimed Valentin's adversary: 'He's taking post horses to get himself killed!'

As with gambling, so with duels. The slightest incidents have their effect on the imagination of the actors so gravely concerned in the luck of the throw! So it was with some anxiety that the young man waited for the carriage to arrive: it was halted on the main road. Old Jonathas was the first to clamber down, in order to help his master alight. He supported him with his enfeebled arm, and attended to him with all the solicitude a lover bestows on his mistress. They were both lost to view in the footpath leading from the main road to the site chosen for the encounter and only reappeared much later, walking slowly along. The four witnesses of this curious scene were profoundly affected at the sight of Valentin leaning on his manservant's arm; pale and dejected, he walked like a man afflicted with gout, his head lowered and not uttering a word. They looked like two old men reduced to equal decrepitude, the one by the passage of time, the other by mental fatigue. The age of the older man was written in his white hair; the younger one's age was quite indeterminate.

'Sir, I did not close my eyes last night!' Raphael said to his adversary.

These icy words and the terrible look that went with them sent a shudder through the real aggressor in this quarrel. He felt himself to be in the wrong and secretly regretted his behaviour. There was something strange in Raphael's attitude, tone of voice and gestures. The marquis made a pause, and everyone imitated his silence. Anxiety and tension were screwed up to the limit.

'There is still time,' he continued, 'to make me a token reparation; but you have to do this, sir, otherwise you will surely die. Just now you are still counting on your skill and have no thought of withdrawing from an encounter in which you believe all the advantage to be on your side. Well, sir, I am generous, I give you fair warning of my superiority. I possess a terrible power. In order to neutralize your skill, to cloud your vision, to make your hand tremble and your heart falter, in order to kill you even, I only have to wish it. I do not want to be forced to exercise my power : to do so costs me too dear, and you will not be the only one to die. If then you refuse to make me an apology, your bullet will fly into that waterfall however practised you may be in the art of gentlemanly assassination, and my bullet, without my aiming it, will go straight into your heart.'

At this moment Raphael was interrupted by a hubbub of voices. In pronouncing these words the marquis had steadily directed at his opponent the unbearable brilliance of his unwavering gaze; he had raised his head and showed as unexpressive a countenance as that of a psychopath.

'Tell him to keep quiet,' the young man said to one of his seconds. 'His voice is twisting my bowels.'

'Enough, sir, say no more . . . These speeches are pointless,' the surgeon and seconds shouted to Raphael.

'Gentlemen, I was fulfilling my duty. Has this young man any last dispositions to make?'

'Enough ! Enough !'

The marquis remained upright, motionless, without for an instant taking his eyes off Charles, his adversary, who, dominated by some quasi-magic power, was like a bird confronted by a snake : he was compelled to sustain the killer's gaze, he could not tear his eyes away.

'Give me some water, I'm thirsty . . .' he said to one of the seconds.

'Are you afraid?'

'Yes. That man's eyes are ablaze; I'm mesmerized.'

'Do you wish to make an apology?'

'It is too late.'

The two adversaries were stationed fifteen paces apart. Each of them had at hand a brace of pistols and, according to the prescribed ritual, they were each to fire two shots at will, but only after the seconds had given the signal.

'What are you doing, Charles?' shouted the young man who was serving as second to Raphael's adversary. 'You're putting the ball in before the powder!'

'I am doomed!' he replied in a low voice. 'You have put me facing the sun.'

'The sun is behind you,' said Valentin in a grave and solemn voice, slowly loading his pistol without worrying either about the signal, which had already been given, or about the care with which his adversary was taking aim.

There was something terrifying about this supernatural self-confidence, which impressed even the two postilions, who had approached the duelling-ground out of callous curiosity. Toying with the power he possessed, or perhaps wanting to test it, Raphael was looking at Jonathas and talking to him at the instant when his opponent fired. Charles's bullet cut a willow branch in half and richochetted on the water. Raphael fired at random and his bullet went through his adversary's heart. Without paying any attention to the young man's fall, he immediately inspected the wild ass's skin to see how much a human life had cost him. The talisman was now no bigger than a small oak-leaf.

'Well, postilions, what are you gaping at? Let us be off.'

*

Reaching France[27] that very evening, he immediately took the road to Auvergne and made for the springs of Mont Dore. During the journey he was struck by one of those sudden thoughts which illuminate our minds as a sunbeam piercing thick clouds lights up a dark valley. Saddening flashes of intuition, implacable shafts of wisdom, throw a fresh light on past events, reveal

27. Savoy did not become part of France until 1860. Raphael has of course to leave Savoy to escape prosecution for the killing of Charles.

us our mistakes and leave no hope of self-pardon. It came to him all at once that the possession of power, however unlimited, did not confer the knowledge how to use it. A sceptre is a toy for a child, an axe for a Richelieu, and for Napoleon a lever with which to move the earth. Power leaves our natures untouched and confers greatness only on the great. There was nothing Raphael might not have done : he had done nothing.

At the baths of Mont Dore he found the same society, still shunning him with the horror that animals show when they scent from afar one of their own kind lying dead. The aversion was reciprocal. His last adventure had filled him with a deep detestation of society. His first concern in consequence was to look for some isolated refuge in the environs of the spa. He felt an instinctive need to draw closer to nature, to simplicity of feeling and the vegetative life to which we so readily surrender in the country. The next day he climbed, not without effort, the peak of Sancy and explored the upland valleys, the aerial heights, the hidden lakes and those rustic cottages dotted about among the mountains of Dore whose severe and rugged charms are beginning to tempt the brushes of our artists. One sometimes finds there delightfully fresh and smiling landscapes which contrast strikingly with the sombre aspect of those desolate mountains. About half a league from the village, Raphael found himself at a spot where nature, as light-hearted as a child at play, seemed to have taken delight in hiding treasure; having visited this picturesque, unspoiled retreat, he resolved to settle there, where he could live undisturbed, as effortlessly as the fruit that ripens on the bough.

Imagine an upturned cone, a cone of granite broadly hollowed out, a sort of punch-bowl whose edges were chipped and cracked in fantastic fashion : here were flat slabs of bare rock, smooth of surface, azure-tinted, with the sun's rays playing over them as on a mirror; elsewhere were cliffs gashed with fissures and cracked by ravines which in many places were crowned by groups of stunted trees twisted out of shape by the winds, while underneath hung blocks of lava which sooner or later the action of the rains was certain to bring crashing down. Here and there were cool and shady recesses from which rose groves of chestnut-trees as tall as cedars, or deep caverns of yellow clay, gaping darkly, their mouths choked with brambles and flowering shrubs, while tongues of green sward stretched out in front of them. At the bottom of this bowl, which may have been the age-old crater of a volcano, there was a pool of clear water sparkling like diamonds. Around this deep basin, bordered with granite, willows, rowans, irises and the thousand varieties of aromatic plants then in bloom, spread a meadow as green as an English lawn; its, fine, tender grass was irrigated by tiny streams which filtered through the clefts in the rocks and was fertilized by the vegetable deposits constantly being washed down by the storms from the higher slopes to the bottom of the valley. The pool, irregularly scalloped round its edges like the fringe of a skirt, covered about three acres; the width of the meadow, varying as the rocks crept up to the water's edge, was rather less; at some places there was scarcely enough room for cows to pass. At a certain altitude vegetation ceased. The granite peaks thrusting into the sky assumed the most bizarre shapes and took on the misty colouring which makes high mountains vaguely resemble clouds. In contrast with the gentle appearance of the valley, those stark, bare rocks offered the gaunt and sterile images of desolation, the dread possibility of landslides, and such capricious forms that one of the outcrops is called the *Capuchin*, so closely does it resemble a hooded monk. At times and turn by turn those tapering needles, those audacious piles, those caverns in mid-air were lit up as the sun moved round to them or in accordance with the play of the light and were tinged with gold, deep crimson or bright pink, or perhaps took on grey or leaden tints. These summits in fact offered a constantly changing spectacle like the iridescent shimmer on a pigeon's throat.

Often, between two sheets of lava which seemed to have been cleft in two by the stroke of an axe, at dawn or sunset, a gleaming sunbeam pierced through to the depths of that laughing riot of blossoms and frolicked in the waters of the mountain lake like the streak of gold which steals through the chink of a shutter and invades a Spanish bedroom, sealed for the siesta. When the sun shone directly above the ancient crater which some antediluvian upheaval had filled with water, its rocky walls grew warm, the extinct volcano heated up once more and this rapid rise in temperature fostered germination, quickened vegetation, coloured the flowers and ripened the fruit in this tiny, forgotten corner of the earth.

When Raphael arrived at this spot, he noticed several cows grazing in the meadow. Having taken a step or two towards the pool he saw, standing where the level ground was at its broadest, a modest dwelling-house of granite faced with wood. The thatched roof of this cottage, in harmony with the site, was gay with mosses and flowering ivy which betrayed its great antiquity. A wisp of smoke, too thin to disturb the birds, wound up from the crumbling chimney. In front of the door was a large bench placed between two enormous bushes of honeysuckle covered with red, sweet-scented blossoms. The walls of the cottage were scarcely visible under the branches of vine and the garlands of roses and jasmine which rambled around at their own sweet will. Unconcerned with this rustic beauty, the cottagers did nothing to cultivate it and left nature to its elvish and virginal grace. Baby-clothes, thrown over a gooseberry-bush, were drying in the sun. A cat was crouched on a hemp-stripping machine, underneath which stood a copper cauldron, recently scoured, with potato peelings scattered around. On the other side of the house Raphael could see a hedge of dead hawthorn whose purpose no doubt was to prevent poultry from pillaging the fruit and vegetables of the kitchen-garden.

There the world seemed to come to an end. That habitation resembled the birds' nests ingeniously built in the cleft of a rock, the combined product of art and heedlessness.

Here nature was simple and kindly, giving an impression of rusticity both genuine and poetic, blossoming a world away from our contrived idylls, with no reference to the universe of ideas, self-generated, the pure product of chance. At the time of day when Raphael arrived there, the sun's rays were falling obliquely from right to left, making the greenery brighter, painting the grey or ochre backdrop of the cliffs with the splendour of its light and the contrasts of shadow, touching up the different shades of green of the trees, the blue, red or white clumps of flowers, the climbing plants with their hanging blossoms, the velvet mosses with their changing tints, the heather with its purple bells, but above all the sheet of clear water in which were mirrored exactly the granite peaks, the trees, the house and the sky. In this delightful picture everything had its lustre, from the glistening mica of the rocks to the tuft of cat's ear hiding in the soft half-light. There was nothing there that jarred: the brindled cow with its sleek coat, the fragile water-lilies stretching like fringes over the water of an inlet over which blue and emerald-green insects were buzzing, and the tree-roots looking like heads of sand-strewn hair surmounting faces of indeterminate shape marked out in the stones. The warm odours rising from the water, from the flowers and the grottoes which made fragrant this quiet retreat, gave Raphael a sensation bordering on the voluptuous.

The majestic silence reigning in this wooded paradise, which may not even have been on the state register of taxable property, was suddenly broken by the barking of two dogs. The cows turned their heads and moist muzzles towards Raphael as he entered the valley, stared at him stupidly for a while and then resumed their grazing. Miraculously perched on the rocks, a she-goat and her kid capered on to a shelf of granite near Raphael, as though to ask him what he was doing there. The yelping of the dogs brought out a sturdy child who stood there gaping; then there came a white-haired old man of medium height. These two matched their surroundings, the atmosphere, the flowers and the cottage. Good health brimmed over in the luxuriance of nature, giving childhood and age their own brand of beauty. In fact, in every form of life there was that carefree habit of contentment that reigned in earlier ages; mocking the didactic discourse of modern philosophy, it also served to cure the heart of its turgid passions.

The old man would have provided a model suited to the virile brush of Schnetz: [28] he had a brown face covered with wrinkles that looked as if they would be rough to the touch, a straight nose, prominent cheek-bones, as veined with red as an old vine-leaf, a gaunt frame and all the signs of muscular strength even

28. Jean Victor Schnetz (1787–1870), a French painter of historical and religious scenes, renowned for their vigour and vividness of their colours.

where strength itself had ceased to exist. On his hands, still horny although he no longer worked with them, were a few white hairs; he bore an air of independence which suggested that in Italy he might have taken to brigandage for love of the liberty he cherished. The boy, a true mountaineer, had black eyes which could look at the sun without blinking, a swarthy complexion and dark brown, untidy hair. He was nimble and self-assured, as natural in his movements as a bird; he was dressed in rags, and his white, fresh skin showed through the holes in his clothes. The two of them stood in silence, side by side, sharing the same feeling, and the look on their faces gave proof of a perfect identity in the equally leisurely life they led. The old man had shared the child's games and the latter had fallen in with the old man's humours, thanks to a kind of pact between two kinds of weakness: departing strength and strength shortly to show itself. Soon a woman of about thirty appeared at the door of the cottage, distaff in hand. A true daughter of the Auvergne, with her high colour, open, smiling face, and white teeth, she had the face and figure, the cap and dress of Auvergne women, big-breasted, speaking patois: in every detail an ideal personification of the country, hard-working, uneducated, thrifty and hospitable.

She spoke a word of greeting to Raphael and they fell into conversation. The dogs quietened down, the old man sat on a bench in the sun and the child followed his mother about, silent, but watching and listening to the stranger.

'You are not afraid to live here, my good woman?'

'What's there to be fraid of, sir? When we stop up the entry, who could get in? No! We've nothing to be scared of! Anyway,' she asked as she showed the marquis into the large living-room, 'what could thieves find to steal in our house?'

She pointed to the smoke-blackened walls, on which the only decoration consisted of coloured prints in blue, red and green representing the *Death of Credit*, the *Passion of Our Lord* and the *Grenadiers of the Imperial Guard*. Disposed in different parts of the room, were an old walnut four-poster bed, a table with corkscrew legs, a few stools, a bread-pan, a jar of salt, a frying-pan and a side of bacon hanging from the rafters; while on the chimney shelf stood coloured plaster saints, yellow with age. As he came out of the house Raphael noticed, among the rocks, a man bent over a hoe who was directing a look of curiosity towards the house.

'It's the man of the house,' said the good wife, with a smile typical of countrywomen. 'There's a field up there he's working.'

'And the old man is your father?'

'Begging your pardon, he's my man's grandfather. He's a hundred and two as sure as he stands there. Why, only a few days ago he took our little lad on foot to Clermont! He used to be a strong 'un; now, he does nothing but sleep, eat and drink. He's always playing with the little lad. Sometimes the little one takes him up the mountain, he can still manage that.'

Valentin formed the immediate resolution to live in the company of the old man and the child, to breathe the air they breathed, to eat of their bread, drink of their water, sleep of their sleep so that their blood should flow through his veins. A dying man's whim! To become one of the limpets on that rock, to save his shell a few days longer by lulling death to sleep became for him the essential principle of individual morality, the complete formula for human existence, the ideal aim in life, the sole life, the true life. His heart was invaded by a surging wave of egoism which engulfed the universe. For him, the universe no longer existed, he had absorbed it wholly into himself. For sick people the world begins at the head of their bed and ends at the foot of it: this beauty-spot became Raphael's bed.

Which of us has not, once in his life, spied on the comings and goings of an ant, slipped a straw into the single orifice through which a slug breathes, watched the darting of a dragonfly, admired the thousand veins, as multi-coloured as the rose window of a cathedral, which stand out on the russet background of an oak-leaf? Which of us has not spent hours contemplating in ravishment the effect of rain and sunlight on a brown-tiled roof, or studied the sparkle of dew-drops, the petals of flowers and the varied denticulation of their calices? Which of us has not drifted into such daydreams, woven round material phenomena, indolent and yet busy, aimless and yet leading to some thoughtful conclusion? Who has not, in short, tried living like a child, an idler, a savage without the savage's hard life? Raphael lived after this fashion for a number of days, having no cares and no desires, feeling a notable improvement in health, an extraordinary euphoria that calmed his anxieties and allayed his suffering. He climbed the rocks and took his seat on a hill-top from which his eyes could roam over a vast tract of country. He stayed there for days on end like a plant in the sun, like a hare in its form. Or else, familiarizing himself with the phenomena of vegetation and the vicissitudes of the weather, he studied the sequence of all processes of change, on the land, in the water and in the air.

He attempted to associate himself with the intimate movement of this natural order around him, to identify himself so completely with its passive obedience that he might come under the despotic law that governs and protects all creatures that live by instinct. He would have liked to cast off the burden of responsibility for himself. Like criminals of former times who, when the arm of the law reached out for them, were safe once they reached the shadow of an altar, he was trying to slip into the very sanctuary of life. He succeeded in integrating himself with the vast, pulsating rhythm of fruitful nature. He had adapted himself to the inclemencies of the weather, lived in the hollows of rocks, learnt the way of life of every plant, studied the flow and ramifications of the streams and grown familiar with the wild animals; in short, he had become so completely one with this animate earth that he had to some extent grasped its meaning and penetrated its secrets. He had come to believe that the infinite forms of being, whether animal, vegetable, or mineral, had all developed from a single substance, that they were the combinations of a single movement: the mighty respiration of an immense being which acted, thought, moved and expanded in unison with whom he too would expand, move, think and act. In some fantastic way he had mingled his life with the life of this rock-pile and had embedded himself in it.

Thanks to this strange fit of illuminism – a pseudo-convalescence similar to the benign onsets of delirium which nature accords as so many halts in the progress of pain – Valentin savoured the pleasures of renewed childhood during the first stage of his sojourn in the heart of this smiling landscape. He drifted along, making meaningless discoveries, starting out on a thousand projects without finishing any one of them, each day forgetting what he had undertaken to do the day before. Having shed his cares, he was happy, and believed that he was saved. One morning he happened to have stayed in bed until noon, steeped in the reverie half-way between wakefulness and sleep which imparts to reality the appearances of phantasy and to chimaeras the firm texture of existence, when suddenly, uncertain at first whether he was not still in a dream, he heard what he had never heard before, the report on his state of health made by his hostess to Jonathas, who came every day to hear it. The good woman probably believed Valentin to be still asleep, and spoke without lowering her voice, resonant like the voices of all mountain dwellers.

'He's no better and no worse,' she said. 'He was coughing all night, I thought he was giving up the ghost. He coughs and spits, the dear gentleman, and it's a pity to hear him. We wonder, me and my man, how he has the strength to cough like that. It breaks your heart to hear it. It's a wicked disease he's got! The fact is he's in a terrible way! I'm for ever afeared of finding him stretched dead in his bed one of these mornings. God's truth, he's as white as a wax Jesus! I tell you, I see him when he gets up, well, his poor body's as thin as a rake. He doesn't smell any too healthy either. But he takes no notice, he's out and about, wearing himself out, as though he had strength and to spare. It can't be denied he has plenty of courage, never to complain! But really he'd be better underground, suffering as he does like the good Lord on the cross! Not that we want that, sir, it's not in our interests. But he might be paying us much less than he does and we'd still be sorry for him. We're not thinking of ourselves. Ah, Lord love you,' she went on, 'you've got to be a Parisian to catch diseases like that. Where do they get them? The poor young gentleman! There's no hope for him, that's for sure. The fever he's got, it's eating him up, it's making him nothing but skin and bone. It's killing him, but he doesn't see it, he's no idea, sir, he don't notice it. But you mustn't grieve, M. Jonathas! You must admit he'll be better off not

273

suffering. Why don't you try having a novena?' she said. 'I've seen wonderful cures through novenas, I have, and I'd be glad to pay for a candle to save such a good, kind man, no more vice in him than a lamb in springtime . . .'

Raphael's voice had grown so weak he could not make himself heard, and so had no alternative but to put up with this appalling babble. However, his impatience got the better of him; climbing out of bed, he came to the doorway.

'You old scoundrel,' he shouted to Jonathas. 'Do you want to drive me to my death?'

He looked like a spectre to the peasant woman, who took to her heels.

'I forbid you,' Raphael continued, 'to feel the slightest anxiety about my health.'

'Yes, Monsieur le Marquis,' said the old manservant, wiping his tears away.

'And you'd better see to it that you don't come here in future unless I send for you.'

Jonathas wanted to do as he was told. But before he withdrew, in the loyal and compassionate look he cast at his master, Raphael read his death-sentence. Dispirited, and made suddenly aware of the true nature of his predicament, he sat down on the doorstep, folded his arms across his chest and let his head droop.

'Sir . . .'

'Go away! Go away!' the sick man shouted.

Early the following day Raphael climbed to the top of the cliff and sat down in a mossy crevice from which he could see the narrow track which led from the watering place to the isolated spot where he had taken up his abode. At the base of the peak he could see Jonathas once more in conversation with the country woman. Some demonic power enabled him to interpret the woman's nods, pessimistic gestures and simple-minded presages of doom; even the fateful words she spoke were borne to him across the silence in the gusts of wind. Sick with horror, he took refuge on the highest mountain-tops and stayed there until evening unable to rid himself of the sinister ideas unluckily reawakened in him by the cruel interest that others were taking in him. Suddenly the Auvergne peasant's wife loomed up before him in person, like a shade in the shades of evening; his eerie poetic imagination, fastening on her black-and-white striped petticoat, suggested to him a vague resemblance with the fleshless ribs of a skeleton.

'Good gentleman, the dew is falling,' she said to him. 'If you stay there you'll rot away like a fallen apple. Better come in. The evening dew's not healthy and besides you've had nothing to eat since morning.'

'God's thunder, you old witch!' he cried. 'I command you to let me live as I please, or I'll move elsewhere. Isn't it enough that you dig my grave every morning without scratching away at it every evening!'

'Your grave, sir? Dig your grave? Where's this grave then? All I want is to see you as spry as grandad, not in the grave! The grave! It's always ready for us before we're ready for it, the grave ...'

'Oh, be quiet!' said Raphael.

'Will you take my arm, sir?'

'No!'

The sentiment which man finds the most unbearable is pity, particularly when he deserves it. Hatred is a tonic which brings one to life and inspires vengeance; but pity kills, robbing the weak of what little strength they have left. Pity is malice turned soft-tongued, contempt wrapped up in tenderness, or tenderness covering up insult. In all these people Raphael found pity: gloating in the centenarian, inquisitive in the child, meddlesome in the woman, avaricious in her husband; but whatever form this pity took, it was always big with threats of death. A poet will make a poem of anything, a dirge or a lyric according to the images that impress him; his exalted soul disdains soft, pastel tints and always opts for clear and vivid colours. The poem dictated to Raphael by this universal pity was one of doleful mourning.

It was clear that he had forgotten how crude natural feelings can be when he had desired to draw closer to nature. When he believed he was alone under a tree, struggling with the obstinate cough which he never mastered without feeling weak in every limb after his fearful efforts, he saw the bright, moist eyes of the little boy, stationed there behind a clump of tall grass like a Red Indian scout and studying him with a curiosity of an urchin compounded as much of derision as of pleasure, and in which callousness is mingled with an interest in God knows what! The terrible greeting of the Trappists: *Brother, death awaits thee!* seemed to be constantly written in the gaze of the peasants with whom Raphael was living. It was hard to tell which he feared most, their unguarded utterances or their silence: everything about them made him feel oppressed. One morning there were two men there in black coats prowling and sniffing around, and eyeing him when they thought themselves unobserved. Then, pretending to have come there for a walk, they put to him some trite questions to which he gave curt replies. He recognized them for the doctor and the chaplain of the watering-place; either Jonathas had asked them to pay this visit, or the people he lodged with wanted to consult them; or else they were drawn thither by the scent of imminent death. Then he had a vision of his own funeral, heard the chant of the priests, counted the candles and from that moment on he could see only through a veil of crêpe the beauties of that luxuriant nature in the bosom of which he had thought to recover his strength. Everything which before had promised him a long life now foretold his approaching end. The next day he departed for Paris, not escaping the melancholy and heartfelt sympathy and good wishes which his hosts showered on him.

*

After travelling all through the night, he awoke in one of the most enchanting valleys of the Bourbonnais. Beauty-spots and vistas went whirling past, as swiftly borne away as the hazy pictures of a dream. Nature displayed herself before his eyes with cruel coquetry. Sometimes the Allier unrolled its liquid, gleaming ribbon of water over a fertile countryside, then hamlets modestly screened at the bottom of a gorge of dark yellow cliffs showed the steeple-tops of their churches; sometimes the water-mills in a tiny valley came suddenly into view after a monotonous succession of vineyards, and there were constantly recurring glimpses of handsome manor-houses, villages clinging to steep slopes, or highways edged with majestic poplars; finally the Loire with its long sweeps of diamond-studded waters wound glistening along its bed of golden sand. An unending picture of delight!

Nature, all animation, vivacious as a child, scarce able to contain the creative ferment and vigour of the month of June, held in its fatal spell the dimming gaze of the dying man. He closed the blinds of his carriage and went back to sleep. Towards evening, after passing Cosne, he was reawakened by the joyful blare of a band and found that a village fête was in progress. The post-house was near the square. During the time it took the postilions to change the horses, he watched the dances of this happy holiday crowd: the pretty village maidens with flowers in their hair flirting with excited youths, and the old farmers ruddy of countenance and flushed with wine. The little children were shrieking at their play, old dames were gossiping and cackling. There was a great din everywhere and the general air of festivity extended even to the costumes and the tables laid for the open-air diners. The market-square and the church were gaily decked; even the village roofs, windows and doorways seemed to have put on their Sunday best.

Like all desperately sick people, impatient at the slightest sound, Raphael could not restrain an angry exclamation, nor the desire to silence the fiddles, to still all that activity, hush all the clamour and scatter all those insolent revellers. He got back into his carriage, his brows beetling. When he looked out on to the square, he saw that the joy had turned to dismay, the peasant women had taken to flight and the benches were empty. On the bandstand a single blind musician persisted in playing a shrill tune on his clarinet. This music without dancers, this solitary old man with his surly profile, his rags and his few wisps of hair, hiding in the shadow of a lime-tree, looked to Raphael like a fantastic allegory of the wish he had made. Torrential rain was falling – one of those sudden, violent storms precipitated by the thunderclouds of June, which pass away as quickly as they come. But it was so natural an event that Raphael, after observing the clutter of greyish-white clouds beings driven across the sky by a squall, did not bother to examine his magic skin. He settled down in the corner of his carriage, and it was soon rattling along the road.

The next day he was at home in his bedroom, by his own chimney-corner. Feeling cold, he had had a great fire lit. Jonathas brought him some letters. They were all from Pauline. He opened the first one without haste and unfolded it as if it had been the dirty grey paper of an income-tax demand. He read the first sentence:

'You have gone! Why this flight, my Raphael ... What! No one can tell me where you are? And if *I* don't know it, who else could?'

Not wanting to read further, he coldly took hold of the letters and threw them into the fire, watching with a dull, lacklustre eye the play of the flames as they twisted the perfumed paper, shrivelled it, turned it over and reduced it to shreds.

Fragments rolled over the ashes and showed him bits of sentences, words, thoughts half consumed by the fire and which it amused him to decipher in the flame as if to afford himself some mindless distraction.

'. . . Sitting at your door . . . waited for . . . Caprice . . . I obey . . . rivals for your love . . . not I, your Pauline! . . . loves . . . no more Pauline then? . . . If you had meant to leave me, you would not have deserted me . . . Eternal love . . . To die . . .'

These words aroused a kind of remorse in him: he seized the tongs and drew from the flames one last fragment of a letter.

'. . . I felt hurt,' Pauline wrote, 'but I did not complain, Raphael! Leaving me far behind, as you did, I am sure you wanted to spare me the burden of some sorrow. One day you will kill me perhaps, but you are too humane to make me suffer. Well then, don't go away again like this. Look, I can face the greatest torture so long as I am by your side. Grief that I suffered through you would be grief no longer: my heart has more love for you than I have shown you yet. I can bear everything except to weep far away from you, not knowing what you . . .'

Raphael laid this fire-blackened shred of a letter on the mantelpiece, then suddenly thrust it back into the hearth. This paper gave too vivid a picture of his love and the life he had led, dogged by fate.

'Go and fetch Monsieur Bianchon,' he said to Jonathas.

Horace arrived and found Raphael in bed.

'My friend, can you make up a potion with a little opium in it which will keep me in a state of continual somnolence without any risk of its constant use affecting my condition?'

'Nothing could be easier,' the young doctor replied. 'All the same you'll have to be on your feet a few hours in the day in order to eat.'

'A few hours?' Raphael broke in. 'No, no! I don't want to be up for more than an hour at most.'

'What are you planning, then?'

'To sleep is still to be alive!' the sick man answered. 'Admit no one, not even Mademoiselle Pauline de Vitschnau!' said Valentin to Jonathas while the doctor was writing the prescription.

'Well, Monsieur Horace, is there any hope?' the old man asked the doctor as he saw him to the front door.

'He might linger on quite a time or die this evening. It's touch and go with him. It's quite beyond me,' the doctor added, giving a shrug of puzzlement. 'Try and keep him interested.'

'Interested, doctor? You don't know him. He killed a man the other day without turning a hair. Nothing can interest him.'

For some days Raphael remained plunged in the nothingness of his induced sleep. Thanks to the material power exerted by opium on our immaterial soul, this man endowed with so violently active an imagination sank down to the level of those sloths that crouch in the depths of tropical forests, camouflaged to look like a lump of decaying vegetation, reluctant to shift an inch even to make sure of some easy prey. He had even shut out the sun, refusing to let daylight into his room. About eight in the evening he would get out of bed; without having any clear consciousness of his existence, he would satisfy his hunger and immediately go back to bed. The hours passed, like chilly, wrinkled beldames, bringing him nothing but blurred images, apparitions, bright shapes against a dark background. He had buried himself in deep silence in refusal of all activity and intelligence. One evening he woke up much later than usual and found that his dinner was not served. He rang for Jonathas.

'You can leave my service,' he said. 'I have made you rich and you will be happy in your old age. But I will not let you put my life at risk any longer. What! You wretched man, I am hungry. Where is my dinner? Answer me!'

Jonathas gave a smile of satisfaction, took up a candle whose flame flickered in the profound darkness of the immense rooms of the house. He guided his master, who walked with robot-like tread, into a vast gallery, the door of which he abruptly pulled open. Immediately Raphael, bathed in a flood of light, was dazzled and startled by an extraordinary spectacle. There were his candelabras, filled with candles, the rarest blooms from his hothouse artistically arranged, a table glittering with silver cutlery, gold plate, mother-of-pearl and porcelain; a royal repast all smoking hot with succulent, mouth-watering dishes. He saw his friends assembled together, and with them women ravishingly attired in low-cut gowns, their shoulders bare, their hair wreathed with flowers, their eyes sparkling, each of them representing a different type of beauty, all of them desirable under the voluptuous disguises they wore. Here was one whose seductive curves were set off by an Irish waistcoat, while another was wearing the wanton *basquina* of the women of Andalusia. One had on the scanty costume of the huntress Diana, while another was modestly but endearingly arrayed as Mademoiselle de la Vallière:[30] but both alike were ready for an evening of wild pleasure. The eyes of every guest were sparkling with joy and sensual pleasure.

The moment the door opened and Raphael, looking like death, appeared before them, there was a sudden burst of spontaneous clapping, which exploded like rockets lit at the candles of this improvised feast. The voices, the perfumes, the lights, the irresistible beauty of the women aroused all his senses and stirred his sleeping appetites. The sweet strain of music from an orchestra concealed in an adjacent room rose above the intoxicating tumult with its flood of harmony and gave a finishing touch to this strange vision. Raphael felt the caressing pressure of a hand on his, a woman's hand, with cool white arms lifted to embrace him: it was Aquilina. He realized that the picture

30. The first mistress of Louis XIV.

280

before him was not insubstantial and fantastic like the fleeting images of his pale dreams; he uttered an appalling cry, slammed the door shut and struck his old servant an infamous blow full in the face.

'Monster! Have you sworn to bring about my death?' he shouted. Then, trembling at the thought of the risk he had run, he summoned up enough strength to regain his bedroom, drank a strong dose of his sleeping-draught and got into bed.

'Devil take it!' said Jonathas as he picked himself up. 'After all, M. Bianchon's orders were to keep him interested . . .'

It was about midnight. At that hour, thanks to one of those physiological anomalies which are at once the astonishment and the despair of the medical sciences, Raphael's face, as he lay asleep, was transfigured by an unearthly beauty. His white cheeks had a bright pink flush on them. His brow, as graceful as a girl's, was expressive of genius. Life seemed to be blooming within him as he lay calm and at rest, like a young child asleep under his mother's watchful eyes. His sleep was an easy one, a pure and even breath was issuing from his red lips, and he was smiling, no doubt carried away in a dream to a land of delight. He was perhaps dreaming that he had reached the age of the patriarchs and that his grandchildren had gathered to wish him yet longer life. Perhaps from the rustic bench where he was sitting in the sunlight, but under the cover of foliage, he could, like the prophet on the mountain top, see the promised land in the serene and distant future.

'Here you are then!'

These words, uttered by a silvery voice, dispelled the nebulous faces peopling his dream. In the glimmer of the lamp he saw his Pauline sitting on his bed, a Pauline embellished by separation and grief. He lay there in wonderment at the sight of that face as white as the petals of a water-lily, but whiter still in the semi-darkness and framed by long strands of black hair. On her cheeks were the glistening traces of tears which lingered there, ready to fall at her slightest movement. Dressed in white, her head bent over him, her body pressing the bed but slightly, she looked like an angel from Heaven, like an apparition which might vanish at a breath.

'Ah! Now all is forgotten!' she exclaimed as Raphael opened his eyes. 'I have only voice enough to tell you I am yours! Yes, there is nothing but love in my heart. Never, angel of my life, have you been so beautiful! Your eyes are like lightning flashes . . . But, believe me, I can guess the whole story! You have sought to recover your health away from me, because you were afraid of me . . . Well now . . .'

'Go away, go away, leave me!' Raphael replied at length in a low voice. 'I beg you, go away! If you stay here I shall die. Do you want to see me die?'

'Die?' she repeated. 'Do you think you can die without me? Die? But you are young! Die? But I love you! Die?' she added in a deep, throaty voice, seizing his hands with a frantic gesture . . . 'They are cold!' she said. 'Is it a delusion?'

Raphael drew from under his pillow the fragment of shagreen skin, as fragile and tiny as the leaf of a periwinkle. He showed it her.

'Pauline, lovely image of my happy life, let us say farewell!'

'Farewell?' she repeated with an air of surprise.

'Yes. This is a talisman which fulfils my desires and represents my life-span. You can see what is left of it. If you look at me once more I shall die.'

The girl thought Valentin had gone mad. She took the talisman and went to fetch the lamp. Under the flickering glimmer playing both on Raphael and the talisman, she examined minutely both her lover's face and the last particle of the magic skin. Seeing Pauline so beautiful, moved by love and terror, he was no longer able to control his thought: the memory of the tender scenes and delirious joys of his passion sprang up in triumph in his long-drugged soul, starting into flame like the embers of a fire banked down but not extinguished.

'Pauline, come to me! . . . Pauline . . .'

A terrible cry burst from the girl's throat and her eyes dilated; her eyebrows, violently contorted by the effect of untold anguish, were drawn apart with horror at what she could read in Raphael's eyes: an onset of frenzied desire, in which she had once gloried. But, as this desire grew, she could feel the skin contracting, tickling her palm as it lay in her hand. Without stopping to think, she fled into the next room, shutting the door behind her.

'Pauline! Pauline!' the dying man shouted as he stumbled after her. 'I love you, I adore you, I want you! . . . Unlock the door, on pain of my curse. I want to die in your arms!'

With extraordinary strength, the last burst of life in him, he battered down the door and saw his mistress, half naked, writhing about on a sofa. She had tried in vain to tear open her breast, and in order to kill herself swiftly, was trying to strangle herself with her shawl.

'If I die, he will live!' she said as she tried to tighten the knot she had made.

Her hair was undone, her shoulders bare, her clothes in disorder and, in this struggle with death, with her streaming eyes and flushed face, writhing in the grip of utter despair, she exhibited to Raphael, already drunk with desire, a body of incomparable beauty which inflamed his frenzy yet more. He threw himself upon her with the swiftness of an eagle swooping on its prey, tore away the shawl and tried to take her in his arms.

The dying man sought for words to express the desire which was devouring his last spark of strength; but only the choking sound of the death-rattle broke from his lungs; each breath he took, fetched from farther within, seemed to come from his very entrails. At length, no longer able to form even sounds, he bit Pauline's breast. Jonathas appeared, terrified by the shouts he had heard, and tried to tear from the girl the corpse over which she crouched in a corner.

'What do you want?' she demanded. 'He is mine. It was I who killed him. Did I not foretell it?'

Epilogue

'AND what became of Pauline?'

'Ah! Pauline? That's what you want to know?'

'Have you ever, on a cosy winter evening, sat at home by the fire-side, indulging in sweet memories of love or youth as you watched the fire eating its way along a log of oak? Here in the half-burnt wood are etched the red squares of a draughts-board; there you see a shimmering cushion of velvet; tiny blue flames run and leap and frolic over the heap of glowing embers. Up comes an unknown painter who adapts this blaze to his use: by some peculiar trick of art he traces in the midst of those crimson or violet tongues of flame a supernatural and unspeakably delicate figure, a fleeting vision that no freak of chance will ever resuscitate: the face of a woman with hair flying in the wind, a profile promising passionate delights – fire within fire! She smiles, fades away and you will never see her again. Farewell, flower of the flame! Farewell, element of the unfulfilled, the unexpected, appearing too soon or too late to materialize as a splendid diamond!'

'But Pauline?'

'You haven't taken my meaning? I will begin again. Make way, make way! Here she comes, the queen of illusions, the woman who passes as swiftly as a kiss, who is as vivid as the lightning flash and who, like it, traverses the heavens like a sword of flame; she, the being uncreate, all spirit, all love! She has materialized in I know not what body of flame; or it may be that flame itself has become, for an instant, a living body at her bidding. Her silhouetted shape has a purity of line that speaks of her celestial origin. Is she not as resplendent as an angel? Can you not hear the airy flutter of her wings? Less substantial than a bird, she alights beside you and holds you in thrall with the terrible fascination of her magnetic gaze; there is a magic sweetness in her breath that compulsively draws your lips to hers. She flits away and sweeps you along with her; your feet no longer touch the earth. You yearn to run your eager, frantic hand just once over her snow-white body, to ruffle her golden hair, to kiss her sparkling eyes. Her perfume intoxicates you and bewitching music holds you in its spell. You quiver in every nerve, you are nothing but desire and painful longing. O nameless happiness! You have touched that woman's lips! But all at once a violent pain awakes you. Aha! you have struck your head against the corner of your bedstead, you have been kissing its brown mahogany, its unresponsive gilding, a bronze ornament or a brass Cupid.'

'But Pauline, my good sir?'

'You still haven't grasped? Well, listen. One fine morning a young man, setting off from Tours on the *City of Angers*, was standing hand in hand with a pretty woman. Linked in this fashion they stood a long time watching, above the broad waters of the Loire, a figure in white, emerging as in a mirage from the heart of the mist like a creation of the water and the sun, or a sport born of the clouds and the air. Water-sprite or sylph in turn, this fluid creature flitted through the air like a word vainly sought that haunts one's memory but cannot be called to mind. She glided among the islands and tossed her head between the tall poplars. Then, towering above them, they saw her shaking the glittering spangles on the countless folds of her dress or displaying the dazzling halo which the sun described round her face. She hovered above the hamlets and hills and seemed to bar the way to the steamer as it churned past the Château d'Ussé. You might have thought she was the ghost of the Dame des Belles Cousines[31] seeking to protect her native Touraine from the invasion of modern technology.'

'Thank you, I understand. So much for Pauline. But what about Fœdora?'

'Oh, Fœdora? You will run across her again . . . Last night she was at the Bouffons; this evening she will go to the Opéra. She's to be found everywhere. She is, if you like, Society.'

Paris, 1830–31.

31. Heroine of a medieval prose romance, *Le Petit-Jehan de Saintré*, by Antoine de la Salle.

MORE ABOUT PENGUINS
AND PELICANS

For further information about books available from Penguins please write to Dept E P, Penguin Books Ltd, Harmondsworth, Middlesex UB7 0DA.

In the U.S.A.: For a complete list of books available from Penguins in the United States write to Dept DG, Penguin Books, 299 Murray Hill Parkway, East Rutherford, New Jersey 07073.

In Canada: For a complete list of books available from Penguins in Canada write to Penguin Books Canada Ltd, 2801 John Street, Markham, Ontario L3R 1B4.

In Australia: For a complete list of books available from Penguins in Australia write to the Marketing Department, Penguin Books Australia Ltd, P.O. Box 257, Ringwood, Victoria 3134.

In New Zealand: For a complete list of books available from Penguins in New Zealand write to the Marketing Department, Penguin Books (N.Z.) Ltd, P.O. Box 4019, Auckland 10.

Some Penguin Classics Translated from the French

Balzac
COUSIN BETTE
Translated by Marion Ayton Crawford

Balzac
EUGÉNIE GRANDET
Translated by Marion Ayton Crawford

Balzac
OLD GORIOT
Translated by Marion Ayton Crawford

Maupassant
SELECTED SHORT STORIES
Translated by Roger Colet

Maupassant
BEL-AMI
Translated by Douglas Parmée

Molière
THE MISANTHROPE AND OTHER PLAYS
Translated by John Wood

Rousseau
THE SOCIAL CONTRACT
Translated by Maurice Cranston

Voltaire
CANDIDE
Translated by John Butt